a
desperate
fortune

SUSANNA KEARSLEY

sourcebooks
landmark

All chapter epigraphs are taken from *The Works of Ossian* by James Macpherson. Francfort and Leipzig: printed for I. G. Fleischer, 1783.

Published by Sourcebooks Landmark, an imprint of Sourcebooks, Inc.
P.O. Box 4410, Naperville, Illinois 60567-4410
(630) 961-3900
Fax: (630) 961-2168
www.sourcebooks.com

Library of Congress Cataloging-in-Publication Data

Kearsley, Susanna.
  A desperate fortune / Susanna Kearsley.
      pages ; cm
  (softcover : acid-free paper) 1. Diaries—Fiction. 2. Jacobites—Fiction.
I. Title.
  PR9199.3.K4112D47 2015
  813'.54—dc23

                              2014044573

          Printed and bound in the United States of America.
                  VP 10 9 8 7 6 5 4 3 2

ALSO BY SUSANNA KEARSLEY

The Winter Sea

The Rose Garden

Mariana

The Shadowy Horses

The Firebird

The Splendour Falls

Season of Storms

For my son,
with love and thanks
for all his help.

"Whoever joins with thee, or stands up for thee,
by doing so forfeits all he hath... What is it to us
that thou callest thy Name Stuart? A Name that will gain
thee no Man that was not bewitched to thee before,
by desperate Superstition, or desperate Ambition, or
a desperate Fortune."
—"Number XXII: The Quaker's Advice to the
Young Pretender," in *The Independent Whig, Being a
Collection of Papers, All written, some of them published,
During the Late Rebellion*, Volume IV, by Thomas
Gordon, London: J. Peele, 1747

CHAPTER 1

M Y COUSIN DIDN'T TRY to catch the bride's bouquet. She knew me well enough to know I wouldn't try to catch it, either.

"Come keep me company," she said, and drew me firmly to one side of all the colorful commotion. "I need to sit."

My father's wild Aunt Lucy, nearly lost in layered flounces of bronze taffeta, tried once to herd us back as we went past. "Oh, girls, you mustn't run away. Go on, get in there. Have a go." Smiling at my cousin, she said, "Third time lucky, Jacqueline, so they say. And Sara, dear," she added in a cheering tone, to me, "there's always hope."

I might have pointed out there wasn't, really. Catching things had never been my strong suit, and it always seemed ridiculous to go through all that effort just to field a bunch of flowers that, while pretty, only showed which of the women at the wedding was the most determined to be married next, not which one would be.

Jacqui didn't give me time to point out anything. She simply answered, "Yes, Aunt Lucy, thanks for that, but Sara isn't feeling well."

And then she steered me off again.

I looked at her. "I'm feeling fine."

"I had to give her some excuse, or she'd have never let us

be. You know the way she is. And I could hardly say *I* wasn't feeling well—she'd only think that I was pregnant."

I had to admit that was true. Jacqui's love life—including her two short-lived marriages, one to a singer flamboyant enough to ensure their divorce had been given a place in the tabloids—was frequently a source of gossip at these family gatherings. She fueled that gossip on her own sometimes when she got bored, and had been known to start a rumor in one corner of the room to see how long it took to travel to another, but this evening she did not seem bored.

I asked, because I couldn't see the man she'd come with, "Where did you leave Humphrey?"

"Over there. He found the punch bowl, I'm afraid, before I had a chance to warn him. Drank three glasses of it."

Uncle Gordon spiked the punch at every family wedding. No one knew with what, but even those of us who'd only ever heard about the hangovers knew better than to drink the stuff. "Poor Humphrey."

Jacqui sighed. "Poor me, more like. I doubt he'll make it into work on Monday, and we've got a sales meeting. That's what I get," she said, "for bringing my assistant to a Thomas family wedding."

I agreed she should have known better. I hadn't brought a date myself, but then I didn't have a Humphrey, clever and good-looking, sitting handily outside my office door. And no one here expected me to bring somebody, anyway.

"Let's find a table," Jacqui said.

We found one tucked quietly off in a corner, half-hidden by one of the faux-marble columns that held up the wedding hall's high ceiling, painted ethereal blue with winged cherubs. The whole setting was a bit over-the-top, but it suited our young cousin Daphne, whose wedding this was. Daphne lived and breathed drama, which made her quite fun in small doses but very exhausting in larger ones.

"All a bit much?" Jacqui asked me. At first I assumed she was thinking, as I was, about the wedding, but then she asked, "How are you coping?" and I understood.

She had always been something of my guardian angel, since I'd been put into her arms as a baby when she had been ten. She was, if one worked out the family tree, more properly my father's cousin, daughter of his youngest uncle, but that made her still my own first cousin once removed, and I had claimed her and was keeping her.

It had been Jacqui who'd first noticed something was a little different in the way I saw the world, and through my childhood and my teens she'd been close by to show me what to do, like an interpreter to guide me through the labyrinth; to pick me up and dust me off if I stepped off the path and took a tumble. And the first year I had spent at university, that awful year when things had started coming all unglued for me, it had been Jacqui who had taken me to lunch with a new author, whose first book she had been editing.

"He's a psychologist," she'd introduced him. "Brilliant book, just fascinating. All about these children who have— how do you pronounce it, Colin?"

"Asperger's." He'd said it with a hard *g*, as in *hamburgers*.

At Jacqui's prompting, he had talked all through our lunch about the syndrome that at that time was believed to lie midway along the sliding scale between the "normal" world and full-on autism, making those who had it all too miserably aware that they were different without understanding why, unable to read and interpret all the complex social cues most other people took for granted—tones of voice, and body language, and the strange figures of speech that made a person say that he had been "knocked sideways" when he hadn't moved at all.

And I had known.

It had, if I was honest, been a great relief to finally put a name to what the issue was. I'd gone for consultations later with that same psychologist, and with my cousin waiting just outside his office door, we'd done the proper tests. He had explained it very clearly, using terms I could relate to.

"You're a programmer, aren't you?" he'd asked me. "You work with computers. Well, if you think of your own mind as a computer, which it is, then your basic architecture is different from most of the other computers around you. You're wired differently, you connect differently, and you run different software on a different operating system. You're like the lone Mac," he'd concluded, "in an office of PCs. They're all running Windows, and you're running OS X."

That had helped. I'd been able to picture that one Mac computer alone on its desk with its own software, processing everything in its own way while all of the other computers, the PCs, shared their incompatible system.

But Jacqui hadn't liked that image. "You don't want to be alone, off in your own corner," she had told me in decided tones. And having helped me put a name to what the problem was, she'd tackled it the way she tackled everything: head on. She'd bought me books and studied on her own, and with a single-minded focus Henry Higgins might have envied, she had tutored me in how to hide the signs, to pass for normal.

"You just have to pretend," she'd said, choosing another analogy, "that you're an alien, come here to learn about earthlings. Our language, our customs, our idioms, all of that. Study and learn them, the way you would any strange culture. But you don't want to *look* like an alien, and that means learning to mimic. I'll show you."

She'd shown me. Most days, I still felt like an alien, if I was honest. But Jacqui had done her job so well these past several years that my own parents, even when faced with the facts, still refused to believe I was anything more than a little bit quirky. And in a family like mine, I thought—bringing my mind firmly back to the present as new bursts of clapping amid shrieks of laughter announced that somebody had caught the bouquet—being quirky was hardly unusual.

"How are you coping?" asked Jacqui again, and I shrugged.

"I'm all right. I could have done without the DJ."

"Yes, well, so could we all. It was too loud for me," she admitted, "so I can only imagine what it must have been like for you."

My senses were…sensitive. Easily jangled and jarred. The wiring of my mind made sounds that other people could ignore strike at me with the full force of a whining dentist's drill. Strong lighting sometimes gave me headaches, certain fabrics rubbed as painfully as sandpaper against my skin, and when all that was added to a room packed full of people, interacting in a way I had to work to understand, then staying calm became a test of my endurance.

Jacqui smiled and took a piece of paper from her handbag. "Here," she said, and slid the paper over to me. "This might help."

Shaking my head, I assured her, "I'm not at that stage yet."

"What stage?"

"The Sudoku stage." Then, because she was still watching me with that expression I'd known from my childhood, I added more firmly, "I'm fine."

I admittedly found it a little endearing that she'd always

fed my addiction to numbers, in full understanding that, when I felt overwhelmed, nothing could calm me like complex equations or, lately, Sudoku—the neat, tidy patterns of numbers in squares, like a warm, fuzzy blanket that wrapped round my mind and was instantly soothing.

It hadn't surprised me that Jacqui had noticed when I'd made the switch to Sudoku. There wasn't much Jacqui missed noticing. And for the past several months she had seemed to have one of the puzzles conveniently tucked in her handbag whenever I'd needed one. But…

"You can stop looking after me," I told her. "Honestly. I'm a big girl now."

"I know that." Her tone told me nothing, but I'd learned that whenever her mouth tightened down at the corners like that, she was being defensive. "And anyway, that's not a puzzle, exactly."

I looked at the page. She was right. These were numbers, but not in an order I recognized—just numbers printed in pairs and threes, with dots between them:

106.62.181.189.68.172.766.86.128.185.64.175.19
.67.164.186.65.47.679.55.173.25.122.13.64.562.215
.128.196.29.56.63

I was already starting to look for the patterns when I asked, "What's this?"

"It's a code. Codes were one of your things, weren't they?"

"When I was ten, sure." I'd been in Year Six then. Our studies had taken us through World War II and the work of the code breakers at Bletchley Park, and I'd been so obsessed with cryptanalysis that, for the whole remainder of that winter, I had written all my school notes in a cipher of my own devising, much to the frustration of my teachers and my parents. "But that was almost twenty years ago."

"Well, I'll lay odds you've not forgotten. That code," she said, with a nod towards the paper I was holding, "is an old one, from the early eighteenth century."

It wasn't actually a code, I could have told her, but a cipher. More specifically, it seemed to be a substitution cipher, in which numbers had been used in place of letters of the alphabet. But I only asked, "And why do you have it?"

"I got it from one of my authors. You've never met Alistair Scott, have you?"

"Who?"

"The historian, Alistair Scott. He's quite famous. He used to be on television all the time."

I took her word for it. I didn't have a television. "And?" I smoothed the paper with my fingers as I focused on the numbers. There weren't many that were higher than 500, so I guessed those might be placeholders, to mark the ends of words.

"He's working on a new book," she went on, "and there's a source he needs to use, but it's in code. He wants someone to break it for him. So I thought of you."

"I'm hardly a professional."

"You need the work."

I paused, and faintly smiled. "I wondered how long it would take before you brought that up. Who told you?"

"Need you ask?"

My mother, then. I looked more closely at the numbers, noting the most common ones were in the 60s. Probably the *e*'s, I thought. The letter used most frequently in English, after all, was *e*. It also was the letter we used most for ending words. If I was right about the placeholders, then two words in this cipher ended in 60-somethings, so again, they were most likely *e*'s. I took a pencil from my handbag. "So she's told you all the details, has she?"

"Only that you handed in your notice," Jacqui said. "You can't keep doing that."

"They wouldn't let me work alone."

"Most people in IT do work in teams."

"I don't." And if the 60-somethings were all *e*'s, that meant it was the 6 alone that mattered, and the final digit didn't count. Testing this, I tried removing all the final digits right across the board, from all the numbers, and put *e*'s where all the sixes were, and spaces for the placeholders. I ended up with:

10.e.18.18.e.17.space.8.12.18.e.17.1.e.16.18.e.4
.space.5.17.2.12.1.e.space.21.12.19.2.5.e

There, I thought. Much less unwieldy. Right then. Twenty-six letters in the alphabet. Except if I were dealing with a simple substitution cipher, in which *a* was 1, and *b* was 2, and so on, then *e* would be written as 5 and not 6. I flipped *e* and *f* round, and got gibberish: *Jerreq hlreqaepred fqblae ulsbfe.*

Jacqui told me, "It would mean a trip to Paris. You like Paris."

"In December?"

"Well, you wouldn't have to go till after Christmas."

"Even worse."

She held her silence for a moment, then she said, "You're right. You'd do much better staying here and moving back in with your parents. That would be a lot more fun."

I wasn't always good at detecting sarcasm, but in this instance just the words alone were all I needed to be certain she was teasing. Glancing up, I tried to straighten out my smile. "Ha-ha."

"No, really. And your mother could invite young men to lunch on Sundays. You could have a lovely time."

"I won't need to move home," I said. "I've got three months left on my lease. I'll find another job."

"*This* one would let you work alone. Besides, he pays obscenely well, you know, does Alistair."

I shook my head. "I couldn't take his money." I flipped a few more letters, moving closer to an understanding of the patterns used by whoever had made this cipher. "This," I said, "is really pretty basic, not so difficult. I've nearly got it. When I've finished here, I'll let you have the key, and you can pass it on to him, and he can do all the deciphering himself, for nothing."

"Yes, well, there's one problem with your logic," Jacqui told me.

"What's that?"

"The code you've got there," she informed me, "is not the one Alistair needs to have broken."

My pencil paused, but only briefly, because I was too far along to just stop. "Then why do I have it?"

"It's sort of a test. I told Alistair you were a wizard with codes and things, and he said if you cracked this one in under a week, he would not only hire you, he'd buy you a bottle of whisky."

I wasn't sure what letter had been flipped with *r*. The first word, with its double *r*, was likely my best clue. It might be meant to be a double *l*, perhaps, or double *t*. Since *t* was the most common English consonant, I went with that. *Jetteq*, read the first word now, unhelpfully. "He knows what this says, then?"

She nodded. "It's out of an old book, or something."

I had only two bits of the cipher left to unravel.

"Tell Alistair Scott," I said, "that if he's buying me whisky, my preference is sixteen-year-old Lagavulin." I jotted the translation down and rotated the paper to slide it back over the table towards her.

I knew that I'd done it correctly when I saw her smile. That was how Jacqui always smiled when I did something to make her proud. "See? I was sure you could do it."

"I'm not a real code breaker."

"Sara." She held up the paper. "You solved this in seventeen minutes. You're good at it."

Probably not good enough, said my inner perfectionist.

Jacqui, who'd known me so long and so well that she likely could hear that voice, too, said, "Come with me tomorrow, I'll take you to meet him."

"To Paris? Be serious."

"Alistair Scott's not in Paris."

"But you said—"

"He only lives over the river, in Ham. It's the job that's in Paris."

She asked me again to come meet him, and of course I told her yes, because I knew she wouldn't let it go until I gave the answer that she wanted. But my gaze stayed on the paper in her hand while we were talking, and I wondered who had written it, and whom they'd meant to warn with those four words. Not me, I knew…and yet the final two words resonated, curiously:

Letter intercepted. France unsafe.

CHAPTER 2

I'D NEVER BEEN TO Ham. It lay not all that far from the grand Tudor palace of Hampton Court, but on the opposite shore of the Thames, the south shore, where the river bent round on itself on its lazy way down into London.

We drove down in the early afternoon, and Jacqui used the time to brief me on the things I should avoid in conversation. "And whatever you do, don't say anything nice about Calum MacCrae."

"Not a problem. I haven't a clue who that is."

"You are joking." She glanced at me. "Oh, right. You don't watch television at all, do you? Calum's a popular history presenter on BBC Four, and a bestselling author besides."

"So a rival of Alistair Scott's?"

"More than that. A usurper." She said the word decidedly. "Alistair was a celebrity once, you understand. The champion of Scotland. He set out to write this tremendous great trilogy, and when the second book came out it struck that magic chord you always hope a book will strike. The stars aligned. The critics loved it, readers too. It hit the charts and stayed there. He was courted by the BBC, their darling boy, presented documentaries for years for them. Whenever they were after someone for a comment about anything to do with Scottish history, it was Alistair they called upon. Then Calum came along, and he was younger, smoother, bolder, with a brand-new book to peddle and a very clever publicist. And before you know it, he'd edged Alistair aside. The BBC stopped calling altogether."

"That must have been upsetting for him."

"Not as upsetting as seeing MacCrae's books sell better than his and win all the awards."

"Are they better books?"

Jacqui was fair in her judgments. "No. Calum's all flash and good hair and tight trousers. His books are entertaining, but he'll be the first to admit that he rarely goes back to the primary sources; he reworks what others have written before him and makes it more colorful, puts his own stamp on it. But because he doesn't footnote, doesn't give a bibliography, you have to take his research and the things he says on trust. And that drives Alistair completely mad. Alistair," she said, "goes deep with his research, leaves no stone unturned, and keeps notes about everything."

"My kind of man."

"Yes, I think you'll get on well. I hope that you do. This is such a huge thing for him, writing this book. For a few years he didn't write anything, nearly gave up. Now he's finally committed to writing the last of the trilogy. I think he views this as his chance to win back his crown, in a way."

I was thinking of that for the rest of our drive into Ham, while I watched the passing sky. I knew that when the sky in mid-December was this clear and blue, it meant the air outside was freezing cold—a lesson Jacqui had apparently absorbed as well, for here, instead of dressing with an eye to fashion as she did in London, she was wrapped up in a warm but shapeless coat that looked about as old as I was, and as we stepped from the car she drew on woolly mittens and a hat.

"He'll be outdoors," was her reply when my expression

couldn't hide my curiosity. "He likes to walk, does Alistair. The last time I was here, last month, he had me on the tow-path, walking all the way to Kingston. In the rain."

There was no sign of rain today, and it appeared there were plenty of places for walking right here in the village. We'd parked near the Common, just steps from the start of the long and tree-lined avenue—now only for pedestrians and cyclists—that would have taken us straight to the ancient stately home of Ham House, if my memory of the map I'd looked at earlier this morning was correct. Instead, we turned the other way and crossed the quiet street to where a double row of trees, some newly planted in among the old, continued that same straight line of the avenue from Ham House, leading out onto the broad green of the Common.

Ham Common, I knew from my previous look at the map, was diverse and large—a mix of wilder wood and open green space, as it would have been from feudal times, when every peasant farming in the village for the lord who owned the manor had the right to let his livestock graze upon the common pastureland, or cut wood from the section of the forest that the lord allowed the villagers to share.

This north end of the Common, like a great expansive pie-shaped wedge of green, crossed by the shadows of the leafless trees that edged it, had been bordered on three sides by streets with elegant old houses that stood back a pace, behind their high brick walls and hedges, gazing out across the Common with an air of graceful permanence.

It was, I thought, the perfect postcard view of what an English village green should look like, right down to the pond at the far corner, with its trailing golden willows and its noisy scrambling ducks; the perfect setting for the white-haired man who stood a little distance off, smoking a pipe and throwing something for his dog to fetch. In his dark green wax jacket and a tweed flat cap, he looked the very picture of an English country gentleman.

Except his voice was anything but English.

"Och, ye numpty," he was saying to the dog, with great affection, "it's behind you."

I had never seen that breed of dog before. Had it been a different color, I'd have said it was a setter, only I'd never seen a setter that wasn't Irish red or English speckled white-and-brown. This one was black. Its wavy coat was marked with chestnut brown on legs and throat and muzzle, with two small brown marks above its eyes that looked like eyebrows. Turning round and round again in search of the dropped object, it snuffed the ground halfheartedly before it caught our scent instead and with a panting grin of welcome came across to greet us.

"Hello, Hector." Jacqui liked dogs well enough, but didn't pat them. Hector had to come to me for that, and when I scratched his ears it set his feathered triangle of a tail in motion.

Jacqui, continuing on, told the man, "We're a bit late, I'm sorry. Did you get my text?"

"Aye. No problem. I never expect you on time."

Alistair Scott was a tall man, well built, with a face that I guessed would have once been incredibly handsome, and still drew the eye. Even mine, and I normally didn't find bearded men all that attractive. His beard, neatly trimmed, was the same ivory white as his hair, also tidily clipped and kept short, and his eyes were a warm, lively brown.

To be honest, though, I didn't notice most of that till later. At the moment, I was looking at the dog. His eyes were warmly brown as well, the little chestnut marks above them giving him a questioning expression, as I asked, "Is he a setter?"

"Aye. A Gordon setter. Hunting dogs, they're meant to be, and Hector would have been as well, if his fool of a first owner hadn't ruined him. She took him on a full day's hunt afore he'd ever heard a gunshot. After that, if anything went bang, he'd tuck his tail and run. His owner didn't want him, then. She sent him to the pound."

"And so you rescued him?"

"Aye. It was never his fault, and you don't cast a life aside like that." Alistair Scott had been walking towards me while he had been talking, and now he bent briefly to rumple the dog's ears himself, with a leather-gloved hand. "He's got lots of good years in him yet." He fell silent for a moment and I wondered, given what my cousin had been telling me, if he was thinking not about the dog but of himself. Then he roused himself and added, "He's a brilliant fetcher still, for all that, but today his mind's elsewhere."

I asked, "Hunting for birds, was she, Hector's first owner?"

"Aye. Pheasant."

"Well, that's why he's stressed, then."

I noticed the pause while both Jacqui and Alistair Scott studied Hector as though they were looking for evidence that he was stressed. I felt sure they would see it. The signs were so obvious.

But to be perfectly clear, I glanced back at the pond, with its flurry of ducks, then I nodded at Hector, who was panting with the corners of his mouth drawn back, his ears tucked closely to his head. "He doesn't like the birds," I said. "You want to take him further down the Common, he'll be happier."

This second pause was shorter, but it gave me time to

realize that I hadn't introduced myself yet, properly, the way that normal people did. I forced myself to look away from Hector for a moment, raised my head and held my hand out. "Pleased to meet you, Mr. Scott. I'm Sara Thomas."

"Alistair." He took his glove off when he shook my hand—the mark, my father always said, of a true gentleman. "And yes, I thought you might be. Shall we?"

As we walked further away from the pond, down the side of the Common, his gaze moved from my face to Jacqui's and back, and I guessed he was trying to find some resemblance. There wasn't one. Jacqui always looked as though she'd stepped out of a fashion plate, her dark hair in its well-cut bob that fell back into place no matter how the wind was blowing, whereas my hair was more frequently a wild and tousled mess that couldn't quite decide if it was blond or brown and, trying to be both, fell in between. It wouldn't keep to any style, so I just kept it on the shorter side and trusted that its shagginess would seem all of a piece with my informal sense of fashion.

I liked scarves, and winter gave me an excuse to wear them daily. I had chosen for today a thickly woolly one in stripes of green and orange with a fringe that hung below the hip-length hem of my old quilted coat and brushed my jeans. If I'd been meeting just with Jacqui, I'd have changed the laces in my boots to green and orange, too, to match, and chosen one glove of each color from the jumbled basket in my entry hall. But first impressions, I knew, were important, and Alistair Scott was a man of tradition, so I'd kept my bootlaces black, and my gloves black, as well. They were kid suede and very expensive, a gift from my mother last Christmas, but I found them stiff. I'd been happy to slide my hand free for the handshake. I kept it free just a bit longer, to give Hector's silky-soft head one more pat as he circled my legs.

"He likes you," said Alistair Scott. "He's not often so friendly with strangers."

"Yes, well, dogs can always spot the dog-deprived."

He smiled. "You haven't got one of your own?"

"I don't have any pets. I wouldn't want to leave them on their own all day, while I'm at work."

My mention of work made him shift topics. "Jacqui," he said, "tells me you're between jobs, at the moment."

I considered this, sliding my glove back on. "Well, that depends."

"On what?"

"Whether I'm working for you."

He looked down at me, smiling more broadly. "You're very direct, aren't you?"

"Sometimes. I'm not a professional code breaker, though. You do know that?"

"Your cousin says you cracked that cipher in seventeen minutes," he said. "At a party."

"A wedding reception. And it wasn't a difficult cipher. I gather the one that you'd want me to work on is different?"

He nodded. "But written the same year. There might be some overlap."

"And it's in Paris?"

"The outskirts of Paris," he told me. "Chatou. It's a suburb, just west of the city itself."

"There's no chance I could do the work here, from a copy?"

"The owner is very…" He searched for the word, until Jacqui supplied it:

"Insistent."

"Aye." Alistair Scott nodded. "*Very* insistent the source can't be copied, or taken away from the house. But she's willing to give you a room for the time that you work on it."

Frowning a little, I asked, "And how long would that be?"

"That depends," he replied, in his turn. "Once you've worked out the cipher itself, it will probably take a few weeks to transcribe the thing."

We had come halfway down the long green of the Common now, midway between the pond end and the road to Richmond, where the cars were passing in a shifting dance of color. "And what," I asked Alistair Scott, "is 'the thing'? Jacqui mentioned an old book?"

"A diary," he said, to correct me. "A handwritten diary, kept by a young lady named Mary Dundas." He gave it the Scottish inflection: Dun-DASS.

I stopped walking when the others did and watched Hector, no longer stressed, bound out to recover the object his master had thrown—a stuffed red canvas cylinder, roughly the size and the shape of a compact umbrella when folded. A remnant of his training days, I guessed. Bird dogs were meant to have soft mouths, and not carry anything hard. Hector brought his prize happily over to me, long tail wagging, and taking the cylinder's toggled end I threw it out again for him.

"Was she someone important, this Mary Dundas?" I asked.

Alistair Scott shook his head. "Quite the opposite. She was, from what I can gather, an ordinary girl. I expect that her diary will be about ordinary things. That's what makes it so valuable."

"How so?"

"You've not read my books," he observed, very certain.

"I haven't, no."

"I write the history of ordinary people. The kings and the

queens and the nobles don't interest me nearly as much as the people they ruled."

Jacqui told me, "This new book that Alistair's writing is all about Jacobite exiles."

She said that as though I should know what those were, and I nearly just nodded and answered with something like "Ah," so as not to reveal my own ignorance, but I was spared that when Alistair Scott asked, straight out,

"D'ye know much at all about Jacobites?"

Truth, in the face of a question, came easily. "No."

"Scottish history, in general?"

"Not much."

"Well now, my country has a complicated past. A group of tribes all trapped together by geography, who'd sooner stab each other in the back than build a nation," was his summary. "And when the Reformation came, religion only made those old divisions that much stronger." He threw the canvas cylinder for Hector, further than my own throw, far out on the green. "The Highlanders stayed Catholic, and the rest turned either fiercely Presbyterian or fell between the two camps and became Episcopalian. And ruling them—or trying to—you had the line of Stewart kings and queens, whose own alliances with France were both a blessing and a curse to them."

"Like Mary, Queen of Scots," I said.

"Exactly. And her son, King James the Sixth, who afterwards became King James the First of England also, when the English Queen Elizabeth the First died with no children to succeed her."

"And King James the Sixth," I asked. "Was he a Catholic or a Protestant?"

"Protestant. As was his son, Charles the First. But Charles

thought a king was above being ruled by his people. They didn't agree. That's what led to the Civil War. After a few years of battles, King Charles made a tactical decision to seek protection from the Scottish Presbyterians. A poor decision, as it happened, since their army held him prisoner, made a deal with England's Parliament, and sold him to them for just under half a million pounds."

"And Parliament beheaded him."

"They did, aye. And put Cromwell in his place, to lead without a king for several years, and in this time the widowed queen with all her children fled to France. The French king was her nephew, her own brother's son, and so he gave her refuge in a palace of her own at Saint-Germain-en-Laye. Now, Charles the First had several children, but you only need mind two: young Charles, who would become King Charles the Second in his turn, and James, his brother. James was sixteen when his father died, and twenty-seven when the English Parliament restored his brother Charles to the throne. As Duke of York, James earned a reputation for himself as a great champion of the navy, a well-respected man, even though unlike his brother he openly practiced his faith as a Catholic. And when James was fifty-one, Charles the Second died, and James was crowned king."

Hector had brought me his toy, and I dealt with it absently, sorting the chain of events in my mind. "But I thought that you couldn't become king, if you were a Catholic."

"That law wasn't written yet. Nor would it be, for another few years. But you're right, it presented a problem. The last time a Catholic had ruled them, a century earlier, things hadn't gone all that well for the Protestants, and there were many in England and Scotland who felt fair uneasy with James on the throne. The only thing that calmed them was the knowledge that the crown would pass to one of James's grown daughters, both good Protestants. But then his second wife, who like her husband was a Catholic, had a son, who having had the fortune and the sense to be born male, would take the place of his half sisters and become the heir. A Catholic heir. Those who had bided their time knew they'd have to take action. The elder of James's two daughters was married to William of Orange, a man of ambition," he said, "and a Protestant."

"Wait." I was vaguely remembering things from a long-ago history class. "Is this the Glorious Revolution?"

Alistair Scott answered, drily, "For some, aye, it might have been glorious. But not for James. A committee of nobles sent word into Holland, to William of Orange, inviting him to come and rule them as king, with his wife Mary as queen. William came, there was fighting, and James—no doubt mindful of what had become of his father—made certain his wife and their wee son were safely sent out of the country, to France, where his cousin the king would protect them. And then he did what he had done as a lad; what his brother had done when the times were against them: he followed his family to exile."

My cousin thought James should have stayed to fight. "Think of how different things might have been if he had stayed."

"Aye, he might have ended up a little shorter, like his father."

"No, really," said Jacqui. "It wasn't the best thing to do. If he'd stayed, then his enemies couldn't have claimed he'd abandoned his kingdom, and William and Mary could never have ruled in his place, and—"

I said, "You don't know that. It might have changed nothing."

Jacqui wasn't swayed. "A king should never run away."

I didn't continue to argue, because I saw Jacqui was doing that thing with her mouth again, being defensive. But Alistair Scott either hadn't yet learned when my cousin was digging her heels in, or else it didn't bother him.

"The problem is," he said, "we want our kings to act like kings, and not like men. King James the Seventh was a man. He had a wife and newborn baby to protect, and he was being asked to fight his own grown daughters, who had taken sides against him. He had seen, firsthand and vividly, the damage that a civil war could do, not only to himself and those he cared for, but to the whole country and its common people. Better he should spare them that and bide a while in France, until the storm had all blown over. It had worked before. I've no doubt James expected the same thing would happen this time."

"But it didn't," I remarked.

"It didn't, no." I wasn't good at judging tones of voice. I only knew that his had changed. He threw the soft red cylinder a little farther this time, and the dog raced gamely after it. "But he wasn't on his own in France. The people who stayed loyal to him—Jacobites, they called themselves, from *Jacobus*, the Latin word for James—they fought with him and bled with him and when he fled, they followed him. The bulk of them, at first, were Irish Catholics, but the Scots were there as well, and even English. It came down," he said, "to what a man believed. What made a king? The will of God, or Acts of Parliament? For Jacobites, the answer was a simple one. A king was born a king, and nothing men could write on paper could undo that. So when James the Seventh died, his son, to them, became the rightful king: King James the Eighth of Scotland, and the Third of England also. And with each new attempt they made to set him on his throne again, their ranks in exile swelled, as men were outlawed for their loyalty to James and came across to join his shadow court at Saint-Germain-en-Laye."

He used the proper French pronunciation, San Zher-MAN en Lay, but I really only registered that briefly.

My imagination had been fully captured by the image of a shadow court—a castle with its king and all his courtiers who were real, yet without substance, moving always as a mirror to their counterparts across the sea.

"That's near Chatou," he said, "the place where you'll be going. Where the diary of Mary Dundas is."

"So then," I said, getting my dates straight, "it would have been James the Eighth ruling the Jacobites when she was writing that diary? The baby whose birth was the cause of the war?"

"Aye."

I looked to the long winter shadows that stretched past our feet from the trees at our backs, and I tried to imagine a girl at that long-ago shadow court. "You still haven't told me," I said, "why the diary's so valuable." And for a writer who claimed that he wrote about ordinary people, his lecture so far had been mostly about kings and queens. When I pointed this out to him, Alistair Scott turned to look at me, smiling as though I had somehow amused him.

"It has, aye," he said. "And you've answered your own question there, in a fashion."

"I don't understand."

"Well now, history is not just the tale of the victors," he said. "It's the tale of the privileged. The men in the mud of the battlefield didn't leave much of a story behind, and the stories they did tell were mostly ignored or forgotten.

The papers and documents that have survived are the ones that were deemed worth preserving, not always the ones that would be of most interest to someone like me. But this diary of Mary Dundas is a treasure *because* she was no one important. Her father was one of the wig makers at Saint-Germain, and her mother was French—we know that much, at least, from the baptism registers. And it appears that, at some point, young Mary was sent to her mother's relations, because when her diary begins—and it starts in plain writing, not cipher— she's on her way back with her brother, to Saint-Germain, coming to live with the Jacobites there. So not only will she be recording the day-to-day life of the common folk at Saint-Germain, she'll be doing it with the keen eye of an outsider. *That's* why her journal's so valuable to me."

I nodded. "I see." And I did see. The girl in that shadow court had her own shape, now. Her own voice, which I could restore to her.

I let my gaze travel over the green of the Common to where a quaint pub stood at one of the far corners, with a tall Christmas tree set up in front of it, cheerful in tinsel and lights, a reminder that Christmas itself was a week and a half away. Christmas, that time of new hope born of winter, when someone like Alistair Scott might imagine it possible to share that rebirth himself.

Second chances, I thought, as my gaze shifted slightly to Hector, the dog who'd been branded as useless but rescued because one man firmly believed that a life shouldn't be cast aside. And although I had never seen Calum MacCrae, much less met him, I suddenly very much wanted to see his works knocked off the bestseller lists by this new book of Alistair Scott's.

I asked, "When would you need me to go to Chatou?"

"Well, as soon as you feel you could—"

"Boxing Day. Would that be soon enough?"

With that decided, my cousin said, "Brilliant." She looked at the pub, too. "I'm actually starting to feel a bit cold…"

"Aye, this standing around isn't good for a body." And whistling to Hector, the Scotsman said cheerfully, "Let's have a walk in the woods."

CHAPTER 3

Another sport is drawing near:
it is like the dark rolling of that wave on the coast.
—Macpherson, "Fingal," Book One

Chanteloup-les-Vignes
January 14, 1732

I T SEEMED ON THAT morning to Mary Dundas that the new
year intended to go on exactly the same as the last, bringing all the excitement, surprise, and adventure she'd come to
expect in her twenty-one years: namely, none.

She had risen at five, as she always did, for her uncle
held to the advice of the physicians quoted in the work of
Rabelais: "To rise at five, to dine at nine, to sup at five, to
sleep at nine," and so he'd run his household for as long as
she'd been part of it.

With the help of the maid she had dressed with her cousin
Colette, as she always did, and they had talked, not of what
they would actually do on that day, but of what might occur
should the wind ever suddenly change its direction and
blow in their favor. Perhaps then the handsome Chevalier
de Vilbray who'd taken the nearby château for the hunting
last autumn and stayed over Christmas would, feeling a need
for companionship, come by to visit. Or maybe their other
near neighbors were even now planning that musical evening
they'd promised to host.

But at breakfast, while Mary had eaten her butter and
bread and fresh milk, as she always did, no invitations had

come to enliven the day and no handsome young nobles had called at the door, and here she was, sitting as usual in the salon in her chair by the window with Frisque, her dog, curled on her lap, and her other two cousins, Gaspard and Jacques, idly debating some trivial point about bridges and which was the longest, and Mary felt certain that anything, *anything*, would be a blessed relief.

"Does it honestly matter?" she asked Gaspard. "Surely each bridge is as long as it needs to be, and serves its purpose as well as the others."

Gaspard, who was four years her junior, his dark hair just recently clipped to allow for the white-powdered wig with its short sides and black-ribboned queue that he thought made him look much more serious, turned now and spoiled the effect with a grin. "That is so like you English, to judge such an intricate thing as a bridge by its function, and no other measure."

"How else would one measure a bridge, but by whether it does what you built it to do?" Mary countered. "And I am not English."

"Half English, then."

Colette, between them, looked up from her sewing and shook her head, setting her bright curls to dancing. "No, no, she is right. Uncle Guillaume is Scottish, not English."

Gaspard blew a sharp puff of air to declare the distinction irrelevant. "What does it matter which nation she claims?"

He looked so very much the part of the young gallant then that Mary had to take great pains to hide her smile, for she was far too fond of him to wish to wound his pride. Instead, she settled one hand on the silken hair of Frisque's warm back and felt the lazy thump-thump of the little dog's tail on her lap. "I claim neither," she said. "I am happily nationless."

Jacques, who would not be fourteen till next month but who was, without question, more thoughtful than all of them, stirred in his own chair. "You can't be."

"Why not?"

"No person can truly be nationless."

Mary knew otherwise. She had been born without a nation—daughter of an exile at the French court of a foreign king who had himself no country and no crown. The fact her mother had been French gave her but partial claim to call herself the same, and she had never tried to do so. Having lived these fifteen years, since she was six, within her aunt and uncle's house, she had adopted French as her first language and adapted to the customs and the fashions of the nation, but while everybody else called her "Marie," in her own mind she was still "Mary," neither Scots nor French, but falling in between.

She plainly said so to her cousins now, and Colette answered, "Silly, if you will not stand in Scotland and you will not stand in France, you will have no place left to stand but in the water that divides them."

To which Gaspard added slyly, "Perhaps *then* our talk of bridges will not bore you."

A swish of skirts and briskly clicking heels announced the entrance of his mother, Mary's aunt, who asked them, "Which of you can possibly be bored on such a morning?" But she knew. Her smiling eyes went straight to Mary's. "You have been too long indoors, I think. Come, bring Frisque. He's half asleep, as well. We'll take a walk together."

"Now? Outside?"

"Where else?" Aunt Magdalene, once having set her mind to something, could be like a plow horse walking in a furrow—difficult to turn. And to be truthful, Mary had no great objection to a walk. If not adventurous, at least it was a welcome change of scene.

She fetched her cloak and muff and changed her slippers for the heavy shoes that better warmed her feet while she was walking, and with Frisque at her heels she trailed after her aunt down the corridor and out the back door.

Outside, the snow lay soft and thick beneath the sleeping vines that climbed the hill behind the line of houses. Come the spring, the sun would bring those vines to life. The vines, in turn, would bring forth vibrant clusters of the little grapes that through the summer and the autumn would enliven the whole village, giving industry and purpose to the villagers who worked towards the harvest and production of the wine that had, for centuries, provided them a living. But for now, the vines lay dormant. And they waited.

Mary, watching Frisque circle and sniff round those leafless vines, felt once again the stir of restlessness and discontent within her breast, and fought to push it down again before her aunt could notice any change in her expression. There was little, she had learned, that could escape the keenly empathetic eye of her Aunt Magdalene.

They walked a little distance without speaking. Mary liked the silence, and the frosted air that smelled of wood smoke, and the view that spread and grew as they climbed higher. She could see, now, clear across the tiled rooftops of their neighbors' houses, clear past the tall spire of the pale stone church of Saint-Roch with its two great bells, across the trees that hid the roofs of the next village, Andrésy, and over the thin curving ribbon of the River Seine, to the dark forest on the shore beyond: the woods of Saint-Germain.

"Marie, my dear," her aunt said—using, as she always did,

the French form of her niece's name, "how much do you remember of your life before you came to us?"

The question caught her unprepared. Surprised, she tried to gather up her thoughts and focused harder on the dark mass of the forest, at the farthest edge of which she knew, although she could not see it, stood the great Château of Saint-Germain-en-Laye—the royal castle in whose shadow she herself had been baptized.

She said, in honesty, "I have few memories."

Those she had retained were like a web of lace, connected in a loose way but with gaps and holes and spaces, and so frail and insubstantial she was never sure how safe they were to trust.

Her mother's face had long since faded from her mind and been supplanted by the image in the portrait hanging here in the salon that showed her mother and Aunt Magdalene as they had looked before they'd both been married. Mary liked that portrait well, but there was little in the pale determined face and calm brown eyes of the young woman who had grown to be her mother that stirred any sense of recognition. It was not her mother's face that she remembered, but the feel of her—the soft warmth of her arms, the firmer softness of her silken bodice over stays, the ever-present tickle of the ruffled lace that edged her white chemise and brushed on Mary's cheek and upturned nose when she was snuggling on her mother's lap.

And there were scents, as well—a whiff of roses, or of lavender. And later still, the scents of sickness, not so pleasant to recall. And that was all the memory of her mother that was left to her. No voice, though she'd been told her mother sang, and she imagined that her mother's voice had been much like Aunt Magdalene's, with warm and pleasant tones that seemed to always be prepared to open easily to laughter.

Of her brothers and her father she remembered something more, but even then, their forms and features had long blurred to indistinction, and their words and voices were reduced to whispers in a language she now rarely used herself, despite her uncle's stoic efforts to make sure she did not lose her English. "Any foreign language," so Uncle Jacques had told her, "is an asset in this world. It will expand your opportunities."

He'd bought her English books, and when the local blacksmith had gone off to Amsterdam and come home with an Irish wife, then Uncle Jacques had happily employed her as a tutor, not to Mary on her own but all the children. Only Mary, though, who'd spoken English for her first six years of life, had truly profited from this arrangement. Colette, Mary's cousin, had no ear for learning languages, and both Gaspard and young Jacques had been too distracted by the fresh blond beauty of the blacksmith's Irish wife to pay attention to their lessons.

Still, the end result had been that Mary, though she spoke in French, could switch to English when she needed to with hardly any accent. And she could at least put meaning to the words that she recalled her father saying, when he'd brought her here to leave her for the final time.

"Now, Mary," he had told her, "be a good lass for your uncle and your aunt, and mind the manners you've been taught, and use the sense that you've been given, and I promise you, you'll have a better life here than I ever could have given you."

At least, that's what she thought he'd said. The years, perhaps, had rearranged his words and phrased them into a more sentimental speech within her memory, the same memory that insisted she'd replied to him, "I want to stay with you." And that his thumb had brushed a tear from her hot cheek, and he had said, "We do not always get the things we want."

She *did* remember, clearly, that she'd cried for him and called him back, and that he had not turned; he'd walked away from her with quick, determined strides, head bent, until her aunt's broad skirts had rustled round to block her vision as the carriage wheels had rattled down the road.

She looked towards that same road now and squared her shoulders as her father had, and asked her aunt, "Why do you wish to know what I remember?"

She had never known Aunt Magdalene to search for words, and yet it seemed to Mary that her aunt was doing just that, in the moment's pause. And then her aunt remarked, "We've had a letter from your brother."

Even less expected. The surprise, this time, stopped Mary in midstep, and made her heedless of the fact that she was standing ankle-deep in snow. She had three brothers. "Which of them?"

Aunt Magdalene said, "Nicolas. Do you remember him at all?"

Her eldest brother. Nicolas. Broad shoulders and a pair of boots. Two hands that tossed her in the air and caught her when she came down laughing. In a voice that hurt her throat a little, Mary answered, "Yes."

"He has returned to Saint-Germain-en-Laye, and now he wishes you should join him."

Mary tried to take this in. Her mind, resisting the attempt, focused instead on little Frisque, who seemed convinced that there was something of great interest hidden underneath the snow that mounded round the rooted base of one staked vine, and had begun to dig in earnest to discover it. A mouse perhaps, thought Mary, sleeping in its winter burrow with its family.

"When," she asked, "did he return?" She'd thought he was in Italy.

Aunt Magdalene paused longer this time. Then she said, "Two years ago."

Mary looked from Frisque to her aunt, well aware her feelings would be plainly written on her face. "Two years? He has been here two years? So close, and yet he has not ever…" She could not continue. She looked sharply down, then up again, and out across the river to the darkly distant forest.

"He has family of his own now," said her aunt. "A wife and children. And a life at Saint-Germain has never been a certain one financially. Perhaps he wanted to be sure that he was well and settled, before sending for you."

Mary nodded, saying nothing, thinking hard and blinking harder, while her aunt, who knew her well, allowed her space to turn things over in her mind. They turned so very quickly that she could not get them sorted, or begin to make much sense of them beyond the simple fact that just beyond those trees, the brother whom she had not seen for fifteen years was even now attending to the business of his day. Perhaps, like her, he was outdoors. Perhaps his gaze was even turned in this direction…

"I did not expect," she said, in that tight voice that hurt her still, "that anyone would ever send for me." And then, because that made her sound too needy, and she was not altogether sure exactly what she needed, she let her forehead crease into a thoughtful frown. "Am I to have a choice?"

"My dear, you always have a choice." Her aunt spoke calmly, in a voice that carried strength and reassurance. "Uncle Jacques and I would never send you where you did not wish to go. But Nicolas does seem to want you with him very much. And Saint-Germain," she said, her own chin lifting in a nod towards the unseen castle past the forest on the far side of the river, "is a world apart from this one. You were too young, I think. You have forgotten how it is to live within a royal court."

A dim remembrance flickered in the corner of her memory: someone's hands—her brother's, maybe—hoisting her up high to see above the heads of others, while a murmur of excitement chased around them like the wind across a summer field. *Look, Mary. Look! The king!*

The flicker died, and left a darkness in its place.

And Mary said, "There is no court at Saint-Germain. Not anymore." The king, if he had ever truly been a king, was gone. The queen, his mother, had been dead for years.

"But there are courtiers still," her aunt remarked. "They will have daughters of your age for you to meet and talk with. And young men with whom to dance." The smile was coloring Aunt Magdalene's warm voice now as she took the few steps needed to draw level with the place where Mary stood, an undemanding presence at her side, but giving comfort nonetheless. "Unless," she said, "you'd rather linger here and battle with Colette to catch the eye of the Chevalier de Vilbray?"

The thought drew Mary from her deeper ones and made her smile, as well. "The chevalier pads his stockings. And his breath is none too pleasant."

Frisque's quarry had eluded him. Abandoning his digging, the undaunted spaniel trundled through the snow towards another vine, his plumed tail wagging. He'd never seemed to mind that his entire world was bounded by this property, thought Mary, and for that she'd always envied him. For fifteen years now, she'd been looking daily to that forest and the wider world beyond it, to the smudge of smoke and rooflines that lay further still than Saint-Germain-en-Laye, past the next bend in the bright river: Paris.

Daily she had looked in that direction and had wished and hoped and dreamed, and all the while she had stayed rooted in this village as securely as these rows of tied and fruitless vines that slumbered here and waited for the sun.

We do not always get the things we want, her father's voice reminded her.

Aunt Magdalene was watching her. "Marie, my darling, you are twenty-one. Your mother, at that age, had met your father, and she would have never done that if she had stayed here."

"I know." Anticipation waged a war with reason in her heart. "But I don't like to think of leaving."

"Then perhaps you ought to view it not as leaving, but returning." Her aunt laid a warm arm over Mary's shoulders. Hugged her close. "We have been blessed to have you with us, but I think that always here"—she tapped her fingers on her cloak, above her heart—"you've had a little voice that calls to you. And maybe now, my darling, is the time for you to let it lead you home."

CHAPTER 4

Thou scarce hast been known to me…
—Macpherson, "Fingal," Book Five

On the road near Poissy
January 22, 1732

H IS EYES WERE BLUE. She marked the fact because her own were brown, just like their mother's in the portrait. And where her hair was brown, as well—a plain dark brown, and straight—her brother Nicolas had hair so fair that when he'd combed the front and sides up over the front edges of his wig, he'd needed hardly any powder to blend all into the same clean shade of white. His eyebrows, too, were fair, as were his lashes, and his features weren't at all like hers. He had her mother's oval face, the same long nose and narrow mouth, the steady eyes that made him look intelligent and thoughtful.

Her face, she knew, was like a heart, more pointed at the chin, and while she'd often been called pretty she'd met no one who, at first glance, had assumed she was intelligent. She didn't really mind. It often worked to her advantage and she'd used it as a shield, having observed that people seemed to value wit above intelligence; vivacity and merriness above demure and shy behavior. Wanting to be liked, she'd learned to bury her own shyness and become another person when in public, one who entertained with turns of phrase and flirted with a confidence she rarely felt inside. It made her popular and sought-after at gatherings and village dances, and had drawn the admiration of a few young men, but it had also kept her safe.

She wore that braver face, so lively and at home in bright society, to guard the smaller girl within her who'd been left behind once, and who'd long ago determined she would never be so vulnerable again.

Except today. Today, that braver face gave no protection. This was Nicolas, her brother, and from earlier this morning when he'd greeted her so warmly with a genuine embrace, to this moment when she sat here pressed so closely to his shoulder in the confines of the horse-drawn chaise, she'd felt every inch that smaller girl. He only had to smile at her, as he was doing now, and she had no shields left to hide behind.

He said, "You always used to do that."

They were speaking English, and for once she felt most grateful that her uncle had insisted she not lose that language, even if she had to think more carefully to answer, "Do what?"

"Frown so that it made this little line, just here"—he touched one finger lightly to the spot between his own pale brows—"whenever you were thinking."

"Oh." She consciously relaxed her forehead, trying to make light of it. "I can't imagine that it happened often, then."

He told her, "On the contrary. You were a small philosopher. I always had to work to make you smile."

"You used to toss me in the air."

"I did. You remember that, do you?" Nicolas looked pleased. "Our mother often scolded me and worried I would drop you, but I liked to hear you laugh."

He would have been just a bit younger in those days than she was now, Mary decided—a young man of eighteen or nineteen—and yet in her memory he'd seemed so grown up, tall and strong in his long coat and boots with the sword at his side. And now he was nearing his midthirties, already showing the softness that men sometimes gained round their middles; the small lines of weariness and resignation that life settled into their features.

"You could not do it now," she said. "You'd do yourself an injury."

His laugh was not like hers. It was a lower sound, and brief, but it stirred memories. "Are you saying that the years have made me weak?"

She shook her head. "But they've made me too old to carry so."

"You're hardly old, my dear. You'll not be two and twenty till July."

The chaise lurched and Frisque shifted in protest on her lap, and Mary seized on that as an excuse to look down for a moment, feeling a tingling warmth at the back of her eyes that she sought to control. He'd remembered her birthday.

She hadn't known what to expect when he'd come to collect her that morning. He had caused quite a sensation in the village by arriving in the chaise, its upright body painted fashionably green with two great yellow wheels that crisply cut the snow, the driver riding as postilion on the near horse of the well-matched pair in harness, looking every bit as grand as the Chevalier de Vilbray's own team and coachman.

Mary's cousins had been slightly disappointed when her brother had explained the chaise was merely hired, and not his own, and yet for Mary when her brother had alighted from the chaise and come towards her with a quick smile and a voice that she remembered, she would not have cared a whit if he had made the trip on foot. It was enough to have him there, and hear him greet her by her name, and feel the warmth as he had wrapped her in his arms.

He had not stayed there long. For all he'd started early in the morning, it had already been midday when he'd come to Chanteloup, and there would still be a long journey back to Saint-Germain ahead of them, so Nicolas had only lingered for the time it took to tend the horses, water them, and let the driver eat and briefly rest while Nicolas sat down to dinner with the family he'd not seen in years.

He'd smiled across the table at Colette and said, "You were a tiny thing when last I saw you, naught but eyes and curls. And you," he'd said, to Gaspard, "were an infant still, all dressed in ruffles."

Gaspard had flushed, not wanting a reminder of the childhood state that he was so impatient to discard, but young Jacques—who of course had not been born at all when Nicolas had paid a visit last to Chanteloup—had made the comment, "Gaspard still wears ruffles."

Nicolas had glanced at the long falls of lace at Gaspard's cuffs and shirtfront. "So I see. He would be perfectly at home at court, with such fine clothes. A match for any gentleman."

And with that Gaspard, too, had been won over.

Even Frisque, who had no love of strangers, had seemed most content at dinner to sit under Nicolas's chair. And even now, as they went rattling in the chaise across the bridge at Poissy, one light touch of Nicolas's hand was all it took to reassure and calm the little dog, who settled once again in peace on Mary's lap.

Her brother said, "He travels well, that dog."

"It is the first time he has traveled."

"Then I'm all the more impressed." He looked at her, and Mary did not know what he was thinking. Perhaps he was contrasting her experience with his; her settled life with all the distance he had traveled, and the places he had lived.

She knew, from what he'd said at dinner, that he and their father had gone with King James to Avignon, a town beyond the French king's jurisdiction.

"Why could he not stay in France?" young Jacques had asked, and Uncle Jacques had told him, "Because when the Spanish war was done, the father of our present king did sign a treaty promising he would no longer recognize or aid King James, but would instead acknowledge none but George, the Prince of Hanover, as Britain's rightful king. I do not think it was a promise that he meant to keep. Our old king was the cousin of King James, and very fond of him, but then the old king died and King James went across to Scotland, where his armies were defeated, and when he returned to France our young king's regent said he could not stay, and so…" His shrug had been expressive.

Nicolas had said, "And so we went to Avignon."

The queen, as she'd been then—King James's mother— had stayed on at Saint-Germain, allowed to keep the royal pension she was paid each year from France, but King James had been forced to seek a welcome elsewhere. Finding Avignon too isolating, he had moved first to Urbino, then finally to Rome, where he'd settled in his new court with the blessing and protection of the pope.

Nicolas had spoken, over dinner, of the ancient curiosities of Rome, and of the palace of the pope, and of the people who were living at King James's court who had once been acquaintances of Mary's aunt and uncle. He'd talked to Mary briefly of her other brothers: Charles, just one year older than herself, and John, four years above that, who had both been sent away to school the year that she'd been left behind, and who were now reportedly in Rotterdam and Spain. And he had told her of their father, who still worked as a perruquier for King James and his nobles, crafting wigs as fine as any made in France or England.

Gaspard, with his newfound love of wigs, had been intrigued. "Do you think Uncle Guillaume would make *me* a wig, were I to ask him?"

Nicolas had smiled. "Well, you would have to go to Rome to do the asking, for my father will not make the journey north. He's too fond of the sunshine and the pleasures of the court, and there is nothing here to draw him back."

Aunt Magdalene had quickly looked at Mary then, her kind eyes always ready to give sympathy, but Mary had already schooled her own face not to show the stab of hurt those words had caused.

"And what was it that drew you back?" she'd asked her brother, in a tone that strove for lightness.

He'd regarded her a moment while she waited for his answer, then he'd faintly smiled and looked away to share that smile with everyone and, lifting up his glass, had said, "I do confess it was the memory of my uncle's fine red wine, for in these fifteen years I've never drunk its equal."

The talk had turned to other things and Mary had not pressed him further, though she would have dearly loved to know the reason why he had returned to Saint-Germain, and why he'd waited two long years to tell them he was back, and why he'd chosen after all that time to come now and collect her.

They were questions that still hung between them now, in the close confines of the horse-drawn chaise, while Nicolas looked down at her and Mary did not know what he was thinking.

So she asked him, and he told her in that same plain, forthright manner, "You are not what I expected."

No, thought Mary. No, of course she wasn't. He would have expected that she'd grown to be the image of their mother, who from all accounts—and from the portrait's evidence— had been a beauty of the court, a woman of accomplishments.

Guarding her reaction as she'd done before at dinnertime, and in a voice as light, she said, "You must be disappointed."

"Quite the contrary." He moved his hand and laid it over hers where it was resting on Frisque's silken back, and gathering her fingers in his own he said a second time, more serious and quiet, "Quite the contrary."

A warmth spread from his touch and, just as Frisque had calmed beneath it when they'd crossed the bridge, so Mary felt the comfort of it now, and felt the tension leave her body and her mind. She'd slept so poorly these past days with all the worry and excitement, waiting for her brother, both impatient for and dreading his arrival, and in truth she had not realized just how weary it had made her till that small but tender action and its show of his approval seemed to lift from her the burden of uncertainty.

In the peaceful moments following, with Nicolas's shoulder pressing close against her own within the jolting chaise, she watched the fall of snow between the branches of the dark trees growing close beside the road, a sign they'd entered the great forest that belonged to Saint-Germain-en-Laye. She had so often looked towards this forest and imagined it, but now she let her eyes drift closed against the sight and wondered if she'd ever felt this measure of contentment in her childhood, with no cares or fears to vex her for the moment, and her brother close beside her, and the sense that she was loved and safe and wanted.

She had slept. The trees were gone, replaced by level farm-land lying thick with shadows in the blue of twilight, and the night was coming on. Already shapes were indistinct; through the front window of the chaise she saw the driver's figure outlined by the yellow braid that trimmed his coat and by the paleness of the powdered wig beneath his hat, but both the horses, being dark, were nigh invisible, the bursts of their warm labored breath appearing in the winter air like shapes of passing ghosts.

In faint confusion Mary raised her head from where it had been resting on her brother's shoulder. "Are we nearly there?" she asked. For surely, if it was now nearly night…

"We were diverted," said her brother, "by an accident. A wagon overturned upon the road, so we were told, and one horse injured, and a rider was sent back to give a warning that the way was quite impassable. We had to turn and come the southern route along the river, which has cost us time and daylight, I'm afraid."

She sat more upright, holding Frisque a little closer. Up ahead, she saw a long and jagged slash of forest showing black between the deep blue-gray of sky and the dark green-gray of the land. It stood some distance off still. "And is that the woods of Saint-Germain-en-Laye?"

"No. No, we are two leagues to the east of Saint-Germain. That is the forest at Chatou. There is a bridge there we can cross."

The shadows of the night had nearly swallowed all the light now, till the blackness of that forest drew the color from both land and sky and flattened them to nothing. Tiny flecks of yellow gleamed and glittered and were one by one extinguished—all the windows of the houses by the river,

Mary realized, being shuttered. Only two small lights were left to burn, to mark the bridge.

She did not relish traveling across that bridge and through the wood so late, but she'd resigned herself to doing it when Nicolas remarked, "I have an old friend at Chatou who keeps a grand house and a grander table, and is always keen to welcome company. We'll stop here for the night."

She masked her own relief with calmness. "If you think it wise."

"I do." She could not see her brother's features in the dimness, but she heard the reassurance in his voice and felt it as he warmly laid his hand on hers again. "I would not have you journey in the dark."

CHAPTER 5

T HE LIGHT NEVER LASTED at this time of year. There had still been a hint of late afternoon sun when we'd landed in Paris, but that had been fading so steadily I was now finding it difficult to read my map well enough to direct Jacqui while she was driving.

I told her, "I think we should keep to the right, here."

"I'm sure we can find it."

"You said you'd been here before."

"Only once," she defended herself, "when Alistair sent me to look at the diary and offer to buy it. And that wasn't in the winter, it was June."

I wasn't sure what difference that made, since a road should lead you to the same place every time you took it, but another concern had distracted me. "You said they'd had a falling out. Claudine Pelletier and Alistair," I added, when she glanced at me.

Claudine, who'd be our hostess here in France, was a photographer who'd closely worked with Alistair on the first two books of his trilogy about the exiled Jacobites of Saint-Germain-en-Laye. I'd looked her up. She was about his own age, early sixties, though the portraits I had found of her online had shown her as a younger woman, mostly—taking photographs herself, the cameras hiding her own features.

Jacqui answered, "That's my understanding, yes. It's all a

bit before my time, I don't know all the details, but I'm told they haven't spoken for some years."

"Is that why she's being difficult about the diary?" After all, the easiest approach, short of buying it, would be to have the whole thing copied. I could take it with me then, and work in private back at home in England, and not inconvenience her at all.

"I've no idea," Jacqui said. "One doesn't argue with Claudine, I'm told, or try to second-guess her. This is how she wants to do it, so it's how it will be done." She glanced at me again and smiled. "Don't worry, though. You'll like Claudine."

The question was, would she like me? She had agreed to give me room and board and space to work within her own house for a month or maybe more, but she might change her mind once she'd met me. She obviously valued the encrypted diary highly, and she'd probably already formed a mental image of the kind of person who'd be sent by an historian like Alistair to do this job. I doubted I looked anything like Claudine had imagined. She might not even let me near the book.

My cousin, if she shared my worries, didn't let it show. She was steering our rental car over a bridge on the Seine, with a lovely old church rising out of the twilight to greet us. "We're here," she said. "This is Chatou."

We came off the bridge onto a boulevard, broad and divided, where buildings of pale stone with sloped mansard roofs and tall, graceful French windows shared space at the edge of the pavement with more modern offices, shop fronts, and flats. I had an impression of tall, bare-branched trees and bright Christmas lights strung over doorways and dangling like icicles over the edges of awnings. They sparkled against the blue light of the evening and made the whole street look decidedly festive.

"It's pretty," I said.

"Wait till you see the Maison des Marronniers."

"That's the name of the house?" I liked houses with names. "Are there actual chestnut trees?"

"Why would you ask that?"

"Because that's what *marronniers* are."

"Ah."

"How can you spend so much time visiting France without knowing the language?"

"We can't all be linguists," she commented. "How many languages *do* you speak now? Twenty?"

"Other than English? I only speak two."

"No, it's more than that, surely? You've French, thanks to Ricky"—my childhood best friend, who'd moved over from Normandy when we'd both still been in nursery school, and in whose house, next to our own, I'd spent most of my after-school hours, in the bustle and warmth of his French-speaking family—"and Swedish, from when you were keen on that Swedish chap. What was his name?"

"Vendel."

"Ah, Vendel, yes. Charming man." *That*, I knew, was pure sarcasm. Jacqui had never liked Vendel. She added, "But then you took courses in German, and—"

"I know a little of four other languages, but I can only speak two."

Jacqui gave me a sidelong look I couldn't read as she slowed the car and steered us through a narrow gate within a high wall fronting on the pavement.

Claudine Pelletier, I decided, must have either married money or been born to it. Because the house that faced us was a cut above the pay grade, I felt sure, of a photographer.

The house was old. Not ancient, but designed with

grandeur and a certain elegance that made me think it dated from the century before the last. And it was much, much larger than I'd thought it would be, stretching long across the garden and rising up a full three stories, with an attic above them, revealed by two round windows set within the steep slant of the slate-gray roofline. There were chimneys—three, that I could count—and rows of gorgeous windows in the classic French style: tall, with lacy black wrought iron balconies for all except the ones at ground floor level, where a broad stone terrace with a carved-stone railing curved along the front facade and dropped a wide and generous fall of grand stone steps to welcome visitors.

The chestnut trees were here as well. We drove beneath a massive one with black and leafless branches as we came into the circle of the drive, and there were others standing like a row of sentinels within the high walls shutting out the larger world with all its noise and bustle. In the twilight, all that pale stone with small accents of dark brick and those grand windows gleaming warm with golden light gave the Maison des Marronniers the look of a château.

It looked like something of another age. It shouldn't have been standing at the corner of a busy street. It should have been out in the country, as it must have been when it was built. It wanted gardens all around it, and the clop of horses' hooves, and graceful carriages arriving with their guests, not our rented Peugeot rolling up to those impressive steps and coughing to a halt.

There had been no one on the terrace when we'd stopped, I would have sworn to it, but when we had stepped out and got our luggage from the boot and turned around again, we met a woman coming down to greet us.

I braced myself a moment, till I realized this was not Claudine, but someone nearer my own age, with straight black hair cropped closely in a stylish cut that framed her smiling face. Her English, when she spoke to Jacqui, was cautious and came with the handshake reserved for acquaintances, not with the *bise*—the light double or triple or even, in some places, quadruple kiss that was used when you'd moved beyond that and become more informal and friendly. "You have had a good journey?"

"Yes, lovely, thanks. Sara," my cousin said, "this is Denise, Claudine's housekeeper."

I should have guessed that a house of this size would need people to run it. I held out my hand for the housekeeper's handshake as Jacqui said, "Sara's my cousin. The one who'll be working here."

Denise smiled. "Yes, of course. You are… I am so sorry, I don't know how you say in English…the *déchiffreuse*."

I answered her in French, to make it easier. "The code breaker, that's right. Though not a trained one, I'm afraid. It's just a hobby."

When she didn't answer right away I worried I'd said something wrong, but then her smile broadened. "You speak French."

"Yes, I do. I learned it as a child."

"You speak it beautifully." And then, to Jacqui, dropping into English for her benefit, the housekeeper repeated, "She speaks French."

My cousin smiled, in turn. "She does. But I'm still hopeless at it, so feel free to use her as a translator." She glanced towards the partly open front door, just behind Denise. "Is Claudine not at home?"

"She is working. But she will be back in time for dinner. Please, come in. I have prepared your rooms."

Ordinarily I traveled light, but taking my cousin's advice

I had packed extra clothes for the longer stay, and I was glad of Denise's help with my spare suitcase. I followed her across the narrow terrace, through the tall doors set with tidy beveled squares of leaded glass, into the entry hall.

There were tropical plants here, in pots, and the fronds of one brushed softly over my shoulder as I came in. I felt faintly on edge, as I always did in houses that belonged to someone else, with unfamiliar rooms around me and the constant worry I might break something, but I steadied myself with a deep breath, enjoying the sudden assault of the warm kitchen smells that were flooding this high-ceilinged area.

The space was a mixture of textures. The floor was a pattern of tiny mosaic tiles, gathered within a striped border so decorative there was no need for a carpet; and there were stone statues, and more leaded glass, and a circular stair winding upwards, set off behind blue stained glass windows and old curving wooden doors standing ajar. More doors opened onto rooms to either side, with the kitchen ahead of us, partially blocked by a short table holding a small Christmas tree hung with bright silver tinsel.

I couldn't do more than glimpse part of the kitchen— cream walls and red brick and dark ceiling beams—because Denise was already ahead of us, leading us through the curved doors to the circular stair, and beginning to climb.

"I put you in the same rooms as before," she told my cousin, "so you have all on this level to yourselves."

The stairs brought us up to the first floor and paused on a corridor of wide-planked hardwood, well darkened with age, before winding up higher, to the unseen floors still above us. The doors here were closed, but Jacqui clearly knew her way around. Not hesitating, she reached for the handle of the nearest door.

"Brilliant," she said. "I adore this room."

My first glimpse told me why. It was a cozy room, not large, with two tall windows hung with heavy curtains that had an almost Tudor look to them and brought to mind the hand-embroidered tapestries and bed hangings at Hampton Court. My cousin, despite her love of modern comforts, had a secret love of anything that looked as though it might have been at home within a castle.

She set down her suitcase and turned to Denise. "That's all right, I'll show Sara where everything is. Thanks."

My cousin had actually taken a step so her one hand was on the door, waiting to close it as soon as the house-keeper left us. Clueless as I might be when it came to many social cues, I recognized this one as a dismissal. Denise clearly caught it as well. With a nod she turned round and was halfway downstairs by the time Jacqui shut the door.

"Why did you do that?" I asked.

"Do what?"

"Send her off like that."

Jacqui stepped out of her shoes. "You were getting that look."

"What look?"

"*That* look. The one that you get when you're finding it all a bit much. When you're tired of trying to socialize."

I briefly glanced in the mirror that hung on the wall just behind her and couldn't see any expression on my face but mild irritation. "I don't have a look."

"Yes, you do. You have many looks," Jacqui assured me. "And I know them all. Besides, I'm sure Denise was quite happy to get back downstairs to whatever she's making. She's really a marvelous cook."

I was not to be sidetracked. "It wasn't too much. I'm not even a little bit tired. And you don't have to nursemaid me."

"Darling, I wasn't…" She stopped in midsentence and closed her mouth firmly, her time-tested method of ending an argument. "At any rate, *your* room's through here. Come see."

She opened a connecting door and led me through into a larger room that spanned the full depth of this section of the house. Two tall French windows faced the front to overlook the drive, with two more facing out towards what must be the back garden. In between those two back windows was the bed, a large one with a flowered white duvet, and lighted sconces mounted on the wall above. And at the far end of the room a fireplace with a writing table and a small uphol-stered chair created an inviting spot beside another beauti-fully carved wardrobe.

I took a few steps in, across a well-worn oriental rug that partly covered the age-darkened burnished floorboards. When I turned to look at Jacqui I could feel the breadth of my own smile.

"I know," she said. "It's all like this. The whole house." Standing in the doorway that connected our two rooms, she pointed sideways at another door set in the same wall. "That takes you back into the corridor. The bathroom's at the far end. If you only need the toilet there's a little washroom just beside the stairs." She glanced at her mobile. "It's just gone six o'clock. Claudine, if I recall correctly, likes to have aperi-tifs at seven. I think I might have a bath and tidy up, if that's all right with you?"

"Of course."

"You won't mind being left alone a minute?"

"Jacqui, please. I'm not a child."

"Right, then. I won't be long."

Alone, I faced the large round mirror hanging just above the fireplace. "I'm not a child," I said again, to no one.

My reflection seemed prepared to back me up on that. I'd chosen my clothes carefully that morning, toning down my use of color so that even in a sweater and a pair of jeans, I nearly looked the part of a professional.

But Jacqui, in her briefing on our drive in from the airport, had assured me Claudine always dressed smartly for dinner. Not a custom that I'd ever understood, and since the food would taste the same no matter what I wore while eating it, I'd never seen the point.

I did, however, see the point of trying to convince my hostess I could do the job that I'd been sent to do. And that meant blending in. I knew the trick of that.

Deliberately I turned my back on what the mirror showed me, found my suitcase, and began to change.

❧

Claudine Pelletier was studying my skirt.

It was one of my favorites, a rich voided velvet on silk chiffon, cut on the bias and wonderfully weighted to swirl round my ankles whenever I walked. I was sitting just now, facing Jacqui and Claudine across the round tea table in the salon on the ground floor—an elegant room lit by sconces and table lamps, with a piano between two tall French windows that faced out towards the front terrace and drive.

My cousin, as ever, was flawlessly dressed with each hair in its place, but it heartened me to see that Claudine appeared to have hair that, like mine, had a mind of its own. Hers was graying attractively, silver strands glittering under the lamplight amid the black, looking like nothing so much as the tinsel that sparkled on the little Christmas tree out in the entry hall.

I could see that tree from where I sat—the twin set of doors to the entry hall had been propped open—and if I turned and looked past Claudine's shoulder I had a straight view through an open arch into the dining room, clear to the back of the house where another door set at an angle led into the kitchen. Denise had been back and forth twice through that door, setting out our aperitifs: sherry and slices of thin bread spread with pink pâté.

Claudine told me now, "It's a very unusual color."

It took me a moment to realize she meant my skirt, not the pâté.

She asked, "Is it violet or blue?"

I glanced down at the fabric. "It's indigo. Blue." I could name nearly all shades of blue. It was my favorite color; the color that made me feel centered and calm.

"Yes, I see." Claudine nodded. "It's lovely." Her English was polished, and she used contractions and idioms with so much ease that I wondered if she'd lived or studied in England, but I didn't ask her. I tried not to ask people too many questions, in case I asked ones they considered too personal.

I simply returned her smile, noticing for the first time that her brown eyes were youthful. That didn't surprise me. Although she'd told Jacqui she'd just celebrated her sixty-third birthday, she looked ten years younger, her face full and all but unlined.

She hadn't asked me anything of consequence since we'd come down—no questions about ciphers, or my background, or my training—and there'd been no mention of the diary of Mary Dundas. Instead we'd talked of very minor things: the weather, and our flight from London, and the color of my skirt. I wasn't sure what purpose this discussion had, and having spent the whole day planning how I could impress her, I was thrown a bit off balance now by being given no real chance to do so.

Jacqui kept the conversation going with, "That's new."

She nodded at Claudine's piano. I'd admired it silently when we had first come in—an older upright, inlaid handsomely and gleaming in the lamplight.

"It wasn't here," said Jacqui, "when I visited before."

"It was in the house, but not this room," Claudine corrected her. "It was half-buried by the papers in my study, but Denise's son takes lessons now and so we moved it here, where he could practice."

Jacqui smiled. "He's quite the little entertainer, that one. It was magic tricks when I was here in June." My cousin had a soft spot when it came to children, and it showed in her tone as she said, "Sara, darling, be prepared. He likes to have an audience."

Claudine agreed. "But now for his school holidays he's gone to have a visit with Denise's parents. So our days are quiet."

I was privately relieved. I didn't dislike children, but being around them made me feel tense and uncomfortable. They were so unpredictable, bundles of energy, frequently loud and demanding attention—and often affection—in ways that I just couldn't give them. If Denise's son was looking for an audience, he'd find me disappointing.

And Claudine would, too, unless I found a way to copy Jacqui's easy way with small talk.

"Surely *that's* new," she was saying to Claudine, her gaze having moved to the painting above the piano, a street scene in winter. "You had a man's portrait hanging there, before."

"Yes, it is new." Claudine smiled. "You have a good memory. The man in the portrait had eyes I wasn't fond of. They would follow me. I sold him and bought this instead."

She lifted her sherry glass. "There are two more things I've changed in this room. Two more things that are new. Can you find them?"

A strange sort of challenge, I thought, till I noticed my cousin was smiling in her turn, and realized that it was a game. Not a game I could play, as I hadn't been here before, but Jacqui's keen gaze was already sweeping the salon expectantly.

"There," she said finally. "The tapestried chair by the fireplace. That's new."

"Yes, and what else?"

Jacqui kept up her visual search of the room, but she seemed to be having more trouble with this final item, whatever it was.

Claudine asked her, "Give up?"

"No. Hang on, I'm still looking. I'll find it. I—"

Her words were interrupted by the sound of the back door into the kitchen being opened and then closed again, while someone stepped into the house. A man's voice called in French, "It's only me."

Claudine half turned. "Luc?" Speaking French herself, she told him, "Come and meet our guests."

Still from the kitchen, he called, "That's all right, I just came for my keys. I dropped my own set in the lane and I can't find them, it's too dark. I need the spare set from Denise. Is she not here?"

"If she's not in the kitchen," Claudine said, "she'll only be upstairs a moment. Come and meet our guests."

His voice was deep. Attractive. "I'm in no condition to meet guests. I've just got back. I need a shower."

"Nonsense. You'll look fine. Come, have a drink with us."

He came through from the kitchen to the dining room

and strode towards us, and my curiosity became a kind of self-conscious confusion.

He was beautiful. There was no other word for it. He wasn't hugely tall, just average height and with a lean and normal build, but he was beautiful. His face had perfect symmetry, as though an artist had drawn half a face and held a mirror to the drawing— straight nose, level eyebrows, and the clean lines of his jaw and cheekbones, broken only by the fact his hair was parted to the side and fell across his forehead to the right. It was nice hair, light brown and cut in careless layers that half covered both his ears and angled down to brush the back of his shirt collar.

I was staring, and I knew it. I was half-aware Claudine was introducing us, in English, and I held my hand out when I was supposed to, and returned his handshake.

Luc Sabran.

I marked the name, not sure I would remember it because I was distracted by his smile. It was symmetrical, as well, both corners of his mouth turned up to the exact same level to reveal an even row of teeth. And then I saw his eyes.

His eyes were very French. They had the kind of heavy lids that made them look both weary and intensely inter- ested at the same time. And they were blue. A clear and perfect blue.

Claudine was telling him, "And Sara will be staying with us for a few weeks."

"In the winter? You are brave." His English was less pol- ished than Claudine's, and had a stronger accent, but I didn't mind. At all.

I wasn't sure what I should answer back, though, and while I was sifting through the possibilities I heard the foot- steps coming down the stairs from the first floor and we all turned to face Denise.

She said in French, "You're back!" and greeted Luc Sabran with an unstudied double kiss that seemed both natural and warm. "And how was California?"

"Full of sunshine. But I've dropped my keys. You have the spare ones?"

"Yes, of course."

She went through to the kitchen and he turned to take his leave of us.

Claudine reminded him, in French, he didn't need to go. "Have an aperitif. Some dinner."

But he shook his head. "Tomorrow," was his promise, "when I've had a chance to rest and look presentable." To us he said, in English, "It was very nice to meet you both. Enjoy your evening."

Watching him walk off was very nearly as absorbing as observing his approach. He walked as all men ought to walk, with a decided swagger to his shoulders.

Whether Jacqui noticed I was watching him, I didn't know, but after Luc Sabran had closed the kitchen door behind him and gone out with his spare keys in hand, my cousin leaned back in her chair and looked across at Claudine with her eyebrows slightly lifting in the way they often did when she was sure she'd won a contest, and she raised her glass. "*He's* new."

CHAPTER 6

W ELL, I COULDN'T DO it," said Jacqui. She took out her hairbrush and sat on the edge of her bed, having dealt with the last button of her pajama top. "If either of my own ex-husbands bought the house next door to mine, I'd kill myself."

"Denise seems not to mind."

"I'm only saying."

I was not about to try debating anything with Jacqui at this hour of the night, not after I'd had rather too much wine, and while I was myself still trying to make sense of what Claudine had told us over dinner about Luc Sabran and why he and Denise had this arrangement.

And my cousin wasn't leaving any room for me to offer an opinion. "It's not natural. You can't be friends with some-one you've divorced. Not really. I should know."

I might have pointed out that neither of her exes was as gorgeous as Denise's, but I only said, "I wonder why they got divorced."

My cousin told me, "Men like that are rarely faithful."

"Men like what?"

"You know. You saw him. He was…"

"Beautiful."

The look she sent me was the one she always used when she was trying to instruct me. "Darling, that man was too masculine," she said, "to be called beautiful."

"What would you call him, then?"

"Hot." Jacqui smiled. "But believe me, he knows it, and men like that aren't worth your time or your trouble."

I knew she was speaking from her own experience, and she was probably right. I'd had relative peace on that front since I'd left university, and I was in no way inclined to revisit the past or repeat my mistakes, but I privately doubted that I could have ever divorced any man who had eyes like that. Whether those doubts showed, I couldn't be sure, but my cousin said, "Sara."

"Yes?"

"Really, I'm serious. That's not a rabbit hole you want to tumble down. Don't get involved."

"I don't get involved. And anyway, I'm here to do a job. That is, I *think* I'm here to do a job."

"Of course you are." My cousin set her hairbrush down. "You're never having second thoughts?"

"Not me. I'm fairly sure Claudine is, though."

"Why would you say that?"

"You were there. I don't think I impressed her much at dinner."

"Nonsense. I thought you did really well at dinner." Jacqui curled her feet beneath her on the bed and leaning back against her pillows said, "You kept up with the conversation and you didn't monologue."

Monologuing was a common habit among those of us with Asperger's. We could, upon occasion, talk an endless stream without allowing anyone to get a word in edgewise, and not realize it.

"I only monologue when something interests me," I pointed out. "We were talking about gardening for most of dinner, weren't we? Not much fear that I would monologue on *that*." I could kill plants at fifty paces just by looking at them. "I'd hoped we'd talk about the diary, or about the Jacobites, or something with a point to it. That's why I'm here. I think she's changed her mind. I think she—"

"Darling," Jacqui cut me off, "you worry far too much. We've just arrived. I'm sure Claudine assumed you'd want to spend your first night getting settled in and rested up."

If that had been the reason why Claudine had kept the conversation superficial, there had been no need. "I want to get to work."

"You want to get some sleep," my cousin countered with a yawn. And then, because she knew from long experience that I might otherwise stay there indefinitely keeping *her* from getting sleep, she reached to switch her bedside lamp off, letting the resulting darkness bring our conversation to a close. "Be patient."

⌇

Patience had never been one of my strong points. The following morning I found myself pacing from wardrobe to bed and then back again, waiting for Jacqui to finish her shower. I'd showered already and dressed in a pair of dark jeans and a fairly conservative white cotton top and I'd tried four silk scarves till I'd found the best one and I'd tied and arranged it a few times until I was pleased with the final effect and I'd put on mascara and done what I could with my hair. And she *still* wasn't ready.

The clock on the chest of drawers told me four minutes had passed since the last time I'd looked at it, meaning it was 7:47 now, and last night we'd been told that breakfast would be served at 8:00.

My whole life I'd been teased by some people and lauded

by others for my fierce fixation on time, but it wasn't a thing I could easily change. And in this instance, turning up late wouldn't just bother *me*, it would also be rude to our hostess. I'd have to go down on my own.

I clenched both my hands and relaxed them, releasing the burst of adrenaline as I reminded myself that I needn't be anxious. I'd only be facing Denise and Claudine, and I'd already met them. I focused on that as I went down the spiral of stairs and across the tiled entry hall. Scents of warm bread and fresh coffee swirled out from the brightly lit kitchen behind the half screen of the small tinseled Christmas tree. Ahead of me, the inward-swinging doors of the salon where we had sat for drinks last night stood open, and the lights had been left on. I went in and turned left through the tall arch in the wall between the salon and the dining room.

I truly loved the dining room. It had a charming shape, with angled corners, and because it was itself set at the rearmost corner of the house it had great rows of windows running all along the back wall and the angle of one corner and again along the side—tall casement windows set with tiny panes of leaded glass, small beveled diamond shapes set at the juncture of the squares, and all contained within a clean narrow double border in two colors, red and gold. I longed to see those windows in the daylight. Last night it had been dark outside while we'd been eating dinner, and this morning it was not yet sunrise and the world beyond the windows was deep blue.

The blue, at least, was calming. And the antique longcase clock that stood between the windows reassured me I had made it down here with six minutes left to spare, although it seemed that I was on my own. Well, nearly. Within the open doorway to the kitchen, sat a cat.

I guessed he was a tomcat from his size, which was impressive. Black all over, he sat fluffed in that particularly vain way tomcats did when they were showing off, and stared at me with contemplative eyes as though deciding what to make of me.

"Hello," I said.

The black cat sat and blinked at me as though I'd spoken in a foreign language, which I realized that I had.

I said, in French this time, "Good morning. You are handsome, aren't you?"

This earned me a faint twitch of one ear as if acknowledging the compliment. I smiled. I had forgotten, living for so long without a pet myself, just how much I liked cats. This one had turned his gaze now nonchalantly to the salon just behind me with a focus that assured me I was hardly worth the bother to investigate.

I laid a challenge down. "Come on, then. Come and say hello and be a proper host. I promise I won't bite."

"*He* might." The man's voice, coming from the salon, caught me unawares. Surprised, I turned but could see no one, not at first. Not till the one door that had been propped open in the farther corner by the entry hall was pushed a little from behind to change its angle, showing me the man who had been kneeling just behind it by a box of tools and working on the radiator. He hadn't been purposely hiding there, he'd just been hidden by the door, and when I'd gone through the salon I'd walked straight past him without even knowing he was there.

Luc Sabran, in jeans and a gray-and-white striped cotton shirt, gave a nod towards the cat and warned me, "Don't let him fool you. He's not to be trusted." He said it good-naturedly, then smiled and added, "Good morning. How are you, Ms. Thomas?"

I said I was well and returned his "Good morning," determined this time not to stare. "And it's Sara."

"I'd come and shake hands, but I'm covered in rust," he said, holding up one hand as proof. "Were you looking for breakfast? Denise just went round to the bakery for more croissants, because Diablo there sat on the ones she made earlier."

Glaring, the black cat replied to this second attack on his honor by stalking indignantly forward and making a tidy leap onto the dining room chair nearest me, giving a short but imperious order that needed no translating. Smoothing the black hair and feeling his back muscles arch and twitch under my hand, I said, "Is that your name, then? Diablo?"

"It goes very well with his character."

"Is he your cat?"

"No." Luc Sabran put one final twist on a screw and sat back on his heels to inspect the results of whatever repairs he had made. "No, he lives with a neighbor just over the lane, but he visits. The food's better here." The radiator was evidently working to his satisfaction now, because he put the tools away and stood and flexed his shoulders and began to walk towards me with that easy stride I had admired last night. In motion, he was even more distracting, and I purposely looked down and concentrated on the cat.

"The treatment he gets here is better, too. Isn't that right, boy?" Luc Sabran had stopped close beside me and his hand came into the line of my vision as he reached down to rumple the cat's ears, his tone and his action affectionate.

Brisk footsteps sounded outside and the kitchen door opened and closed and Denise said, "Do *not* make a fuss of that cat. I still haven't forgiven him."

Diablo rather smugly pressed his head up into Luc Sabran's cupped hand and closed his eyes as Luc said, "But you will.

You always do. That's why he still comes round." He gave the cat's head one last scratch and moved into the kitchen himself, past Denise to the sink where he turned on the taps and began to wash, scrubbing the cat hair and rust from his hands. "Did you get any chocolate ones?"

"And if I did?"

"Well, I did fix the radiator for you. And you won't find many tradesmen who would come out on a Sunday before sunrise, no matter how nicely you ask them. And none," he said, with certainty, "who'd do the work for coffee and croissants."

"All right, then." She was smiling. "But you'll have to set an extra place. And be nice. Was he being nice?" she asked me.

Luc answered for himself, "Of course I was. What kind of a question is that?"

The dynamic of how they behaved with each other was more like good friends than ex-husband and wife, I thought. Nothing like how Jacqui and her own exes behaved. From where I stood in the dining room, the open arch of the door leading into the kitchen created a frame for them both as though they were performers and I was their audience, and I admittedly watched them with interest, searching for some sign that my first impression was wrong. I could usually spot tension, even if I didn't always know its cause. Denise and Luc weren't tense, they were relaxed—they joked and smiled without a trace of animosity. I found that very curious.

Denise told Luc, "With you, it's never something that I take for granted."

Luc grinned and took a tea towel in his hands to dry them as he looked to me for help. "Was I not being nice?"

"You were. He was," I told Denise.

I couldn't catch the nuance of the look he sent her then,

but I assumed it held a hint of vindication or was smug, because she knocked him down a peg with, "Well, just see that it continues while she's here."

Again he looked to me. "You're here how long?"

I didn't know for certain. "It depends. A few weeks, probably. Perhaps a month."

Luc told Denise, "I'm sure I can behave well that long. Noah, I'm not sure of. He'll be after her to help him practice English all the time."

"He'd do better," said Denise, "to have her help him practice his own grammar. Sara speaks French really well."

Luc's smile was brief to match his nod. "Yes, I did notice."

It surprised me just a little when he said that, because from the moment I'd addressed the cat in French I'd ceased to notice we were speaking in that language—I'd been more wrapped up in following the conversation. The cat himself had obviously tired of the attention I was showing him, and with a stretch he slipped down from the chair, rubbed past my legs to mark me as his new possession, then stalked off with purpose into the salon.

Denise said, "Now he's had his breakfast, he'll be off to have his morning nap. He likes the softer chairs."

"And warm croissants," Luc added, coming back again into the dining room with plate and cup in hand to set a place for himself at the table.

It was eight o'clock now, properly. The light was changing, brightening, the soft blue world beyond the leaded windows turning violet and then lavender with pink around its edges, very beautiful. It turned the little beveled shapes between the squares of window glass to diamond drops that glittered round the room like tiny jewels. It showed me, too, more details of the view of the back garden: bare-branched trees and what appeared to be a high hedge all around it, with the silhouettes of a small scattering of rooftops showing over that and close behind.

"Which house is yours?" I asked Luc without thinking what reason I might have for wanting to know.

"That one there, at the end of the lane."

I could see little more than the peak of a roof and the bump of a chimney. It didn't look large.

"I am two steps away," he said. "And just behind, that's the house where Diablo lives."

"How does his owner mistreat him?"

He looked at me and raised one eyebrow slightly in a move that, while it spoiled his facial symmetry, was nonetheless attractive. "Pardon?"

"You said the treatment he got here was better."

"Ah. Yes, well, he isn't mistreated so much as neglected."

"Neglect is a form of abuse, surely."

Claudine Pelletier spoke up from the salon behind me as she made her way through from the entry hall. "I agree, but tell me, whom are you discussing?" She was simply dressed this morning in a finely knitted roll-neck sweater and a pair of jeans, but though her clothes were not much different from my own she looked more elegant. I put it down to how she moved, with easy unselfconscious grace.

Denise replied, "Diablo. He's been making a nuisance of himself this morning, as usual, and Luc has been defending him, as usual."

Luc told her, "I wasn't defending him." Then turned to me once again to confirm the facts. "Was I defending him?"

"No, you were saying he couldn't be trusted."

Luc nodded as though vindicated. "There you see? She speaks the perfect truth."

His statement sobered me for reasons he would not have understood. I looked away, and met Claudine's small smile.

"Denise informed me you spoke French," she said, "but I didn't expect that you'd speak it so well. I'm surprised your cousin didn't mention it."

"It wasn't a requirement of the job. At least, it was my understanding that the diary—or the part that's not in cipher—is in English. Is that right?"

"Yes. There is a single entry that begins the diary, all in English, so one would expect the cipher will be based in English also."

Denise, setting down a bowl of fresh fruit salad on the table, asked me, "Could you solve it if it were in French?"

"I think so, yes."

"What's this?" Luc looked from one face to another, his one eyebrow raised a fraction in the same way it had been before. "What am I missing? What's all this about a diary?"

Claudine told him, in the briefest terms. His eyebrow lifted higher and he looked at me.

"So this is quite a skill you have. A gift."

"I'm not a professional."

Claudine said, "Even so, you must have done very well to win Alistair's confidence. He can be hard to impress. He is…" Pausing for thought, she half turned as my cousin came into the dining room, looking her usual smartly dressed self in the wake of her shower. Switching smoothly to English, Claudine told her, "I was just speaking of Alistair and of his drive for perfection. How would you describe him?"

"A thorn in my side," Jacqui said with a smile, as she greeted Claudine with the double kiss. "Sorry I'm late." When she reached to shake Luc's hand across the wide table and wish him good morning as well, it reminded me I hadn't yet washed my hands after petting the cat. I excused myself, using the moment to step out of everyone's way and enjoy the warm peace of the kitchen.

It was the best kind of a kitchen—high ceilinged, with dark wood beams holding the plaster above, and a scrubbed stone floor under my feet, and tall multipaned windows to let in the light. On one wall an old fireplace, painted the same rich cream color as most of the walls and the cupboards, spoke of the age of the house and the time when that hearth would have been used instead of the enameled cooker—venerable itself, and likely wood-burning, but clearly still in use from the two pots that steamed and bubbled on its cast iron surface.

There were modern appliances, too, and a TV tucked off to one side on the worktop, but I liked the fireplace and old-fashioned cooker the best. I could happily have eaten breakfast here, amid the clutter of utensils at the sturdy-looking table in the center of the room, but from the scrape of chair legs and the clink of tableware I knew that everyone was taking up their places in the dining room and I would have to join them.

The table in the dining room was long and could have seated ten if called upon to do it, but there were only five places set. Ordinarily I would have picked the chair that had me facing Jacqui, for I found it easier to have her face to focus on if I felt overwhelmed in conversations, but this morning I sat down beside her, focusing instead on Luc.

His eyes were very blue.

The conversation had moved on while I'd been in the kitchen. The talk was all in English now, so Jacqui was included, though Denise appeared to find it fairly challenging to follow what was being said.

Claudine, in her educated English, was attempting to explain to Luc the background of the Jacobite community in France and how they'd come to live in exile here, with agents from the government in England sent to spy on them.

I would have found it incredibly difficult, living like that—never knowing if one of your friends had been threatened or bought off and turned to the enemy's side, or if even your family could truly be trusted. The spies, from all that Alistair had told me, had been everywhere. Somebody's servant or cousin or priest and confessor could be in the pay of the English King George and his government, opening letters and selling off secrets.

And if one was caught, the results, on both sides, could be deadly.

The levels of spying and counterintelligence had caught my interest so deeply I'd spent the past week or so reading about them, until I knew most of the spies' and the spymasters' names—could have probably spotted them, from their descriptions, had I been alive back then. This was just part of the way my brain processed things: nothing by half measures. Every new interest became an obsession.

But at least it meant I could contribute to this conversation over breakfast, filling in a detail that Claudine could not remember, and then going on to properly set out the full chronology of what had happened after King James moved his shadow court to Rome, and those who had been left behind had struggled in the wake of the Queen Mother's death to keep up their community at Saint-Germain-en-Laye.

The first time Jacqui kicked my ankle I assumed she'd done it by mistake, but when she did it for a second time I realized what I was doing. I reined in my thoughts, put a check on my monologue, and was self-consciously searching for some way to back out with some shred of dignity when Jacqui smiled reassurance.

"You're going to have *me* looking over my shoulder," she told me, "with all of this talk about traitors and spies."

"I'm sorry. I do tend to ramble on a bit."

Across the table, Luc Sabran looked from my cousin's face to mine. "You don't need to apologize. Go on, I find it interesting. I didn't know this history."

All throughout my monologue Denise had kept herself in nearly constant motion, back and forth between the kitchen and her own seat next to Luc. She said to Jacqui now, in careful English, "While Sara is here with us she must go visit the château."

My cousin, smiling still, said, "Sara will most likely be too busy with her work to do much touring."

Luc shrugged and raised his coffee cup to drink. "Perhaps that is a thing for Sara to decide."

It seemed to me he held her gaze a moment longer than he needed to. For a moment, even though I knew it was ridiculous, I almost thought I felt a trace of tension in the air between them.

Claudine smoothly cut across it with a comment aimed at me. "But yes, of course, today is Sunday and you've only just arrived. Perhaps you'd like to visit Saint-Germain-en-Laye?"

"Or we could maybe take a walk around Chatou?" suggested Jacqui.

All the faces turned towards me made me feel uncomfortably the center of attention, and I couldn't give an answer because honestly I didn't know what choice to make or whom to please or what they all expected me to say.

Luc asked, "What would *you* like to do?"

Direct and simple, in a tone that brought my gaze round

to the perfect angles of his features, and to those blue eyes that in that moment seemed to anchor me.

I found my voice with ease then. And I looked from Luc to Claudine and I said in total honesty, "I'd like to get to work."

CHAPTER 7

Then shall the traveler come…
—Macpherson, "Temora," Book Two

Chatou
January 23, 1732

T HE HOUSE WHERE THEY had passed the night was large
and grand with many rooms, yet Mary had awakened
feeling restless. She had taken Frisque outdoors but it had
been too cold to stay there, and since Nicolas seemed to be in
no hurry to depart she had been left with little option but to
find some way to pass the time within this house of strangers.

They were pleasant strangers, certainly. The master of
the house, Sir Redmond Everard, had welcomed both her
brother and herself on their arrival with as much warmth
as if they had been his family, and had fed and entertained
them all the evening with so little inconvenience that
one would have thought they were expected guests. Sir
Redmond was an Irishman of middle age whose educated
voice held little trace of the same accent as the blacksmith's
Irish wife's in Chanteloup-les-Vignes. It was not clear to
Mary how he'd come to know her brother, but she'd gathered from their conversation they had many friends in common at the former court of Saint-Germain-en-Laye, among
the exiles, though Sir Redmond had come over much more
recently than most. She'd gathered, too, he had left an estate
of worth behind him in Ireland, for his manners were the

manners of a gentleman by birth, and all the things within his house were very fine.

She liked his drawing room the best. Not for the carpets and tapestry hangings and wainscoting, nor for the richness of furnishings—walnut-tree tables, and chairs with stuffed cushions and footstools, and even a cage with a red-breasted linnet whose twittering song had enlivened the evening while Mary and Nicolas had sat with Sir Redmond and his wife playing at cards. No, she liked the room best for its books: seven shelves of them, carefully dusted and ordered by binding and looking, to her, like a wonderland.

There had been few books in her uncle's house: a Bible, and a book of plays by Molière that she and all her cousins had delighted in performing of an evening, with appropriate theatrics; three English sermons purchased by her uncle to help Mary practice reading in her native language, and two books by the Countess d'Aulnoy—one her famous novel of the Count of Douglas, and the other a collection of enchanting fairy tales that had delighted Mary until her Aunt Magdalene had one day found her reading them and promptly had reclaimed the book from Mary's hands with the remark, "These are *not* meant for children."

She'd obeyed her aunt, of course, until she'd reached her sixteenth birthday, when she'd judged herself to be grown-up enough to read the fairy tales. She'd learned them all by heart, and in the nighttime with her cousin Colette close beside her in the bed they shared, she would recite them and embellish them, and when she had told all the Countess d'Aulnoy's tales she started to invent her own, of princes and forbidden love, enchanted lands and twists of fate and such romantic tragedy that often at the end of them Colette would be in tears.

One night last November, when Mary had finished a story, Colette had remarked, "You must marry a man who will take you to Paris, for you could charm the writers of the great salons with your own tales, and I could charm the men who came to listen, and so find a wealthy husband of my own."

That had long been Mary's dream as well, but she was practical. "It will be the other way about, for you will marry before I do."

"Why?" Colette had asked. "You are the elder."

Mary had explained with patience, "I am not your sister. And your parents will have need to see you settled with a husband and a dowry before giving thought to me."

"Then I must set myself at once to win the heart of the Chevalier de Vilbray," Colette had said, not all in jest. "I saw him riding to the hunt today. He is in truth as handsome as they say he is. Perhaps one day he'll meet me in the woods, as the prince met the peasant girl in tonight's tale, and fall madly in love with me."

Mary, who at that time had not yet seen the chevalier, had allowed herself to daydream of chance meetings in the woods with him herself. She'd smiled. "Well, if he sweeps you up onto his horse the way the prince did to the peasant girl, I trust you'll sweep yourself back down, for such encounters rarely end so well in life as they do in the fairy tales. Real men are not so chivalrous."

"I'll not permit you to be cynical. You cannot tell the tales you tell and not believe in chivalry."

"I do. But the Chevalier de Vilbray—"

"—will make a charming husband," Colette had completed Mary's sentence. "And when we are married, he will carry me to Paris and I'll bring you with me, and you'll be the new sensation of the literary salons. You will be adored by all and have so many famous lovers and so many grand adventures that your memoirs, as you write them, will run into several volumes, all of which of course you'll dedicate to me. Now," she'd said, "tell me the ending again, where the prince reappears when the princess was sure he'd abandoned her, for that is my favorite part, and I'll try not to weep."

It had seemed strange to Mary last night in this house in Chatou to sleep all by herself in a bed, without Colette beside her. And she knew that it would have been equally strange for Colette.

When Mary had said her good-byes before driving away in the closed chaise with Nicolas, Colette had hugged her the hardest. And late last night when Mary had retrieved a night-gown from her portmanteau she'd found a parcel wrapped in paper nestled in the neatly folded clothes, addressed in pencil in her cousin's careful writing: *For your memoirs*.

It had been a book with all its pages blank, exactly like the one in which her uncle kept household accounts, with cloth boards and a leather spine, and with it had been a cylindrical traveling pen set, the ink well and talc in small sections that screwed one on top of the other beneath the long section that held three plain quill pens with neatly carved nibs.

An extravagant gift, and had Colette attempted to give it before she had gone Mary wouldn't have taken it, knowing how much the small pen set alone must have cost. But last night she had held it and been grateful for the sentiment behind the gesture, and the small connection that it gave her to the place she'd left behind, and she had brought both book and pen set down this morning with her to Sir Redmond's drawing room, where she sat now, the book laid open to its first page while she wrote the details of her journey here with Nicolas.

For if she was in truth to have adventures, she decided, that was where they should most properly begin.

Frisque did not like to be ignored. When Mary had first started writing, he had flopped upon the carpet on his back with all four feet up in his most engaging attitude, attempting to convince her that he needed her attention, and when that had failed he'd alternately pounced upon her shoes and tugged and worried at the hemline of her gown until she'd met his needs halfway by rolling, with her foot, his favorite wooden ball across the floor so he could chase it and retrieve it. She could do this without thinking, because Frisque retrieved things brilliantly. Each time the ball rolled off across the carpet he would hunt for it quite happily, tail wagging, bring it back and lay it down exactly at the right spot near her foot so she could kick it out again.

This went on for some time, and Mary had managed to put down her summary of what had happened the previous day, from the time she had set out with Nicolas right through their evening with Sir Redmond Everard, and she was just starting into the details of what she'd done so far today when she felt Frisque return, so she aimed a kick at where the ball should have been and discovered it wasn't. Instead she connected with softness and fur and was met with a swift bark of protest.

She left off her writing midword to bend down and apologize, petting Frisque to comfort him. "Where is it, then?" she asked the dog. "What have you done with it?"

Frisque cocked his head in a quizzical way.

Mary told him, "The ball. Where's the ball?"

It was one of the three words, together with *outside* and *food* that could spur the small dog to immediate action. That he expected her to follow him was evident from how he trotted off a few steps, wheeled and bounced and wheeled again, and with a sigh she stood and went where he was leading her, across the room to where a high-backed settee faced the fireplace. The settee was broad and deep, richly upholstered with silken embroidery over the wool of the cushions and arms and the tall curving back, trimmed with braid and a dainty bell fringe that brushed over Frisque's ears as the little dog pushed underneath, scrabbling with his small paws in an effort to reach the ball wedged underneath the low rail that connected the settee's carved legs.

"Idiot," she told him with affection, "you won't get it out like that, it's too far back." She knelt and nudged him to the side with one hand while she reached beneath the settee with the other, feeling for the ball. Out in the entry hall the bell beside the front door rang and Frisque gave the low rumbling woof he used when threats felt close at hand, his louder barking always kept reserved for challenging those things that were too far away to answer him. She stroked his head and shushed him, warning him to silence, for she did not wish to be a nuisance to their host and hostess. Frisque gave one more grumble but obeyed, and when the door into the drawing room was opened he made no sound, though his ears twitched forward.

"…comfortable in here," Sir Redmond Everard was saying as he showed an unseen guest into the room. A woman, from the rustle of her gown and petticoat; the click of smaller heels across the floor.

Mary, feeling anything but comfortable, debated what to do. They had not seen her crouched behind the tall settee, and as embarrassing as her position was she knew she should stand and announce her presence before they began to—

"There," Sir Redmond said, "now we have privacy."

Behind the shelter of the settee Mary sank back on her heels and felt her cheeks flame as she tried hard *not* to think of why a married man might wish to be in private with a woman not his wife. If she had felt uncomfortable before, it had been nothing to the level of discomfort she felt now, and she could see no easy end to it that let her keep her dignity, although her mind was whirring in its search for one.

Sir Redmond told the woman, "I'd expected Mrs. Farrand."

"Mrs. Farrand has been taken, sir." The woman spoke in English with a pleasant lilt. Her voice was clear and confident, and sounded young. "When last she crossed to Dover she was met there by a Messenger who had been sent to stop her and arrest her as a spy, and she's been taken now to London to await examination."

"She's in prison?"

"Aye, sir."

"That is most unfortunate."

The woman's voice acquired what Mary took to be the slightest edge. "You underestimate her, sir, if you imagine Mrs. Farrand will tell anything of value to the government, however ill they treat her."

"Then you know her?"

"Aye, I do, sir."

"And have you brought any proof of this?"

"I have. My introductions, which were given me when I passed through Boulogne."

There was a pause, and the faint crinkle of a paper being smoothed along its folds. Sir Redmond commented, "From Father Graeme *and* from General Gordon. These are both good men. How do you come to know them, Mistress—?"

Clearly he was waiting for her name, but she did not supply it. Her reply was simply, "You'll forgive me, but as Mrs.

Farrand was herself so recently betrayed, I would prefer to keep my own connections private. They are good men, as you say. And I do know them, as their letters prove."

"Well then, that must suffice." Sir Redmond's voice held admiration and amusement. "Come then, give me what you've carried all this way. Unless you've got them in your stays, as Mrs. Farrand always carried them? Should I turn round?"

"They are not in my stays, and I can do the turning round, if you will give me but a moment." She had evidently sewn whatever they were both referring to within the lining of her gown or petticoat, for Mary heard the rustling of the fabric as the woman turned, and then the tearing of a seam, and the crinkle of paper again.

Frisque, growing bored, reached with his paw again beneath the settee's legs in an attempt to gain his ball, and Mary pressed more firmly on his head to quiet him and hold him to his silence while she closed her eyes and sent a wish to any fairy godmother who might be like to listen that Sir Redmond and his guest would soon conclude their business—or that a convenient hole might open in the floor beneath herself and Frisque, and so end her embarrassment.

The woman said, "There are five letters, and the latest cipher, for the one that Mrs. Farrand carried with her is no longer safe to use."

"Of course. I'll—"

What he was about to say was interrupted by a fall of footsteps in the corridor, and then the door swung open and Sir Redmond's wife exclaimed, "Oh, do excuse me, dear, I did not know we had a guest."

"My wife," Sir Redmond made the introductions, "this is Mistress—"

"Jamieson," the woman now replied, in friendly tones,

after what Mary thought had been the faintest pause. "It is an honor, Lady Everard."

The knight said, "Mistress Jamieson is a great friend of Mrs. Farrand."

"Ah, dear Mrs. Farrand," said his wife. "I have not seen her for some weeks. Does she not travel with you?"

"She is indisposed, just at the moment," was the younger woman's answer, and Sir Redmond's wife made sounds of sympathy that made it plain she was not privy to her husband's business and was unaware that Mrs. Farrand—and indeed the woman she was being introduced to—were in fact clandestine couriers.

The younger woman carried on, "But knowing I would be in this vicinity, she asked me if I'd stop and ask your husband for a letter that attests to the good character of her son Thomas, who does seek to marry a young lady at Calais whose father yet requires convincing."

"Yes, of course. For Mrs. Farrand, anything. You'll do that for her, won't you, darling?"

"Yes, of course," Sir Redmond played along, still with the tinge of admiration in his voice. "Do have a seat here, Mistress Jamieson, and make yourself at home, and I'll away up to my chamber and compose just such a letter."

"On your way, my dear," his wife put in, "perhaps you'll take a moment to assist me in explaining to the groom what's to be done about the harness, for he does not seem inclined to take direction from a woman."

"And you left him standing, did you?"

"For the moment." As though mention of the groom had then reminded her of something else, Sir Redmond's wife asked, this time of their guest, "Have you a driver waiting? I will have a warming drink sent out to him, for it is very cold this morning."

"No," said Mistress Jamieson, "I do not have a driver. I took lodgings in the town last night and walked from there."

"My dear! In such a wintry wind?"

"I am accustomed to the cold, for I was raised in it."

Sir Redmond's wife said, "Nonetheless, I'll have the maid brew tea for you, that you may warm yourself while you are waiting."

"Thank you. That would be most kind."

Sir Redmond told her, "I'll not keep you waiting long." And then both he and Lady Everard went out and closed the door behind them, leaving the young woman standing squarely between Mary and escape from her predicament.

She might have stayed there stuck another hour had Frisque not wriggled free just then and, cheerfully evading all her efforts to recapture him, gone bounding in an energetic path across the drawing room to give a wagging welcome to this new potential playmate.

"Well, hello," said Mistress Jamieson, in evident surprise. "Where did you spring from?" And when Frisque was not forthcoming with an answer, she went on, "Come here then, you're quite safe. I'm not about to bite. And you can tell that to your mistress, for she cannot be so comfortable down there upon the floor."

Mary rested her forehead a moment in shame on the seat cushion of the settee before gathering up what remained of her tattered pride, pushing herself to her feet so her shoulders and head were entirely visible over the back of the scrolled piece of furniture, braced for whatever might come.

CHAPTER 8

My soul brightens in danger…
I am of the race of steel; my fathers never feared.
—Macpherson, "Fingal," Book Three

Chatou
January 23, 1732

THE WOMAN SHE WAS facing looked to be about her own age, slender and of middle height, with features that could not have been called beautiful and yet held a vivacity that made them pretty—lively eyes lit with a keen intelligence beneath arched eyebrows the same dark brown color as the curling hair that had been swept up from her face and neatly fastened underneath a plain lace pinner.

Mary cleared her throat and said, "I do apologize."

"That's quite all right. I used to hide behind chairs often as a child. The trick is keeping back so that your shoes are out of sight."

"I wasn't hiding. I was… Frisque had lost his ball, you see, and I was only trying to retrieve it when you… Well," she finished, knowing how ridiculous it sounded.

"Are you French?" the woman asked, her head tipped slightly to one side as though she were trying to place Mary's accent. "Or Irish?"

"My father was Scottish, my mother was French." She remembered her manners and put out her hand as she stepped round the settee and forced herself forward. "I'm Mary Dundas, Mistress Jamieson." And having properly managed the more formal greeting, she said, "I'll just…go. I should go."

"Nonsense. You were here first. You were writing," observed Mistress Jamieson, looking down now at the journal and pen on the table where Mary had earlier sat.

"It was nothing of importance," Mary said, aware how foolish any chronicle of her "adventures" would appear to this young woman who, from all the evidence, was living one herself; for if in truth the other woman, Mrs. Farrand, had been taken and arrested as a spy, then stepping in to carry messages across the Channel in her place in such a time of danger called for courage of a kind that Mary could not hope to claim.

She could but marvel at the realization that this young woman, although near to her in age, was so beyond her in experience and confidence. And energy, she added, as she watched while Mistress Jamieson began to move about the room with Frisque an ever-bouncing bundle at the hemline of her gown.

"Indeed," Mistress Jamieson said as she trailed a hand over the spines of the books on one shelf, "so few women write anything, that when one does it can never be deemed unimportant."

"Truly, it was nothing more than my own private thoughts."

"Then pray, don't let me keep you from them."

Mary wasn't sure if that was meant to be an invitation or a firm command, but since the answer either way was to reclaim her chair and carry on where she'd left off within her journal, she decided it was best to do exactly that. It was a great relief, in fact, to bend her head and hide her reddened cheeks as she took up her pen again and dipped it in the ink while she read over what she'd so far written for her first attempt for this new year beneath the simple heading "January":

Upon the 22nd came my eldest brother Nicolas to my uncle's home at Chanteloup-les-Vignes, and after dinner we began our journey to his home—and my new one—at Saint-Germain-en-Laye, he having hired a splendid chaise for the occasion with a driver and two bay mares matched in all but that the near one had white forelegs and the other had no white at all upon her. Though the day was cold my heart was made the warmer knowing all my years of praying for such a reunion had at last been heard and answered, and with my brother as companion and so many fine and strange things to be seen within the woods through which we passed, I was well satisfied, the only complication rising from a wagon over-turned upon the road that made it necessary for our driver to divert some several leagues around the obstacle, and causing us to break our journey at Chatou, where lives a noble gentle-man of Irish birth who knows my brother well. Sir Redmond Everard, for so his name is, seemed not in the least put out to have us thus descend upon him. He and his good lady made us welcome and installed us in fine chambers, and a maid was sent to help me dress for supper, and a better supper I have never had, set out so cleverly and with so little notice, and a wine Sir Redmond told us he'd had sent him from Bordeaux, which we agreed with him was very fine, though privately I would confess I'd hold my uncle's wine to be superior. Supper being done we then amused ourselves at play upon the cards. There being three of us (for Lady Everard declined to play but chose instead to sit apart and so be entertained) we played the Renegado with Sir Redmond and myself aligned against my brother, though he, with great skill, confounded both of us and left us all in laughter. So to bed, and up the morning of the 23rd at sunrise to attend to Frisque. I thought to walk some little way along the river, but the freezing wind defeated us and drove us back indoors where I—

The narrative broke off there, where she'd risen to help Frisque retrieve his ball. She tried now to retrieve the thread of it, without including the embarrassing details of what had happened in the meantime:

—made the acquaintance of a fellow guest of our good host: a woman by the name of Mistress Jamieson who carried to Sir Redmond correspondence of a secret nature, which she carried hidden on her person. I suspect the name she gave him may be false, she having earlier declined to give a name at all and only acquiescing when his lady entered in the room and wanted introduction, but Sir Redmond, if he does suspect the same, seems yet well satisfied. I do perceive, from having seen him toast King James's health last night at supper, that Sir Redmond is himself a Jacobite, and so this woman's errand doubtless serves that same king who has long been favored with the love and loyalty of my own father and my brothers, and in whose lost palace I am soon to take up residence.

"Where did he lose it, then?" asked Mistress Jamieson.

Mary looked up, startled, with her pen still resting on the paper, and for a confusing moment she believed the other woman had divined what she was writing.

"I do beg your pardon, but—"

"The ball. Where did your dog misplace it?"

"Oh." Relaxing, Mary pointed out the place. "Beneath the settee."

The other woman found the ball and set it freely rolling. Frisque chased after it, delighted, and retrieved it for the woman who seemed happy to indulge him. Mary could have warned her that the little dog could play this favorite game all day, but there was no need after all because just then the promised tea arrived, delivered by a housemaid who on seeing Mary went and brought a second porcelain cup to set in place upon the little lacquered tea table. To Mary, who had only drunk tea twice before in all her life, her aunt not being fond of it, it was a fascinating thing to watch the housemaid set things out so carefully: the silver pot that rested in its stand above the warming flame, the water jug and sugar dish with gleaming silver tongs, the little cups so delicate in Chinese blue and white and sitting neatly in their saucers with a matching common bowl in which to empty out the dregs.

Too late she realized that her admiration had betrayed her inexperience, for when the housemaid had again departed, Mistress Jamieson asked in a tone that did not condescend but rather held a trace of understanding, "Shall I pour?"

"Yes, please," said Mary.

Mistress Jamieson was clearly expert at the art of serving tea and Mary watched her carefully and marked the steps in order, so in future she could mimic them.

Her cousin had accused her once of being like an ape. "You always watch," Colette had said, "and then you copy so completely it's as if you've shed your own self and become another creature altogether, like the fairies in the tales you tell, who change their form according to their fancy."

To which Mary had replied, "And how else would I hope to learn if not by imitation, since my life conspires to limit my experience?"

The life of Mistress Jamieson, thought Mary, must have

done very much the opposite and bathed her in experience, for how else could so young a woman seem so self-assured and in control? Mary observed her closely, noting how she took her seat, arranged her skirts, and squared her shoulders all at once, as graceful as a falcon perched at rest upon her block, fully aware and in command of all around her. Even Frisque obeyed the quiet word she told him and lay down with rare obedience to settle with one paw at rest upon the hemline of her gown.

Mary held the little bowl-like teacup balanced neatly on her fingertips, the way the other woman did, and drank with care, deciding that unlike her aunt she rather liked the taste of sweetened tea. She cleared her throat. "Are you from Scotland, Mistress Jamieson?"

"I am."

"I've never been to Scotland."

"Have you lived in France your whole life, then?"

"I have."

The other woman looked at Mary as though trying to imagine what that would be like, to spend one's whole life in one place.

On the table between them the cards from last evening's play still lay untidily stacked. Mistress Jamieson set down her cup and gathered all the cards into her two hands, at first seeming only to want to align them, but then as though the feel of them within her fingers altered her intent, she loosely shuffled them and turned the top one over to reveal the knave of hearts. Her mouth curved faintly in a private smile before she turned the card again and slipped it in among the rest. "Have you no wish to travel?" she asked Mary.

"Very much the opposite. I wish it more than anything, but women cannot up and see the world when we so choose.

That is," she stammered as she realized that the other woman had just come some distance on her own, "I mean—"

"No, you are right in that," said Mistress Jamieson. "And I was told so bluntly as a child—a woman cannot travel with the freedom of a man. The road does rarely welcome us, preferring we should stay at home, but I have found the remedy is simply then to move my home itself to other places, and so gain a different view."

Mary, feeling happy to have found some bit of common ground to stand upon, remarked, "I am now in the midst of doing so myself."

"Oh, yes?" The other woman's eyebrows arched a fraction, as once more she drew the knave of hearts from deep within the pack of cards and put him back again and shuffled all, not seeing Mary's nod.

"Yes. My brother, whom I have not seen for many years, did come to fetch me home. We only stayed our journey here last night because we were delayed upon the road and it became too dark to travel, and my brother is acquainted with Sir Redmond, who was kind enough to take us in. But later on this day I'll have a different view, as you do say, from quite a different window." She was trying to sound confident, but some of her uncertainty must have yet wavered in her tone, or so she guessed from watching Mistress Jamieson look up with eyes that seemed to take her measure.

"Do you travel far this day?" the Scottish woman asked.

"Not far. My brother lives at Saint-Germain-en-Laye."

The lovely eyebrows arched again. "At Saint-Germain?"

"Yes. Do you know it?"

This time when she drew the knave of hearts she seemed to do so without paying any heed to it, as though her mind were otherwise diverted. Without answering the question,

Mistress Jamieson said lightly, "It is not a place for keeping private thoughts." And then, on noticing that Mary did not seem to understand, she gave a nod towards the journal lying open on the table. "You will have to guard that well, for Saint-Germain is full of prying eyes and those who love exposing secrets." But she smoothed the warning with the kindness of her tone, and asked, "And will you go no further in your travels?"

Mary gave a tiny shrug. "I am dependent on my brother and must wait for his indulgence, naturally, but someday I should like to go to Paris." She'd have felt a fool to say aloud the reason why; to lay her childish fantasies and dreams before this woman, so she aimed instead for something like sophistication. "I am told the men there are the handsomest in all of France, and very gallant."

Mistress Jamieson looked down and traced the corner of the card she held, the knave. "Aye, there are handsome men in Paris." For a moment it appeared the other woman's thoughts had drifted far afield, before they were summarily recalled. Laying the knave faceup on the table, she set down the other cards and reached for her forgotten tea. "And men of wit and learning, which are also handsome qualities."

Mary tried to match the grace with which the Scottish woman held her teacup, as she said, "I fear I have no qualities that would impress a man of wit and learning, so I must make do with one who has a handsome face." She'd said it brightly, all in jest, but in the pause that followed, Mistress Jamieson appeared to be considering the matter.

Straightening the edges of the stack of cards she turned the top one over to reveal the ace of hearts, and set it on the table with the waiting knave so that the two were touching one another with their edges overlapped. She said to Mary,

"Any man deserving of your notice will need nothing to impress him but that you should be yourself, and any man deserving of your love will see you as you truly are, and love you notwithstanding."

Such advice, thought Mary, must be spoken from experience. The only ring the other woman wore was on her right hand, not her left—a ring of gold wrought in a curious design of two hands clasping a crowned heart, and looking nothing like the wedding ring her own aunt wore, but Mary could not keep herself from asking, "Are you married, Mistress Jamieson?"

Again, as when she'd given Lady Everard her name, there was the faintest pause, too brief to be much noticed but enough time to arrange her thoughts. She raised her cup to drink. "And if I were, I should not own it."

"Why is that?"

Above the teacup's rim the level gaze seemed to assess Mary's intelligence. "Come now. You overheard me speaking to Sir Redmond, and you clearly are no fool, so then you know what I am doing."

Mary flushed a bit to be reminded of her accidental indiscretion, but she answered just as plainly. "Yes."

"Well, then. Had I a husband whom I loved, that love alone would lead me to deny him, lest my actions bring him also into danger."

Mary, frowning just a little, said, "But if you had a husband…"

"Yes?"

"Forgive me, but if you did have a husband and if he loved *you*, how could he then permit that you would put *yourself* in danger?"

Another pause, and then a shrug. "My mother likes to

say some people choose the path of danger on their own, for it is how the Lord did make them, and they never will be changed." Emptying the settled tea leaves from her cup into the common slop bowl, Mistress Jamieson continued, "If I had a husband, and if he loved me, then he would understand my nature and not think that he could sway me by withholding his permission, for he'd know I cannot stay beside the hearth and tend my needlework when those I love risk more in their adventures."

At that moment Mary felt convinced that Mistress Jamieson was all at once the bravest and most fascinating woman she had ever met, and emptying her teacup in her turn she reached to take her pen in hand and started searching through the lines she had last written in her journal for the places where she'd mentioned Mistress Jamieson by name, and with a new respect for secrecy began to strike them out so as to leave no written record that could carelessly incriminate this woman she admired.

Mistress Jamieson, observing her, remarked, "There is a better way to guard your secrets, when you write. Would you like me to show you?"

"If you speak of ciphers," Mary said, "you need not waste your time, for I am sure I never could remember anything so complicated."

"He never rode that never fell," the other woman answered, but since Mary had not ever heard that proverb she was unsure what it meant till Mistress Jamieson translated it more simply: "Nothing venture, nothing have. Come, take a clean page from your journal—tear it out, for you must keep it loose—and we'll devise a cipher. Is there tea left in the pot?"

"Yes, I believe so." Mary rose in what she hoped was a fair imitation of the other's competence and grace. "Shall I pour?"

The cipher proved to be a simple thing for her to master after all. She had converted her own name and Frisque's to numerals by the time Sir Redmond's wife returned to keep them company, at which time Mary closed her journal altogether with the ciphered sheet set at the place where she'd been writing, laying it aside as Lady Everard went over to inspect the little linnet in its cage.

"Will not you sing for us this morning?" Lady Everard addressed the bird, and tapped a finger lightly on the bars. "You've had your breakfast, give us payment. Don't be selfish."

Mary said, "Perhaps he's sad."

The older woman clucked her tongue. "What reason has he to be sad? He's warm and fed and fussed over."

"But you have set his cage beside the window," Mary pointed out, "where he may see the wider sky, and any bird on seeing that would want to try his wings in it."

"He'd freeze were he to try his wings out there this morning." Lady Everard turned from the linnet's cage and settled in a nearby armchair and remarked, "You do that very neatly, Mistress Jamieson. I can no more play at cards than I can shuffle them, though dear Mr. O'Connor has been trying to instruct me in the simpler games."

The Scottish woman, who had once again been idly shuffling through the pack of cards and drawing out the knave from time to time, stopped the repeating motion, looking up to ask, "Mr. O'Connor? You'll forgive me, I'm acquainted with some members of that family, and I wonder…"

"Do you know him, then?" Sir Redmond's wife looked pleased. "He comes with Colonel Brett quite often here to visit with us. Mr. Martin O'Connor, of the Mine Adventurers Company."

Mary, who was watching Mistress Jamieson, saw

something that looked strangely like relief and disappointment intermingled cross the other woman's features as she answered, "Ah. Then no, I do not know him."

"He's a very charming gentleman," Sir Redmond's wife continued. "Very charming, though my husband has his doubts about his teaching me to play at cards." She turned a little to address her husband who was entering the drawing room. "Is that not right, dear?"

"Oh yes, very likely," he indulged her, though he could have hardly known what she was referencing, a fact they both acknowledged with a shared smile of affection.

"I was saying," she informed him, "that you had your doubts about Mr. O'Connor teaching me to play at cards."

Her husband nodded. "Most emphatic doubts. O'Connor is an unrepentant sharper, and I fear he'll teach you all his means of cheating."

"Mistress Jamieson, although she does not know him, is acquainted with some others of that name."

"They are more honest men, I hope?" Sir Redmond asked the Scottish woman, jokingly.

"I fear," said Mistress Jamieson, "the unrepentant sharpers do outnumber honest men within that family." Setting down the pack of cards, she stood and shook her skirts to smooth them, startling Frisque who leaped to stand alert himself, tail wagging with anticipation. "Do you have the letter, then, for Mrs. Farrand?"

"Yes, I have it here." He made to hand it to her, but his wife delayed him.

"But you'll not be leaving yet so soon?" she asked the Scottish woman. "You must stay to dinner." Turning to her husband, she said, "Darling, do persuade her she must stay to dinner."

Any effort he could have put forward to persuade her was cut short by the distinctive sound of horses' hooves outside and wheels that crunched and squeaked upon the snow, and looking through the window nearest to her Mary saw a covered carriage with a driver sitting huddled in his cloak upon his box, his hat drawn low upon his forehead as he turned the mismatched team of horses—one a chestnut, one a bay—to smoothly halt before the house. A man, no doubt Sir Redmond's groom, came briskly out to greet him, and the two spoke briefly before the groom turned again and headed round the house.

Lady Everard peered out as well, with interest. "What now?" she asked her husband. "Who is this? Are you expecting someone?"

"No, not I. But here comes Evans now, to tell us," said Sir Redmond, as the tramping of the groom's boots could be heard approaching from the rear part of the house. "What, Evans, who is come?"

The groom, ignoring Frisque's excited sniffing at his boots, touched his forehead respectfully. "Beg pardon, Sir Redmond, my lady," he said, and looked to Mistress Jamieson. "It is your driver, madam, come from Paris. He desires me to remind you that the morning is a cold one and he asks you would you very kindly hurry."

Mistress Jamieson, who during this had also looked out through the window, turned her head to show the same small, private smile she'd given when she'd found the knave of hearts within the pack of cards. "I do suspect he said it rather less politely."

"Yes, madam," the groom replied.

Sir Redmond's wife stared in open surprise at the form of the driver outside. "He is insolent."

Smiling still, Mistress Jamieson told her, "Aye, frequently."

Taking the letter Sir Redmond held out to her, she took her leave of them, wishing them all a good day, and on seeing that Frisque had begun a small circling dance on the floorboards, observed, "Your dog needs to be taken outdoors, Mistress Dundas. Come, wrap yourself well and walk out with me."

Mary wished her own cloak was as elegantly cut as Mistress Jamieson's, and had a fur-lined hood. Outside, the air was so intensely cold it burned her lungs when she drew breath, then turned that breath to steam when she exhaled.

Beside her, Mistress Jamieson stepped lightly in the snow as though accustomed to the cold. "You said your brother came to fetch you home. Where were you previously?"

"With my uncle and my aunt, who raised me." It was difficult to speak in such a cold wind.

"I have always lived in other people's houses," said the Scottish woman. "As an education, I do highly recommend it. But," she added, "you were right about the linnet, Mistress Dundas. Some things weren't meant to live in cages." They were halfway to the carriage now. She stopped and turned to Mary. "And the sky is very wide." Her smile was warm. "I hope you get to try your wings in it."

With all her being Mary wished she could have found an eloquent reply, because it seemed to her that such a rare and memorable encounter should be marked with words less commonplace than "Thank you" and "I hope you have a pleasant journey." But the better words, as always, were eluding her.

And Mistress Jamieson seemed not to mind. "And you," she said. "A safe trip home." And giving one last pat to Frisque she turned and walked away.

The driver had dismounted and was standing by the carriage door, and Mary could now see he was a tall man and broad shouldered in his snow-flecked cloak and polished boots, for all he stood there hunched against the cold. He raised his head as Mistress Jamieson approached, and Mary saw his face was handsome, made more handsome when he grinned.

He spoke, and though she stood too far from them to be completely certain she had heard his words correctly, she'd have sworn that in a deeply pleasant Irish voice he'd told the Scottish woman, "See now, this is why I cannot leave you anywhere. You never will sit still."

And Mistress Jamieson said something in return that Mary could not hear at all because the other woman's back was to her, but the driver laughed aloud and offered Mistress Jamieson his hand and helped her climb into the carriage with a solid sort of masculine protectiveness that set off a strange longing within Mary that she might, at least once in her own life, have a man who took such care of her.

But it was what she witnessed next that she marked most, for in the moment just before the driver swung the carriage door closed, Mistress Jamieson reached up from where she sat inside and took his darkly handsome face in both her hands and kissed him, and the golden ring upon her right hand briefly caught the light as he returned the kiss but swiftly, so that any who were watching from the house would have seen nothing but a driver taking care to see his passenger was safely seated.

Then he closed the carriage door and turned and tipped his hat to Mary, climbing once more to his box and taking up the reins to turn the horses back the way they'd come, along the road that Mary knew would lead at length across the bridge and over the horizon, into Paris.

She stood and watched the carriage out of sight, and stood there longer with her feet cold in the snow until the dancing rhythm of the horses' hooves had ceased to echo in the air and all the frosty silence fell again around Sir Redmond's house.

And then she sighed a breath that turned to mist before the wind stole past and scattered it to nothing, and with Frisque reluctant at her heels she turned and headed back towards the house where, at the window, hung the caged bird that for all its comfort had that morning chosen not to sing.

CHAPTER 9

I HAD EXPECTED MORE.

Which wasn't logical. I'd known that there would only be a single diary entry in plain text, and Alistair had told me he'd learned little from it but the names of Mary and her brother and the fact they'd been acquainted with Sir Redmond Everard, a famous Jacobite who'd lived here at Chatou. Not in this house, of course. I'd asked Claudine already, and she'd told me the Maison des Marronniers had not been built until the middle of the 1800s, and by her best guess Sir Redmond's house would have been closer to the river, where the oldest buildings of the town had stood. It didn't matter, really, but I liked to keep the details straight in my own mind.

I could have wished Mary Dundas had put more stock in minor details, but I knew, again, that wasn't realistic to expect. I hadn't honestly believed that she'd have kept a note of all that had been done and said by whom to whom. Most people didn't, as a rule. I'd seen it done sometimes in novels, where the characters would keep a diary or write a letter that read like a narrative, complete with perfect dialogue, but even in the best of novels that device could never quite convince me, and I'd find myself detaching from the text enough to think, "She'd never write that down in that way. No one would."

No, I thought it far more likely that a person in real life

would summarize a conversation as Mary Dundas had done, and simply write:

She proved to be the bravest and most fascinating woman I have ever met, and we did speak awhile of things both great and small, while drinking tea.

No more than that, and having not been in the room while they were speaking, I would never have a clue what all those "things both great and small" had been.

I didn't even know the other woman's name. "What would you say that is?" I asked Claudine, and pointed to the name that had been scored through several times in ink to render it illegible. "Harrison? Mistress Harrison?"

"Possibly." She leaned in for a closer look, and placed her hand directly on the page.

I felt my mouth fall open but I caught myself in time and didn't comment. I'd assumed, from her refusal to allow the diary to be moved or copied, that Claudine would have concerns about the way that it was handled. I had done a detailed search on how to work with paper artifacts. I'd hunted down a shop that sold supplies designed for libraries and archives, and I'd built myself a kit of sorts to bring with me—a desk-top beanbag pillow to support the diary in a way that spared its fragile spine, and little leather weights to gently hold the pages open while I worked. And even though the current state of research seemed divided as to whether the advantages of wearing gloves outweighed the disadvantages, I'd erred upon the side of caution and brought several pairs of cotton gloves to keep the paper safe from the potentially destructive oils that, regardless of how many times I washed my hands, remained on my own fingers.

I might simply have concluded that Claudine was one of those who thought that gloves were not desirable or necessary when one touched old paper, and that keeping one's hands clean and dry was all that was required, except I'd seen her not five minutes earlier spill coffee on that same hand when she'd set her cup down on the desk, and all she'd done was wipe it dry with tissue, and that hand was now laid full upon the diary.

The coffee on the desk had been enough to make me wonder, with the diary sitting open so close by, but I had held my tongue then too, recalling Jacqui's years of telling me that pointing out another person's faults was rarely wise. And it was Claudine's diary, after all. Not mine.

I looked away deliberately and focused on the other features of the room instead. I liked this room. It was much smaller than the others I had so far seen within the house, and set just off the entry hall across from the salon, so that its windows—there were two, set close together—overlooked the narrow terrace and the front drive with its chestnut trees. The floor was done in hardwood in the same herringbone pattern as the salon and the dining room and overlaid, as they were, with an oriental carpet, and the walls were painted warmly yellow, making things feel cozier. I liked the desk, too. It was large and serviceable, made for work and not for decoration, and had room enough for me to set the diary on its pillow in the middle with my working papers and my pencils to the right, and still leave ample space for the ceramic table lamp that squatted to the left, its large shade angled perfectly to cast light where I needed it.

But best of all, there was no second chair in here—no place for someone else to sit and socialize while I was working. I could work, as Jacqui had assured me I'd be able to, alone.

My cousin, knowing I preferred to work with no one else around me, had considerately stayed to drink her coffee in the dining room, where I could hear her talking now in English with Denise and Luc, no doubt attempting to keep them both there as well, and let me have my breathing space.

But it was Claudine's house, and Claudine's diary, and I couldn't tell her not to come along, and not to touch it.

"Yes, I think it might be Harrison," she said at last, and straightened.

As her fingers left the page I looked for any signs of damage to the paper and found none, although I knew such damage could take time to show.

"Your cousin," Claudine told me, "when she came last June to see this, could not make that word out either. Nor this one."

"That's 'Frisque.' See how she writes her *F*'s, and then the *s*? It's probably a dog's name, as she says that she 'attends to' Frisque by walking outside in the cold, and then they both come back indoors. A dog's the only pet that people walk and bring indoors again. At least the only pet that I can think of."

"So she had a dog? How very clever of you, spotting that."

I didn't think it all that clever. I had seen some samples of old documents, old handwriting, and I'd been braced to find this entry of the diary tricky to transcribe, but in fact Mary Dundas had written her words in a very clear hand. It was fairly elaborate, and she wrote her *l*'s and her *t*'s in a manner that made it a bit of a chore to tell one from the other, but still it was perfectly legible.

Claudine leaned over again to touch three little blots in the margin. "And what are these, do you think? Numbers?"

"They could be." I'd brought a magnifying glass with me

as well, on the advice of the shopkeeper from whom I'd bought my archival supplies, and I lifted it now to examine that part of the page. The three marks had been meant to conceal what she'd written beneath, as she'd done with the name of the woman she'd met at Sir Redmond's. "Yes, they're numbers. That's eight, and that's nine. And that last one," I said, "might be ten. I'm not certain."

"A key to the cipher, perhaps?"

"Not the key. That would be on its own separate paper, it's probably lost. But the numbers might still be a clue of some kind." I had glanced at the pages that followed—no words, only numbers divided by points, looking just like the cipher that Alistair had given Jacqui to test me with. Only it wasn't the same. "I don't know, it's a lot of effort to go to for something so commonplace," I said, choosing to ignore that I'd done much the same thing years ago when I'd encrypted all my school notes. "She'd have had to work out what she wanted to write down, and then translate it into cipher. All these pages. That would take a lot of time."

Claudine remarked, "She must have had her reasons."

I, for one, could not imagine what would make an ordinary woman keep a diary in the first place. I could never see the point in taking time in which you could be doing something, and then simply wasting it by writing down the things you had already done. But Mary Dundas clearly had not shared my view.

Her diary was the size and thickness of a modern hardcover novel, with a leather spine and worn cloth-covered boards and pages turned a golden beige by time, and with a texture of fine ribbing that I gathered was a feature of the way that it had been produced. The color of the ink had changed, as well. It would have once been black, but time had faded it to brown, though it was dark enough to stand out easily against the page.

For all its age and wear, someone had taken quite good care of it. And judging from the way that she had handled it this morning, I was fairly sure that person had not been Claudine.

I asked, "How did you come by this? It's not a family heirloom, is it?"

"No. Oh, no, my family does not keep such things. They are not sentimental for the past. But several years ago here in Chatou there was an antiques market, and I saw this in a stall and thought that it might be of interest to…" She coughed, and raised her cup to take a drink of coffee. "It looked interesting. Can you break the cipher, do you think?"

"I'll do my best."

"I'll leave you to it, then." She closed the double doors as she went out, and I was left in blissful solitude—the thing I had been wanting all along.

I turned the diary to the first page written in the cipher, and began to work.

❧

It should have been a simple thing. Mary Dundas had told me so herself, in words so plain I could not misinterpret them:

And she observing I was writing private thoughts advised me there were ways to write in secret, and when I replied I had no head for ciphers she assured me any person could devise one using anything to hand, whereon she crafted one upon the spot so simple in design that I do presently intend to follow her advice and practice it.

"So simple in design," the diary promised, yet three days had passed and I had come no closer to unraveling the cipher that another woman had devised "upon the spot" while drinking tea. It drove me to distraction.

I had barely noticed Jacqui leaving Monday. She had smiled and kissed me lightly on the head and given me a hug and seeing I was well absorbed in work, had tiptoed quietly away to drive herself back to the airport. If the house felt slightly different with her gone, I'd scarcely noticed it. I'd socialized when necessary, sharing an aperitif with Claudine every evening before joining her at dinner, where I'd let her take the lead in conversation, which so far had touched on local wines, the euro, and photography, three things that I knew little of myself, so it was natural for me to be the audience for her impromptu and impassioned lectures.

If I had not seen Luc Sabran—which to be honest I *had* noticed slightly more than other things—it was because he had returned to work after the holidays, and truly it was just as well to not have the distraction.

It was bad enough the cat had found a way to sneak into my workroom when he wanted to, and even though he was a cat and therefore understood the rules of solitude, it still was disconcerting to glance up and find he'd settled in his favorite spot atop the box of files by the windows and was watching me, the way cats did, with steady and unblinking eyes.

I felt the weight of his stare now and raised my head to meet it with my own. "Well then, *you* try it. See how you get on," I challenged him.

He twitched an ear and wisely did not answer.

"Fine then. Don't be so judgmental." In frustration I turned back to the first entry of the diary and read through it for what seemed the thousandth time in search of clues.

What cipher could a person craft that would be "simple in design" and "using anything to hand"? What would a person have "to hand" in those days in a house belonging to a man of some estate? I didn't know what room they had been sitting in, for Mary never mentioned it. The drawing room, presumably. There was no way to tell. They'd been drinking tea, which meant there'd been a tea service: a tea tray, teacups, lumps of sugar. Totally unhelpful. A design upon the teacups? It was possible. There would have been a fireplace, with its andirons and tongs and pokers. And because Sir Redmond was a man of means and education, there might have been books.

If there'd been books, I thought, and if they'd used one as the basis for their cipher, I was in deep trouble, for the key they'd chosen could be anything: a passage from a poem, or some rare religious tract. Odds were I'd never track it down.

Not giving in to that depressing thought, I pulled my mind back forcibly to focus on the other possibilities. The dog, I thought. Or something that the dog had with it. Or the number of wood panels on the door…

The knock that interrupted didn't fully register at first. I knew Denise's knock by now—she usually knocked lightly in an effort not to startle me, not wishing to intrude.

I said, "Come in," in French, and she put her head round the double doors.

"How does it go this morning?"

"Not well."

"Oh," she said. "Well, anyway, I'm leaving in a minute. If you want a little lunch before I go…perhaps some soup…"

"No, thanks. I'm fine."

"You have to eat." That was the mother in her talking now, I knew. She stood with hands on hips in the same stance that my own mother struck whenever she was getting set to tell me that I'd been indoors too long.

Denise, predictably enough, said, "You have been too long in this one room. You need a change of scene. Your brain can't work without fresh air."

Which from a scientific standpoint was debatable, I knew, but her suggestion of a change of scenery struck me suddenly as something that might be a good idea. Often when I labored on a tricky bit of programming, I found if I switched tasks to something simpler for a little while, my brain had time and space to better concentrate upon the more important problem.

And ever since it had been first suggested to me Sunday morning, there was one much simpler task I'd added to my list of things that needed doing. "Is it very difficult," I asked Denise, "to get from here to Saint-Germain-en-Laye? Is there a train?"

She nodded. "Yes, the RER. But you don't have to take it. I can drop you on my way, it isn't far. I'm nearly ready. I just have to make a phone call first, then we can go. All right?"

The cat Diablo stared down from his perch atop the box of files and dared me to.

"I'll get my coat," I said.

CHAPTER 10

D ENISE DROVE FAST, AND played the radio—both things
I found distracting, but today I was distracted even
more by my imaginings.

The road to Saint-Germain-en-Laye looked much like
any other road, but I was busy seeing it the way it would
have been when Mary Dundas and her brother had presumably set out that afternoon from the house of Sir Redmond
Everard. In Mary's time—I'd worked it out—a horse and
chaise could travel at an average speed of 1.65 leagues an
hour, to use the standard reckoning for leagues in Paris,
every district having its own measurements. And Chatou,
from its center, lay approximately 1.7 leagues from Saint-
Germain-en-Laye, which meant it would have taken Mary
and her brother, in the winter, just above an hour to reach
their final destination.

In the car, it took us fifteen minutes. Slightly less, the way
Denise was driving.

We crossed the river by a long bridge, turned and wound
our way around and up a road still edged with the remainder
of the old town walls, then back along an avenue with trees
cut in a box-like hedge and round again to where the old
château sat facing down the huddled buildings at the center
of the town. There was a church directly opposite with regal
steps and pillars that looked every bit as old as the château,

and both those buildings had retained their grandeur—but the modern world had crept right to their doorsteps.

Denise had pulled in to what looked like a long bay for buses to pick up and drop off their passengers. Pointing ahead she said, "There is the entrance. Or if you don't want to go inside just yet, go through there, through that big gate, and down and around through the park and along the terrace— the long path overlooking the river. It's really a beautiful walk, and the fresh air will help you change your thoughts," she said, using the French phrase for clearing one's mind. With a glance at her wristwatch she asked, "Will two hours from now be enough time?"

I wasn't about to impose my own schedule on hers. "Tell me what time I need to be back here, and I'll be here."

"Three o'clock," she said. "Be back at three."

I said, "Thanks," as I climbed from the car and she gave me a wave and was off again. The broad stretch of pavement in front of the château was practically empty, which suited me fine. I had never done well in the jostling confusion of crowds.

The château rose squarely in front of me, solid and soaring, designed to impress, yet it looked slightly lost. Like the house at Chatou it seemed fully aware that it should have had grander surroundings; as though it had slumbered and woken to find itself here at the edge of a street crowded round with tall mansard-roofed buildings, an outdoor café and the broad entrance into the underground RER station bookending the church on the opposite side, and it wasn't quite sure how to manage the fact that the world had moved on.

It was built of that same pale stone that looked ivory in some lights and golden in others and gave French châteaux their own beauty. Today there was no sun to make that stone glow, only clouds in a flat winter sky, and the walls of the château thus robbed of their light had a dull ochre cast to them, only relieved by the contrasting red brick that trimmed the round walls of the turrets and towers and framed the tall arched rows of windows that lined the two uppermost stories, reflecting no image but that of the overcast sky.

Hardly welcoming, but then the point of my trip here today wasn't to be made welcome. It was to learn the layout of the château and the grounds, to walk where Mary Dundas had once walked, so if I ever broke her cipher and began to read her diary entries I could understand them better.

Alistair considered it unlikely Mary's brother and his wife and children would have lived within the château proper, because most of the apartments there were taken up by influential Jacobites and those who'd served the young King James's mother while she'd lived. It was more probable, thought Alistair, that Nicolas Dundas on his return to Saint-Germain-en-Laye would have found lodgings for his family in the town that had grown up around the château walls to house the varied tradespeople and servants and supporters of the exiled royal court. But even so, the château and the people who had lived there would have been a daily feature of the life of Mary Dundas, and whatever events she described in her diary would need to be placed against that backdrop to be viewed in proper context.

I used my mobile now to take a few snaps of the château. When I got back to Chatou, I could create a file of photographs to reference when I was transcribing the diary. *There*, I thought. *Pure optimism.* Jacqui would be proud of me. She always told me I was far too quick to give up hope.

Moving in closer, I photographed some of the details: the balconies edged with stone railings that ran in a long line across the facade, and the carved stonework over the massive main entry doors set at the end of a narrow stone bridge leading over the dry grassy moat. Then I crossed that same bridge myself and went in.

I'd been warned by Denise that the château was now a museum, but in my mind I'd pictured something much like Hampton Court—rooms made to look as they'd looked in the past, with paneled beds and tapestries and those great portraits in which all the faces looked so much the same that to tell them apart was a challenge. But this wasn't anything like that. The château had been entirely repurposed as a museum of archaeology, the old rooms all refitted with exhibits showing finds from Paleolithic times through the Bronze and Iron Ages, and the Romans to the early Modern era. They were probably important finds, but honestly I paid them no attention. I was more absorbed in searching out the little plaques explaining what the rooms had been originally, and in finding features that appeared to have survived unchanged, most notably the stairwells with their stone steps and their intricately vaulted stone-and-redbrick walls and ceilings, and the leaded windows looking out towards the central courtyard.

I liked courtyards—the sense of seclusion, of echoing quiet and peace—and this one, when I managed to make my way out to it, wrapped me in all the sensations I loved. The château itself wasn't square; it was more an elongated pentagon, meaning the courtyard had five high enclosing sides shutting it off from the commonplace world. Four of these had beautiful cloister-like repeating arches with more arches above them, four stories of glittering windows surrounded by pale stone and edged in red brick, with round towers to mark the interior stairwells set into each corner. The fifth side of the courtyard, most lovely of all, was the wall of a chapel, with windows more beautiful than all the others, tall windows of restful green glass that soared heavenward inside their frames of stone tracery.

I had the whole courtyard alone to myself, and I could have explored any part of it, but I was drawn to that chapel, which inside was even more impressive—long and filled with quiet light from those tall narrow windows, and designed so that the vaulted ceiling's weight was borne entirely by the walls so there were no supporting columns needed here to spoil the perfect open beauty of the nave. A huge rose window filled the western wall, but at some point it had been covered over from the outside and its glass had been removed to show the stone of what I guessed to be the wall of some addition to the castle, though the sunburst wheel of intricate stone tracery remained. And best of all, at least for me, where once the altar would have been there stood a glassed-in case that housed a model of the château, built in miniature.

I had a thing for models. Not only was it easier for me to understand things when they were presented to me in their concrete form and not the abstract, but the mathematical precision and exactness used to build to scale were pleasant to my eye. This model was a fascinating thing. Raised up to table height, it was so detailed and extensive that I had to walk the whole way round to view the full expanse of the château as it would have appeared at the end of the seventeenth century, not long before Mary Dundas was born.

I hadn't realized it was so large. I'd thought this massive pentagon of rooms that I'd just toured through would have been the greatest part of it, but in the model I could see the pentagon—the "old château"—was nothing but a small bit at the western end, eclipsed by what the label on the model's case described as the *Château-Neuf* or the "new château" that

spread right to the Seine. The model showed its grand pala-
tial walls, with tower-like pavilions marking out the corners,
and the perfect mirrored symmetry of all the steps and ter-
races that led down to the river. Clearly there was more for
me to see outside.

I took a careful set of photos of the model, checked the
time, and seeing I had twenty-seven minutes left before I
had to meet Denise, I left the quiet refuge of the chapel and
the courtyard and went out again, across the little bridge that
spanned the moat, and round the corner through the tall
black iron gates into the grounds.

I should have been more fond of French formal gardens.
They were, after all, about order and symmetry—man tam-
ing nature by shaping it to his unyielding design—but I didn't
like wide-open spaces with nothing around me to serve as a
shield, so to stand in a garden like this made me feel unprotected and far too exposed. I preferred English gardens—the
overgrown corners with tree branches hanging however they
pleased, and the tucked-away benches with hedges and warm
brick walls guarding my back.

There was nowhere to hide here. What hedges there were
barely came to my knees and the broad expanse of gravel I
was standing on was *too* broad and too open for my comfort.
Even the facade of the old château, stately and large as it was,
stood too many steps distant to offer me shelter.

This side of it was longer, more imposing than the side
that faced the street, as though the castle was more conscious
of its need to make a statement here. It stood above the geo-
metric landscape with a silent sort of majesty that almost
made me feel a little sorry for it, wasting all that effort to look
regal when the only person noticing was me.

In fact, if I were pressed to put a name to how the

château looked to me from here, I would have settled on the word *forlorn*.

The wind, as if to underline the thought, blew in a colder gust that chilled my ears and made me hunch deeper in my scarf. I walked the long way down to where the wide path met an iron railing at the top of the steep bank that dropped to meet the river. And all that way, from where the old château's walls ended to the point where both the railing and the path were tied together by a building of red brick and old white stone that looked like one of the pavilions, there was nothing else remaining of the grandly sprawling "new château" depicted in the model in the chapel. It was as if a child's hand had swept a castle built of blocks aside without a care, replacing everything with houses and apartments set in rows behind a high obscuring hedge.

The pavilion itself had been repurposed into a hotel and restaurant, too upscale for me to feel comfortable venturing in off the path for a look, in my old coat and scarf and laced boots, so I stayed by the railing and stood for a moment to focus my thoughts on the river. At least *that*, I thought, couldn't be taken away. The view might have changed, with its bridges and cars and the skyscraper sprawl of the Parisian business hub of La Défense looming out of the mist just ahead, but still the olive-colored Seine wound through it all as it had done in Mary's day.

Perhaps she'd stood just here and watched boats sliding by on their slow way upstream to Paris, like the long barge I was watching now. Perhaps she'd felt the same wind blowing strongly from the west, and heard the black crows calling roughly to each other from the slope below, above the sweeter trilling of the unseen birds that hid amid the tangle of the ivy-covered trees.

The crows I could see. There was one large crow perched very near to me, on the high hedge at the corner of the old pavilion, but the birds that attracted me most were the magpies. My mother had no love of magpies and chased them relentlessly out of our garden, but I'd always liked their bold plumage—the white and blue-black in predictable patterns that set them apart from their cousins the crows.

The ones here were scattered along the path, flying and flapping and hopping and searching the gravel for scraps as I made my way back up the broad promenade, a group of them gathering as I repeated the childish rhyme in my head, counting each bird I saw: *One for sorrow.* That suited the château, I thought, with the mist and the bare lonely trees and the hard gravel shifting beneath my feet as a reminder that nothing was permanent.

I went on counting:

Two for joy. Three for a girl, four for a boy, five for silver, six for gold…

Another magpie settled on the ground amid its fellows, casting a dark eye in my direction.

Seven for a secret never to be told.

"You might be right," I told it. If I couldn't break the cipher, then whatever Mary Dundas had experienced here would be lost to history altogether and remain a secret. Mary, who had lived and breathed and walked within this shadow court of Jacobites, whose voice I had the power to restore, would stay instead forever silent. The worry and weight of frustration began to close in again. So much for "changing my thoughts," I conceded. I may have spent two hours out of my workroom, but I'd achieved little to show for it.

Eight for a wish, was the next magpie. *Nine for a kiss.* Hardly likely. The tenth took a hop from the ground to the edge of a large round low fountain not far from the gate where I'd entered the grounds. *Ten a surprise…*

"There you are." A man's voice, speaking French. A familiar voice.

Looking round sharply, I saw Luc Sabran strolling in through the gate with a casual ease that, because it was so unexpected, completely unsettled me. I had to take a moment to absorb the new turn of events and adjust, as though trimming the sails of a ship in response to a change in the wind.

He was several steps closer now. "So you decided to see the château after all." With a smile and a glance at the clouds passing swiftly above, low and dark, he said, "Not the best day for it. What did you think?"

I could see his eyes now, and they helped me recover my balance. I wanted to bluntly ask what he was doing here, but I thought that might be rude, so I simply replied, "I'm not too keen on what they've done inside. The courtyard was beautiful, though. And the chapel."

"You've been to see the terrace?" he asked. "There by the river? It runs nearly two thousand meters along, with the forest behind it. A nice place to walk when the weather is better."

"I saw it. I didn't try walking it. I only went there," I told him, and pointed back down to the far distant railing. "I wanted to find all the parts of the château I'd seen in the model."

"The model?" He tucked his hands into the pockets of his leather jacket.

"In the chapel."

"Ah." He gave a nod of understanding. "Right, I had forgotten. But those buildings are all gone. This old part is all that's left now, and the pavilion of Henry IV at the end of the path where you were, and perhaps a few cellars. The rest was all lost in the time of the Revolution. All royal lands then were taken as national properties."

"Yes, well, the nation," I said, "should have taken a bit better care of them."

Something in that evidently amused him, because he smiled. "You wouldn't have made a good revolutionary."

"Probably not. I don't like to see things destroyed. It would have made me sad to see the château being taken down."

"But this is how life is, yes? It moves forward, and the sadness of those times, it is now gone."

But not entirely, I thought, as I looked up at those dark windows, gazing out across the gravel at the barren, leafless trees. The old château hadn't lost all of its sadness. I felt it and shivered a little and turned from the fountain, now drained for the winter and empty.

I looked at my watch. It was 2:58. Only two minutes left till I'd promised to meet Denise where she had dropped me off. "I have to leave."

"OK." Still with his hands in his pockets, Luc fell into step just in front of me and to the side. That was actually where I liked people to walk—I felt shielded from all the uncomfortable empty space but not too crowded. Relaxing a little, I asked, "Do you work here?"

He shook his head. "No, my proper office is in La Défense, not far from here."

I was very familiar with La Défense, having done business there once, for a former job.

"But Wednesdays," Luc went on, "I work from home. That's why—"

"I have to wait right here," I interrupted.

"OK." Luc stopped with me on the pavement. Looked around. "Why?"

"I'm supposed to meet Denise."

We were exactly at the place where I'd been told to be, in front of the château and right across the street from the old church with its grand steps and portico, now sheltering a scruffy group of youths who didn't look at all religious. The traffic had grown busier.

Luc said, "I don't think you are."

"I am. She told me to be here at three o'clock."

His answer was to hold his right hand up the way a person did when swearing on the Bible, so that I could see the ring of car keys dangling from his fingers. "That's what she told me, as well." He smiled and flipped the keys into his fist again and moved a step in front of me to take the lead. "Come on," he said. "I'll drive you home."

I didn't understand.

I said so. "I don't understand. Why did Denise send you?"

I saw the lifting of his shoulders in the faint shrug that was such a quintessential French expression. "She couldn't come herself. She's gone to Chinon."

"Where is that?"

"The Val de Loire. Her family's there, and she and our son Noah always have their Christmas Eve in Chinon. Normally they come back the day after, but this year I was away as well, and so Denise left Noah with his grandparents to have a short vacation. She's just gone to fetch him home."

He'd had the luck to find a parking space a few steps round the corner in a street that ran beside the old château. He stopped beside a dark red Peugeot hatchback and unlocked the doors as I tried working through the logic of what he'd just told me.

It was possible, I knew, that I'd been told all this before—Denise could easily have talked about her plans to go to Chinon and, depending how absorbed I'd been in working on the cipher, I might not have paid attention. All she'd said this afternoon when she had come into my workroom was, "I'm leaving in a minute," which could certainly imply that I was meant to know where she was going, and presumably the phone call she had made before we'd left had been to Luc, to make sure there'd be someone here to meet me.

"But," I asked him, "why did she send *you*?"

He paused with a hand on the passenger door handle, turning to look at me. "Sorry, I'm not thinking. If it makes you too uncomfortable to drive with someone you don't know—"

"It isn't that." I shook my head, deciding that it really wasn't something I could easily explain to him. My cousin often said that men were clueless, and in this instance that seemed to be the case. If Luc thought it was normal for his ex-wife to arrange for him to meet me, clearly he had not shared my experience with couples who'd divorced. Even Jacqui, who'd be happy not to be in the same time zone as her exes, kept a faintly jealous eye on all their new associations, and she never would have volunteered them to chauffeur another woman.

Luc was waiting.

"Never mind," I said. "It doesn't matter."

Usually, if I were honest, I *did* feel uncomfortable in cars I wasn't used to, though this morning in Denise's car I had been too distracted by her driving speed to notice. And as I settled now into the passenger seat of Luc's car while he swung my door closed and walked round to his own, I felt a sense of the familiar that distracted me as well, until I put my finger on its cause.

"Is this a Peugeot 207?" I asked him as he slid behind the steering wheel.

"It is. An old one, though: 2009."

That would explain things. I nodded and said, "Jacqui's second ex-husband had one of these, only his was a coupe cabriolet, not a hatchback."

"I wanted that one, too." Luc smiled as he released the handbrake. "But Noah was still small and there was no place for his car seat."

As we moved off from the curb I cast a glance into the back and saw a child's booster seat. "How old is Noah now?"

"He's nine years old. Nine and two-thirds, if you ask him." He had seen what I was looking at. "When he turns ten he plans to set that booster seat on fire, I think. He knows it is the law for him to use it, but he hates it."

So then Noah was a law-abiding rebel. Like his father, I decided, for although Luc drove with care he had a sure touch with the gear lever that made me think he would have much preferred an open road where he could shift into top gear straightaway instead of being trapped within these winding streets that slowed his speed.

He was wearing jeans again today. I liked his legs in jeans, though in the confines of the car their muscled length was stretched so close to mine I had to force my gaze elsewhere to keep from staring.

We were crossing the bridge now, and leaving the château behind.

"Does she have very many ex-husbands, your cousin?" he asked.

"Only two. They were both very difficult men."

"This is why she is able to take on such difficult authors," he guessed, "like this Alistair Scott. Denise tells me that he and Claudine have a history."

Not knowing the details, I didn't have any real comment on that. But, "I wouldn't say Alistair's difficult, really. He's just very focused. That's not a bad thing, for a researcher."

"No." I felt Luc's sideways glance. "No, it isn't."

We drove for a moment in silence, until something struck me.

"Why Wednesdays?" I asked.

"Pardon?"

"Why do you work from home Wednesdays?"

He paused as though having to search back in our conversation to find the stray comment he'd made that had led to my question. "Oh. Noah still has Wednesday afternoons off, so it's necessary."

I had a vague and distant memory of my childhood friend and neighbor, Ricky, when he'd moved across from France, complaining that in Britain he was made to go to school on Wednesdays, so I gathered it was normal here for schoolchildren to have a midweek holiday. But Luc was talking as though Noah lived with him all week, not just at every other weekend, and that seemed to me less normal. It was probably rude just to ask, I knew, but curiosity outweighed my manners. "So, where does your son live? With you, or Denise?"

"We share custody. Alternate weeks. We switch over on Mondays. It's becoming more common in France, this arrangement," he said. "It's better for Noah, I think. And for us. You don't have children?"

"No." I'd have found it much easier winning my battle to *not* watch his legs if they hadn't been constantly working the clutch and the gas pedals as he changed gears, but I managed to pull my gaze up in time to catch his small shrug.

"They take work, they keep you busy." Once again he briefly looked in my direction, this time with a smile, and added, "Noah more than most. You'll likely have him underfoot when he discovers what you're doing. He'll think code breaking is cool—he'll want to help you."

I returned the smile to be polite, and looked away. I didn't dislike children, but I wasn't all that keen on being "helped" by one. And when it came to something like the breaking of a cipher, there was no real help a nine-year-old could give me.

Or at least, that's what I thought on Wednesday afternoon. By Thursday night, on New Year's Eve, I'd learned that I was wrong.

Chapter 11

THE DAY BEGAN WITH rain, which by the early afternoon had lost its steady patter and become a dismal mist that clouded everything outdoors in gray and now and then was spattered on the windows by the fitful wind.

Inside, the house was quiet.

With Denise not back from Chinon yet, my breakfast with Claudine had been as simple as our meal the night before, with us both managing to serve ourselves from what she'd left behind for us to eat and clearing up the table when we'd finished. Claudine had gone out somewhere just after that and I had taken full advantage of the solitude to start my work, refusing to be beaten by the challenge of that single line:

> *…when I replied I had no head for ciphers she assured me any person could devise one using anything to hand, whereon she crafted one upon the spot…*

Because if Mistress Harrison—or whatever her name had been—could craft a cipher on the spot, then I could do the same thing in reverse. Or so I'd told myself. My confidence had waned and I was feeling now the rumbling of faint hunger in my stomach that reminded me I hadn't stopped for lunchtime, but I stoically ignored it and bent closer to the fresh page in my notebook where I copied out more numbers from the cipher in the diary into tidy penciled rows and searched for patterns.

I'd completely bored Diablo, who had draped himself across his box of files by the window, turned his head away and closed his eyes disdainfully, the twitching of his tail the only sign he wasn't actually asleep. That, and the swivel of an ear, as though he'd heard something beyond the range of my own senses.

I was in the middle of re-ordering a row of numbers when I heard it, too: a faint repeating simple tune, like something from a synthesizer. Gradually it gained in volume, growing nearer. On his box, Diablo shifted, opening his eyes to watchful slits. The music stopped abruptly on a click, as though whatever had been playing it had been snapped shut, and from the entry hall outside my workroom I could hear the lightly purposeful approach of footsteps on the tiles.

The door, which I had left ajar so that the cat could come and go, swung inward as a boy came in, his whole attention on the cat. "Diablo!" he said, stretching out his arms, and to my great surprise the tomcat rose and arched and leaped straight into them, allowing himself to be made a fuss of in a way that I'd have thought he'd find undignified. I must have made a sound, because the boy turned then and noticed me. An adult faced with that sort of surprise might well have dropped the cat; the boy held on more tightly to it as he said, "*Bonjour, madam*," recovering his manners. Speaking carefully in English he continued, "I am sorry to derange you. I look for… I *was* looking for Diablo." Shifting the cat to one side, he came forward and held out his hand. "I am pleasured to meet you," he said. "I am Noah."

Of course he was. Noah Sabran had his mother's black hair and his father's blue eyes. He seemed small for a nine-year-old, but he looked healthy and filled with the energy most boys contained at that age. He came right to the side of my desk for the handshake.

Returning it, I told him, "It's 'disturb.' To be 'deranged' in English doesn't mean the same thing that it does in French. In modern English, anyway. So you'd say: 'I am sorry to disturb you.'"

"I am sorry to disturb you," he repeated, with a nod at the correction, as he gathered up the cat against his chest. I heard the rumbling as the cat began to purr. "Thank you, madam. Good-bye, madam." He made a swift retreat into the entry hall and left me on my own again.

I felt both relieved and a little surprised that he hadn't displayed any interest in what I was doing. The diary spread on its cushion, its pages held open with small leather weights, dominated my desk but was vulnerable to any person who thought it looked curious, and children in my experience liked to explore things by touch. Then again, it admittedly wasn't that easy to touch things while holding a cat.

I carried on working. It took several minutes before my brain—no doubt egged on by my stomach—connected enough dots to realize that Noah Sabran being here in the house meant Denise must be home, and Denise being home meant a better than average chance I would be greeted with food if I found my way into the kitchen, and food would restore both my spirits and my concentration. I set down my pencil.

The kitchen was warm from the wood-burning cooker and lit with a brightness that banished the wet gray world outside the multipaned windows, creating a cozy and comfortable haven of cream-colored walls and red brick and dark beams, with the old vintage cupboards and old flagstone floor and, in front of the fireplace, a plain sturdy table where Noah sat petting Diablo and playing a video game.

Denise was busily unpacking bread, fruit, and vegetables from an assortment of bags, but she paused to greet me cheerfully, saying in French, "Did you hear us? We tried to be quiet and sneak in the back so we wouldn't disturb you. I knew you'd be working." She said to her son, "Noah, this is Madame Thomas."

Noah had set down his video game and was standing politely and watching me with those blue eyes that were so like his father's.

I nearly replied that we'd already met, but I caught myself just in time, realizing from what Denise had just said that her son hadn't told her he'd been in my workroom ten minutes ago. And from how he was holding his shoulders, so square and so still—like my cousin did when she was bracing for something unpleasant—I guessed he'd be happier if Denise didn't find out.

"Hello, Noah," I said, still in French, as I held out my hand. "How are you?"

He blinked and accepted the handshake. "I am very well, madam. Thank you."

"Sit down," said Denise. "I was just getting Noah a snack, would you like one?"

Her "snack" was the same as the ones I'd been served in the home of my childhood best friend—bread and butter and chocolate in generous proportions, except with a hot mug of coffee in place of the milk Ricky's mother had given me then. I could feel my inner self regressing happily to that remembered time, that other kitchen where I'd spent so many afternoons in warmth and comfort, lovingly accepted as a member of the family.

Denise asked me, "How did you enjoy your time at Saint-Germain-en-Laye? Did you find inspiration?"

"No, but it was very interesting."

"And Luc came to meet you at the proper time? He wasn't late?"

Across the table from me Noah said, "Papa is never late."

His mother smiled. "Well, not with you. And not for meals. But when he's working he forgets to watch the clock sometimes."

I told them both, "He was on time. A little early, actually." I didn't bother saying that I'd been surprised to see him, because if in fact Denise *had* told me yesterday that she'd be heading off to Chinon, I was not about to look a fool for having failed to listen.

Noah, looking vindicated, fed the cat a bit of bread beneath the table. "Did he bring his motorcycle?"

"No. He drove a car."

"I like the motorcycle best," his son said. "It goes very fast."

A rebel then, as I'd suspected. If I'd needed further proof, just watching how he made sure that his mother wasn't looking before breaking off another bit of bread to give Diablo told me he was fond of testing boundaries. The cat looked furtive, too. He'd sunk so low on Noah's lap his eyes and ears were all that showed above the table's edge.

I smiled a little, and when Noah smiled back I reasoned he was probably acknowledging the bond between conspirators.

Denise, who hadn't noticed, brought the coffee pot across to fill my cup again, and glancing out the windows said, "He won't be riding it today, not in this weather."

"He can ride the motorcycle in the rain," said Noah. "There are tunnels on his way to work."

I gave in to my growing curiosity. "He works in La Défense, he said. What does he do?"

"He's a financial accountant for Morland Electronics," she told me. "It's an English company, do you know it?"

The bloodred Morland logo was familiar to me. "Yes."

"Luc's brother works for Morland, too, in California. They have offices worldwide. In Luc's division, here in Paris, they do tactical and sonar systems special for the military and defense."

"But Papa doesn't build them. He just keeps the books."

Denise corrected Noah patiently. "It's rather more than that. Your father has to manage and prepare all the reports. He does the budgeting and forecasting and keeps the ledgers balanced. It's important."

"But it's still too many numbers," Noah said. "I'd rather do what Uncle Thierry does."

Denise was smiling as she said to me, "*My* brother, Thierry, chooses not to grow up, ever. He still helps our aunt and uncle with their hotel, as he's done since we were both at school. He will be Chinon's oldest bartender, I think."

"He lets me help him," Noah said.

"Oh yes, he always likes to have your help. It means less work for him." She kissed him lightly on the head. "And if you're such an eager helper, you can help me with the decorations for tonight."

I couldn't think why she'd need decorations for tonight until I realized it was New Year's Eve—the feast of Saint-Sylvestre here in France. At my friend Ricky's house they'd always had a full-on party, filled the house with neighbors, but Denise assured me things at the Maison des Marronniers weren't that elaborate.

"Claudine likes to do things simply. There will only be

the five of us." She handed me a small box. "Here, I'll give you the balloons, if you don't mind? Noah will waste them all by popping them."

I disliked the sound of balloons popping, so I was careful to blow them up slowly, to Noah's frustration. Diablo, unimpressed by my efforts, retreated to a shadowed corner of the salon while we strung the paper banners that said "*Bonne Année!*" above the lovely windows of the dining room, and fastened clusters of balloons to all the chair backs, and hung stars of silver glitter where Denise directed us to hang them while she set the table with fine china and cut-crystalware and candles with more silver stars and glitter balls strewn round them for good measure.

By the time Claudine arrived home from wherever she had been, we'd nearly finished with the salon, too, and everything looked festive.

"This is perfect," she announced, and hung her coat up in the entry hall before she spread her arms to give a double kiss to Noah. "You've been busy, darling. Aren't you clever?"

"Madame Thomas helped."

"Then she is clever, too." Claudine included me in her warm smile and joined us in the salon, looking up towards the ceiling. "All we need now is the mistletoe."

We British liked our mistletoe at Christmas, but in France it was a ritual of New Year's Eve, as I had learned in childhood.

Noah said, "Papa is bringing it."

As if on cue, the sound of footsteps scuffed against the stone walk in the garden at the back. Before the rear door to the kitchen opened on a gust of wind and slammed again the boy had started running, and Luc barely had the time to shake his coat and clear the rain from it and step into the dining room before he had to kneel to intercept a flying hug.

"Papa!"

With both their heads so close together it was even easier to notice the resemblance. It was more than just their eye color—I saw it in the angle of their jawlines and the quickness of their smiles. Luc hugged his son back tightly with his one free hand—his other hand was taken by a plastic-handled shopping bag that bulged.

"You got my messages?" asked Noah.

"Yes, all five of them."

Denise, who'd come through from the kitchen also and was standing in the arched door with her apron smudged from cooking, said, "I can't believe I didn't think to get it at the market. We were right there."

"It's no trouble finding mistletoe," Luc told her.

Noah asked him, "But the blowpipes! Did you find the blowpipes?"

"Yes, of course. *And* hats. See here." Luc reached into the shopping bag and pulled a pointed party hat from deep within it. "Look, it has a light that flashes if you push it there. And this," he said, "is even better. This is mine." He drew it out and put it on his head—a rather ridiculous novelty hat made of shiny foil card with a small sprig of mistletoe stuck to its brim.

"Very subtle," said Denise, but as he stood and handed her the bag she kissed him anyway, a friendly kiss that looked no different from the one he coaxed from Claudine when he came through to the salon to give her a proper greeting. Then he was in front of me, and smiling, so I kissed him too, as lightly as the others had. His face was cold and smelled of wood smoke and the damp outdoors. I liked it. I liked him.

"I have a hat for you as well. And you," he told Claudine. "Yours has a light on it, like Noah's."

Claudine thanked him. "Very kind of you." Her tone was dry. "But if it's all the same to you, I'll wait and wear it after dinner."

"As we all should," said Denise, removing Noah's hat and nudging him affectionately forward. "Go and keep Papa from getting into trouble while I finish cooking dinner. You can show him your new card trick."

"Not another one?" Luc's groan sounded real, but the way Noah grinned in reply made me realize his father was teasing and everyone knew it.

"It's a good one," the boy promised. "One of the waitresses at the hotel showed me."

Luc grinned in his turn. "Hanging out with the waitresses, were you?"

"He'll claim it was only professional interest," Denise said, "but notice he never asks *me* if I know any tricks with the cards I can teach him."

Her son turned to look at her. "Do you?"

"I might have learned one or two when I was your age."

"Did they have cards when you were my age?" Noah asked. For all my difficulty reading people's tones and their expressions, I was fairly sure from looking at him that he hadn't meant that as an insult. Children his age sometimes had no proper sense of history as a timeline—to them, everything that happened in the years before their birth was "history," tangled dates that intersected freely without context. I remembered asking my own mother one day after school how many traitors she had gone to see beheaded at the Tower.

Denise replied in the same tone my mother had used then, "Oh yes, when we weren't hunting dinosaurs for dinner, we played cards. Of course we had them. How old do you think

I am?" She smiled and added, "People have been playing cards for centuries, my dear. They're not a new invention."

Something struck my memory, hard.

Forgetting all about Luc's kiss, or that he was still standing close beside me, I excused myself. I crossed from the salon into my workroom, pulled my gloves on, and with care turned back the pages of the diary to its start.

Upon the 22nd came my eldest brother Nicolas... I followed down the neat handwritten lines: *Sir Redmond Everard, for so his name is, seemed not in the least put out to have us thus descend upon him. He and his good lady made us welcome...* Further down, my finger stopped. I'd found it: *Supper being done we then amused ourselves at play upon the cards.*

They had been playing cards, perhaps in that same room where Mary Dundas had the next day sat and talked to Mistress Whatever-her-name-was, who had crafted there "upon the spot" a cipher using something close at hand.

I sat, and slipping off the gloves reached for my pencil once again, and started setting down a simple substitution cipher using varied values for a suit of cards. It nearly fit. I tried with aces high and aces low, and padded extra numbers round the real ones, just as numbers had been added in the first test cipher Alistair had given me, for camouflage. It nearly worked. The letters still spelled gibberish, but something in the patterns that they made now gave me hope.

Perhaps, I thought, the fault was mine. Perhaps the cards that Mary had been playing with were different from our modern packs of cards. I turned my chair around so I could use Claudine's computer, neatly tucked into the corner of the room behind my working desk. A quick search on the Internet bombarded me with facts and speculations on the origins of playing cards, but cross-referencing my sources left me fairly sure our modern packs—with fifty-two cards split into four suits of clubs and diamonds, spades and hearts—had been established by the 1500s here in France, a full two hundred years before Mary Dundas had come along. She wouldn't have been playing with a joker, since those hadn't yet been added to the pack, but all the other cards would have matched those I was familiar with. So if cards *were* the basis of her cipher, all I had to do was figure out which order she had used them in.

Returning to my study of the diary, I stared hard at the three blotted numbers in the margin that appeared to be eight, nine, and ten, as though by staring I might force them to give up their secrets, but they stubbornly stayed blot-like and unhelpful.

All through dinner my mind remained fixed on the puzzle. I failed to appreciate all the fine food that Denise had prepared for this most festive meal at the end of the year. We had champagne and oysters, smoked salmon on toast and roast pork and a platter of delicate cheeses, with wines for each course and a chocolate log cake for the finish, but I didn't register all of the tastes. And I stayed on the fringe of the talk, only answering when I was spoken to, which to my great relief wasn't that often.

Claudine and Luc had a discussion about some French folk singer she had once photographed whose name meant nothing to me, so I happily kept out of that, and then Noah was kept busy answering questions about what he'd done with his grandparents, which once again was a topic I wasn't expected to have an opinion on, leaving my mind free to think about playing cards and how one might work them into a cipher.

I was focused on this when I felt a soft tap on my forehead, and I glanced up as a second something hit me very lightly on my cheekbone. From his seat across the table from me, Luc grinned as he lowered his toy blowpipe with its ammunition of small wads of paper. "You make an easy target when you're thinking. Denise wants us all to move into the salon. Would you like brandy?"

In the salon, Claudine dimmed the lamps to let the fairy lights and decorations show and shimmer. Opening the doors of a tall cabinet, she revealed a television that I hadn't known was there, and soon a program called *Le Plus Grand Cabaret du Monde*—"The Greatest Cabaret Show in the World"—was working hard to entertain us with a dazzling cavalcade of international performers seeking to outdo each other with their acts of song and dance and acrobatics. There was a magician, too, who managed complicated things with scarves that briefly captured Noah's interest, but when that was done the boy returned his own attention to his handheld gaming console.

"What is that you're playing?" asked Luc.

"Robo Patrol."

Denise explained to Luc, "It was a gift from Uncle Thierry."

"Yes, of course it was. Your brother only gives gifts that make noise." Luc held his hand to Noah. "Can I have a go?"

Noah shook his head, not looking up from his game. "Uncle Thierry said that it is not for you. He says you are too old to play it."

"Uncle Thierry is older than I am."

"He seems a lot younger."

"Not mentally," put in Denise, and Luc answered by raising his toy blowpipe, aiming it in her direction and pinging her with a small wad of bright paper.

"Just give me the game."

Noah handed it over and waited, and smiled when the synthesized music trailed off on a flourish. "You died."

"I'm only wounded," said his father, and the music started up again.

Claudine curled into her armchair and said, "Noah, why don't you show me your new card trick?"

I was finding it difficult focusing with all the movement and noise from the cabaret program combined with the sounds of the video game and the room's conversation, so I only had half an eye on the boy as he rummaged in one of his pockets and drew out a pack of cards, but when he said, "I just need to take some of them out, first," and Claudine asked, "Why?" I recovered my focus in time for his answer.

"Because this trick's done with a pack like you use when you're playing belote, when you first take out all of the cards between one and six."

I sat more upright. I doubted that anyone noticed, because they went on with what they had been doing around me, but if all the gears in my brain had been audible, there would have been an explosion of noise that stopped everyone else in their tracks. I excused myself quietly. Crossed to the workroom.

The lines from the first journal entry of Mary Dundas leaped insistently into my view:

Supper being done we then amused ourselves at play upon the cards. There being three of us (for Lady Everard declined to play but chose instead to sit apart and so be entertained) we played the Renegado with Sir Redmond and myself aligned against my brother...

Renegado. The computer took a moment to oblige me, but eventually it told me renegado was a form of the once-popular game ombre, in which the eights, nines, and tens were removed before play, thus creating a forty-card pack.

I turned round in my chair again, seeking the small blotted numbers marked down in the margin, to make very certain they still read the same as they always had: eight, nine, and ten.

It was not just the cards on their own, I thought, feeling the warm spreading thrill of discovery. No, it was the *game*.

"Clever you," I applauded the long-faceless woman who'd crafted this over a tea table so long ago. It *was* simple, as Mary had said, but with all the right twists to avoid being obvious. Taking my pencil in hand I began to work through the results, reading over the rules of the card game again and fine-tuning the whole thing before I applied what I'd learned to the first line that Mary had written in cipher. The patterns made sense now, and words started shaping themselves from the numbers.

I nearly missed hearing the knock at my door.

It was open, and Luc had stepped into the room by the time I looked up. He was wearing his hat with the mistletoe stuck to the brim. From across in the salon behind him I heard a man singing along to the musical strains of the can-can. "It's midnight," said Luc. "Happy New Year."

I met the blue of his gaze with a smile that felt brilliant from my side. "I've got it!" I told him. "They did it with playing cards, and they had played renegado, so they took out all of the eights, nines, and tens, and each player's dealt nine cards to start with, so that means you have to begin with the ninth letter, and now I've got the whole key to the cipher. I've got it!"

He looked at me a moment, as though something in my features held him fascinated, then he left the doorway and came forward in two strides and leaned across the desk and bending down, he kissed me. It was not the same as when I'd kissed him before dinner in the salon. This was warmer, lasted longer, and the pressure of it changed and deepened, lingering as he drew back to smile into my eyes.

"Come have champagne. We'll celebrate," he said.

I heard my cousin's warning voice flash briefly through my mind: "That's not a rabbit hole you want to tumble down. Don't get involved." And then I pushed that voice aside and took the hand that Luc was holding out.

"All right," I said.

I left my workbook on the desk, where the first words of Mary's secret diary lay reclaimed from silence, written out in plain text for the world to read:

At three o'clock, my brother came to fetch me with the news that I was wanted…

CHAPTER 12

They best succeed who dare.
—Macpherson, "Fingal," Book Three

Chatou
January 23, 1732

F RISQUE HAD FALLEN ASLEEP. Mary might have done likewise, for dinner had been a large meal and a full hour after they'd finished, her body was still wanting time to digest it. And now she'd been called to this room where the air was uncommonly warm from the fierce fire Sir Redmond kept stirring to life with his poker and tongs, and the ponderous tick of a longcase clock's pendulum lulled her with every swing closer to slumber. What saved her from falling asleep was the fact that the chairs in this small upstairs chamber were favored with cushions as firm as their rush-bottomed seats, and while Frisque had the softness of Mary's own lap and the satiny folds of her skirts to surround him in comfort, she was forced to sit upright or risk an undignified fall to the hearth rug.

Her brother had taken a seat in the armchair beside her and stretched out his boots to the fender, and now with a long sigh Sir Redmond sat too, on her other side. Taking a bright silver snuffbox from one of his pockets, he followed her gaze to the two portraits hanging in narrow gold frames just above the dark wood of the mantelpiece.

"Very good likenesses, wouldn't you say?" he asked Mary.

She couldn't be sure, since she recognized neither the boy nor the girl in the portraits. She wouldn't have guessed at their ages—they looked to be no longer children, exactly, and yet not quite adults. The girl, with her lovely large eyes and her delicate features and curling brown hair crowned with flowers, gazed straight from the canvas at Mary and smiled. She was holding more flowers in one of her lady-like hands, and her richly blue gown was embroidered in gold with a light fall of lace at the edge of her sleeves. The boy, who had similar features, was looking away with one hand on his hip, with a chest piece of armor strapped over a red coat with gold braid and buttons. His hair was brown too, though in his case the long fall of curls was more likely a gentleman's periwig much like the ones Mary's father had made, in the style men had worn at the time of her birth.

She asked, "Are they relations of yours?"

"Relations of…? No, my dear." Sir Redmond seemed to be hiding a smile as though she had amused him. "No, I can claim many grand things in my lineage, but to my knowledge I've no claim to royalty. That," he said, giving a nod to the portraits, "is our good King James when a boy, and his sister the Princess Louise Marie, God rest her soul."

Mary had no memory of the princess, having been not two years old when smallpox had descended upon Saint-Germain-en-Laye and struck the young King James and his beloved sister, among others. But she'd heard the stories. Mary's aunt had often spoken of the day the princess died, when no one told the ailing king for fear that knowing he had lost his only sibling and his close companion would destroy his own will to recover. Her aunt, who had a weakness for a tragic tale, had said to Mary once, "You've never seen a man in such pain as the king was on the day they judged him well enough to hear the sad news. He had loved her so, and it was terrible to watch his grief."

The king had then been four and twenty years of age, the princess not much younger than herself, thought Mary. Looking to where Nicolas was sitting with his gaze upon the shifting fire, she wondered whether he would grieve her death so deeply, if she were to die as the princess had died, before she'd truly had a chance to live.

She doubted he would have considered her his close companion, nor was she his only sibling, but he'd thought enough of her to fetch her home to live with him, which told her he must hold her dear, or else he would have left her where she was and not increased his household burdens and expenditures.

As though he felt her watching him, he turned his head and smiled a little. "You were nearly named Louise Marie. Our mother much admired the princess."

Sir Redmond with his focus on the portraits said, "She was a lovely child. As was the king. And I gather his own sons, the princes, are handsome as well. Is that not so?"

"They are fine lads, both of them." Nicolas nodded. "The king and queen dote on them."

"God bless them and keep them. A family," Sir Redmond remarked, "is a very great thing." He opened his snuffbox and held it to Mary. "It's fine Barcelona, my dear, you may take it with no fear of sneezing. No?" He offered it next to her brother, who did take some, dipping a small measure out of the box with a tiny pipe. Sir Redmond leaned back in his chair and did the same, tapping the snuff to the back of his hand before sniffing it in and replacing the box in his pocket while taking his handkerchief out. He did not sneeze as many men did, but he did wipe his nose before saying again, "Yes, a family's a very great thing, Mistress Dundas. Do you not agree?"

Mary looked to her brother, and feeling the warmth of his encouragement beside her answered, "Yes, sir, I do. Most wholeheartedly."

"For my own part, there is little that I would not do for the love of my family," Sir Redmond said. "Their cause is my cause; their need is my own. Do you feel the same way?"

Mary wasn't entirely sure why the older man wanted to know her opinion, but she told him, "Yes, sir."

His eyes held approval. The fire had started to settle, and taking the poker in hand he leaned forward to stir the flames higher. "Your family has long served the king, Mistress Dundas. If he were in need of your services now, would you help him?"

She frowned faintly, not understanding. "I'm sure I could be of no help to the king."

"If you could be," he pressed her, "what would you do then? Would you honor your family and keep to their path?"

She glanced sideways at Nicolas only to find he was looking deliberately into the fire, and away from her. Mary said slowly, "I hope I would always remember my family and honor them, sir, if I could. But I—"

"Ask her more plainly," said Nicolas in a low voice to Sir Redmond. "She has the intelligence to understand."

Still confused, Mary looked to the Irishman who smiled kindly and set down the poker.

"There is at this moment in Paris," Sir Redmond told Mary, "a man whose affairs are of interest to King James. This man is now sought by the English, and must be protected. I do have a plan for this, but I require your help."

"My help?" Mary considered this such an unlikely request she was frankly astonished. "But how?"

"I can tell you no details beyond that you would be expected to live for a short while in Paris, my dear, and to keep a great secret. It's very important."

She felt a small thrill in her breast. *Her* help. Keeping a secret. Mere hours ago she had talked with and watched Mistress Jamieson, feeling quite certain she'd never be able to be as adventurous nor half as brave, and now here she was being told she might be given the chance to do just that. And in Paris, where she'd so long dreamed of going.

Sir Redmond asked, "Will you do it?"

"Yes." She got the word out before indecision could hold it back. "Yes, sir, I will."

"Splendid." Sir Redmond turned his attention to Nicolas, who was still watching the fire.

Mary thought she knew, now, why her brother had seemed so distracted. He clearly was not in approval of Sir Redmond's plan of her going to Paris and would have preferred she returned with him to Saint-Germain-en-Laye, although his loyalty to king and cause left him duty bound not to complain. She was trying to find the right speech to assure him her choice would amount to no more than a minor delay of his plans, when Sir Redmond spoke first.

"You were right, sir," he said to her brother. To Mary, he added, "He told me last month you'd be perfectly suited to take this assignment, and so you are."

Mary's hand stilled on Frisque's sleeping back. She looked quickly at Nicolas and this time caught the corner of his sideways glance before it slid away again.

A log fell splintering in the fire and something deep in Mary splintered too, and fell in flames as hot and searing, but she struggled not to let the sudden pain inside her show in her expression as the longcase clock began to chime.

"What, four o'clock already?" asked Sir Redmond. "You must soon be on your way, sir, if you hope to make it home by dark."

Her brother stood. "I'll see my sister to her chamber first."

She did not speak to him the whole length of the corridor, nor he to her, but when they reached her chamber she set Frisque down on the carpet by the bed and, turning from her brother so he would not see the hurt she knew was showing plainly in her eyes, asked, "Am I to remain here, then?"

"Sir Redmond and his wife are very kind."

She nodded slightly. "Do be sure to give my compliments to your good lady and your children."

"Mary."

"I am sorry that I shall not have the chance to meet them, but—"

"'Tis only for a little while. A few weeks, possibly, until the man is moved to safer quarters." When she did not speak in answer to that, Nicolas continued, "When Sir Redmond said he needed a young woman who spoke French and yet whose loyalty was absolute, I thought…"

"You thought of me. I understand." She understood too well, she realized. "So, when this is finished, this affair in Paris, where will I go then?"

"Then you will come, as I have promised you, to live at Saint-Germain."

She did not want to ask the question, but her heart was bound to know the answer. "Tell me, if Sir Redmond had not needed me, if there had been no use for me, would you have still been moved to write the letter that you wrote? Would you have wanted me to come to you?"

His pause was a more honest answer than his words.

"Yes," he said. "Of course. You are my sister." Then to fill the silence that came afterwards he carried on, "There is no danger in what you are being asked to do, I can assure you. I would never have consented to it otherwise, nor placed you in harm's way." And as her silence stretched, he added, "If you wish to reconsider…if you do not want to go…"

You always have a choice, her aunt had promised her. And Mary squared her shoulders as she made one now. "I'll go."

"Come then and heal my conscience, for I'll not away until I know that things are well between us."

She could not let him see her face the way it was, because she knew it was not so much different from the face she'd shown her father when he'd left those many years ago, but time if nothing else had given her the gift of hiding how she felt inside by doing what her cousin Colette had so truthfully observed—the conscious mimicry and masking of her own self with another form, the way the fairies in the tales she loved assumed an alternate appearance to disguise themselves. She closed her eyes a moment, blinking back the futile tears of disappointment that she would not have betray her, and allowed the poise and grace of Mistress Jamieson to settle round her shoulders like a robe before she turned.

Her brother, knowing her but little to begin with, did not seem to mark the change. He seemed relieved, and when she crossed to him he kissed her cheek and asked her, "Is there anything you need me to have sent to you? A new gown, or some shoes with pattens for the Paris streets?"

She meant to tell him no, there wasn't anything, but suddenly the linnet in the drawing room downstairs began to sing, a pure exquisite burst of sound that drifted up the stairs to where her brother stood and waited for her answer.

It was not a joyous song, but one of wistfulness and

longing, from a creature forced to ever view the world behind the gilt bars of its cage, to never know the taste of freedom. Mary, with her thoughts on Mistress Jamieson, received that plaintive song as though it had been sung for her alone, a herald's call reminding her that this might be her only chance to spread her own wings to a wider sky.

She raised her chin and met her brother's gaze with new determination. "I should like a cloak," she told him, "with a fur-lined hood."

CHAPTER 13

Protect the friends of your father: and remember the chiefs of old.
—Macpherson, "Fingal," Book Four

Paris
February 1732

THE MAN HAD RETURNED to the window.

She saw the faint glow of his pipe in the dimness beyond the glass, fading and burning in time with his breathing. She hadn't seen *him* yet, not clearly, but she'd seen his shape at the window on no fewer than three occasions this evening while she'd been arranging her things in this chamber that was to be hers, at the front of the house. The man's house stood opposite, which on this small narrow street meant that there was not much to divide them. Had he tossed a stone to her she could have caught it with ease, she decided, especially as his room was on the first floor of that house, straight across from the lodgings that had been secured for herself and the others in rooms on the first floor of theirs: six fine rooms, fully furnished, with two rooms on the ground floor underneath that gave them private access to the street, so they were not obliged to use the common stairs shared by the other tenants. The rooms below were also where the maid, the cook, and the cook's boy would do the best part of their labor, for Sir Redmond having dealt with every hazard had arranged things so that Mary and the man whom she'd be helping to protect would have no cause to leave their house to seek their meals.

That sounded over-grand to her, now that she thought of it: "the man whom she'd be helping to protect." She was not truly a protection for him, merely a small piece of his disguise. Those who were searching for him would be looking for a man alone, she had been told, not one with family.

"When he does arrive," Sir Redmond had explained, "you'll greet him as his sister, and the servants will assume that is the truth of your relationship."

"And then?"

"That is the whole of it, my dear. You'll stay there with him until we are given word where we're to send him. That may take some weeks, I fear." He'd stressed the need for secrecy. "His liberty depends upon it. There are many who would seek to find him and so claim the rich reward that's offered by the English."

"Would it not be safer," Mary had suggested, "if he were concealed somewhere away from Paris?"

"Men are better hidden in a crowd than in the country. It is yet the time of Carnival in Paris, when all within that city are well occupied with feasting and with revelry, and we have found you lodgings in a house in Saint-Germain, where you will further be protected by the Fair that does begin a few days hence."

Mary had looked at him, confused. "In Saint-Germain? But—"

"Not in Saint-Germain-en-Laye, my dear, but Saint-Germain in Paris." He'd explained it was a quarter of the city that had nothing to connect it to the palace or the town where she'd been born and where her brother had returned to live, except that they both honored the same saint and so did partly share his name. Sir Redmond, being then with Mary in the room that held his books, had found a map in one to show her. "See now, this is Saint-Germain. It takes its name from this old abbey at its center, Saint-Germain-des-Prés. It's now primarily a prison, I believe, although the ancient church and abbey palace yet remain in use. And here"—he'd moved his finger slightly—"is the place where every year they hold the Fair, beginning on the day that follows Candlemas and lasting till the eve before Palm Sunday."

Mary had begun to feel excitement at the prospect of a fair, until Sir Redmond had reminded her that she would not see much of it. "I'd rather that you did not venture too far from your lodgings, and then only when it cannot be avoided."

It was not, she thought, the way she had imagined seeing Paris.

She had dreamed of a city of beautiful buildings and gardens and bridges that gleamed in the sunlight, and churches with bells that rang over the river that wound past tall houses and streets paved with stones. She had dreamed of the salons and lively discussions, of places of learning and shops filled with wonderful things. She had so far seen none of it.

All the way in on the road from Chatou she'd been closed in a chaise with Madame Roy, the dour-faced woman who had been selected to serve as her chaperone. They had been shuttered away, kept from seeing the things they were passing until they'd arrived in this tight narrow street and had entered these rooms where she had to take Sir Redmond's word for the fact that the old abbey church of Saint-Germain-des-Prés even stood where he'd shown her it did on the map, a mere few streets away, for outside her own window the tight line of houses leaned so high that she could see nothing beyond their walls.

Only the slow-burning glow of the pipe of the man in the grimy house opposite.

Mary yanked at the calico curtains that hung at her window and drew them together to gain herself privacy.

Frisque, who'd been battling the fringe of a carpet in front of the clothespress, turned now with a wag of his tail as the chaperone entered their room with a purposeful rustling of linens and silk.

Madame Roy was a tall, middle-aged woman, healthily formed, with an unsmiling face deeply pitted from smallpox and straight hair the color of pewter confined by a cap with long lappets that hung to her shoulders. She spoke perfect French, though her accent was one Mary hadn't been able to place. Mary couldn't be sure Madame Roy was the woman's real name, because Mary herself had been given the alias "Mademoiselle Vasseur" for her time here, so she would match "Monsieur Vasseur," the man who would pose as her brother.

The chaperone held in her arms the two new gowns Sir Redmond had ordered for Mary. Both were finely made and of the latest fashion called the *robe volant*—unstructured at the front and with a long front seam that, instead of dividing over the petticoat as in the old style, stayed closed nearly all the way up, parting only above the waist to show the ribbons and ties of her stomachers. Both gowns had lovely broad pleats spreading down in the back from the shoulders, and full sleeves gathered at the elbows into soft cuffs trimmed with scalloped falls of lace, and both were styled in bold damask prints, one a richly olive green and one the color of ripe plums.

Madame Roy explained her entrance with, "I have to hang them in the clothespress."

"Here, let me," Mary said too quickly, for she'd left her journal and the pen case lying in an open drawer within the clothespress, being too distracted by the pipe smoker to properly conceal them. As she gathered up the folds of gowns and petticoats from Madame Roy, she added, "I fear I've not been a very sociable companion. Do forgive me."

"I have rarely been accused of being sociable myself." A twist that might have been a smile turned up the corners of the older woman's mouth. Her eyes looked pewter gray as well, and Mary found them difficult to read. "It is a tiring thing to travel. I expect you'll feel more settled once your brother has arrived."

The man who was to be her brother came by coach next afternoon.

He was, to her surprise and pleasure, rather like her brother in appearance—of the same age and the same build and of middle height like Nicolas, and with an oval face as frank and friendly. He wore a short white-powdered wig that made a contrast to his darker eyebrows, and his eyes were hazel green and large, inclined to narrow slightly when he smiled. He smiled often.

He spoke educated French, a scholar's French, and had the manners of a gentleman.

"My dear Marie," he greeted her as smoothly as an actor, with a warm embrace as genuine as if he had in truth been her own brother. "It is good to see you well."

He gallantly removed his cloak and passed it to the waiting maid together with his gloves, and climbed the stair with Mary to their suite of rooms where he proceeded to warm every corner of that space with personality. He charmed the servants, one and all, made Mary laugh, and even coaxed a proper smile from Madame Roy. Frisque, being not as fond of male companionship, was harder to impress, but by the week's end even he was coming round a little.

Mary played her part as well as she was able. She knew nothing of this man but that his name was Jacques, or so she had been told, and she could hardly ask him questions in this house where they were never on their own together, but she nonetheless reached some conclusions of her own.

She did not think that he was French. He spoke without a hint of accent, but his choice of words was often not in keeping with the words she would have chosen, and at breakfast on the third day he stopped speaking in the middle of a sentence with a sudden look of vague surprise, as though he either had forgotten what he was about to say, or did not know the phrase for it. She finished off the thought for him and teased him for becoming so distracted, hoping humor would keep any of the servants from perceiving his small stumble, and he smiled at her in gratitude, but from that moment on she was convinced he was not French.

And while he clearly did not labor with his hands, he had the faintest callous on the middle finger of his right hand as a man acquired from daily taking up a pen or pencil.

She herself was gaining something similar from writing in her journal every evening, after supper but before Madame Roy came to bed. It was a peaceful moment she looked forward to, alone with pen and candle and the blank page of her journal as she worked the simple cipher Mistress Jamieson had made for her, to write her thoughts in private.

I am inclined to think, she wrote, *that Jacques may be a poet or a satirist, and persecuted by the English for his bold attacks on them. In truth he has a cutting wit and keeps us all amused.*

The candle dipped and danced, caught in a stray draught that had seeped with stealth around the window frame, for outside it was growing colder from the darkness and the bitter wind that chased between the houses, down the narrow street. The street, she knew now, had a name: the rue du Coeur Volant. The street of the flying heart. Quite a romantic name for such a mean and deplorable thoroughfare; and yet at night all its ugliness faded, subdued by the light of the lanterns that caught the bright clothes of the revelers passing beneath on their way to and from the great Fair Saint-Germain in the next street but one.

Mary rose now and crossed to the window to watch them a moment and tried not to yearn quite so strongly to follow them, telling herself there would be other years, other fairs, other chances. She leaned on the glass so she would not be forced to see her own reflection in place of the wider world, much like the linnet confined to its cage might press one eye close up to the bars and so fool itself.

Frisque whined at her feet as though sensing her mood and she bent low and lifted him up so that he could see, too. Through the glass and above the hard wind she could hear mingled shouting and music.

"It's all right," she told the dog, holding him tightly. "It's still an adventure."

A tale for her memoirs.

A small speck of light caught the edge of her gaze from the dark of the tall house across the street. Turning her head just a fraction, she watched till she saw it again, to be sure: the faint glow of a pipe held by someone who stood at the opposite window, now fading, now burning, in time with his breathing.

❧

"I'm certain," said Jacques the next morning, "there's nothing at all to be causing concern."

She had broken her strict rule of keeping in character, speaking of nothing but trifles. She'd risen yet earlier than was her custom and waited for Jacques in the breakfast room so she could ask him to speak with her privately. No easy thing in this house, but they'd managed to find a small passage between rooms with no one about and the servants well busy below.

"He was at the window on the day before you came as well," Mary went on. "I did think nothing of it then, for people often take an interest in new neighbors, but I've thought about it since, and I do fear he may be watching us."

"Watching you, possibly. And who could blame him?" Jacques smiled in his charming way. "No, I have faith in our friends. I have lasted some months without being discovered, I've truly acquired an instinct for possible danger. And here, I sense none."

But she still felt uneasy.

He told her, "I'll prove it. I'll take you to Mass."

Mary shook her head forcefully. "No, we are not meant to leave the house."

"My orders were not to leave it unless it could not be avoided," he answered her smoothly. "And I'd be a very poor brother indeed if I put you in peril of losing your soul. You are Catholic, I take it?"

She paused, and then nodded.

"Well then. I shall order a chaise," he assured her, "to carry us safely to church and then home again. We will be perfectly safe."

And they were. Madame Roy went as well, and although it took Mary some minutes to quell the uncomfortable feeling of being exposed, the great beauty at last of the church with its frescoes and colored-glass windows and music that filled the whole soaring interior, fit for a choir of angels, allowed her to conquer her fears.

They returned the next week also, and in all the days between she saw no sign of the man watching from the window of the house across the street. The days settled into domestic routine, and she ceased writing anything down in her journal because there was nothing of note to record.

So on Wednesday the thirteenth, when Jacques said at dinner, "The cook's boy says there is to be a new play in the rue de Bussy this night, just round the corner. An excellent pantomime. Shall we attend?" Mary managed no more than the smallest of protests, her own faint misgivings soon calmed by the thought of Sir Redmond's advice that a man could hide best in a crowd.

And oh! The relief to be out of the house. Mary had to contain herself, trying to act with a confidence that would befit Mistress Jamieson were she to walk in a Paris street, here in the snow with the joy of the Carnival atmosphere spilling on all sides around her, the sounds of the Fair and a gentleman guiding her through it, her hand safely held in his arm with Madame Roy an ever-watchful presence just behind.

They found the playhouse without any incident and joined the crowd inside, and Mary watched enraptured as the clever pantomime unfolded, set to music that spoke for the silent actors as they told the tale of lovers kept apart by an unyielding mother who preferred a suitor much less worthy for her daughter. There was poignancy and laughter—mostly laughter, as the better suitor bested his dim-witted rival at each turn and finally won his mistress and her mother's good opinion.

Mary had not ever seen a play performed before. For her, this was the Paris she had dreamed about, at long last spread before her in its glory and its opulence. The candlelight and costumes, and the music and the mirth within the playhouse, made her feel as though a veil had been drawn back to show her Paradise. Jacques looked at her and smiled and turned to Madame Roy. "I would not cut her pleasure short. Let's walk back through the Fair."

The older woman nodded her consent, and when the pantomime was finished they walked down together through the throngs of people to the grand and covered spectacle that was the Fair of Saint-Germain.

If Mary had been dazzled by the play, she was near ecstasy while walking through the Fair. It was a tiny village in itself all held beneath a wooden roof, with rows of open wooden stalls and balconies and stairs, the whole lit warmly with what seemed a thousand candles, some suspended from the ceiling overhead. Each stall held something new to see or buy— the vendors selling everything but books and weapons, or so Madame Roy maintained. There were performers here as well; they stopped to watch a man who juggled knives, and marveled at the flash of steel and his dexterity. They watched a couple dancing to the playing of an oboe, and a woman who walked lightly on a rope strung between balconies as though it were the ground itself, and did not fall.

And pressed around them seemed to be the whole of Paris, glittering as brightly as the finery contained within that festive place.

"Take care," Madame Roy warned, "for with the nectar come the wasps. Guard well your purses."

Mary, who had no purse to be careful of, felt free to simply wander and enjoy.

She was well satisfied and weary when they finally took the turning at the Fair's end and walked through the little laneway to the rue du Coeur Volant and started up towards their lodgings.

With the Fair behind them it was quieter. The street for once looked empty and the wind that had so often chased between the houses now had changed direction and was blowing from the east, and so was blocked by the high walls. When Mary hummed a lilting line of music she remembered from the pantomime, it seemed to echo back to her as happily.

A little way ahead, she saw the cook's boy had come out to sweep their front step clear of snow, and when he noticed their approach he stood and held the door for them and waited, letting lamplight from within slant welcoming and warm across the frozen ground.

Mary felt quite warm enough already. She had taken off her gloves to cool her hands a little in the air and started to push back her hood when suddenly a man burst from the shelter of a doorway she was passing.

Startled, Mary had no time to move aside. He roughly shoved her, snatched the kid gloves she was holding in her hands, and took off running.

Jacques reacted angrily. "Stop, you—!"

"Thief!" Mary cried in French across his words, alarmed as much because he'd spoken English as because she'd lost her favorite gloves.

The man who swiftly moved from close behind them seemed at first to have been born directly of the shadows. She saw but a passing blur of gray and heard a low cry as the thief was caught and briefly overpowered and released with flailing speed into the night, and then her gloves were being offered to her, held within the bare hand of a tall man in a gray cloak, whose bent head concealed a face already hidden by a dark three-cornered hat.

In height and in form he looked much like the coachman who'd come to collect Mistress Jamieson, but when she finally found her voice to thank him for his chivalry, the stranger partly raised his head to show a pair of eyes as hard as any she had seen, set in a face that was not handsome. With a silent nod he crossed the street ahead of them to enter through the doorway of the house that faced their own. The door closed after him, and Mary stood and stared at it, while Jacques and Madame Roy both sought to reassure themselves she was not harmed.

The cook's boy, who appeared to have been shaken by the whole adventure, held the door still wider as they hurried her indoors.

"My dear, you're trembling," Jacques observed.

"It is but shock," said Madame Roy, "and quickly cured with brandy, warmth, and bed."

The brandy helped, but it could not completely chase away the cold she felt within her. Upstairs she did a thing she rarely did and took Frisque with her into bed and curled her body round him for the comfort of his warmth. She did not need to draw the curtain back to view the window of the house across the street, nor look to see the glowing light of the man's pipe against the dark, for now she knew not seeing it meant nothing.

He was in that room. She knew it just as surely as she knew the color of his cloak. The hardness of his eyes.

And all the pleasure of her lovely evening had now vanished with the knowledge that in all the time he'd walked so close behind them in the shadowed street—and possibly before that—she had never once suspected he was there.

CHAPTER 14

I FEAR THE MAN ACROSS *the street…*

I set my pencil down and sighed as once again the labored notes of the piano in the salon broke my concentration. Noah had been practicing the same arpeggio for several minutes now without much sign of progress. Getting up, I crossed to close my door, which didn't stop the sound but muffled it enough that I could turn my focus back to my deciphering of Mary's words.

After two days I was getting faster with my work, having gained a better eye to tell her sevens from her nines, and I was starting to develop a good sense of how she phrased things. Her cadence was clear from the first line I'd finished deciphering, just after breakfast on New Year's Day:

At three o'clock, my brother came to fetch me with the news that I was wanted, and of the lies he told me I hold that to be the hardest to forgive.

I'd had to edit that and put the commas in and the apostrophes, and modify her spelling. She had written "aclock" for "o'clock" and used a *y* for "lyes" instead of "lies," but those were easy things to sort in context. Easier than Mary sorting out the tangled circumstances of her life. It must have been a blow to learn her brother hadn't wanted her for who she was, but only for the use that he could put her to. And while she didn't list the lies he'd told her, it was obvious that he'd been less than honest about why he'd brought her to Chatou. The "wagon overturned upon the road" that had supposedly diverted them and made them go the long way round could not have been an accident. Sir Redmond had been waiting all along for their arrival.

He had said as much to Mary, as she'd written in her diary:

On the 24th arose to find Sir Redmond had obtained a bed for Frisque, with the apology he had not been informed beforehand that I'd have a dog with me, or else he would have had the room more properly arranged. "Did Nicolas then tell you that I would be on my own?" I asked, and "Aye," said he, and told me that my brother had informed him full a week ago that we would be arriving on the Tuesday as we did, which did show faith I think upon my brother's part, since having not yet met me grown, he could not have known then if I would suit his purpose. Happily—and Jacqui, when I'd read the entry to her on the phone, had seemed to think that word had held some sarcasm—*Sir Redmond tells me I am perfect for the part I am to play, not only for the fact I do speak French but for the simpler fact that no one of the former court at Saint-Germain-en-Laye will know my face should they encounter me in Paris, nor suspect that I am other than what I will then appear to be: a woman living with her brother. I shall take it to be practice for the day my brother Nicolas has promised, when I will indeed go home with him, though I confess I do not fix my hopes upon the coming of that day.*

I didn't, either. Which was why, when I had read that entry New Year's Day, I'd called my cousin.

"It isn't noon yet," had been Jacqui's protest, in a husky voice that told me she'd been out late celebrating. "Have a heart."

"She hasn't gone to Saint-Germain-en-Laye."

"I'm sorry?"

"Mary," I explained. "She's being sent to Paris."

I could hear the creak of bedsprings as though she'd rolled over. "Sorry, what? Who's Mary?"

"Mary Dundas, in the diary. She's—"

"What, did you break the code?"

"Cipher. And yes, but—"

"That's wonderful!" Jacqui was sounding awake now. The bedsprings creaked a little louder, and I guessed that this time she was sitting up. "Just wait till I tell Alistair. He'll be so pleased."

"He may not be, that's what I'm saying. Mary Dundas hasn't gone to Saint-Germain-en-Laye," I said a second time. "Her brother lied to her, and now she's being sent to Paris on some sort of secret mission for the Jacobites. He's promised he'll bring her back afterwards, only I don't think he will. When she writes 'Saint-Germain-en-Laye' it makes a long, specific set of numbers in the cipher, and I've had a quick look through the diary and she doesn't mention it much after this."

"Well, she wouldn't, though, if she were living there," Jacqui replied. "I mean, I wouldn't say, 'Here I am in London, and I'm going to the hairdresser today, here in London, and after that I'm going to have dinner at the restaurant on the corner, it's in London, too…'"

I saw her point and took it, but that didn't stop me arguing, "But if she *doesn't* go to Saint-Germain-en-Laye, then what she's written in this diary won't be what Alistair Scott needs to finish his book, and I can't take his money for doing a job on false pretenses."

"Darling," she told me, "you worry too much."

"But it wouldn't be honest. I think you should tell him at least, so he'll know about Mary and Paris."

"All right, then. Tell *me* what you've got from the diary so far. Tell me more about this secret mission Mary's being sent on."

I had read her the few entries I had deciphered, that ended with Mary's remark about not having much hope her brother would keep his word.

"But," Jacqui had reasoned, "we don't know for certain he didn't. We don't even know that she made it to Paris, yet, do we? She's still at the home of this Sir Redmond whomever."

"Sir Redmond Everard. I looked him up. He came from Tipperary, and he died in France around 1740, so eight years or so after Mary first met him." I had started a reference sheet of all the people that Mary was mentioning, for my own use, and I'd reached for it. "He was the last baronet of his family line. I couldn't find more than that, but I didn't search all that hard, really." I hadn't let myself be too distracted from the task at hand.

And Jacqui hadn't cared much. "What I mean is, you've just started this. I don't think we can leap to any judgments or conclusions yet. Why don't you carry on, and if you find firm proof that Mary didn't go to Saint-Germain, *then* I'll tell Alistair, and we'll let him decide what you should do. All right?"

It had seemed very logical advice. "All right."

We'd briefly talked of other things and wished each other Happy New Year, and then I got back to work.

I hadn't mentioned anything about Luc or his New Year's kiss. She wouldn't have approved. Besides, in retrospect it seemed to have been nothing too important, since it hadn't changed the way we interacted. When he'd dropped in after lunch on New Year's Day and I had offered him a handshake he'd accepted it without a sign of having been offended that he wasn't being greeted by the double kiss, the *bise*, and when he spoke to me directly he still used the formal way of saying you—*vous*—rather than the more familiar *tu* that French speakers dropped into as a sign that your relationship was growing closer.

I'd been fine with that, I'd told myself. I didn't like entanglements to start with, and it was enough to have his perfect face and blue eyes to enjoy when I was looking at him, even if they tended to distract me. I'd been looking at him later on that evening, while we had aperitifs in the salon and everyone, including Noah, shared their New Year's resolutions. Claudine's had been, to my surprise, to give up smoking, to which I'd remarked, "I didn't even know you smoked."

"I'm very secretive," she'd told me, with a smile. "But it is not good for my health, and I'm not getting any younger. Noah? What's your resolution for this year?"

He was drinking ginger ale in place of wine, but still he held his glass with a sophistication older than his years as he replied, "I'm going to learn to play tennis."

Denise had asked, "Why tennis?"

"Uncle Thierry plays tennis."

I'd watched Luc smile slightly. "Uncle Thierry plays all sorts of things. And this is an expensive resolution for your mother and myself, if we will have to buy you lessons."

"But Mama can teach me. Uncle Thierry says she used to play as well as he does."

To which praise Denise had raised her own glass in a toast and said, "Well, there you are. That will take care of my own resolution, too, for I would like to lose some weight."

"You say that every year," said Noah, "and you always stay the same."

When Luc had laughed, Denise had turned the tables with, "And you?"

"I am resolved to grow a mustache."

Denise hadn't thought that was a good idea. "It will make you look like one of those old villains in the silent films."

"All right, then. I will travel less, and stay at home more."

Noah had approved that with a heartfelt nod before he'd looked at me. "Madame Thomas?"

"I don't make resolutions," I had told him.

"But you must. It's a tradition."

I'd considered it a moment, till I realized I was taking too long to decide, and since it wasn't something I'd be bound to do at any rate, I copied what Denise had said. "I'd like to lose some weight."

I'd seen Luc shake his head. "Too easy. That one has been claimed already by Denise, and anyway like her you hardly need to. Try again."

I couldn't tell if he'd been teasing or if he was serious, but on the off chance that it was the latter I had answered him more honestly, "I'm going to find a job."

Claudine had offered me the plate of little toasts spread with pâté. "But surely," she had said, "this is the perfect job for you to have."

I'd guessed, from how she'd smiled, she'd meant that lightly, but again I wasn't sure.

"It isn't permanent," was all I'd said, and suddenly Luc's face across the table had seemed too distracting, and I'd looked away from it.

The next day, Friday—yesterday—he'd been at work and I'd had no distractions whatsoever. Only Noah, who had wandered past my workroom now and then, his presence heralded by the repeating tune of his Robo Patrol game, like the ticking of the clock that had been swallowed by the crocodile in *Peter Pan* and warned of its approach.

It hadn't bothered me too much, though, and my work on Friday had been steady, following Mary Dundas as she finally left Chatou for Paris.

The 28th I did depart, she'd written, *with the woman who was sent to be my chaperone, Madame Roy, who smiles little and speaks less but is in every other way agreeable. Her face has been disfigured by the smallpox which no doubt accounts for some of her demeanor. As we left, the bird was singing loudly at the window which I took to be a hopeful omen. Lady Everard herself remarked upon it when she came to farewell us, believing (for Sir Redmond has so told her) that I was but going to rejoin my brother, having lingered with them for no other reason than to give my brother's wife more time to ready my new rooms. Sir Redmond seems most careful that his wife should be kept sheltered from his Jacobite activities, and I suppose he does this because, much like Mistress Jamieson, he does not wish his actions to put those he loves in danger.*

I had paused here with a certain satisfaction to take up the list of names that I'd been keeping and write firmly "Mistress Jamieson" in place of "Mistress Harrison." It was, when I looked back at that first entry in the diary that was written in plain text, quite clearly "Jamieson." The woman who had thought this cipher up while drinking tea now had her proper name restored and duly noted, if that had in fact been her true name.

By bedtime Friday, I had settled in with Mary to the house in Paris, on the rue du Coeur Volant.

She had described the household neatly, with the six rooms on the first floor of the house and the two ground-floor rooms beneath, linked by the private staircase with a door out to the street. She had not named the cook, nor the cook's boy—who from what Mary wrote of him appeared to be not actually the cook's son but an older teenaged boy assigned to help her in the kitchen with the heavy work—but she did name the maid, Yvette, and Madame Roy of course, and there was Jacques.

And so here I was, pencil in hand, picking up where I'd been interrupted by Noah's belabored arpeggios from the piano.

I fear the man across the street…

I concentrated, studying the numbers. The piano playing stopped, and in the blissful silence I was finally able to complete the line:

I fear the man across the street is watching us.

Another interruption—a soft knocking at my door.

"Come in," I told Denise.

She had her coat on. "We'll be leaving in a minute," she announced. This time, I'd paid attention when she'd rattled off her plans at breakfast, so I had remembered the rough schedule of her day: she would be driving Noah first to his piano lesson, then he had a birthday party to attend, while she went to the cinema. "We should be back by three o'clock. I've left you soup and cheese and bread, and there is still some chicken if you're very hungry."

"Thank you. Is Claudine at home?"

She shook her head. "She has a wedding. Saturdays are always very busy for her." Giving me a long look she asked, "Have you been outside at all since yesterday?"

"I wasn't outside yesterday."

"Well, if you want to get some fresh air, take a walk, the keys to the back door are in the soup tureen," she told me, "in the kitchen."

"All right."

She hovered for a moment. "It is beautiful outside. The sun is shining."

"Yes, all right." I kept my eyes fixed on my work.

"And Luc is home, I think, if you need anything."

I only nodded this time, and she must have left it there because the next time I glanced up she had already gone. Returning to the diary, I continued, learning Jacques had not shared Mary's doubts about the man across the street.

To prove to me my worries were unfounded he conveyed us all to church, where I was much soothed by the music and the liturgy. So back again and welcomed by a dinner from our cook as fine as any I have ever had, and then a peaceful afternoon and evening, and to bed.

The next two entries were as regular as that. She'd settled in, I thought. And knowing she might be in Paris for a while to come, I took a break and turned once more to the computer, searching out old maps of Paris that would help me get a better sense of where she was and what the streets around her had once looked like.

She'd been on the Left Bank in the Latin Quarter, and in studying the old maps and the modern ones I noticed many of the streets had stayed the same. Including Mary's, which while it had changed its name to rue Grégoire-de-Tours, still had the same tight, crowded look of the original. I felt a sudden urge to see it. To the empty room I said aloud, "I need to go to Paris."

Luc is home, Denise had said, *if you need anything.*

It took me under five minutes to gather my mobile, a notebook and pen, put my coat on, and slip out the back door. I made sure the house was locked, taking the keys from the soup tureen with me. The green metal door in the garden wall stood halfway open and I passed through easily into the lane, where the trees grew across in an arch at the end, where Luc's house stood.

It wasn't an overly large house. I noticed that much, even in my fixated state, and as I climbed up the steps to the covered front porch I could see an old-fashioned bell hanging beside the door. Ringing it soundly, I stood back and tucked my hands into my pockets and waited.

Luc came to the door wearing jeans and a pullover. If he was surprised to see me standing on his doorstep, he was too polite to let it show. "Hello," he said.

"I need to go to Paris."

For a moment he just looked at me, and then he reached behind and took his leather jacket from its peg upon the wall and shrugged it on. "OK."

CHAPTER 15

H E DIDN'T HAVE A car today. "Denise's wouldn't start," he said, as he walked down the front porch steps with me, "and Noah had his lesson, so I let them borrow mine. But we could take the RER, the train. It goes to Châtelet–Les Halles and joins the Métro. Where is it you need to go?"

"Could we take that?" I pointed to the motorcycle parked beside the house, a sinuous thing of black leather and chrome.

He raised an eyebrow. "The Ducati?"

"Noah says that it goes very fast."

"It does," he said, and smiled. "You'll need a helmet."

I had only ever ridden on a motorcycle once, behind the brother of a school friend. He had taken me quite slowly up the street where we'd all lived and round and back again. I'd thought it so exciting at the time, but it was nothing like the feel of being on a busy road in winter in the middle of a stream of cars all driving on the wrong side. It was not that I felt unprotected—Luc had found a helmet for me and an extra leather jacket he'd insisted I wear over mine for safety, and he had loaned me gloves that were too large but very warm, and I was pressed so close behind him on the seat he blocked the wind. Not being used to this, I hadn't known where to put my hands, but Luc had solved that problem for me, taking my arms and wrapping them around his middle. "Hold on tight," he'd said, and so I did.

It was a thrilling feeling. The Ducati had a power that chased up my legs and made me feel a part of it; a part of Luc as well, as we were forced to move as one, to lean in unison at every change of lane and every turn. The road dived into tunnels and I loved that even better, loved the feeling of enclosure with the ceiling dark above us like the sky at night and little rows of lights like stars to either side that flashed by in a calming rhythm, drawing us along. I almost hated coming up again to sunlight, but my disappointment vanished when I saw the Arc de Triomphe dead ahead of us—that huge iconic stone arch in the middle of its always-busy roundabout, a massive circle of confusion ringed by trees and buildings, old and modern intermingled, though in honesty I only saw a blur of branches, pale walls, and the high gray mansard roofs that were so wonderfully Parisian.

Here the street turned into cobblestone and made the ride more perilous, and I held on to Luc more tightly as he slowed and wove between the whirlpool lanes of cars, passed round the shadow of the looming heavy arch, and neatly zipped off onto the broad Avenue des Champs-Élysées. This, with its expensive shops, was one of Jacqui's meccas, but while I'd been here before I'd never been here at this time of winter, so I was surprised to see the row of wooden vendors' stalls with open fronts and peaked roofs, like small white-painted chalets strung in a line along the pavement, with signs proclaiming it the "*Paris Village de Noël*"—the Christmas Village. There was more to read on those signs but I only registered the "*Artisans et Arts*" part before we had turned again and my attention was distracted by the Eiffel Tower on our right and by the sunlight catching the gold statues on the columns of the bridge as we crossed over to the Left Bank of the river Seine.

The parking gods of Paris smiled kindly on us, leaving us one space for the Ducati in the row of motorcycles parked beside the church of Saint-Germain-des-Prés, a lovely ancient church of pale stone with a soaring tower that allowed it still to hold its own in that great boulevard of buildings that rose six and seven stories high. The pointed tower with its belfry rose above them all.

I wasn't sure if this was the church Mary Dundas had written about in her diary, the one where she'd gone to hear Mass, but I wasn't inclined to run the gauntlet of the group of tourists milling round the entrance to go in. There were too many people on the pavement for my liking, too, all pressing past and chattering, weaving through a cluster of more Christmas Village vendors' stalls at this side of the church.

Seen up close, the stalls showed their simple design—like white boxes with peaked roofs and flaps at the front and sides that had been lifted and propped open to reveal whatever wares lay inside on display—but they'd all been made festive with fairy lights strung round and warm lights within and green garland with tinsel roped up and down over the peaks of the roofs in a glittering line. Some stalls offered jewelry and some offered food or warm wine or embroidered white linens. One had a display of fur hats in a rainbow of colors, and one had been stacked full of glass jars of honey of different varieties, claiming that it would add years to your life and more life to those years. But the stall that attracted my eye was the one with the strings of pashminas and bright woven scarves. There was one scarf draped over a hanger, a beautiful fringed scarf of cornflower blue shot with silver that made me slow my steps and feel my pocket for my wallet, but apparently of all the things I'd thought to bring, my wallet wasn't one of them.

I found the pen, the notebook, my small booklet of Sudoku puzzles, and the mobile—took them out to make quite certain there was nothing else in either pocket—and had put them back and was preparing to move on when Luc strolled over, chivalrously carrying both motorcycle helmets by their chin straps, one slung over his left elbow and the other in his left hand. He asked, "Which is it you want? The blue one?"

"That's all right, I have a lot of scarves. It isn't necessary."

"When did it become a crime to want what wasn't necessary?"

I was left to try to form an argument to that while Luc stepped up to greet the woman in the stall. He'd pointed out the scarf to her and paid for it and had it wrapped and handed me the parcel by the time I could reply, "I only meant that I'd survive without it."

With a shrug he said, "Surviving life is not the same as living and enjoying it."

I couldn't really argue that, and anyway it was too late—he'd moved into position as he'd done before, a half step to my side and just a little bit in front of me, and with his easy stride began to clear a path for us along the pavement through the crowd. I followed him and frowned a little, realizing the only thing to do was tell him thank you. "Thanks," I said. "I'll pay you back the money."

"You will not," he told me. "That's a gift."

"But you don't have to give me gifts."

"I do. It's New Year's, it's tradition."

"But—"

We'd reached the curb now and Luc stopped and turned to look down at me, smiling his perfect symmetrical smile. "Are you always this difficult?"

I thought about that a moment and answered him honestly. "Yes."

His smile briefly turned to a grin, but he seemed to be trying to hide that by looking instead at the cars passing by on the Boulevard Saint-Germain. When he looked back at me he only had a faint curve to his mouth. "Give it here, then."

He held out his hand for the paper-wrapped parcel and I passed it over, not really wanting to have him return it but realizing that was the logical consequence of all my arguing.

"Thank you. Now take this." He handed me my helmet, leaving both his hands free while he opened the parcel and drew out the length of blue shimmering silk. Taking hold of it firmly he reached to arrange it around my neck, tucking the ends through to make a loose knot. "There," he said, folding the paper into a small square that he tucked deep in one of his pockets, "you've worn it, it can't be returned, and I won't take your money. You'll just have to keep it." He reclaimed my helmet, and held it as effortlessly as before in his left hand. "Now, where are we going?"

The scarf felt soft against my neck—as soft as the worn lining of the borrowed leather jacket that I still had on because I liked the feel of it layered over my own thinner coat. The sleeves were long enough that I could draw my hands back up inside them when the wind blew cold. I did that now, and looked around to get my bearings, trying to remember what I'd seen on the computer maps.

"Well," I said, "there was some sort of Fair that was held here in Mary's time. She mentions it in her diary, seeing all the people coming and going from it, although I don't know if she ever went to it herself. But just in case, I ought to have a look. According to the maps it's a big market now, just over there I think." I nodded left. "So I'd like to walk that way, and then Mary's street should be just beyond that."

We crossed over. It was hard to miss the market. It stood grandly at the end of a short side street—a great covered building with banner ads draping the walls with their pale colonnades and a two-tiered tile roof and *Marché Saint-Germain* spelled out in large letters over the arches around the main entrance. The old Fair, I thought, must have been as imposing in its day. It, too, from the pictures I'd seen on the Internet, had been housed under one roof in a large building that dominated the space, drawing crowds.

"Do you want to go in?" Luc asked.

"No." Busy places like that were my private idea of hell, but I didn't elaborate. "I only wanted to see it."

He stood there and looked at the building too. "Is it important to see things in person, for what you are doing?"

"For me it is, yes." With a slight frown, I tried to explain. "When I'm working through what Mary wrote in her diary, she talks all the time about where she is and where she's going, but I can't construct places in my mind when I'm just reading about them in words. If I go to a place, I can follow those words," I said, "let them direct me, and then I find it easier to form a mental image. Otherwise I get confused."

Which probably, I thought, was far more information than he either needed or had asked for. I fell silent, feeling suddenly self-conscious.

"There are maps," Luc said. "And these days on the Internet you can get down to street level, real photographs, and navigate around."

I didn't tell him that I found most maps too crowded and confusing, and that even with the online ones he'd mentioned I still couldn't get the details I was after. All I told him was, "It's not the same."

I drew my mobile out to take some pictures and he waited in his undemanding way and let me take the lead. We strolled down the length of the front of the market and down its far side to the little street running behind it—the rue des Quatre Vents, meaning the street of the four winds—and that, in its turn, led us right to the old street where Mary had lived, here in Paris. It wasn't a long street—the old rue du Coeur Volant was just a single block long, and so narrow in places there scarcely seemed space for a single car to squeeze between the old buildings.

The buildings made a solid line—I counted seven stories with the ground floor and the garret in the buildings on my left, and those that faced them weren't much lower. Some were old but all were painted white or freshly plastered, with a scattering of restaurants and small businesses providing bits of upscale color, burgundy or blue or black, and of the cars parked in a tight line further up the narrow street the foremost was a Jaguar. Not the rough street that it had been, then, in Mary's day.

But still, the older buildings had an inward lean towards the top that made them look Dickensian, and it was not too difficult to stand here and imagine Mary at one of the windows on a winter afternoon like this one, watching the dark windows of the houses that stood opposite…

I fear the man across the street is watching us.

The wind crept cold along my neck. I shivered, and Luc, patient at my shoulder, broke the spell by asking if I was too cold.

I nearly told him no, but it occurred to me he might have asked because he might be starting to feel cold himself, so I gave a safe answer. "I'm nearly done," I told him. I tried to be quick with my photos, then turned to him. "There, we can go now."

"Go where?"

"Well, I'm finished. I really just needed to see Mary's street."

Luc was smiling again. "But we only just got here. I tell you what, let's go get something to eat. There's a good restaurant just round the corner. You'll love it, I promise."

I *was* hungry, but I hadn't brought my wallet and it didn't feel right asking him to pay. I'd actually been in this sort of situation once before with colleagues at a former job, and I tried thinking back to what I'd told them then because whatever way I'd phrased it had worked rather well without offending anybody…but I didn't get the chance to use it now, because Luc said, "Come on, I haven't eaten lunch. I'm starving." And I realized that the reason he had missed his lunch was probably because I had descended on his doorstep and insisted that he bring me into Paris.

I could have tea, I decided. That would not be an enormous imposition, and although I'd missed my own lunch I could wait until I got back to Chatou to eat a proper meal.

The restaurant was indeed around the corner, as he'd said, right where the Street of Four Winds emptied into a small square with busy traffic, lots of tourists passing on the pavement, and a tiny island at its center from which a tall bare-branched tree stretched upwards to the sun.

The restaurant's name, Les Éditeurs, was spelled out in neat letters on its long red awning, but I was distracted by the tree. "Are those books hanging from the branches?" There were several of them, worn and tattered, yellow from the weather, hung like ornaments in clusters.

Luc explained they were a tribute to the fact there had

once been so many publishers and bookshops in this area, along with all the authors, French and foreign, who had lived and worked in Saint-Germain-des-Prés. And when we stepped inside the restaurant, it was clear the owners also had a fond spot for this literary history.

There were walls of bookshelves—books above the door-ways, next to tables, even stacked over the staircase as the waiter showed us to the upper floor. It was a classy place, made warmly intimate with lamplight and dark wood and little tables meant for two. The waiter led us to the end of the long upstairs room where four such tables had been set close to each other in a line along a red leather banquette, watched over by the oil-painted portrait of a young and pretty woman of another era.

Luc asked for and to my relief received the end table by the window, and before the waiter had a chance to hold the chair for me I'd claimed the banquette seat instead, with bookshelves just behind me and a wall against my shoulder that allowed me to feel safe and not exposed, and space for our motorcycle helmets to rest on my other side, on the ban-quette, like an extra defense. Besides which, when I looked up now I didn't really see the room or any of the other peo-ple in it; all I saw was Luc, his head bent as he read the menu.

There was no need to read mine. I set it down and to the side. "I'll have a pot of tea."

"That's very English of you. If you're very hungry there's a steak with cheese potatoes here that's excellent."

"The tea is fine."

He looked up from the menu then, his eyebrow lifting slightly. "Just the tea?"

"That's right." It would have been a lie to say I wasn't hungry, but it was the truth at least to say, "That's all I need."

He studied me and I felt sure his gaze dropped briefly

to my scarf before he told me, "Here in France it is a New Year's custom for a man to take a woman out to lunch. It brings us luck."

I cast my mind back over all the holiday traditions of my childhood neighbors. "You've just made that up. It's not a custom."

"Well, it ought to be." He nudged my menu card towards me. "You can pay for my lunch next time."

There was no one sitting right beside us but from the tables just behind Luc came a swirl of appetizing smells that weakened my resolve. "Do you promise?"

"Word of honor."

"You just lied about the New Year's custom."

His mouth curved, then straightened. "I swear on the head of my son." His blue eyes were disarming.

I gave in then and ordered the risotto. The waiter brought us bread and nuts and olives as an appetizer, and Luc nudged them all towards me. "I was worried you had changed your mind about your New Year's resolution, and were starting on a diet after all."

I shook my head. "I never stick to diets. I've no willpower."

"Your other resolution was much better."

"What was that?" I had forgotten. Working on the diary had pushed less important details from my memory.

Luc reminded me, "To find a job."

"Oh. Right."

"What will you look for? What, in your view, is the perfect job?"

I took an olive from the dish between us. "One that lets me work alone."

"You said that very quickly. Don't you like to work in teams, then?"

"No." I didn't give an explanation, but I did admit it was a problem. "Most programming jobs involve teamwork."

"You program computers?"

"Yes. Why?"

"Nothing, it's nothing. I think it's a very good job for an amateur code breaker," he said. "My brother is also a programmer."

I nodded in the way I'd noticed people did when making small talk, but I had no interest in Luc's brother. I *was* interested in Luc, though, which for me was quite unusual. Since I'd left university, relationships with men had all conformed to the same pattern: I would meet someone I found attractive, one of us would ask the other out for dinner or for drinks, we'd spend some time together—maybe several evenings or a weekend here or there, but never longer than a month—then I would end it. Neat and tidy and controllable.

There had been four men, all nice enough, but never had I taken any interest in their lives beyond the time we'd spent together. Never had I taken any notice of their gestures or their habits or the little things about them, but with Luc I noticed everything. I really wasn't used to that. Nor was I used to being curious enough about his life to ask, "How many brothers do you have?"

"Just one. And you?"

"There's only me. My parents were both only children. They enjoyed it, so they wanted me to be an only child as well."

He broke a piece of bread and asked me, "And did you enjoy it as they'd hoped, to be the only one?"

"I didn't mind it."

"I don't know what that would be like," he confessed, "to have no one to argue with."

"I always had my cousin."

"Yes, I can imagine she'd be very good to argue with."

I couldn't tell from his expression whether he was serious or teasing, but I wondered something else. "Is it that you're worried that your son's an only child? Is that why you want to know whether I like it?"

It seemed when his left eyebrow lifted like that I'd surprised him, though not necessarily in a bad way. He smiled. "Children teach you worries that you never knew you had, it's true. But no, that isn't why I asked. I—" He was interrupted by the sudden ringing of his mobile, in his pocket. He excused himself to check the number, made a face and said, "This one is work, I have to answer it. I'm sorry."

When my cousin got a business call while eating at a restaurant, she would answer it while sitting at the table. Luc was either too polite or just too private to do likewise. Pushing back his chair, he told the caller in a low voice, "Just a moment," and sent me a nod I took for reassurance as he headed for the stairs.

The room seemed large without him. Large and busy. Where before I'd noticed only Luc, I now became aware of all the other people sitting at their tables, all the other conversations. I tried finding something steady I could focus on and settled on my water glass, which worked until the waiter brought another couple to the table right beside our own. The woman wore a rich floral perfume and sat too close beside me on the leather banquette, and I pulled our motorcycle helmets closer to my leg to make a kind of shield as I rummaged in the pocket of my jacket for the one thing that I knew could calm me down at times like this, when all my senses were on overload.

I'd brought the little booklet of Sudoku puzzles with me when I'd come to France. I hadn't had to use one, until now.

I was half finished with it when Luc took his chair again. "I'm sorry about that. We're in the middle of an audit."

"That's all right." I closed the booklet with my pen inside to mark the page, and tucked it back into my pocket.

Luc had noticed. "You like numbers."

"I like puzzles," I replied.

The waiter brought our drinks, and I sat back to give him room to set them down. Luc watched, and smiled.

"Me, too," he said. And reached across to pour my tea.

CHAPTER 16

The dagger glittered in his hand. He whistled as he went.
—Macpherson, "Fingal," Book Five

Paris
February 1732

THE TEA IS COLD," warned Jacques as Mary joined him at the breakfast table.

"I am sorry to be late." She'd overslept a little, having passed a night so filled with restless nightmares of light-footed thieves and shadows sprung to sudden life that chased her ceaselessly through empty streets, that she suspected she'd have done much better never to have slept at all. Her gown and hair were tidy but she felt disheveled on the inside and disordered in her thoughts.

Jacques stood and waited while she sat, then took his chair again and said, "Had you been half an hour earlier you would have found the tea no warmer. It was cold when it was set upon the table. I was thinking to complain, but Cook is nearly at the limits of her temper as it is, and I am doubtful our new housemaid has the wits to boil water."

"New housemaid?" Mary turned her head. "Why, what's become of Yvette?"

"She has not come today, but claims an illness and has sent her sister in her place, together with a note of explanation that has little satisfied our Cook."

"How do you know all this?"

He smiled. "I know our new maid's name is—"

From the kitchen below stairs Cook bellowed, "Christiane!" and Jacques paused only briefly before finishing his sentence. "Christiane. The rest I've pieced together from Cook's mutterings, for she has done the better part of serving me my breakfast."

"Could not she use the boy? He's served us once before."

"Ah. Well, the boy, you see, is ill as well, although his illness is the kind that comes when lads of his age who imagine themselves men do overestimate their tolerance for drink. To his credit he did come this morning, but in such a sorry state that Cook dismissed him with a lively lecture which I no doubt could recite to you. So we are left with Cook and—"

Cook called "Christiane!" more forcefully, and Mary sought to hide her smile and nodded.

"Christiane," she said.

"Just so," said Jacques. He looked robust this morning and well rested, as though what had passed last night had left him unconcerned. But Mary, when he asked if she'd slept well, felt bound to answer him with honesty.

"I did not, sir. That man, the one who stopped the thief— you saw where he does lodge?"

"Across the street, yes."

"In the very house where lives the man I fear is watching us. The man of whom I spoke to you before."

He met her gaze with one intended to be comforting. "But surely I did put those fears to rest for you? And surely it was Providence to send us such a neighbor at an hour when we had need of him, for had I been the only man defending you last night, my dear, your gloves would be long gone and sold already for a pretty coin, to grace another's hands."

She might have pressed her case with more persuasion had the door not opened just then to admit a woman Mary took to be their temporary housemaid, Christiane, who looked to be a little older than the sister she'd been sent to take the place of, though she had the sort of face that having once begun to show its age now made it rather difficult to judge if she were in her thirties or beyond that. In youth, thought Mary, she would have been beautiful—pale-skinned, large-eyed, and delicate. But time with all its drudgery had left her simply pretty, with a hardened edge that showed now in the tight line of her mouth.

On seeing Mary at the table, the maid fetched a new plate from the sideboard before offering the breads and cheeses, fruit preserves and pâté. Mary, having little appetite, took only bread spread thinly with sweet butter, and not relishing the prospect of cold tea asked, with a nod towards another silver pot still on the sideboard, "Is that chocolate?"

With a silent nod the maid moved to retrieve it.

Jacques said to Mary, "Your dog is not under my feet, as he usually is of a morning. Whatever has happened?" His feigned concern was meant to make Mary smile, and it did. There at first had been little love lost between Jacques and Frisque, and although they had since warmed to each other, the dog sometimes curled himself under Jacques's chair where he seemed to await the best moment to suddenly let out a bark.

"Frisque has stayed abed with Madame Roy, who had a slight headache last evening and wanted the rest."

"Ah. He'll be the very cure for her, no doubt. He—" Breaking off, he swore a sudden oath as Christiane behind him stumbled, lost her hold on the small pot of chocolate, and sloshed steaming liquid down the sleeve of his fine velvet coat. As with the thief the night before, surprise made him forget he was supposed to speak in French. "Faith, woman, have a care!"

To Mary's great relief it seemed the English words were lost on Christiane, who was already flustered past the point of noticing such trifles, dabbing with her apron at the dripping splotch until Jacques shooed her off in irritation, whereupon she scurried altogether from the room as though she knew no other course to take in such a situation.

Mary said, "Come, let me see it," for she had been witness to an accident of this kind with her cousin only last September, though it had been coffee then, not chocolate, and the coat involved had been plain wool, not velvet. As Jacques held his arm towards her for inspection, she reminded him in quiet tones, "You must take greater caution, sir, when something does surprise you. You have spoken English twice now, and such lapses could prove dangerous."

"I know, I know." He had recovered now, though he still frowned. "Can it be put right, do you think?"

He meant the coat, she realized. "Yes, I do believe so. But it must be sponged before the stain takes hold. The maid will likely melt in tears if you descend upon her," Mary said, "but I can take it to her, if you like." She took the coat from him and left him sitting at the table in his shirt and stock and waistcoat while she went where Christiane had gone, down by the narrow back stairs to the kitchen.

Cook was grumbling and preparing to go out, her cloak already firmly tied around her shoulders. "I'm sure I do not know, madam," she said when Mary asked her where the housemaid was. "But if you find her, you may freely keep her. I have errands I must run, else we will have no food for dinner." And with that she went out by the servants' entrance at the back, into the shabby-looking courtyard that connected by an alley to the street.

Mary called out to the maid and getting no reply searched briefly through the downstairs rooms but found no sign of Christiane, and all the while she knew the stain was settling more tenaciously in Jacques's velvet coat, and so at length she took a sponge herself and wet it in the washing basin in the kitchen, spreading out the coat upon the table near the window where there would be better light. The wind had risen outside and it whistled past the window glass and set the small panes rattling in their frosty wooden frame, but on the hearth the kitchen fire worked bravely to spread warmth, and Mary, who liked kitchens to begin with, felt quite comfortable. She would not wish the hardships of a servant's life, but neither was she happy being idle, and in doing something useful now she gained some satisfaction. She'd begun to make some progress with the stain when she felt cold air at her back and, turning, saw the door had blown inward. Evidently Cook, for all the forcefulness of her departure, hadn't pulled the door behind her hard enough to spring the latch. Mary set the sponge aside and crossed to where the door was swinging open on its hinges, letting in a chilling swirl of wind. For an instant, as she grasped the handle of the door to tug it closed again, she felt a stab of childish apprehension that there might be something hiding just behind it, some menacing creature from one of her fairy tales waiting to pounce, but of course it was only imagined. There was nothing behind the door. Nor was there anything lurking outside in the courtyard, and Mary relaxed with a smile as she swung the door to.

From directly behind her, a man's arm reached forward, his bare hand completing the motion to slam the door all the way shut.

And he slid the bolt home.

Mary felt the scream swell in her throat, but it wouldn't come out. Fear and panic had rendered her dumb. But not paralyzed. Wheeling, she felt the rough brush of the intruder's sleeve on the skin of her cheek as he withdrew his arm again, standing too close to her, sprung as before from the shadows, from nowhere, his hard eyes as merciless as they had been in her nightmares last night.

"Do not strike me," he warned. He spoke English, but not like an Englishman.

Mary had not even realized she'd lifted her hand to defend herself, but on the threat of his words she arrested the motion and let her hand fall to her side.

"And keep quiet."

Her mouth had gone dryer than dust, but the galloping beat of her heart had apparently dislodged the lump in her throat and she knew that she could, if she'd wanted to, scream with a loudness to bring down the walls, but her wits, although all out of order, retained enough sense to know little would come of it. All she'd accomplish by calling for help would be to bring Jacques down to help her, and Jacques was no match for this man.

He was dressed as he had been last night, in the gray cloak and three-cornered hat, though the cloak was pushed back now to show a wool coat of a similar gray, trimmed with wine-dark red on the broad collar and cuffs, and not one but two sword belts that crossed at his chest. There was snow on his shoulder. She did not know why that should draw her attention, except it seemed vital she focus on something and she was not brave enough to shift her gaze the few inches to look at his face, even though she could feel he was looking at hers.

He asked, still in that accent that rolled its words thickly and yet seemed familiar somehow, "What's your name?"

"Mary." Why she had answered him that and not told him "Marie" she did not stop to analyze, counting it enough of an achievement she had answered him at all.

"Mary. Where is he?"

The snow on his shoulder was melting. It struck her as something impossible that this man, seemingly carved out of shadow and ice, could melt anything. It was the fire, of course, she thought, and her mind traveled an uneven course back in time to another fire, with both her brother and Sir Redmond Everard sitting before it, and Sir Redmond telling her of the man she knew as Jacques, whose affairs were of interest to King James. "This man is now sought by the English," he'd told her, "and must be protected."

Protected. She clung to that word and its purpose—her purpose—although she could not think of what she could do to fulfill it.

The last snowflake melted to nothing against the gray wool and she looked from the place it had been to the eyes of the tall man in front of her, and though she still heard the fear in her own voice she forced out the words, "Where is who?"

When her uncle's vines froze in the winter, the first morning light turned the edge of the ice a pale blue, a reflection of cold sky that had not yet thawed to the sun. This man's eyes were exactly like that, Mary thought. Like a hard, killing frost.

When he frowned she flinched backwards in spite of herself, but his frown wasn't aimed at her. Angling his head to the side, he appeared to be listening. He hadn't made a move to touch her, his mere presence proving force enough to hold her in her place, and even when he took a step aside now Mary didn't feel that she had been released. She kept her back pressed to the bolted door, as she had done from the beginning, and she barely dared to breathe.

She heard, above the lower whistle of the wind and the stern rattle of the window glass, the slightly mismatched clopping of a team of horses from the street. The sound drew nearer till she fancied she could hear the heavy roll of wheels behind.

The man said curtly, "Come." And still not touching her or needing to, he motioned her to walk before him from the kitchen into the front entry hall. The horses' hooves and rolling wheels drew level with the house and stopped, and never had a silence felt more ominous.

The man stopped too, and leaning close to Mary's side said, "Do exactly as I say. Whoever knocks upon that door, you tell him you are in the house alone, and send him off again. Do not allow him in."

He backed away from her and melted to the shadows of the wall, but she was very much aware of him when she first heard the scuff of booted footsteps and the almost lively knock. She did not wish to answer it at all, but she was more afraid of what was waiting at her back than of whatever lay beyond the door, and so she tried her best to gather her composure as she turned the handle, easing the door open just enough to show her face.

The man who stood on the front step looked reassuringly friendly. He was of middle age and height and rather handsome, in the wig and clothing of a gentleman. The carriage he'd arrived in was more handsome still, its driver sitting hunched upon the box, the horses steaming in the winter air. The man removed his hat and bowed and greeted her in French, "Madam, good morning. I am sent with an important message for Monsieur Vasseur, that I am told I must deliver to his hand."

Her mind was racing with such speed it failed to register connections, and it took her half a moment to remember that "Monsieur Vasseur" was Jacques. And half a moment more to bring to mind what she'd been told to say, although she could not bring herself to say it, for she feared that by so doing she might send away their only hope of rescue.

Mary realized half in horror that the man upon the step was now advancing. He was smiling and his hand was on the outside of the door, and in that instant while she wavered without knowing what to do, he had stepped through somehow and joined her in the entry hall, completely unaware what danger waited for him there.

She panicked then and shook her head against the stranger's cheerful smile and said, "You cannot be here. You must go."

"Not yet." He closed the door more gently than the man in gray had closed the kitchen door. This was a gentleman. His manners and his voice remained as charming as they had been on the step. He was still smiling when he locked the door, and when he drew the dagger. "Take me where he is, this man who calls himself Vasseur."

Her heart resumed its wilder beating, only now it weighed so heavily within her chest she could not move at all, the way a rabbit frightened by a passing hawk might freeze so it would not be seen. But this man was not passing. And he saw her very plainly.

He had turned the dagger till he held it sideways like a sword, and raised it now to touch it to her throat. "He is not worth your life," he told her. "He—"

She did not clearly see what happened next, for everything was sudden, swift, and shocking.

She was conscious of the movement at her side, the sweep of gray that knocked the other man aside and drove him hard against the wall. And when the other man as quickly turned his dagger on the man in gray, she saw the deadly flashing of a longer knife that slid along the bottom of the other's blade and trapped it at the hilt and forced it up and back behind the other's head, and was withdrawn in one quick forward motion that concealed its violence so efficiently that Mary did not know until the other man had fallen and she saw the blood begin to pool around him on the floor that he'd just had his throat cut.

The man in gray turned round, and though he breathed more quickly he was every bit as in control as he had been before. "Up." He nodded at the stairs behind her. "Go." And when she did not move at once he spurred her on with, "*Now.*"

She did not know how her legs carried her, they trembled so alarmingly, but he was close behind her on the stairs and she could not stop for she felt certain he would not. She was proved right when, as they reached the upper floor, he did not pause nor break his stride but only called out, "Mr. Thomson!"

Jacques, as was his custom after breakfast, had been sitting reading in the parlor, but he rose now with his book in hand and looked from Mary to the man behind her.

Run, she would have told him if she'd had a voice. Instead he stood his ground and frowned and said, "Mr. MacPherson." He was speaking English too, now. "I did wonder who was at the door. Has something happened?"

"Aye." The tall man moved past Mary. "Get your things. There is no time to waste. You have to leave."

CHAPTER 17

His sword is like a beam of light upon the warrior's side.
But dark is his brow; and tempests are in his soul.
　—Macpherson, "Fingal," Book Three

Paris
February 14, 1732

HER HANDS WOULD NOT stop shaking.

It was left to Madame Roy to tie the tapes of Mary's petticoat and fit the second gown over the one she wore already. They'd been told in no uncertain terms they could bring nothing with them but the little they could carry in their hands, or wear, and having been allotted but five minutes to prepare themselves they'd had to work at speed, a thing that Mary was incapable of doing in her current state.

"He killed a man," she said again. She'd said it twice already but Madame Roy only nodded as she'd done before, with patience.

"Yes, I know, dear. Put your gloves on."

"He" was in the chamber next to theirs, with Jacques. No, Mr. Thomson. Mary found the change of names confusing, and her brain was having difficulty holding to the details. Mr. Thomson. And the man in gray was Mac…MacSomething. He was Scottish, then. Her father had been Scottish, though this hard man's voice was nothing like her memory of her father's voice. Her father's had been pleasant, even soothing, but this man's was—

"Are ye finished?" He was standing in the doorway.

Madame Roy spoke back to him in English, only Mary was surprised to hear her accent and her intonations sounded much like his. "We're nearly done, aye."

"Where's your book?" he asked, and Mary stared at him uncomprehending until he repeated with more emphasis, "Your book. The one ye write in."

When she still could not reply he muttered something that she took to be a curse and crossing to the bed began to shift the bolster and the pillows. Frisque, who until now had been content to sit amidst the blankets and observe the bustle and confusion, rose to bark a protest. The Scotsman swung his gaze towards the little dog, and Mary found her voice.

"Do not harm him!"

Madame Roy had finished with the fastening of Mary's cloak and let her hands drop lightly onto Mary's shoulders as if she would hold her back from interfering, but the potent rush of terror and protectiveness would not let Mary hold her tongue. "The book is in the clothespress."

It was underneath the linens but the Scotsman found it easily and slipped it with the penner into one of his coat pockets before turning once again towards the bed, where Frisque was barking still. "The dog," he said to Mary, "cannot come."

"I will not leave him." She could feel her chin lift even though she was afraid, and for a moment they stood staring at each other.

He was not a handsome man. His face was formed of stubborn angles, none of which was even, and his mouth at one end slanted up and downward at the other, and his eyes held not a hint of warmth. They measured her impatiently. He said, "It will be trouble."

She did not back down. "You said that we could bring

what we could carry," was her argument. "And I can carry him."

With a frown the man reached down and scooped the barking dog into his one large hand with no apparent effort. Frisque, whether from prudence or his love of being held, wisely fell silent, though his feathered tail began to wag. The Scotsman exhaled tightly in what could not quite be called a sigh, and turning from the bed closed the small distance between him and Mary, thrusting Frisque into her hands. "But nothing else," he said. "And we go *now*."

He seemed to have a knowledge of the house and all its rooms that hinted this was not the first time he had been inside. She'd been afraid that he would lead them down through the entry where the dead man lay and where, beyond the door, the coach might yet be waiting in the street outside. But he did not. He took them by the back stairs Mary had used after breakfast, that went straight into the kitchen. Mary stumbled on the stairs, her limbs still numb and unresponsive and her movements made more cumbersome by being bundled in two gowns at once like a stuffed doll, but she'd regained her balance and was holding Frisque more tightly by the time the man glanced back.

Just standing in the kitchen made her stomach twist unpleasantly. She focused for a moment on the soiled coat, still lying where she'd left it on the table by the window, but it seemed quite far away from them and he had on another now, so really she supposed it didn't matter.

"Come," the Scotsman told them, sliding back the bolt he'd fastened earlier and easing the door open to allow them access to the courtyard. "Quietly."

Mary, through the fog that had encased her brain, observed that from the tone in which he spoke there always seemed to be a silent threat appended to his words, so that one could, if one were moved to make a game of it, attach the words "or else I'll kill you" to the things he said and have them fit as though he'd spoken them aloud.

They followed him along the back walls of the row of houses and so out into the street some way behind the waiting coach. She little noticed where he led them—through what streets or for how long—but in the end they found themselves within another sheltered courtyard tightly crowded by the high dark walls of other houses, and they climbed another narrow twisting stair into a set of cold and sparsely furnished rooms. The Scotsman was the last to enter. Bolting shut the door he turned and told them, "Find a seat."

"Or else I'll kill you," Mary murmured to herself. He stood too far from her to hear her, Mary knew. His gaze swung briefly to her, studied her dispassionately for a moment, then moved on.

The fire within the room had been allowed to burn so low that it was little more than embers in the fireplace. Madame Roy crossed without asking for permission and took up the poker from the hearth to stir the fire to stronger life. The Scotsman took no notice. He was standing now at one of the room's windows, looking out.

Madame Roy said to Mary, "Come and sit here by the fire, child." She said it first in English, then when Mary did not move from where she stood, repeated it in French, and slowly Mary did as she was told and with Frisque in her arms she took a seat upon the stool Madame Roy had set near the hearth.

The Scotsman without turning round told Madame Roy in English, "Keep the fire low."

"The lass has had a fright. She must be warmed or she'll fall ill. Do you have brandy?"

"No." His focus stayed upon whatever he was watching through the window. Mary noticed he was standing back just far enough that he would not be easily observed by someone looking in. And then she saw the little table to the one side of the window, and the pale clay pipe that rested on it, and she knew exactly where they were. For all the walking they had done, they'd ended up a stone's throw from where they had started, in the house across the street, and in the room where he had stood for all those nights and watched them, as he now was keeping watch upon the street below.

A woman's shrill scream tore the silence, followed by another and another in hysterical succession, growing louder as though suddenly a door had been flung open to eliminate a barrier between them and the frantic sound. And like a boulder tumbling downhill it started others tumbling, too—the scream was answered by the shouts and calls of neighbors and the nervous clopping shuffle of the hooves of horses, and the creak and thud of countless windows being opened.

Jacques—or rather, Mr. Thomson—said, "I take it that will be our Cook returning. Not the kindest welcome for her."

Madame Roy glanced up sharply. "They will never think she did it?"

"No," said Thomson. "The servants of course will be questioned, but none of them will need to fear the police." His voice, too, Mary thought, was not properly English. It had a faint lilt to it, as of an accent he'd long learned to mask.

Madame Roy said, "You seem very certain."

"I am. The police have been very well bribed since I came into France. I suspect they have known all along where I am, but they turn a blind eye for the twin joys of lining their pockets and thwarting the English." He comfortably settled himself in the room's only armchair, which oddly sat some distance off from the fire. "The English ambassador writes to the head of the Paris police, who replies that he's confident I am not here, then turns round and surprises his wife with a new diamond bracelet. It's all very civilized. No, the police will not bother the servants for finding a man lying dead in the house, unless..." He looked to the man by the window. "That man you dispatched was not from the police, I hope?"

"No."

Mary saw the dead man's face again and felt the knife's blade at her throat. She fought the cold by gathering Frisque closer, and the dog whined.

"Keep him quiet," said the Scotsman.

Mary murmured to herself, "Or else I'll kill you."

Thomson, hearing but the last two words and thinking she had spoken them to him, misunderstood and sought to reassure her. "No, my dear, he never would have killed me. I'm of little use to anybody dead. The English, though, would no doubt pay a rich reward to one who could deliver me into their hands. That would be why he brought the coach, to spirit me away, though I'll be deuced if I can think how he discovered me."

The Scotsman said, "Ye called out in a public street. In English. And your kitchen lad was there to hear ye do it."

"But—"

"The lad sleeps in a room above the tavern near the Fair."

"You keep yourself informed," said Thomson.

"'Tis my business to." He still had not turned round. "This morning when I saw the lad arrive for work he was too drunk to stand. I made inquiries and discovered that last night he had a tale to tell, and found an eager audience in one who bought him drink to hear yet more."

"I'm sorry," Thomson said. "It was most careless of me, to be sure, but I did not intend—"

"Among that tavern's patrons is an English spy who gains his secrets by seducing foolish women. I had him pointed out to me some days ago, together with a woman he so used some years ago and made his wife." He did turn slightly then. "This morning she was in your house. I did not see her enter, but I saw her leave. She wore the clothing of a housemaid."

Thomson raised his eyebrows. "Christiane?"

"Aye, that's her name. He sent her in, no doubt, to gather proof of who ye were. She must have found it. Did she speak to ye in English?"

Thomson paused and flushed a little and he did not answer with a lie, but neither did he tell the truth of how he had betrayed himself at breakfast. "No."

Mary glanced at him and felt the Scotsman glance at *her* before he carried on, "Then she had likely matched your face to your description and was satisfied. She went off in a hurry, and I guessed she'd gone to fetch her husband." With a shrug he turned again and finished with, "Now she's his widow."

In the street below them the commotion was expanding, growing louder, but it seemed a distant thing to Mary on her stool beside the fire. She felt so cold now she'd begun to tremble from it.

"So," said Thomson with a sigh, "we must now travel south." The silence he received as a reply seemed not to trouble him. He stretched his legs before him and in contemplation of the buckles of his shoes remarked, "I should have much preferred to wait until we were more certain of our welcome, but I see there's nothing to be done but make the best of it. When would you have us leave?"

"Not yet." The light had changed its angle very slightly at the window and the Scotsman shifted with it, staying just beyond its reach. "We'll move at night."

"Move where?" Thomson asked, but once again his only answer was the silence of the room. He smiled. "You're not a trusting man, Mr. MacPherson."

Madame Roy said more than that, but briefly, in a language Mary did not understand, but then in honesty the three of them were making little sense to her with all this talk of leaving.

Mary found her voice and told them all, "I cannot travel with you." She could feel them turn to look at her, and to be plain she added, "I was told to come to Paris, only that, and when I'm no longer needed here, then I am to return to…" She came near to saying "Saint-Germain-en-Laye," but she caught herself in time because in spite of her confusion she remembered there were some things she was charged with keeping secret. "…to my family."

Thomson asked, "Who told you this?" His tone was friendly, even sympathetic, but she could no longer freely give her trust. However amiable he'd been as a companion these past days, he was a stranger to her, as were both the others. And it seemed they'd all been keeping secrets from her, too.

She answered without answering. "The person who did send me."

"Well, that person did not tell you all," said Thomson, "for there always was a larger plan in place to put to use if we should be discovered, as we have been. But I can assure you you'll be safe with us. Mr. MacPherson is a most efficient guard. The very best, I'm told." His tone altered subtly from calming to curious. "Who was it that sent you, may I ask? Sir Redmond Everard? It was Sir Redmond, was it not? Or was it General Dillon?"

Mary held her tongue, and Madame Roy reminded both the men, "The lass has had a trying day."

The Scotsman had observed this whole exchange with an impassive face so empty of expression Mary could not guess at what he might be thinking. When he moved, it was to leave the room and pass into the one beyond, returning in a moment with a pewter cup, his fingers lightly holding it suspended by the rim.

He stopped in front of Mary, holding out the cup to her. Whatever was inside it had a scent so strong the vapors on their own were like to set her eyes to watering.

Madame Roy said something that to Mary sounded much like "Oushki-bah"—strange words indeed, but spoken with approval; and the older woman added, "That will heal the evil that does ail you."

Mary could not look above the level of the cup.

The Scotsman's hands were clean. It struck her odd that they should be so clean when he'd just killed a man, and yet they were. The hand that held the cup was strong and square with well-formed fingers. But beneath the broad cuff of his gray wool coat, along the ruffle of his sleeve, she saw the spattered stains of blood.

They held her gaze transfixed. She was aware of Thomson asking, "How the devil did you come by whisky in this place?"

The Scotsman, true to form, ignored him. Mary watched that clean hand and the bloodstained sleeve come closer still to offer her the cup, insistent.

"Take it," he instructed her. "The day's not over yet."

They left in the dead hours of night, in the dark, slipping over the Seine by a bridge that allowed her a view of the towers of Notre Dame, looming above them and seeming alive with a thousand stone eyes she could never escape. Her own shadow changed form with the sway of the glass-enclosed candle lamps strung in a line down the larger streets, and at her back came the larger black shadow of Mr. MacPherson, who'd changed all his clothes but his hat and his boots and had traded his cloak for a brown horseman's coat with its collar turned down like a cape at his shoulders and full pleats that made the coat swing when he walked. He looked none the less menacing, Mary decided—not even when weighted with most of their traveling gear, for he carried the straps of their two leather portmanteaus over his shoulders together with a long cylindrical case that he'd slung in between them, and this with the already cumbersome burden of his two crossed sword belts that carried a regular sword in one scabbard and one in the other that looked like none Mary had seen, with a hilt woven much like a basket of silver that would have completely enveloped his hand.

Where the longer, lethal knife was Mary did not know, but she knew well that he did have it, for she'd watched him clean it; watched him wipe the crusting smudges from the blade and make the steel gleam sharp again with oil, until Madame Roy gently had distracted her attention. Mary did not wish to ever see that knife again.

She drew the softness of her cloak more tightly round herself and Frisque. The dog's warmth in her arms was of great use now as she only wore one gown, the other being packed with all her extra things into one of the portmanteaus Mr. MacPherson had supplied. He'd seemed so well prepared for revision of their plans that Mary would not have been in the least surprised to find he had already hired a coach and driver for them.

Thomson had expected that as well, a fact made clear by his reaction to the news of where they now were headed. "But," he'd told the Scotsman as they'd earlier prepared to leave the shelter of his rooms, "it would be safer for us, surely, were we in a private coach, perhaps with you as driver?"

"Aye, they'll think the same. And they'll be watching for us."

Mary, with a frown, had said, "But you seemed sure that we had naught to fear from the police."

"We don't." He had not said another word till now, as they came within sight of a marvelous building trapped tightly between narrow streets, a medieval château with a round stone-walled turret at one corner and great doors that stood open to give a view into the courtyard beyond.

In a low voice that could not be overheard by others but themselves, MacPherson said, "Wait there." And then he was gone.

Madame Roy looked at Mary's face and smiled slightly. "This is the Hotel de Sens," she said, speaking in French as they took up their places where they had been told to stand, beside the open doorway. "It was built for archbishops and once housed a queen and her lovers, and though that was a long, long time ago, this still has the look of a castle, do you not think?"

Mary was not in a state to admire the building as she might have otherwise done. It had clearly been repurposed as the office for the public coaches traveling to all the parts of France, for even at this hour of the night—or early morning, rather, since it was approaching four o'clock—the streets and courtyard bustled with activity, with torchlight and the call of voices, mostly male; the fall of booted footsteps on the cobblestones, the grind and roll of wheels, and restless stamping of the horses.

She had never seen a diligence. Her uncle, who had journeyed in one, had described it as appearing very like a coach, but being longer and in all dimensions larger, and the vehicle before them now was definitely that. It looked, by torchlight in the darkness of the early morning, very large. The huge heavy wheels at the rear were her own height, and even the smaller and more nimble front wheels were sturdily built. Besides the central closed compartment, which looked fully long enough to carry several passengers, there was another partly open box set at the front, protected by a leather curtain, and on top was seating for a handful more, though given the extremes of weather those who traveled outside would have had to be of hardy constitution. At the back end of the diligence a great curved covered basket held the luggage of the passengers, and at the front stood seven horses waiting with impatience in their harness, the postilion's large black jackboots strapped in place upon the nearside mare who flicked her tail and twitched an ear to Mary as though waiting for the order to be off.

Thomson, beside her, adjusted his hold on the deal-box he'd carried the whole way across from the rooms they had waited the day in. Much like the portmanteaus, it had appeared from the back room with no explanation, though Thomson had instantly taken control of it and ever since had been loath to let go of its handles. It wasn't a large box—her uncle had used one quite like it to hold all his papers—but Thomson had guarded it closely enough Mary guessed it contained something he deemed of value.

She watched as the Scotsman returned with his sure, easy stride in the company of a much shorter and older man who helped consign both the portmanteaus into the basket. She noticed, though, Mr. MacPherson chose not to relinquish control of the third leather cylinder strapped to his back, nor his swords, but conveyed them himself to the netting assigned for that purpose. Then turning, he motioned the others to come.

Mary looked at the diligence, and at the horses, and felt a small stab of misgiving. MacPherson's three-cornered hat blocked out the glare of the torchlight and cast a black shadow that hid his eyes, but she was no less aware of his steady regard as she turned to face Thomson and covered her worries with petulance.

"Is it permitted," she said in a tight voice, "to ask where you're taking me?"

"Certainly," he said, remembering this time to answer her as she had spoken, in French. "We are bound for Lyon."

Lyon. Mary's heart dipped. It was such a long way to travel, so far from the dream of her bright life in Paris, the dream that beckoned to her all these years from the hazy horizon.

And yet…it was thinking about that horizon that helped her to muster some courage. The mare stamped hard upon the cobbles, breathing steam into the frosty early morning air, and Mary lifted a hand to the hood of her fur-lined cloak, gathering it closely round her face to hide her features.

Mistress Jamieson, she told herself, would not have felt afraid. She would have welcomed the adventure, turned her face towards the wider sky and never looked behind.

So Mary tried to do the same. She took the gallant hand that Thomson offered her and stepped as lightly as she could into the waiting diligence and took her seat with perfect nonchalance. She tried to keep her gaze fixed forward, only forward, taking on the poise of Mistress Jamieson as though it were another cloak that made her fears invisible.

But as the massive public coach began to lurch and roll along the cobbles, Mary couldn't help herself. She turned her head, against all her intentions, and looked back. The lights of Paris seemed already to have dimmed and lost their promise. And the wider sky ahead of them looked very dark indeed.

CHAPTER 18

THE INCANDESCENT BLUE OF twilight had already started its descent, and all along the row of little Christmas Village chalets on the Champs-Élysées strings of beautiful white lights were coming on, as though they wanted to illuminate our way. The slight curve of my visor turned those little lights to stars, and their reflections swiftly chased across the sleek black surface of Luc's helmet as he briefly glanced to see the way was clear before he changed lanes. Holding tight to him, I tried to look where he was looking, at the Arc de Triomphe rising brightly in its floodlights just ahead of us, but my eyes kept returning to those fairy lights that draped the white chalets. I couldn't help it.

There was something in their beauty and the rhythm of their passing that was making me feel warm inside, and happy—though the happiness, I knew, had been a steady growing thing inside me all the afternoon. I knew the source of it. I'd felt this way before, although I hadn't felt it with such strength in years, this feeling of attraction and anticipation; *liking* someone. There had been a time, before I'd learned how to contain it and control it, when this feeling would have frightened me because I would have feared that it would end, and I'd be hurt. But now, the certain knowledge all relationships *would* end, and I could choose the time to end them, left me free to just enjoy the rich sensations that I felt when one began.

At the moment, here with Luc, with the Ducati roaring underneath us and the cold air rushing past and all the little lights like stars around us, it felt very much like flying.

It was really, I assured myself, the perfect situation. I would only be in Chatou for another month at most, and then my work with Mary's diary would be done and I'd be gone, which made a neat and perfect end date for a romance, if I did choose to indulge in one. Apart from which, Luc seemed to understand the time I needed for my work, and with his son and his ex-wife already here to keep him company, he didn't seem to be the kind of man who'd place demands on me, or try to hold me back when it was time for me to leave. He'd likely only shrug and smile and say "OK," the way he did to everything.

My cousin's voice spoke from a distant corner of my mind, made fainter from the effort of attempting to push past my pleasant thoughts with her more rational advice: *That's not a rabbit hole you want to tumble down.*

But I was already some distance down that hole and falling ever faster. By the time we reached the first of the long tunnels and the motorcycle dived into the close embrace of the low-ceilinged arched walls with the long and steady line of lights that flashed past with the rhythm of a heartbeat, I was too far down the rabbit hole for saving. I leaned forward, wrapped my arms more tightly round Luc's waist and, with my head turned sideways, let my helmet rest against the safety of his back. And went on falling.

❧

Noah didn't want to go to bed. Each night, except for New Year's Eve, he'd gone upstairs at 9:15 without complaint, but now it was 9:43 and he was still downstairs wandering round from one room to the other; only this time he didn't have his video game with him, so there wasn't the synthesized music to serve as a warning, and when he came into my workroom it startled me.

Noah apologized, not bothering to try to speak in English. "I am looking for Diablo," he explained. "I cannot find him." He looked sad.

I'd always been puzzled when books about people with Asperger's claimed that we didn't have empathy. True, I might have trouble sometimes guessing how another person felt, but sadness was an obvious emotion and an easy one to spot most of the time. My problem wasn't that I didn't understand their feelings, only that I didn't have a clue how to respond to them. I never knew the proper thing to do or say. I wasn't good at comforting.

He said, "I thought he might be here, with you. He likes this room."

"I haven't seen him." Which, considering Diablo was a cat, meant very little. Cats were good at hiding.

"Oh."

I hesitated as I looked at Noah. He looked *so* sad. And he hadn't interrupted me, not really. I'd just finished work on one of Mary's entries in the diary and had set my pencil down to rest my hand a moment. She had not had much to say. The diary entry had been short and dull, a recap of her second trip to Mass, and I'd learned nothing from it other than that she had liked her new green gown. Mary hadn't named the church they'd gone to this time, either, which at least had made me feel less guilty for not taking on the crowd of tourists at the church of Saint-Germain-des-Prés this afternoon, because she might have never gone there. I was happy with the way I'd spent my time in Paris, anyway. So happy, to be honest, that my concentration wasn't what it should be, and I found it easy now to set my work aside completely to help Noah take a look around the room. The cat, as I'd suspected, was not there.

I said, "He must be somewhere. Where else have you looked?"

His shrug was very French, a smaller mirror version of his father's. "Everywhere. In all his favorite places. There is only the one room he likes upstairs, but I can't go in there alone, not without a grown-up, and Maman is busy doing laundry and Madame Pelletier is in the bath." His eyes were like his father's, too, and fully as persuasive.

"I'll come up," I offered, which if not exactly comforting must still have been the right response, because he brightened. "Truly?"

"Yes, of course." I rose, and let him lead me out and up the winding stairway. As we climbed, I asked him, "Are you sure he's even in the house? Perhaps he's gone home to his owner."

"You can't own a cat. Cats don't like to be owned."

This was news to me. "No?"

Noah shook his head, certain. "Papa says that cats choose the people they want to be with; you can't force them to stay if they don't want to stay. And they only belong to themselves," he said. "That's why Diablo prefers to live here, because we understand that."

"I see." We were at the first floor, now, where my bedroom was, but we simply stepped round to the next flight of stairs and kept climbing. I hadn't been up this far yet. It was my understanding Denise and her son had the attic suite on the third floor, while Claudine's rooms were just above mine, but the second-floor room Noah led me to, although directly on top of my own and the same general shape and size, wasn't a bedroom. When the light was switched on I saw cameras and tripods and lamps and reflectors; a sleek modern desk and a couple of stools and framed photographs everywhere, telling me this must be Claudine's own workspace—her studio.

I paused on the threshold. "You're sure you're allowed to be in here?"

"If I'm with a grown-up." He'd already entered the room and was moving around with the easy assurance of someone who knew it well, peering behind canvas backdrops and under the desk and in what I assumed were the cat's favorite places. I wasn't much help to him, mainly because I was busy admiring the photos that hung on the wall.

I had seen all the photographs Claudine had taken for Alistair's books, of course, but those were landscapes and streetscapes and buildings, while these for the most part were portraits of people, some done in full color and some black and white. They were people I didn't know—strangers—except for one man in a black-and-white image, caught halfway in shadow. A big man with dark hair turned gray at his temples.

There were at least three other portraits of Alistair Scott hung beside and below it, but this one attracted my eye because, while all the others were formal and posed, this one captured a quieter moment, more private. He seemed unaware of the camera. He sat in a chair by a window, its casement propped open to some sort of breeze that had lifted the simple sheer curtain and let in a soft slanting angle of light. He was reading, his head slightly bent to the paperback book that he held in one hand, while his other hand cradled the stem of a wineglass that still had some wine in it. There was a second glass, also half full, on the table set under the window beside him, as well as a second chair pushed back as though someone had only just stood and walked out of camera range. Or as if that person was the one taking the picture.

It wasn't the usual sort of a portrait one saw of an author, I thought. It was intimate.

"He isn't here," Noah said.

Turning, I saw his eyes filling with tears and that made me feel even more useless because I still didn't know what I could do. So it helped that the next thing he said was, "He's lost."

Then at least I knew I could correct him. "We don't know that. All we know is we can't find him," I said, using simple logic, "but that doesn't mean *he* doesn't know exactly where he is."

Noah paused to think this through. I wasn't sure if it made sense to him, but it did stop the tears.

Relieved, I carried on, "So, where else—"

I didn't get to finish. I was interrupted by a thump, a thud, and a shriek from Denise in the room underneath us. My room.

Noah, as always, was faster than I was. His feet seemed to barely connect with the stairs, and he made a loud thump of his own at the landing in front of my bedroom door. I came more cautiously, not sure of what I would find.

Denise smiled as we entered the room. She had bent to recover a basket of clean folded sheets that had dropped to the floor and now lay on its side with its contents disheveled and half on the carpet. "I'm sorry," she told us, "I'm fine. I just opened the wardrobe to put the new sheets in, and this beast decided to pounce from on top of it."

Noah looked where she nodded and let out a squeal of his own, only happy. "Diablo! You found him, Maman!"

Denise, in the middle of righting the basket, said, "I didn't realize he was lost."

"He wasn't. Madame Thomas said he wasn't, and he wasn't. Were you?" Noah asked the cat, now sitting very innocently near my bed. "You knew exactly where you were."

The cat, without denying or confirming this, blinked back at him.

"Thank you, Maman," said Noah, and he hugged his mother tightly. Turned to me. "Thank you, madam." He hugged me too, so quickly there was no time for me to respond. Which was, I reasoned, just as well. I wasn't good at hugging, either.

Diablo didn't seem to have a problem with it. He allowed himself to be scooped up without complaint. As Noah bounced off with Diablo cradled closely in his arms, Denise smiled and remarked, "Noah likes you."

I wasn't sure what to reply but it didn't much matter, since she didn't leave any time before adding, "And so does his father. That jacket he loaned you today was his favorite. He never lets anyone touch it."

She said that the same way a school friend might point out a boy in your classroom who fancied you. Maybe, I thought, I was doing a poor job of reading her tone and was missing the jealousy. Then again, she didn't look out of sorts. She was putting the clean sheets away on the shelf of my wardrobe, without any cat this time lurking on top to surprise her. She swung the doors closed and said, "These few belong in the next room, the room where your cousin stayed. Then I'll be out of your way."

In honesty, I didn't really want her to be out of my way. I liked Denise. And there was something I wanted to ask her, so when she moved into the small adjoining room I trailed behind her. The bed here was stripped to the mattress, and Denise explained, "I should have done this right after your cousin left, but I got sidetracked with my trip to Chinon and since then it slipped my mind."

I watched her shake out a sheet. "Would you like me to help you?"

"You needn't bother," she said. "I can manage."

"It isn't a bother." I'd always enjoyed making beds. I enjoyed the precision of centering sheets on the mattress and smoothing the wrinkles and tucking things in, and I'd always felt soothed by the feel and the smell of fresh bed linens. Taking the end of the sheet Denise handed me, I stretched it over the bed and asked, straight out, "Why did you and Luc get divorced?"

Even to my ears, that sounded too blunt, so I added, "It's only that you seem to get on so well with each other. Like friends. And you're nice, and he's...well, he's..." I faltered, not sure I should tell her I thought he was "hot," as my cousin would say, but Denise seemed to know what I meant.

"Yes," she said, smiling, "he certainly is. And we are friends. We've been friends a very long time, since my parents brought me from Chinon to Paris. I wasn't much older than Noah then, and I was lonely. Luc's desk was beside mine at school. He was good-looking then, too," she told me, "but I never saw him that way. I still don't."

"But you married him."

"Yes, well, we did a ridiculous thing, once. There might have been wine involved. Maybe a lot of wine. And I had just broken up with a boyfriend, so partly I wanted to be reassured that it hadn't been me, you know? That I was worth being loved by a man." With a shrug she selected a blanket and shook it out, passing one side of it over to me. "It was stupid, but there you are. And I got pregnant. My parents were *not* pleased, but Luc...well, he tried to make everything right. To take care of me. And for a while, I let him," she said. "But you can't make a spark where there isn't one. We don't belong with each other like that. We both knew it. The day of our wedding I knew it, but I didn't want to hurt Luc any more than he wanted to disappoint me, so we didn't say anything. Then on our first anniversary—there might have been wine involved then, as well—we finally sat down and said what we felt, and we felt the same thing, so we fixed it."

I thought about Jacqui's divorces: the tears and betrayals, the lawyers and arguments, and all the anger that lingered. This didn't sound anything like that.

Denise said, "I can't say we made a mistake, because out of all that we got Noah, so really we did this amazing, good thing. But we're better as friends than as husband and wife. I'm not sure I'm meant to be married at all. I'm too fond of my freedom." She tucked in the blanket and reached for the duvet. "And Luc, he deserves to be properly loved."

We all did, I thought. And I didn't doubt Luc would eventually find someone he could love back, but I didn't have any illusions that it would be me.

I'd been told in no uncertain terms why I couldn't have lasting relationships, and though the words had been hurtful they had at least kept me from being hurt further by letting me take a more practical view of the way I approached men, and what I expected.

So it was enough that Luc liked me, I reasoned, and that I liked him. And whatever developed between us while I was here working would be a nice memory to take with me when I went home.

Still, I couldn't help feeling a small pang of wistfulness, as though I'd seen something in a shop window I wanted but couldn't afford. And for once I was glad that my Asperger's made my reactions mixed up sometimes, making me laugh in a sad situation—because when I straightened my side of the duvet and looked at Denise, all she saw was my smile.

CHAPTER 19

I love thee not, thou gloomy man. —Hard is thy heart of rock,
and dark thy terrible brow.
—Macpherson, "Fingal," Book One

Fontainebleau
February 15, 1732

S HE FELT, NOT FOR the first time, very glad she had developed the ability to hide her inner feelings. When the Scotsman fixed his gaze upon her with that disconcertingly detached expression that might have been carved of stone, she parried with her brightest smile. He did not move a muscle of his face, but briefly dropped his gaze to Frisque, who from a comfortable position curled on Mary's lap looked back at him as well, ears pricked and waiting.

Had she kept the corner seat she'd started with, she would have been across from Mr. Thomson, who was certainly more amiable to look at and converse with; but Madame Roy had suffered from the movement of the diligence, and when they'd stopped for dinner at midday Mary had changed seats with the older woman, giving her the corner place where she at least could lean her head against the seat back for relief. So Mary, for the hours since, had faced Mr. MacPherson.

They were not the only passengers. A frilly-looking woman and her two grown daughters, nearly Mary's age, were also going to Lyon. They'd come aboard at Villejuif, and having taken one look at the Scotsman planted squarely at the center of the one seat, the protective mother had assigned her daughters to the other, next to Madame Roy and Mary, and for her own part had sat pressed as much as possible into the farther corner.

Mr. MacPherson, Mary thought, had that effect on people. Even with his leather case and swords stowed safely in the net provided for that purpose, and dressed in clothes that were both well made and respectable, he still looked fierce. It did not help that he was plain of face, his features made more unattractive by the hardness of their angles and the absence of emotion in his eyes. In looking at him for the past few hours she'd come to realize that his gaze seemed more intense because his eyelashes were fair. His hair was fair as well. He wore no wig, and from the hair that was not covered by his hat at sides and back she judged it to be only slightly less fair than her brother's, gathered firmly in a queue tied with a plain black band at his collar, disregarding fashion for the sake of practicality.

She felt Frisque's tail begin to thump against her lap and smiled to think the little dog was wagging at the Scotsman, not the slightest bit afraid of him and fully primed for play. Another man, she thought, might have reached out to pet the dog, or smiled at least. Mr. MacPherson only turned his stony gaze towards the window.

There was little there to see. The sun had set and it was nearly fully dark outside. They were arriving, so the driver had announced, at Fontainebleau, where they'd be stopping for the night. Two days ago, Mary would have thrilled at the romance of visiting Fontainebleau—an ancient village set deep in the forest that, just like the forest at Saint-Germain-en-Laye, was home to the French royal hunting grounds; where every autumn the King of France brought his bright court to a palace so beautiful it might have graced any fairy tale Mary could dream of, with gardens and fountains and statues that seemed, it was said, to draw breath. But it wasn't two days ago. Now, Mary found she could summon no interest in Fontainebleau.

Having only slept fitfully for a few hours last night on a hard sofa while she'd awaited the signal to leave, she was sure any gladness she felt in the prospect of stopping was only because she craved rest, and because it would give some relief to Madame Roy, who'd passed the afternoon in stoic silence, uncomplaining but uncomfortable, her pallor and closed eyes the only evidence she felt unwell. Mary herself would be grateful to stop being jolted around for a while. She'd developed an ache in her neck and her back felt as stiff as her stays and her hair was beginning to fall from its pins so she had to keep raising a hand to repair it.

She was weary as well from the effort of keeping up bright conversation. With Madame Roy feeling poorly and Mr. MacPherson refusing to try to be sociable, it had been left up to Mary and Thomson to talk to the three women sharing the diligence with them. And after dinner, when Thomson had nodded off and stayed that way for an hour or more following, Mary had been left alone to converse as politeness demanded. The mother in particular was much inclined to gossip. Having chattered for some time about her daughters and their various accomplishments, she'd turned to asking questions about Mary and her "brother"—for despite another change of surname forced by the new papers of identity they carried, they'd maintained that false relationship and were now Mademoiselle and Monsieur Robillard. Mary, with all her experience making up stories to entertain, had put that skill to good use by inventing a fictional family with numerous cousins, connections, and lively, amusing adventures by which she diverted the woman's more personal questions and rendered them harmless.

Asked why they were going to Lyon, she'd answered in vague terms that led into tales of a cousin who'd traveled much farther than that, into Muscovy, and of the wonders he'd seen. And when asked where they'd stayed while in Paris, she'd taken a morsel of fact and embellished it freely. "Our friend, the Chevalier de Vilbray," she'd said, making use of the dashing young nobleman who had so captured the eye of her cousin Colette this past winter, "has a beautiful home there. Do you by chance know the chevalier?"

The woman had said in reply, much impressed, "I regret I do not."

"He is handsome," so Mary had told her, omitting the fact that his breath was unpleasant. "And kind. When he heard we were coming to Paris, and he being yet in the country, he wrote to his servants to place his entire house at our disposal."

The woman and both of her daughters had thought that was gallant indeed, and the younger of the daughters had asked, "And where is his house, pray?"

The question had not given Mary much pause, for she'd quickly remembered the street in which one of the great literary salons had been held, and she'd named it and added, "It's quite near the Palais-Royal." Which had served to impress them still more, and they'd begged for more details about the chevalier.

She'd spun them a few stories, using the princes and heroes that she had created in all the tales she'd told Colette for the framework of her re-imagined Chevalier de Vilbray, so that in the end he'd resembled the true man in nothing but name and the cut of his wig, having gained much in charm and intelligence.

Thomson had stirred in his corner and woken and caught the tail end of one fanciful story. He'd asked, rather sleepily, "Who is this, now?"

"The Chevalier de Vilbray." She'd hoped that her eyes would be warning enough, for she could not have said any more. "I was saying how grateful we were that he'd loaned us his house for our sojourn in Paris."

"Ah, yes." Thomson had rubbed his eyes with one hand, catching on to the game. "He is quite a remarkable man, the chevalier."

The three women traveling with them had been in agreement, the mother remarking to Mary, "I wonder, my dear, that you aren't half in love with him."

Frisque, at that moment, had nuzzled her fingers and Mary had glanced down, a movement that must to the others have looked demure.

Thomson had teased, "I believe you've struck close to the mark with that arrow, madam."

And the others, except for Madame Roy and Mr. MacPherson, had laughed.

Mary found herself wondering now whether Mr. MacPherson had ever laughed, even in childhood. She couldn't imagine it. Nothing about his hard line of a mouth seemed prepared to allow it, not even the edge that appeared to twist upwards a fraction, because it was balanced by the grimly downward slant of the opposite end. Mary couldn't imagine him being a boy. Or a baby. It seemed quite impossible.

But in this instance she had to concede that he might not have laughed for the reason he'd missed the remark altogether, because they were speaking in French. It had gradually started to dawn on her that he did not know the language, for since she had been in his company she had not once heard him speak it himself, and when they had been joined by the other three women he'd seemed to with-draw even further from all interaction. Nor was he traveling under a French name. While their new identity papers made Thomson and Mary the Robillards, and Madame Roy was continuing as Madame Roy, it was telling, thought Mary, that Mr. MacPherson was now styled a Spaniard, assuming the name of Montero.

She wasn't sure "señor Montero" could truly speak Spanish, or anything other than English, but she was increas-ingly certain he couldn't speak French.

She was trying to think how to test her suspicion when finally the diligence rolled to a halt, and the driver dis-mounted and came round to open the door, and from that moment Mary was only concerned with assisting Madame Roy down the step into the yard of the coaching inn, where the fresh air could begin to revive her. The yard was alive with activity, light spilling warmly in slabs from the doorways and unshuttered windows above as the innkeeper and his staff came bustling out to receive them. A handful of boys set to work to unharness the eight weary horses, rewarded by whinnies and snorts and the tossing of reins as the animals, freed from the traces that galled them, were led to the stables. The driver, who must have been nearly as weary from riding postilion the whole way from Paris, was helped by two men as he started unloading the baggage and parcels.

Mr. MacPherson was there as well, taking his swords and the long leather case from the netting up top before anyone offered them, and moving over to take up the two portman-teaus and Thomson's deal-box. He made them all look rather weak and superfluous, Mary decided, although she *was* being of use to Madame Roy, who leaned on her heavily as they were shown up the stairs to their room.

It relieved her to see they'd been put in a room of their own, for she'd been half afraid they'd be forced to share space with the chattering mother and daughters—or worse yet, with Thomson and Mr. MacPherson—for this was the first time she'd stayed at an inn and she had little notion of what to expect, beyond what she had read in her various stories.

The room they'd been given was comfortably sized, with a bed and a little round table and two rush-backed chairs, and a fireplace that, while not large, sent enough warmth from its little fire into the room to push back the cold evening air seeping in round the tall frames of the frost-speckled windows.

Madame Roy sat gratefully onto the bed. "Thank you, my dear, for your help. I can manage a post chaise, but I fear the motion of anything larger has never agreed with me. No, no, you've no need to fuss over me. I'll be fine again once I've had sleep."

"But you'll miss supper."

"I've no appetite for supper. If you send a maid up with some broth and bread, that will be more than ample. Leave the dog here, if you like," she added. "I'll share my meal with him and we can keep each other company."

Frisque seemed content with that arrangement, snuggling deep into the blankets of the bed while Mary, with assistance from the looking glass above the mantel, made what small repairs she could to her appearance and went down to sup.

She found the other women there before her, sitting waiting in the little parlor open to the dining room. The fireplace here was decorated finely with a mantel of mahogany and topped with polished candlesticks that, with the others set in sconces round the room, created quite a brightness.

"Mademoiselle," the elder of the daughters, who was close to Mary's age, enticed her over to their table, holding up a pack of cards. "Do come and play piquet while we are waiting. Both my sister and my mother have refused me."

Mary liked to play piquet. It was her favorite game, in fact—fast-paced and often favoring the player who possessed the better memory. But after such a long day's journey, following so closely on the drama of the day before, and having had but little sleep since they'd been forced to flee their lodgings in the rue du Coeur Volant, she would have much preferred to sit in peace until the landlord called them to their meal. Her hesitation must have shown enough that Mr. Thomson, entering the room behind her, sought to save her by remarking in apologetic tones, "My sister only rarely plays at cards."

It was not Mr. Thomson, though, who drew her eye. It was the tall man walking in his shadow, and aware of his unwavering regard that seemed dismissive of all cowardice, she strove again to cloak herself in courage that was not her own. She crossed the room as bidden, took her seat, arranged her skirts, and squared her shoulders all at once, in imitation of the graceful Mistress Jamieson.

She said, "I make exceptions in good company." And showed a most deliberate smile to the young woman opposite, who in delight held out the pack of cards so they could draw to see who would be first to deal.

If not entirely good company, it was at least diverting. Both the daughters and their mother kept a constant conversation going, moving from one topic to another with the flightiness of butterflies, and yet they were too friendly in their speech to be annoying. Thomson settled in an elbow chair beside the fire and set to charm the women by appearing to be interested in anything they told him, while the Scotsman, having neither the ability nor will to charm, apparently preferred to stand. He stayed close to the doorway that stood open to the dining room, his shoulder to the door frame in an attitude of ease. It was, so Mary reasoned, only logical that after being forced to sit so long in close confinement in the diligence, a man so tall should wish to give his limbs relief by standing, but she wished he might have found a place to do it that did not put him directly at her back. She had to fight the fleeting chills that brushed the bent back of her neck when she was looking at her cards.

There was a strategy to piquet that appealed to her and helped her keep her focus. There were cards to be discarded and exchanged, and calculations to be made from what the other player first declared in terms of what they held—how many cards of the same suit, or the same rank—that let her guess at what they had been dealt, and so make choices of her own in play that gave her the best chance to win the tricks.

In the first hand she was able to not only win the tricks she led, but steal one for an extra point. And in the second she found herself with that rare hand that had no court cards in it—a *carte blanche*.

She carefully kept her face neutral while thinking. Declaring a carte blanche would gain her an instant ten points, and would bar her opponent from later declaring a *pique* or *repique*, but it came at a cost, for to claim a carte blanche, she would have to reveal her whole hand—turn the cards round, though briefly, and let her opponent see all for that moment. Which meant that the woman she played against would then have gained the advantage in play. Mary weighed both the possible gains and the risks, and deciding that one did not balance the other she chose to say nothing, selecting three cards and exchanging them silently as though the ones she'd been dealt had been ordinary.

Her caution was rewarded as the cards she gained in her exchange turned out to be the king and queen and knave of diamonds, giving her the whole eight cards available in that suit, which allowed her to not only score well in the declarations, but to so control the play that she won nearly all the tricks, and thus the hand.

The younger daughter teased her sister, "You would be advised, I think, to charm our fellow guest, here, into aiding you by giving you some signal as to what Mademoiselle Robillard is holding in her hand." She cast a smile past Mary's shoulder at the Scotsman to include him in the joke, but must have had no answering response, for Mary saw her smile falter, and the mother in a faintly disapproving tone remarked to Thomson, "Monsieur Robillard, your man does not believe in conversation, so I see."

"You will excuse him," Thomson said, "for it is only that he finds our language difficult."

The mother asked, "Is he not French, then?"

"No, he comes from Spain. I have associates in business there who asked if I would find him a position in this country."

"Ah." She gave a nod.

The elder daughter, sorting through her cards, said to her sister, "You converse a bit in Spanish, do you not? At least you seemed to understand our Spanish dancing master well enough." It was no more than playful banter, but the younger of the sisters rose to it, obligingly attempting something to the Scotsman in the Spanish tongue, to which he answered curtly. She replied and drew him into an exchange that, although brief, displayed his fluency, while her own knowledge clearly had its limits, for she often seemed uncertain of her words. At length she gave up altogether.

To her mother and her sister, speaking once again in French, she said, "He has a more provincial accent than our dancing master, but I would suppose that is a function of his class, for he is clearly not a gentleman. How kind of Monsieur Robillard to take him on."

Her mother turned to Thomson. "Yes, indeed. In what position does he serve you, for in truth he seems quite fierce for a valet?"

Mary observed that Thomson had been caught off guard and had to think about his answer, so she sought to turn attention from him with a bit of teasing of her own. She told the other women, "He may seem fierce, but I promise you señor Montero is not half as hardened as he looks. He's rather soft beneath it all. Quite sentimental. Frisque, my dog, adores him. And he never will admit it but I'm told that he writes poetry."

"Indeed." The mother looked towards MacPherson, and her daughters followed suit with interest, making Mary glad that he was standing at her back and so she could not see his face, although she knew he had not understood what she had said.

She bravely carried on, "Oh, yes. And reads it, too. Which does remind me," she said to the younger sister, "could you ask him, please, if he has finished with the book I loaned him lately to assist him in his efforts to learn French? I confess I do speak nothing of his language, and you manage it so beautifully."

Well flattered by this praise, the younger sister said, "Of course," and asked a question of the Scotsman, who after a weighted pause responded with an answer that seemed longer than the others he had given.

Satisfied, the younger sister translated, "He says that it is safe upstairs at present, and that after we have supped he will be pleased to fetch it for you and return it to your room, if that would suit you."

Mary felt like saying that it wouldn't suit her in the least. She had no wish to have to face him in her room, even though Madame Roy would be there. It had been a gamble, certainly, to try to get her journal back in such a sideways fashion, but she'd seen no more straightforward way to ask for its return without resorting to the use of English, which might have betrayed their new disguises, for in truth there seemed no place where they might not be overheard if she'd confronted him. Except, perhaps, within a private room.

She felt the pricking on her neck again, and buried the strong urge to rub her hand against her nape. Instead she briefly gave attention to the game she was still playing, as the elder sister made a declaration of three tens.

"Not good," said Mary, in the customary answer, as she countered with her own four queens. And then, encouraged by the simple fact her voice had sounded calm, she told the younger sister, "Do please tell señor Montero that he needn't put himself to so much trouble. I am sure my brother could deliver me the book."

She played her cards with studied concentration while the message was conveyed in Spanish, and she tried to keep that concentration when his answer seemed as long and full of detail as the one he'd given previously.

"What I *think* he said," the younger sister told her, "is that it's no trouble to him, and he knows the book is of importance to you, so he would be easier in his own mind if he returned it to you by his own hand. He *did* say he enjoyed it,

I could understand that much, and that he has some questions on the text he wishes to discuss with you."

"Well," Mary said, and sought to smile. "I'm sure that will prove something of a challenge."

She had lost the hand. She lost the next one, too, so though she won the next three and thus won the game itself, she felt off balance all through supper, tasting little of the food or wine, and when they'd parted company and gone up to their rooms she could not make herself relax.

There was no point, she knew, in trying to do anything at all until he came to bring the journal to her. Frisque had raised his head with keen anticipation when she'd entered, but seeing she was in no mood for play he'd tucked his head into the blankets as before, content and warm beside the sleeping form of Madame Roy. The older woman's gown and cloak were neatly hanging in the clothespress, and she seemed so very peacefully asleep that Mary did not have the heart to wake her, so instead she lit a single candle from the hearth and set it on the small round table near the center of the room. And waited.

From her short experience, she'd half expected that the Scotsman would move like a ghost and somehow make it down the corridor without her hearing his approach, but he did not. She heard the even measure of his footsteps coming nearer, and had ample time to meet him at the door.

He did not wait upon the threshold like a gentleman to be invited in, but gave a short nod and stepped forward so that she was left no choice but to step back and let him enter, or be flattened.

In English, in an undertone, he told her, "Shut the door."

Or else I'll kill you, Mary finished in her mind, which raised an inner smile that eased a little of her nervousness. She did as he instructed, and then turned to find him standing at the center of the room already, looking round as though he had a vague distrust of everything within it.

Frisque had raised his head again, and now the little dog rose to his feet and wagged his tail with such a force it set his body shaking. Mary, fearing he might bark, crossed quickly to the bed and took him in her arms. There was no way she could avoid the Scotsman, nor could they converse and keep their voices low as caution would require unless she moved to stand quite close to him, so with reluctance Mary did just that. The deeper shadows cast by the lone candle and the low flames of the hearth made harder angles of his features, but she faced him squarely anyway, and said, "You have my journal."

Without answering, he drew the book and penner from his pocket, and as wordlessly he set them on the table.

Frisque was squirming. Mary, settling the dog, said, "Thank you."

"Your brother," said Mr. MacPherson, "is Nicolas Dundas?"

She knew she'd written down her brother's first name in her journal, in the single entry that she'd made in English before switching to the cipher. As to how he had deduced their surname, Mary did not know, but she could see no reason to deny it. "Yes."

He did not ask about the cipher, which at first she thought was strange, until she reasoned that if he had read that first long entry he'd have known about her morning spent with Mistress Jamieson, and how she had devised the cipher, and the purpose of it. All he said, after a frowning pause, was: "I would have your word that what ye write within those pages is for your eyes, and none other."

Mary looked at him in some surprise. "You have it."

She'd expected him to question her more closely; to demand to know the contents of the entries she had written, and perhaps even compel her to reveal to him the cipher. All he did instead was study her a moment with that gaze she could not penetrate.

She held that gaze unwillingly, but did not look away, and in the end he broke the contact and looked down at where the journal lay, and with one square and well-formed hand he slid it closer to her, in an action that was also a decision.

"Then guard it," he said to her. "Burn it or bring it. Don't leave it behind."

Which appeared to be all he would say on the subject. But when Mary thought he would leave her he paused again; brought his gaze back to hers, and for an instant she thought she discerned something searching within it, as though he were faced with a conflict of facts he was seeking to reconcile.

"You are accomplished," he told her, "at cards."

Having no notion how to reply to a compliment from this inscrutable man, she could only say, "Thank you."

"You had a carte blanche in the second hand."

Mary thought she had some faint idea, then, where he was heading with this line of talk. And she could have explained to him what her intention had been in not claiming the carte blanche, but telling him *that* would in turn have revealed near as much of her mind and true self to him as claiming carte blanche would have revealed all of her cards to her gaming opponent, and Mary did not wish to be so exposed. She retreated instead, as she'd done for so long, behind that useful mask she had learned to adopt, of the pretty and witty but none-too-intelligent female. "How silly of me," she said, "not to declare it. I must be more tired than I realized."

His gaze could no longer be read, at least not by the

candlelight. Giving the short nod she'd noticed he gave in the place of a bow, he said nothing further but turned and departed.

She bolted the door when he'd gone. Frisque whined and Mary hushed him with her mouth against his soft fur.

"It's all right," she soothed the little dog. "He scares me, too."

CHAPTER 20

M Y TEMPER, THOUGH I didn't often vent it, was my least attractive feature. Had I been at home I would have let loose with a stream of every swear word I could muster, but because I was in someone else's house I held it in and fumed in steady, burning silence.

It took a lot of effort, so much so I didn't notice the by-now-familiar sound of Noah's video game music until he was standing in the doorway of my little workroom, and when I glanced up there must have been a lot of anger in my eyes because he physically stepped back a pace, and instantly I felt remorse.

"Good morning, Madame Thomas," he said, speaking careful English. "I am sorry to disturb you. I will not disturb you more. I do not want to be disturbing."

I was briefly puzzled by his repetition of the word *disturb* until I realized I had taught it to him on the morning we'd first met, and he was probably just showing me that he'd remembered.

"No, it's fine," I said. "I'm only frustrated by something here. It isn't about you."

"Ah. Good. I'm looking for—"

"Diablo. Yes. He's there." I waved a hand towards the boxes by the window, where the cat had been curled up in comfort, staring at me for the past half hour as though convinced I'd lost my mind. Perhaps I had. I said to Noah, "Take him." Which of course meant: *Take him with you when you leave,* but Noah only lifted up the cat and stood there by the window, watching me.

He asked, "Is frustrated the same as *frustré?*"

"Yes, it is. The very same."

"I am sorry you are frustrated."

"It's fine," I said again, and then because it wasn't fine and there was no one else to let off steam to, I went on, "It's only that she's changed the game. She based the stupid cipher on a card game, and I had it sorted out, but now she's gone and changed the game, I think, and I can't figure out to what."

He blinked at me a moment. Then he simply said, "OK."

It was the best thing anybody could have done to break my mood. He sounded so exactly like his father that I couldn't help but be amused. I said, "You didn't understand that, did you? Any of it?"

Noah shook his head.

I switched to French, and in less aggravated terms explained the problem.

"Oh," said Noah. "Can I help?"

I nearly told him no, he couldn't help at all, he was too young to be of any proper use to me…and then in time I caught myself, recalling that it had been Noah's offhand mention of discarding cards that had been key to my decrypting Mary's cipher in the first place, so I said, "All right."

I'd read in books of people "lighting up" when they were happy, but I'd never had a sense of what that meant, because a person couldn't really light up. But the change in Noah's features when I told him he could help me made him seem more animated. Brighter. Maybe that was what the books were on about.

I shifted my chair to the side so he could come and stand beside me. "See this list? It's all the different card games people played back in the early eighteenth century. The time when this cipher was written."

"Where did you find these?"

Why did children ask the most inconsequential questions? "On the Internet. Now, I've got through this list to here," I said, and pointed to the place. "So when I ask you to, just read me the next game that's got a star beside it, and then tell me what the numbers are beside that name, all right?"

"OK." He took the list into his hands, a move that shifted the black cat held in his arms so that Diablo's face was level with my own. It was a little disconcerting being stared at by a cat, and definitely not my normal solitary working pattern, but at least I'd lost the anger and could turn my focus fully on the task at hand.

"All right," I said to Noah. "Read me out the next one."

"Whist," he told me, with exaggerated emphasis upon the *wh* so that it came out: "Wuh-hist."

"And the numbers?"

"Two and twelve."

I set to work with those.

"I like this other name," said Noah. "Lanterloo. It's funny. It's a funny word to say." As though to prove it, he repeated "Lanterloo" in different tones at different speeds.

I interrupted him. "You did say you would help me, yes?"

"Of course."

"Well, that's not helpful. Does it have a star beside it?"

Noah peered down at the list. "No."

"Then it isn't one we need to know."

"What does the star mean?" Noah asked.

I wasn't used to having someone asking questions at my

shoulder while I worked. "It means that cards are taken from the pack before they start to play that game. Like in belote." I realized that he didn't know the help he'd been to me already, so I told him how his comment New Year's Eve had set me on a course to solve the cipher.

He was smiling. "Really? Did I really help you?"

"Yes. Perhaps you'll be a spy when you grow up."

"I wouldn't like to be a spy. They're like assassins," Noah said. "They can't have friends."

The perfect sort of job for me, then. "Is that right?" I only said this because Jacqui always said it, I had noticed, when she was absorbed in something else yet wanted to appear to be involved in someone's conversation. And it worked. While I was focused on my numbers, Noah rambled on about some comic book, and I paid no attention. When I'd finished, he was finishing as well.

"...so it was only that his family had been killed and he was left alone and that's why he became a hit man, but he wasn't really bad."

"That's nice," I said. "The next one, please."

"Why do you only want the games where they take cards out first?"

One saving feature of his questions, I conceded, was the fact they were direct enough that I could answer easily. "Because she used a game like that to be her key the first time round. It makes the cipher trickier. I'm guessing she'll have made another game like that her key this time, as well." If I was wrong, I thought, at least I'd have eliminated several possibilities among the many. Evidently people in the eighteenth century had loved their card games.

Noah frowned. "A key like in the door?"

"In a way. A door key can unlock a door, a cipher key

unlocks the cipher, but it doesn't look the way a door key looks. In this case it would be a piece of paper, where she wrote a list to show what number stands in for what letter." Which was simplifying things, because of course some ciphers used more complicated keys.

"Why," asked Noah, "is it called a cipher?"

In his arms the cat had changed position, rolling so his head was upside down but with his gaze still steady on me as though he was also interested.

"I'm not sure anybody knows, exactly. The word itself comes from an old French word, *cifre*, which comes from an earlier Arabic word meaning zero, and later we used it to mean any numeral, so people might just have begun to use *cifre* to mean secret writing like this, that used numbers."

He nodded. "You like ciphers, madam?"

"I like puzzles."

"Papa always says I'm a puzzle." He flashed a grin. "Maybe that's why you like *me*."

I did like him, actually. It didn't hurt that he had the same eyes as his father, but just on his own he was still pleasant company. "Maybe," I said. "But I'd like you still more if you'd read the next game with a star on that list. And no silliness this time, just read me the name."

"OK." There was a pause as he searched down the list, then he made an odd snorting noise.

"Noah."

"I'm sorry."

"Just read me the next name."

He giggled.

I sighed. "Noah."

"Sorry. I'm sorry, madam."

"What's the name, please?"

He looked at me, trying to hold in the giggles enough to be able to get out the word. "Gleek."

And even I had to admit that was funny.

It wasn't gleek, though, in the end. It was one of the games further down the list: piquet.

"Two, three, four, five, six, and seven," read Noah. "And eight. What's the eight?" he asked. "Why is it separate?"

"Each player's dealt eight cards," I told him. I worked through the numbers and to my relief saw words appear: *Upon the 14th…*

"Does that work?" asked Noah.

"Yes, that's the one."

"We found the key?"

I didn't mind including him, because it seemed to make him happy. "Yes, we did."

He cheered with such exuberance it brought Denise into the doorway. "What," she asked, "is going on in here?"

"I'm helping," Noah said.

"Well, come and be some help to me," his mother told him. "I have breakfast dishes to be dried."

He didn't argue, though he didn't move as quickly as he could have to the door, and when he'd reached Denise he turned back for a moment and said, "Thank you for allowing me to work with you, madam."

"You're welcome."

Denise smiled at me and said, "I'll keep him out from underfoot." And then she closed the door and left me to myself.

My little workroom was decidedly more quiet. Which was fine. I worked much better on my own, with nobody distracting me, and Noah, although likeable, was constantly distracting me. But even so, the room felt oddly empty with him gone.

❧

"The problem is," I said to Jacqui, as I held the phone against my cheek and frowned, "they're miles away from Saint-Germain-en-Laye, and heading to Lyon, and I don't think they're going back." I'd only had to read the first long entry in the diary in the new piquet-based cipher to be sure we'd moved beyond the realm of doubt. "This isn't going to be what Alistair is hoping for."

"Perhaps he'll like this better," said my cousin. "It would read just like a thriller."

"Jacqui."

"No, I mean it. First they have a woman sent to spy on them, and then a man gets killed, and there's a bodyguard involved, and now they're on the run with false names? Sara, honestly, it sounds like gripping stuff."

"It isn't what he wanted." I stayed firm upon that point. "You promised you would tell him. You said if I found for certain that they didn't go to Saint-Germain-en-Laye, then you'd tell Alistair."

"I will. I will. I'll let him know."

"Well, do it now. I'll wait for you to ring me back."

"I'll text you," Jacqui compromised. She'd tried for ages to get me to text more, her preferred way of communicating, but I liked to hear the voice of people I was talking to.

"All right," I said. "I'll wait right here."

Right here was at my desk, with Mary's diary open to the end of her last entry and the first lines of her next one. My transcription, rough in pencil, lay where I had left it to the side, and now I picked it up and read again what she had noted down about what must have been a frightening two days for her, beginning with her breakfast on the fourteenth and continuing right through until she'd gone to bed at Fontainebleau. She'd blended both days into one long entry—perhaps partly because with no sleep to speak of in between, the days had felt like they were one, but also because she hadn't had her diary on the evening of the first day. The man who smoked the pipe, Mr. MacPherson, had been carrying it in his pocket. From what she had written of the way he was behaving, I'd concluded that he was some sort of bodyguard, although I knew the word in that sense hadn't yet been used in Mary's day. But he was clearly there to watch the man whom Mary had first known as Jacques, and of whom she had written now:

His true name it appears is Mr. Thomson, though the reasons for his hiding his identity are not made plain to me, and it is likely never will be, for it seems of all the people so involved in our disguise I am the only one designed to not know all. 'Tis very certain Mr. M— knows most of any of us, and is the least natured to reveal it.

That she feared and yet was fascinated by Mr. MacPherson was made evident all through that entry by the way she wrote about him, nowhere more so than towards the end when she described how he'd returned her diary:

…so as promised after supper came he to my chamber and returned it in his customary way, without the benefit of nice-ties, and only asked my word that I would keep it private, which I freely gave him. I believe he distrusts everyone and puts his faith in nobody, for which he has my pity, though 'tis sure he would not welcome it. I follow his example now, for since he read the first part of this book and is no fool, he may have made a full discovery of the cipher and so read the

*rest, so I now use this newer cipher which I pray will guard my
privacy. I would not wish that he should know my thoughts
so well, for though Frisque seems to think him harmless I am
certain that we never shall be friends.*

I was happy that she'd been allowed to keep the dog and
take it with her on their travels. It would have been hard for
Mary Dundas if she'd had to be alone among so many strangers, and so far from home, without the company of Frisque.
She never said what sort of dog he was, but from the paintings I'd seen of the time and from her mention of him lying
on her lap I guessed he was a miniature spaniel of some kind,
with floppy ears and silky fur.

I saw him clearly in my mind, as clearly as I pictured Mary
and her traveling companions: Mr. Thomson, at the lower
end of middle age and charming in a gentlemanly way; the
older Madame Roy, her features marred by smallpox scars
as Mary had described her, yet not all unkind in spite of her
more structured ways; and more clearly than any of them,
Mary's stone-faced nemesis, the tall Mr. MacPherson, who
had killed a man in front of her without remorse and was by
her account the only one of them who had a full sense of the
plan that had been put in motion, and that they were now
required to follow.

I was frankly curious about that plan myself, and I'd have
loved to follow Mary as she found out more about it. If I left
her now, I knew I'd always wonder what had happened—
what adventures she had lived, and what became of her.

So when my mobile pinged to let me know a message
had arrived, and I read Jacqui's text that said: *Keep going!*
with a smiley face, I felt a rush of great relief and wasted no
time picking up my pencil to continue my transcribing of the

diary, Mary's words now like a voice that I heard speaking to me clearly in my mind.

Which meant that later on that evening, I began to worry for her when I reached the entry that began:

We find ourselves again in danger…

CHAPTER 21

Let them move along the heath,
bright as the sun-shine before a storm…
—Macpherson, "Fingal," Book One

En route to Saulieu, in Le Morvan
February 17, 1732

T HE DILIGENCE WAS CROWDED. There had only been
the seven of them yesterday, when they'd departed
Fontainebleau at first light and so entered into Burgundy,
to dine within the ancient walls of Sens and carry on along
a mostly level road that kept within a valley and crossed riv-
ers on the way to the old city of Auxerre. There they had
stopped the night, and Madame Roy, revived a little by their
easy day of travel, had slept soundly and been well enough to
come to early Mass at the Cathedral of Saint-Étienne while
they'd waited for the horses to be harnessed to the diligence.
They had been joined this morning at Auxerre by three men
who had journeyed down from Paris by the *coche d'eau*, or
"water coach," that traveled by the river Seine.

The new additions to their number made a motley trio:
one a merchant with a most impressive wig and fine lace
cuffs and an unfortunate dependency on snuff that made him
sneeze at frequent intervals. He brought with him a servant
who, poor fellow, was consigned to ride outside within the
partly sheltered box that hung upon the front end of the
coach, protected somewhat from the wind but still at the full
mercy of the snow that swirled around them as the coachman

strapped himself into his jackboots on the rearmost nearside horse, took the long whip and all the reins into his hands, and started out just as the sun came up, at seven.

The third man was an Englishman, quite young and lean of limb and featured rather like a ferret. Mary thought he grew more ferret-like, in fact, the more he spoke. He knew no French beyond "hello" and "please" and "thank you," and those spoken in a rude indifferent accent, but discovering the merchant and the elder of the frilly sisters spoke some part of English he proceeded to regale them with his stories, little knowing that at least four other persons in the diligence were listening and understanding all.

He seemed to hold his English ways to be the best, comparing what he'd seen and done in France since his arrival some few months ago to what he held superior in London. Paris streets were, by his reckoning, too narrow and too dangerous and lacking in the footways he so prized in London streets. The city of Auxerre, where they'd just spent the night, was dirty and had nothing to commend it in his view, nor to remark upon, despite the fact that Mary in the short time she had spent there had admired the cathedral and a Benedictine monastery and a stately clock tower that showed the movements of the sun and moon.

The merchant for a time chose to debate him in his views, until they fixed upon a shared dislike of Spanish foreign policy, which then occupied them for some time.

The elder sister, during this discussion, sent several apprehensive glances at the Scotsman, sitting as he'd sat the day before, in stoic silence, before finally she felt moved to tell the other men, "Señor Montero is from Spain."

The Englishman broke off and asked, "Is he indeed?" He looked with newfound interest at MacPherson. "Well then, sir, not meaning to offend, I'm sure. Your country and my own have long been foes, but we need not be." And he held his hand outstretched.

MacPherson's cold gaze slanted down to view that hand a moment before lifting to regard the Englishman impassively, but otherwise he did not move.

The elder sister coughed into the briefly awkward silence and explained, "Señor Montero speaks no English."

"Does he not?" The Englishman withdrew his hand, but in a sharpish movement that alarmed Frisque, so the little dog laid back his ears and gave a warning growl, a thing that Mary had not ever seen him do before.

She soothed him with a brief word and a rumple of his ears, but she was inwardly quite pleased to know he did not like the Englishman. By dinnertime, she had decided she did not much like him, either.

It was obvious he'd set himself to charm the elder sister, but he did not do it honorably. Through the meal he touched her arm and bodice most improperly and made it seem by accident, and while they waited to reboard the diligence he moved to stand quite close to her as though to shield her from the weather, but his hand roved then as well and Mary saw him do it. For her part the elder sister, plainly flattered, was not trying to discourage him, but when they took their seats again the mother made both daughters sit with her beside Mr. MacPherson, reckoning the Spanish devil better than the English one.

Madame Roy, who'd been suffering again upon the very hilly roads they'd been traversing since Auxerre, looked none too pleased to see the Englishman sit beside Mary, but she could do no more than give Mary a faint warning glance before she turned her head again into the corner of the diligence and closed her eyes. An hour later, she had gone so pale that Mary felt compelled to take her hand and hold it reassuringly.

It seemed her fellow travelers, now warm and full from dinner and lulled by the constant rocking of the diligence and rumbling of its wheels, were all asleep. She'd been surprised to see the Scotsman, sitting just across from her, lean back and close his eyes as well, for he had seemed to her a force of nature that did not need things so commonplace as sleep. And yet he slept. His features stayed as unforgiving and his mouth as grim as when he was awake, his body resting yet not resting, with his fine hands curled to partly open fists upon his thighs.

She was so absorbed in studying him that she did not notice that the Englishman beside her was awake until he bent to open the small wooden foot stove at their feet to touch a twist of paper to the embers glowing in the metal pot within, so he could light his pipe.

Madame Roy stirred and moaned and Mary knew she could not let him smoke, or else the older woman would be made to feel yet sicker, but there was no one awake for her to call upon to serve as a translator. It was risky, Mary knew, to speak in English, but the needs of Madame Roy outweighed the need for caution in this instance, and she was accustomed to pretending to be that which she was not, so she affected a much thicker accent than was purely necessary, seeming to have but a little knowledge of the English language.

"Please," she told him, "not to smoke."

The Englishman, still bending forward, turned in some surprise. "I beg your pardon?"

"Not to smoke," she tried again, and motioned to the corner. "Madame Roy is ill."

"I see. All right, then." Letting down the pierced lid of the foot stove, he sat upright and looked down at her with speculation in his eyes.

The Scotsman's eyes had opened, too, and Mary felt his brief regard before his eyelids closed again and he appeared asleep.

The Englishman remarked, "I did not know you spoke my language."

Mary shrugged. "I speak it but a little."

"No, indeed you speak it well." He wore the smile that sought to charm, although to her it had a predatory edge that left her cold.

He was perhaps five years her senior, still a young man yet he had acquired that air of subtle boredom that marked men of some experience. His likely had been gained through self-indulgence and debauchery, she thought, since he had none of the appearance of a man of wealth or industry. He wore the proper sort of clothes, the proper shoes, the proper wig, and yet they did not sit upon him well. Nor did his smile: it failed to touch his eyes, which always seemed to try to see a step ahead of where he was, and so stayed ever watchful, almost sly.

The diligence lurched suddenly. The Englishman put one hand on her leg, as if by accident, then drew it quickly back again as Frisque began to growl.

"That's quite a watchdog you have there, mademoiselle."

She stroked Frisque's head to quiet him. "I do not know this word."

"A dog who guards you."

"Ah. Yes, he is good."

"I have a dog at home in London," said the man, "that would I fear eat this small one for breakfast."

Mary forced a smile and said, "I do not understand," because she did not want to talk to him.

Their conversation had awoken the French merchant who sat on the Englishman's far side, and he now stirred and yawned and said in English, "I am much surprised, monsieur, that you do not go back to London, since you find so little here to please you."

That remark, made drily and in jest, produced a broad smile from the Englishman, who looking Mary up and down deliberately, said, "There are *some* things in France that please me." Turning in his seat to face the merchant, he went on, "Besides, I cannot leave your country yet, while I stand set to make my fortune."

That did rouse the merchant's interest. "How is that?"

"I seek a fugitive." He slipped his unsmoked pipe into the pocket of his coat. "A man my Parliament would gladly hang, if they could get their hands on him, and for whose capture they have offered a reward that I intend to claim."

"And he is here in France, this fugitive?"

"He is. His name is Thomson," said the Englishman. "John Thomson."

Mary's feet were by the foot stove yet she felt a sudden rush of cold that settled in her marrow, and her hand upon the dog's soft head fell still.

The Scotsman kept his eyes closed but she noticed his right hand had moved a little up his thigh so it was covered by a loose fold of his horseman's coat. Her own hand had grown tighter in its grip on Madame Roy's, until the older woman squeezed her hand by way of reassurance. Mary breathed, and tried to go on breathing normally.

"He's been in France," the Englishman went on, still speaking to the merchant, "since October last past, when he fled from London with a fortune of his own—five hundred thousand pounds, they reckon, robbed from the investors of the Charitable Corporation, some of whom were driven since to bankruptcy and suicide."

The merchant clucked his tongue. "For shame."

"Indeed. Though I admit I cannot curse him altogether, for his crime provides me with the means to line my pockets, as you see."

"And do you know where he is now?"

"He *was* in Paris," said the Englishman. "I had a friend there by the name of Erskine who was sure he knew the place. Well then, come in with me, says I to Erskine, and we can divide the profits, but the fool did tell me no, he'd put his trust in the police, whom he had plans to bribe. Good luck, says I, for I have contacts of my own who tell me Thomson has left Paris and has headed south. And I am on his trail." He settled back against his seat with satisfaction, and remarked, "It is no different, really, than a common hunt, and I have hunted nearly every quarry you can name."

"Ah, yes?" The merchant showed a quickened interest that revealed they'd hit upon another thing in common. "What do you most like to hunt, monsieur? The fox? The bear?"

"The boar, I think, does make a worthy adversary."

For nearly half an hour after that the two men traded stories of their hunting prowess, while the others slumbered on or seemed to, leaving Mary sadly isolated in her disappointment at discovering that Thomson was no better than a criminal.

She looked at him with different eyes, as though the light by which she viewed him had been changed forever and she could see nothing but the parts that lay in shadow. Frisque sensed her change of mood and licked her hand but she was not to be consoled. She'd had too many disappointments lately, Mary thought. Too many people who had played her false and let her down.

She felt the prick of foolish tears and let her own eyes close to hold them back so nobody would see them fall…but even as her lashes drifted shut she saw the Scotsman's eyes had opened once again, and he was watching her.

～✦～

At supper at Saulieu they heard the howling of the wolves from deep within the forests of the Morvan, and their land-lord told them how in wintertime, as it was now, the starved wolves sometimes ventured from their lairs to lie in wait for passing travelers. When Frisque demanded Mary take him outside after supper, she kept close beside the door and kept her eyes turned to the forest that lay dark beyond the city walls, where still the wolves howled eerily. The moon was entering its final quarter and the stars were half-obscured by clouds that moved by stealth and seemed to drive the wind before them, for it stung at Mary's frozen cheeks and burned her eyes.

She smelled the pipe smoke first. She stiffened, for she did not wish to see Mr. MacPherson, nor yet any of the people who had brought her into such a business. Loyalty to king and country she could understand, although the king and country she was being asked to bear allegiance to were ones she scarce could call her own. Yet theft was theft, and there could be no honor in the robbing of the innocent, no matter how well cloaked it was in patriotic purpose. She had cast her lot with criminals, and Thomson had this morning stood at Mass beside her and received the Host and he had done it as though his soul was pure white as the snow that Frisque was turning round and round upon this moment. It was, Mary thought, a hard thing to forgive.

She had kept silent for the most part since they'd stopped here, and declined an invitation by the elder of the daughters to repeat their play at cards, and over supper she had spoken only when directly spoken to, and risen when it was polite to do so and retreated to her room, and would have been there still had not Frisque now demanded to come out.

The pipe smoke swirled its scent again from somewhere close behind her, and she braced herself and turned prepared to face Mr. MacPherson. But it wasn't him at all.

It was the Englishman.

His name was Stevens. Mary wondered what he would have thought to know the fugitive he hunted had been sitting to his right hand all through supper, and had passed him salt and bread.

He said, "You're brave to come outside, mademoiselle, after the tales we heard at supper."

Mary drew the warm hood of her cloak about her face and lied to him. "I do not understand." Perhaps, she thought, if she repeated that enough he'd let her be.

"The wolves." He came another step until he stood beside her, looking out where she was looking. "I have hunted wolf before. It is a most diverting sport, yet dangerous."

"To hunt," she said, "is dangerous." She said it in a simple tone, as though to make it seem she were repeating what he'd said and nothing more, and yet he took it as a warning. Or a challenge.

"Not if one approaches it with thought," he said, "and planning. Do you know what I liked best about the wolf hunt?"

Mary shrugged apologetically and said, "I do not underst—"

"The cubs," he said, as though she had not spoken. "I

did find it most diverting, hunting wolf cubs, for they are too young and innocent to know how to behave when they are hunted. They will run not in a line but in a circle, and soon tire and think to go to ground to hide themselves, not knowing that is no way of escape. The trick is that you have to draw the mother off with hounds, or else she'll sacrifice herself to save her litter," he explained. She felt his hand brush lightly on her back, as though it were by accident. He smiled. "And there is little sport in sacrifice."

Frisque had finished with his necessary business. Turning round, the dog caught sight of Mr. Stevens and began to bark as though he sought to argue with the Englishman.

The sound shook Mary from her frozen state, and telling Frisque to hush she quickly lifted him and held him tightly.

Stevens said, "I see you have your fierce protector."

Mary did her best to smile to show she had not been at all affected by what she was half afraid had been a cleverly directed threat. She told him simply what she'd said before, when he had given Frisque slight praise. "Yes, he is good."

"I was not speaking of the dog." The Englishman smiled one last time and bowed and turned and left her, and in leaving gave a nod to the tall man who had been standing in the shadows by the doorway of the inn, behind them both, the glowing bowl of his own pipe a stab of burning red against the darkness.

Mary gathered Frisque against her heart and moved towards the doorway, and MacPherson struck the ashes from his pipe and let her pass, but as she crossed the threshold he fell into step behind her casually, as though it were his place, and for the first time since she'd met him Mary felt a little safer knowing he was at her back.

CHAPTER 22

I WAS STARTING TO AGREE with Jacqui that the diary read more like a thriller than a chronicle of everyday events.

We find ourselves again in danger, Mary had confided, *in the form of Mr. Stevens who did join us at Auxerre and who appears to have discovered Mr. Thomson's true identity, or at the least suspect it very strongly. He has friends in Paris, so he said, who told him Mr. Thomson headed south, and I do fear they've also told him that he travels with a sister, for tonight he told a tale of hunting wolf cubs that did seem to me an allegory meant to warn me nothing good would come of an attempt to sacrifice myself to shield another. Though I am not certain that was his intent, I do suspect it, and I warrant Mr. M— suspects it also, and I hope that this encounter does not have its end in violence.*

She'd described this Mr. Stevens in some detail and had written of their journey from Auxerre to Saulieu so minutely I could all but see the people crowded in that diligence and feel the sense of Mary's disappointment when she'd learned that Mr. Thomson was no grand romantic outlaw but a fraudster and a thief.

I had the sense as well that, while she disliked Mr. Stevens, she was nonetheless in sympathy a little with his purpose, since she'd added:

He did tell us of the poor investors driven sadly into bankruptcy and ruin, and there must be a host of people now in

London injured by this swindle of the Charitable Corporation
who do nightly pray to see its architect brought home to justice.

By Monday night I'd come no closer to an understanding of "this swindle of the Charitable Corporation." I had looked it up online, and read reports to the committees of the House of Commons and the House of Lords, and academic articles and snippets out of history books that analyzed the workings of the scandal and the men who'd been involved in it—but as with many things, the more I read, the less I understood.

The problem with hindsight, I thought, was that there were just too many documents. And when they touched on the issue of stockbroking, I was at sea.

As I passed through the kitchen Denise, chopping something to bits on the worktop, looked up. "Heading out?"

"Yes."

"You should wear your coat," she advised me. "It's cold once the sun sets."

"I'm not going far. I'll be back before dinner."

In the tops of the tall bare-branched chestnut trees in the back garden a chattering cluster of swallows was gathering, filling the air with the sound of their wings as they rose and resettled, preparing to fly. They were likely midway through migration, those swallows. A long way from home.

Through the trees and above the gray wall at the end of the garden I saw a light burning a warm golden welcome upstairs in the window of Luc's house. I passed through the door in the wall and went out to the lane and along underneath the low archway of branches. His car was parked where it should be, at the side of the house, and the lights were on downstairs as well. As I climbed the short flight of curved steps to the porch I could hear Noah laughing—a small, friendly sound in the darkening evening that tugged somewhere under my rib cage.

I reached for the dangling cord of the old-fashioned bell Luc had hung to the side of the door. It was rusted from being exposed to the weather, but I liked the clear sound of its ring.

When the door opened I felt surrounded by warmth from the light in the entry hall and the quick genuine flash of Luc's smile as he stepped to the side and invited me in.

I had not yet been inside the house. It reminded me of my aunt's mock-Tudor cottage: a central hall plan with two rooms at the front and a kitchen behind and a staircase that climbed from the back of the hall to the bedrooms above. I knew that the door at the back, at the foot of the staircase, led into the kitchen because of the smells of roast chicken and some sort of vegetable drifting out from it. The front entry hall was narrow and I felt the brush of Luc's arm on my own as he swung the door shut again, then turned to me as though waiting for me to decide what the form of our greeting should be.

We had moved past the handshake, I thought, so I led with the *bise*. He was due for a shave and smelt faintly of Scotch, but it wasn't unpleasant. "I wasn't aware you wore glasses," I told him.

"I need them for reading. I'm old."

"Thirty-two isn't old."

"You've been learning my secrets." He looked at the handful of papers I'd brought. "Do you need me to take you somewhere?"

"No." As much as I wanted to physically follow where Mary had gone, it would not have been practical. Going to Paris was one thing, but driving across all of France was another. Besides, she was moving too quickly and not staying long enough in any village or town to make seeing those places of use to my work.

I said, "I need your help with a stock fraud."

He honestly had the best smile. Through the frames of his glasses I saw his eyes crinkle a bit at the edges. "OK." With a nod to the room just behind, he said, "Come have a drink."

It was not a large sitting room, but it was cozy and comfortably furnished with lamps and a slouchy brown sofa and chairs and low tables that looked like they wouldn't much mind if you set down a drink on them. Luc had been doing just that. On the table in front of the sofa he'd set a large Scotch glass beside a ring binder of papers. He closed the ring binder now, sliding it off to the side as he shifted a small stack of newspapers and a one-armed robot built out of LEGO bricks to tidy up. He had left me a choice between taking the armchair or sharing the sofa. I sat on the sofa.

He took off his glasses, still standing, and sliding them into the breast pocket of the plain white cotton shirt he was wearing, he asked, "What would you like? I have sherry or whisky or rum or *épine*…"

"What's *épine*?"

"It's homemade, from the leaves of the blackthorn."

"You made it yourself?"

"Noah helped. It's not bad."

I opted to try it and watched while he crossed to the drinks cabinet in the front corner beside the big window that looked to the front of the house. He must do something other than sit at a desk, I decided. He had to belong to a gym, or go running. Men didn't stay lean with long muscles like that just by sitting around all day working with numbers.

I knew. Every office I'd worked in was full of men glued to computers, and there was an obvious difference between those who did nothing else and the ones who stayed active.

I glanced round the room for a clue as to what sport he played, but I didn't see anything, so I just asked him.

He shrugged and said, "Different things. Racquetball. Football. I walk. You?"

"I'm not good at sports."

"You can walk, surely? We'll take you walking some weekend," he promised me, "Noah and I. When the weather is good."

I was frankly surprised how appealing that sounded. "All right."

"Now," he said, coming back to the sofa and setting my glass down in front of me, "what is this stock fraud you're needing my help with? I won't go to jail for this, will I?"

The sound of electronic Robo Patrol music preceded the light creak of footsteps that came down the hall. Noah asked us, "Who's going to jail?"

"No one," Luc said. "Madame Thomas needs me to help with her work, I think."

Noah greeted me very politely, but said as though he were correcting his father, "*I* help with her work."

Luc said, "Well, come and help, then. But first get the red bowl of nuts from the dining room, will you? We might as well try to convince Madame Thomas we have a few manners."

Obligingly Noah crossed over the hall and returned with a small dish of almonds and set it down carefully, and would have squeezed himself onto the sofa between us if Luc hadn't told him to sit in the chair. I was grateful for that. I liked Noah, and I liked Luc, but I was feeling a little hemmed in and I needed my personal space.

"Now," said Luc to me, "how can we help you?"

I set down my notes and attempted to put them in order. "The Charitable Corporation," I said, "was a British corporation formed supposedly to make small loans to poor people who needed money. In exchange, the poor people put items in the corporation's warehouse as security, and when they paid the loan back then their items were returned."

"So, like a pawnshop," was Luc's summing-up.

"Exactly like a pawnshop, really. Only the directors of the corporation started running some sort of a fraud, taking money for themselves, and they were speculating with the shares and buying stock in this"—I showed another paper to him—"the York Buildings Company, and it all went bad and people lost their savings and the corporation's banker and their warehouse keeper took off into France, and it's the warehouse keeper, Thomson, who the woman in the diary is supposed to be protecting, and she's really angry with him now for what he's done, but I don't have a clue exactly what it was he did." I had to stop for breath. "They lost me," I confessed, "in all the rates of interest and the price of shares, and…well, I just don't understand it. And I thought, you're an accountant, maybe you can tell me what was going on."

Luc turned one paper slightly on the table, put his glasses on again, and read it over carefully.

I took a sip of my *épine*. It was a lovely, honey-colored liquor, very sweet and with the pleasant taste of almonds. It was also very strong. I wasn't used to drinking anything but wine or sherry, and with those I knew how much to drink without it having an effect. *Épine* was different. It kicked straight into my bloodstream and I set it down with care.

"OK," said Luc, "I see. It's not so complicated. Just forget about the interest and the price of stocks, it doesn't matter. This is very simple. I can show you."

He did just that, and in the way that I always found easiest when I was learning new concepts: by teaching with actual objects. Calling on Noah to bring him four cereal bowls, Luc set them on the table in front of us; designated them his warehouse, stock shares, lending bank, and marketplace, and proceeded to show me how a corporation like the one that Thomson worked for was supposed to operate. He used a handful of his own business cards in place of stock certificates, almonds for his merchandise, and coins from his wallet to represent cash, moving all of them round in the four bowls to show how things all ran smoothly until he began scooping out coins from the "bank" for himself. At first he was able to cover this by putting more "stock certificates" into play and selling the pawned items from his warehouse, thus earning more coins to cover his losses, but in the end Noah grew frustrated with him for messing things up.

Luc agreed it was all out of balance. "The more I try to make things right, the worse it gets, and if I keep on doing this my money will be gone, and then my warehouse will be empty, and the only thing that I'll have left is lots of paper stock things," he said, using Noah's term, "that aren't worth anything."

"That's silly," Noah said. And giving up on things financial, he resumed his game of Robo Patrol and tuned us out while Luc, his lesson done, leaned back and calmly ate an almond.

I was processing.

He looked at me. "Did any of that help?"

"It did." I thought I understood it now more clearly. "So the banker and the warehouse keeper, Thomson, and the other men in league with them, just helped themselves to money, only nothing new was going in the warehouse that could balance the amount that they were taking out."

"That's right."

"And then they sold more stock to try to cover what they'd taken, and when people in the Parliament got wise to this and asked to see their books, they just ran off. Well, Thomson did. The banker, too."

Luc said, "That's what it sounds like, from that article you've got there."

I was quiet for a moment while I processed this some more. I took a sip of my *épine*. "And all the people who'd invested money…"

"Their certificates were worthless. There was nothing left to pay them with."

I gave a nod. I got it, now. Except for one thing. "But," I said, "they didn't only take a few coins, Thomson and the banker. The report said they took something like five hundred thousand pounds."

"A lot of money," Luc agreed. "Especially in those days."

"Yes, but where did it all go? What did they do with it?"

Luc shrugged again, and reached for his own drink. "I would imagine only two men ever really knew the answer to that."

"Thomson and the banker."

With a nod he said, "And both of them are dead."

❧

He walked me back. It wasn't necessary. Even with the darkness in the lane there was still light enough to see by, and it wasn't far to go. But he'd insisted, and in honesty I hadn't really argued. It felt nice to have him walking here beside me, hands in pockets, with his shoulder brushing mine. Men sometimes made me nervous but with Luc it was more simply being aware of him—very aware, as I'd felt in his house, when he'd sat with his arm on the back of the worn leather sofa, behind my shoulders, never touching me but simply *there*.

I'd nearly answered yes when he'd invited me to stay for dinner, but I knew Denise had been at work the past few hours cooking something fairly finicky. I didn't want to disappoint her, so I'd said, "I have to go."

His son had said, "Tomorrow, though. You'll come tomorrow, won't you?"

"Well..."

"You have to," Noah had informed me. "It's Epiphany. We're having dinner here."

"Yes," Luc had promised him, "they'll all be here tomorrow night."

I must have looked a little undecided because Noah had sweetened the offer with, "We'll have balloons. And a king cake."

It had been years since I'd last celebrated Epiphany in the traditional French way. Or eaten a king cake. "I'll be here," I'd told him.

He'd hugged me in parting the way he'd done last night, and I'd hugged him back, trying not to look awkward. And Luc, as he'd lifted his coat from its peg, had said, "Go do your homework. I'll just be outside in the lane for a minute."

And now here we were.

I liked lanes. They felt close and embracing, like tunnels. This one had a high hedge, thickly green, on one side and the stepped concrete wall of Claudine's garden running the length of the other, with bare-branched trees standing attentively all down it, screening the view of the château's eclectic assortment of roof angles and the warm lights gleaming down from a few upstairs windows. The ground underneath us was level, a long strip of patchy green growing between the broad parallel tracks worn by car tires, so there was no reason I should have felt I was walking on something unsteady. I blamed the effects of my glass of *épine*. And the man walking next to me.

"So I've been thinking," he said as we came to the door in the wall. "If you're not busy Saturday, I thought you'd like to come with me and Noah when we go to his piano lesson. It's not very far, just up the road a bit in Carrières-sur-Seine. His teacher isn't fond of parents sitting in, she says we're too big a distraction, so while Noah takes his lesson we could have a walk around. There are some good places to walk there."

"I'd like that."

He opened the door for me, swinging it inward and into the garden. "Good night, Sara."

He started the *bise* this time, but when his mouth brushed my cheek for the second time it hovered there for a moment, and paused, and then slowly slid sideways to cover my own. I was already turning to meet it, to welcome it, loving the rush of sensation I got from that one gentle touch. Then it ceased being gentle, and I loved that, too. I was dimly aware of Luc pulling the door shut again, closing both of us back in the silence and peace of the lane, leaving both of his hands free to hold me.

Somewhere, in the middle of that still and perfect moment, wrapped in warmth, I thought: *I will remember this.*

I knew it to be true: I would remember this when other, more important things had faded from my memory. I'd remember how the evening air had breathed its cold against my cheek, and how a car had revved its engine in the unseen street behind me, and how Luc Sabran had tangled one hand in the hair behind my ear to hold my head supported while he kissed me.

I'd remember, too, the way he'd moved that same hand when the kiss had ended, combing back the curling hair along my temple with his fingers.

"Till tomorrow," was his promise, as he reached again to turn the handle of the green door in the wall, and this time when he swung it open for me I passed through and somehow crossed the lawn with less than steady steps and made it to the back door of the kitchen without once looking behind me, for I knew that if I'd stopped at all it might have been a long, long time before I'd left that lane.

CHAPTER 23

Ye sons of the chace, stand far distant…
—Macpherson, "The War of Inis-Thona"

Chalon-sur-Saône
February 18, 1732

I MUST CONFESS I KNOW not what to do with him," said Thomson.

He was speaking to the Scotsman, who was walking at his side in front of Mary and Madame Roy as they climbed the sloping road towards the citadel. Their travel in the diligence had been disrupted on the day before by one horse falling lame and forcing them to slow their pace, so when they had been meant to dine at Beaune they had not reached that place till after nightfall, and instead of reaching Chalon on the river Saône last night, they had arrived here late this morning and were now faced with the prospect of a full day's wait before they would be able to change over to the river barge—the diligence *d'eau*—that would convey them the remaining way to Lyon.

Mr. Stevens had seemed little inconvenienced by the change of plan. When he had joined them at Auxerre he clearly had not known that he was traveling alongside the same man he had been following, for otherwise he would have been a fool to speak so freely of his plans to them, but Mary felt quite certain that before that day was done he'd grown suspicious, and the comment he had made to her about the wolves at Saulieu had been proof. He'd dogged their steps all yesterday and kept close by all evening, watching them with an increasing interest Mary did not like. Which was the reason she was outdoors in the open air now, climbing to the citadel, instead of sitting with the mother and her daughters in the comfort of the new inn's parlor, by a pleasant warming fire—because both Mr. Stevens and the merchant were within the parlor also, talking politics as usual. And hunting.

Madame Roy, even fatigued from travel and the days of sickness and poor eating, climbed more strongly than did Mary and was not the least bit winded, as though she'd been bred to steep terrain. The four of them were now above the main part of the houses of the lower town, and being where they were no longer likely to be overheard so long as they spoke low, they were now briefly able to converse in English.

Thomson said, "If, as you say, he knows—"

"He knows."

"—then he does not yet feel so certain of that knowledge in his mind to rouse himself to action, else he would by now have taken me."

MacPherson merely cast a sideways look at him as though he felt it hardly needed saying that there was another reason why the Englishman had not yet tried to lay a hand on Thomson. A tall, ill-tempered, very Scottish reason.

Thomson said, "I know how you would wish to deal with him, but surely there are other ways. You cannot simply kill the man."

He fell to silence, thinking.

Madame Roy glanced sideways at the little dog in Mary's arms and smiled and said in French, "You've spoiled that beast. God gave him four legs and he never gets to use them."

Mary answered her in French as well, explaining, "Frisque

was spoiled before he came to me. I'm sure it is too late for him to be reformed." She snuggled him against her and the little spaniel licked her chin and nestled in the warm folds of her cloak.

At least the dog, she told herself, was yet a true companion and not likely to deceive or disappoint her as the others had.

She'd found it very hard today to keep up the appearance of normality. She'd kept on seeing Nicolas's eyes as they had looked on their last parting at Sir Redmond's—how he'd sworn he'd never put her in harm's way, when he'd have surely known he'd just consigned her to the keeping of a murderer, a thief, and…well, whatever Madame Roy was. Mary truly did not wish to know. The less she knew, the simpler it would be for her to keep her conscience stainless and not share their guilt.

Madame Roy observed that the dog did not look old, and Mary replied, "He is nine. He was a great pet of our neighbors' children, but last winter they fell very ill of…very ill. Two children died, as did their father."

"A most grievous loss. What was the illness?"

Mary hesitated briefly. "It was smallpox."

Madame Roy, who very clearly from the scars upon her own face had an intimate acquaintance with that illness, made no comment in reply but only nodded.

Mary told her, "After that, the mother took the three surviving children and went home to her own people, where there was no room to keep the dog."

"No room?" The older woman looked at Frisque. "But he's so very small."

"Some people," Mary said, and could not keep from glancing at the Scotsman walking silently and unaware in front of her, not understanding what she said in French, "think only of the trouble that an animal will bring them, and they do not want the burden." Which was true enough in his case. He had told her at the first she could not bring the dog. She looked away, recalling how the little dog had whimpered when her neighbors had gone off without him, and how desolate he'd been without the children. Like her father when he'd left her, none of them had looked behind—no faces peering from the windows of the coach for one last glimpse of their abandoned playmate—and when Frisque had whined and barked to call them back, it had fair broken Mary's heart and raised her own pain from that place where she had long since sought to bury it.

We do not always get the things we want.

She knew her father's words were true, and yet she pushed them down again into that grave where she'd now also buried all her brother's promises.

"To people such as those," she said, in hopes her words concealed the hurt that lay beneath them, "small things are the easiest to leave behind."

They'd nearly reached the level of the citadel, a great imposing fortress which they did not try to enter but instead, upon MacPherson's lead, ceased walking and upon a level place turned round to contemplate the view they now commanded—roofs and steeples huddled safe within the old town's walls beneath them, and the gate they had come in by, and the curving width of river with its bridges and small island, and the plain that stretched beyond that to the distant row of ridges capped with white.

After a moment, Thomson asked, "What lies beyond those hills?"

The Scotsman answered him, "Geneva. And the Alps."

"And where is Lyon?"

Nodding to the right, along the river's course, MacPherson told him, "There."

"Is there another way to travel there from here except by water?"

"Aye, but if he's close upon our heels it matters little how we go."

"So then the trick of it," said Thomson, "is to make quite sure he's not upon our heels." He gave some thought to this, and then remarked, "If you'd brought more whisky I'd have said we ought to get him drunk enough that he would lie abed too late and miss our departure in the morning, but I doubt we could at any rate persuade him not to be suspicious of a friendly drink when we are none of us too friendly with him. Nor could he be tricked into a drinking contest unless we could tempt him with a wager—and apart from my own head upon a platter I have nothing I can wager that he'd want enough to set aside his caution."

MacPherson's gaze stayed level on the distant line of mountains as he told them, very sure, "I do."

⁂

"One cannot fault the food in France," said Stevens, as he pushed his plate away from him. "And this, although no rival for our English gin, is very good indeed. What did you call it?"

At his side, the merchant named the liquor: "marc," although in proper form the *c* stayed silent so it came out simply "mar."

It was made, Mary knew, by fermenting, distilling, and aging the leftover skins, seeds, and pulp of the grapes after they had been pressed to make wine, and her uncle had prized it, but Mary did not like the taste of marc. It was too strong. When Thomson had requested and received a bottle of it from the landlord for their table, she'd declined the offer of a cup and kept instead to the plain wine they had been served with supper.

"Sometimes it is not so good," the merchant said, "but this, the Marc de Bourgogne—or of Burgundy, as you would say—it is the very best."

"A good end," Stevens praised it, "to a good meal." He drank long and studied Mary boldly while he did so.

She was now the only woman at the table, since the other two young ladies had been hastened by their mother to excuse themselves the moment that their plates were empty, pleading the long journey and tomorrow's early start as explanations for their quick retreat upstairs, though Mary knew it had been Stevens's sly persistence in attempting to lay hands upon the elder of the sisters in improper ways beneath the table that had spurred the mother into taking such an action. Madame Roy had taken supper in her room again, as had become her habit of an evening on this journey, and was up there now attending to the dog.

Mary would have much preferred to have been upstairs as well, for of the men within this room there was not one she wanted to spend time with, Thomson having lost her trust, MacPherson having earned her fear, the merchant being a great bore and an uncaring master to his servant, who had taken early to his own bed from the cough he had developed in his days of being set to travel outside on the diligence, exposed to all the worst of winter's wind and weather; and lastly Mr. Stevens, being the embodiment of everything that Mary found unpleasant.

She'd have gladly left them all and let them bear each

other's company without her interference, but she had a part to play, and with the younger of the frilly sisters gone upstairs she knew her role was even more important to the plan they'd laid in place.

"Your brother," Stevens said to Mary with the faintest stress upon the second word, "has chosen a good drink for us. Do tell him I am grateful."

Mary gave a nod to show she understood, and translating his words to French she passed them on to Thomson who was sitting to her left. Receiving Thomson's brief but courteous reply she turned that into purposely imperfect English, telling Stevens, "He is very happy you are thinking this, monsieur."

She saw a mingling of amusement and acceptance in the Englishman's expression, as though he meant her to know that he knew well this whole performance was unnecessary. "Tell me, mademoiselle, how is it you speak such good English while your brother knows it not at all?"

She borrowed from a story she'd invented once at bedtime for her cousin, and adapted it to give herself the background of the heroine. "Ah, is very sad, monsieur. Our parents, they are dead when I am very young, and so my brother has to take the business of our father, but he has no one to care for me, so I am in the convent placed. And in the convent," Mary said, "a nun from Ireland was, who teached me English."

"Did she really?"

"Yes." She hoped he did not ask her where the convent was, because she did not have a ready answer. In the fairy story she'd created, it had been in a far-off and magic land without a name, but she could hardly use that portion of the tale. "But in a few years all is well again. My brother came."

The best thing about telling stories, Mary thought, was that one could reshape them as one wished, and change the ending to a happy one. "He takes…he *took* me home."

"And where is home?" asked Stevens.

Mary faltered, but her tiny pause was neatly covered by the fact the Scotsman chose that moment to excuse himself and stand and leave the room, which actions proved enough of a distraction to the Englishman that Mary gained the time to call to mind the birthplace of that famous authoress she so admired and whom she sought to emulate: Madame d'Aulnoy. "Barneville-la-Bertran," Mary named the little village in the north of France and trusted it was small enough that Stevens would not know it.

To her great dismay the merchant said, "Ah yes, I know this place." He turned to Stevens, and in English added, "It is near Honfleur, in Normandy."

"I see." And letting his gaze slide with seeming non-chalance from Mary to the man beside her, Stevens said to Thomson, "And what is your business, sir?"

She held her breath. She almost dared not look at Thomson, fearing he would fall into the trap that had been set for him by answering in English, as he'd done before by accident, or simply by revealing he had understood the question. He did neither. With a faintly puzzled frown, he shrugged and looked to Mary, asking her in French, "What did he say?"

She breathed, and felt a mingling of relief and admiration that she smothered as she might have snuffed a candle flame, reminding herself stiffly that however kind and charming she'd found Thomson, he was not a man to be admired. He was a fraudster.

If she shielded him now it was only because she felt bound

by the pledge she had given Sir Redmond: he'd asked her to help and she'd told him she would, and whatever else happened she would not go back on her promise. Her word. She'd have little else left of her honor, she knew, if the identities and crimes of her companions were exposed. Her safety now was tied to theirs—if they were caught, there would be none who would believe she was an innocent accomplice. And by joining in their plan tonight, she knew she'd lost the right to claim full innocence.

She fixed the mask—invisible to all except herself—across her features and began to translate Stevens's last question for the benefit of Thomson. She had barely made it halfway through before the Englishman's attention was again diverted, this time by the calmly self-assured return of the tall Scotsman.

He was carrying the leather case he'd carried out of Paris—the long cylinder he'd stowed each day atop the moving diligence. The case itself was interesting. It had been made to open not along its length but round its middle, and not hinged but merely fastened on with straps and buckles so the whole top half could be detached and lifted off and set aside. He sat and did that now, revealing to them all the long and polished barrel of a gun.

"Ah, yes," said Mary, breaking off her speech as though she'd only just remembered. "Yesterday I tell my brother how you like to speak of hunting, and he thinks you might enjoy to see the gun señor Montero brings from Spain."

MacPherson had the gun out of its case now, holding it vertically balanced with one strong hand. Mary knew nothing of guns, beyond their basic structure and their function, but she didn't need to look at Mr. Stevens's face to know this one was special. A thing men would covet. It was handsomely made of some richly dark wood, with an ivory-tipped ram-rod and fine engraved scrollwork in silver and gold, and an elegant guard to the trigger.

"May I?" Stevens stretched a reverent hand towards it, and MacPherson passed it over, looking on with an impassive face as Stevens stroked one hand along the piece and said, "It has been rifled, also. Here," he told the merchant in the man-ner of a man compelled to share a great discovery, "see these spiral grooves that have been cut within the barrel? These do place a whirling action on the bullet so it spins upon its axis in its flight and so does bore the air as keenly as a screw, and travels straight and true and with prodigious speed. I have heard tell of these," he said, "but never seen one."

Mary guessed the merchant had not understood the whole of what the Englishman had said, but he too appeared capti-vated, leaning close to look at the engraving work, admiring the scrollwork of the lock.

They might have been children, thought Mary, entranced with a pretty new toy. It *was* pretty. She had a good view from her side of the table of the silver plate near the shoulder end, fancifully etched with a swan drifting past on the moat of a castle set deep amid trees. But the gilt mount at the front end of the trigger guard was cast in the shape of a wolf's head, reminding her keenly that this was designed to bring death.

Stevens, mingling praise and insult, said, "This is no Spanish gun." Looking to Thomson he asked, "Is it German?"

Again Thomson kept to his role and gave a convincingly French shrug while turning to Mary and waiting while she played *her* part in turn, doing the translating. Thomson was then free to ask the same question of Mr. MacPherson in Spanish—though Mary suspected that Thomson's command of that language did not match the Scotsman's, who when he replied sounded quite like a native. Still, with the younger of the sisters gone upstairs there was no one remaining who spoke any Spanish at all, so it was left to Thomson to turn what MacPherson had said into French, and then Mary turned that French to English, and so in this ungainly way Mr. Stevens at length got his answer.

"He wins it in Switzerland. But it is made in Vienna," said Mary.

"Wins it?" Stevens frowned a little. "Wins it how?"

Again the question went round from Mary to Thomson to Mr. MacPherson and back again. This time, when Mary paused to try to phrase her own reply a little more inexpertly, the merchant seemed to leap to the conclusion she was only being modest, and because he was a Frenchman too and understood what Thomson had just told her, he attempted to come to her aid by telling Stevens on his own: "He won it in a game of drinking."

"Ah." The war showed for an instant on his face, between his wanting to possess that rifled long gun and his grudging but pragmatic realization that MacPherson, being larger, would perhaps have the advantage in a competition.

And that instant was enough. The Scotsman spoke again to Thomson, seeming nonchalant, but there was something in his tone that sounded rather like an insult of his own. And so it was.

"He says," said Mary, when the words had come to her through Thomson, "this gun is for the brave, and this is why he wins it. It is not a gun for cowards. He says one day maybe someone comes who proves himself to be…" She knew the phrase, but for the purpose of disguising her abilities she turned now to the merchant and repeated it in French and asked for his advice in choosing English words.

The merchant had grown slightly flushed and seemed a bit uncomfortable with what was yet to come, but still he told her, "I would say, 'the best,' or no, 'the better man.'"

She nodded. "Yes. The better man." Returning her attention to the Englishman, she added in her sweetest tone, "And he does not believe, monsieur, that you will be this man."

A flash of something dangerous was there and gone so rapidly in Mr. Stevens's eyes that if it had not also raised a dark flush on his cheekbones Mary would have thought it had been but imagined. He passed the rifled gun into the Scotsman's hands without so much as glancing at him. Then with slow, deliberate movements he reached for the bottle of the strong, fierce-tasting Marc de Bourgogne. He filled MacPherson's glass, and then his own, and turning to MacPherson raised his own glass in a mocking gesture.

"Well, then," he said, and with his gaze locked upon the Scotsman's, drained his glass and set it with a thump upon the table in an open challenge. "May the best man win."

Chapter 24

I am in the land of strangers, where is my friend…?
—Macpherson, "The Battle of Lora"

On the Saône
February 19, 1732

THE GUN WAS IN its customary place amid the baggage of the diligence *d'eau* when they set out next morning for their journey down the river Saône, but Mr. Stevens had mysteriously vanished.

"It is odd," the merchant said, as though still trying to make sense of it. "I'd formed the strong impression he was bound, as we were, for Lyon. It was indeed most fortunate that when we helped him to his room we spied that note upon the table and so learned he'd booked his passage on the coach this morning for Dijon, for as it was we had but barely half an hour to get him onto it. And it was fortunate also that señor Montero was not in the condition Mr. Stevens was, for even with my man to help it took the three of us together to convey him with his baggage to the coaching yard. 'Tis no small feat to move a man when he is all but senseless. I fear," the merchant added, "he will have a rough day's journey, but at least when he awakes he will be where he planned to be."

He spoke in French now, for with Stevens gone there was no longer any need for him to speak in English, so his words would have been lost on the tall Scotsman sitting now across from Mary; though from how MacPherson sat with his eyes closed, his head resting carefully against the wall at his back, she was not at all sure he'd have paid much attention at any rate.

The movement of the diligence *d'eau* could not have helped. The river had an undulating current that was proving to have much the same effect on Madame Roy as had their travel over hilly roads by land, which had made Mary wonder why the older woman had been chosen to accompany them, given she could not have harbored any love of traveling.

This diligence upon the river was, to Mary's mind, more pleasant than the one that went by road. In form it was a long and shallow barge, towed from the riverbank by horses with a driver, while on board another bargeman did the steering with a pole. The covered cabin, pleasantly appointed with long benches for the seating, had glass windows all around that gave a view of the scenery slipping away to each side, which in a better season might have been quite beautiful but now was half-obscured by a thick dewy mist that hung above the riverbank and fields.

The merchant's servant was at least allowed to sit within-doors for this section of the voyage and was huddled now at his end of the bench across from Madame Roy. He looked a mirror image of her misery, his cough grown deep enough to rattle in his chest alarmingly and make the mother of the daughters look at him with disapproval.

Turning that same disapproving look upon the Scotsman now, the mother said, "It is a most disgraceful vice, to drink for sport. I'm glad I was not there to see it. And I do hope you," she said to Mary, "did not have to see it either."

Mary reassured her she'd seen little of the drinking contest beyond its beginning. "I went early to my bed. I had a headache."

She had claimed that headache first because it had been prearranged within their plan that she should do so, once the contest had begun, to give a proper cause for Thomson to remove himself until the threat from Stevens had been dealt with. And once Thomson had escorted her upstairs and gone along to his own room and she'd been left with Madame Roy, the still-pretended headache had become a way for Mary to avoid the need to enter into conversation.

Mary had not wished to talk to Madame Roy, nor to the others. She had played the part they'd asked of her and wanted to do no more after that but get to Lyon, where she hoped their journey would be at an end and she would be released and then…

And then what? Mary did not know. She had no money and no friends here, and her brother and Sir Redmond having happily abandoned her to such an expedition could now hardly be relied upon to offer her a rescue.

In all the years she'd yearned for an adventure, she had not dreamed that when one finally did arrive, she'd find herself so ill equipped to meet it. In the darkness of her room last night, curled lonely in her bed with Frisque a sleeping weight upon her feet, she'd closed her eyes and felt the slow, despairing tears come anyway.

She'd felt the mattress dip as Madame Roy had sat beside her, and a cool and soothing hand had stroked the hair back from her forehead, lending sympathy. "The best thing for a headache is to sleep," the older woman had advised, and Mary, mastering her tears, had kept her eyes tight shut and nodded.

Madame Roy, she knew, was one of those involved in keeping secrets from her, and so not deserving of her trust, but while she did not want to like the older woman there was something in that touch upon her forehead that brought comfort.

Mary's voice had sounded very small when she had said to Madame Roy, "My mother used to do that."

And the older woman, giving no reply, had gone on stroking Mary's hair back from her forehead, very gently, till the blissful dark forgetfulness of sleep had finally claimed her.

She had woken to discover that, perhaps in retribution, her pretended headache had become a very real one. It had worsened as the morning had progressed and felt like steady pounding hammers at her temples now.

The Scotsman likely had a headache also, Mary judged from how he kept so still and silent, but she could not muster any thoughts of pity for him. Nor had her own feelings of self-pity long survived the break of day, when they had yielded to a quiet growing anger deep inside her that seemed driven by the cheerful conversation Mr. Thomson had been having with the merchant just as much as by the dull and throbbing pain within her head.

He had no right to be cheerful, Mary thought, no more than any of them had a right to use her thus—not Nicolas, nor yet Sir Redmond, nor the three who traveled with her now. She had no reason to feel sorrowful; no reason to despair or weep. They were the ones who had transgressed, and if she was yet bound to keep their company, she was not bound to pay them any more than common courtesy—to speak when she was spoken to, and play the role assigned to her until they came to Lyon, when she'd find some means to part with them.

She felt a rising confidence in that resolve. She was no child, to be required to always follow orders. She was nearly twenty-two years old, a woman. Mistress Jamieson could not have been her senior by more than a few years, after all, and she had found resourcefulness enough to cross the Channel on her own and in disguise, upon an errand that was certainly as daring as the one that Mary faced, and full as dangerous.

Frisque stirred upon her lap and turned a circle and lay down again, himself a little out of sorts. He wanted room to run, she knew. She patted him and rumpled his soft ears and said, "Be patient."

At her side the younger of the daughters said, "He's very well behaved, your dog. I long have wanted one myself, only Maman will not allow it. See, Maman, how sweet he is?"

Her mother said, "Yes, very sweet. But dogs may not be put into a cupboard when you tire of them, with all your other playthings."

"That is most unfair," the younger daughter countered. "I am nearly seventeen, and not a child."

"When you are married and it is your husband's problem, you may have a dog," her mother promised.

"I should prefer a dog," the younger daughter told her, "to a husband."

Her mother thought that foolish. "Every girl does need a husband to take care of her; to love her and protect her. What do you think, Monsieur Robillard?"

The question interrupted Thomson in his conversation with the merchant, but he took it in his stride and turning asked, "I beg your pardon?"

"Would you not wish to see your sister marry well?"

The fact that such a thought had never crossed his mind was plainly written on his features as he sought to frame the proper answer, none too certain of the conversation he was being asked to join.

The mother pressed him further, "You would surely not

desire she should be always your companion, with no chance to know the joys of being someone's wife."

"No," he said, "I—"

"Truly," said the mother, with a knowing air, "I do suspect you'll one day find your noble friend, the good Chevalier de Vilbray, has stolen her away from you, for as I do perceive he has already claimed her heart."

The elder daughter, who'd been saddened earlier that morning by the loss of Mr. Stevens in their company, revived now with a wistful smile. "He'd certainly lay claim to mine," she said, "if he behaved to me as gallantly as he has done to Mademoiselle Robillard. Come, mademoiselle, do share another story of your handsome chevalier and his adventures, for the morning is a dreary one and all of us need cheering."

Mary felt little inclined to tell stories, but neither did she want to spread her own ill mood to those who had no part in causing it. Pushing the pain of her headache aside, she started to weave a new tale of a voyage on which her invented Chevalier de Vilbray—who now had grown taller as well as more chivalrous than his original—found himself traveling with villains and thieves who intended him harm. It was one of her most inspired stories and filled with excitement and intrigue, and when it had finished the mother and daughters and even the merchant were rapt with attention and greatly impressed.

"Well!" The mother leaned back as she let out the breath she'd been holding. "Your friend the chevalier is certainly one of the bravest of men."

"Yes," said Mary. "He is."

At her side, the young sister had taken a pencil and paper from out of her pocket and was noting down the key points of the story. "My aunt," she explained, "will be highly diverted by this when I write to her next. You don't mind if I tell her?"

"Of course not." Her tale finished, Mary was just on the point of allowing her own eyes to close when she stopped. Her aunt… "Do you write to your aunt very often?"

"Oh, yes. She is widowed, you see, and has little in life to amuse her, and when we are traveling she finds it lonely to not have us near, so I write little letters and post them whenever I can. I shall send her the next from Lyon."

"Very kind of you," Mary acknowledged, but absently, her own mind traveling now on a new course of thought. *Her* Aunt Magdalene and Uncle Jacques were not wealthy, but were she to write them a letter they surely could manage the small price that they'd have to pay to receive it. And were she to ask for their aid they'd be sure to do what they were able to do to assist her.

Lyon was no village, she knew, but a city—much larger than any of the places they'd stopped before this. If Mary could get to a church and a priest she could make her confession and still keep her oath to Sir Redmond. A priest would not put Mr. Thomson in danger, because being bound by the sanctity of the confessional, he'd be unable to pass on the details of what Mary told him; yet having once heard those same details, a priest would most certainly also be bound, at the risk of her soul, to protect her from further exposure to vice. She could ask for protection until Uncle Jacques could arrange for her safe return to Chanteloup-les-Vignes.

Hope found a small fertile place to take root in her heart.

As if sensing the change in her mood, Frisque grew restless again. He turned thrice in her lap this time, pawed at her skirts, and then suddenly gathered his haunches and leaped from her lap to the knee of the Scotsman across from her. Mr. MacPherson's strong leg did not look like a comfortable bed for the dog, but Frisque turned round and settled upon it decidedly, tucking his nose firmly under his paws.

Mary had at first been too surprised to react, but before she could lean forward and retrieve the dog the Scotsman's hand descended on Frisque's back and stayed at rest there, holding him securely. To anyone who had no notion of MacPherson's nature, such a gesture might have seemed to be protective and endearing, but to Mary's eyes it was but an example of the Scotsman's way of keeping everything around him firmly under his control.

And although Frisque had not the sense to feel uncomfortable beneath that hold, for Mary it was growing more important to break free of it.

&

She wrote the letter late that night, when they had stopped to sup and sleep at Mâcon. Madame Roy had grown accustomed to the sight of Mary writing in her journal and made no remark upon it when she took herself to bed. And when the older woman's breathing slowed and deepened into slumber, Mary dipped her quill into fresh ink and on a new page wrote a careful message to her aunt and uncle, ever mindful that her letter, once she'd sent it, would be passed from hand to hand and might be read by unintended eyes, particularly as it must be carried close by Saint-Germain-en-Laye, which was, as Mistress Jamieson had warned her, "full of prying eyes and those who love exposing secrets."

Notwithstanding that, she could not write in cipher, for her aunt and uncle would not know the key to it. She could but choose her words with purpose, hoping they would look between the cheerful lines and see the desperation that had driven her to write them.

I pray you do not tell my brother, she included, taking the contrite tone of a child who had been warned against a course of action and who'd acted anyway and viewed that rash decision with regret; although her aunt and uncle would of course know that was not the truth of what had happened— *for he will be justly disappointed*.

She kept her obligation to her brother and Sir Redmond and did not give any details of her traveling companions; did not even tell their number. All she wrote was:

I am told that at Lyon we will be finished with our journey, and I will be most content to stay and wait for your arrival.

But wait where? she wondered. Lyon was a large place, and although the merchant, having been there many times before, had obliged her by describing several of the major sights he thought she should not miss, she still had no idea where she would be lodged, or what the nearest church might be where she could seek to make confession to a priest and beg protection.

For a moment Mary hesitated, sifting in her memory through the places that the merchant had described, and then she dipped her quill in ink again and carried on:

I understand there is a great cathedral at Lyon, named for Saint John the Baptist. I intend to make my way there and petition for assistance from the priests, who will, I trust, be able to direct you where I may be found.

There, she thought. That should suffice. Her page was nearly full now, and she closed her letter simply.

You will find me greatly changed and none the better for my travels, I do fear, but not so changed that I am yet prevented from remaining your most faithful and sincerely loving niece,

She signed her name and tore the page with great care from her journal. Then she folded it and sealed it and addressed it and secreted it between the pages of her journal while she finished her long entry for that day and evening.

There the letter stayed all through the night, till the next morning when she rose a little earlier than was her custom, and with the excuse of taking Frisque out for his necessary business, went downstairs alone.

She had observed the mother and her daughters wakened early, and this morning Mary was in hopes of finding some brief chance of speaking to the younger daughter and of asking her in private, as a favor, if she'd carry Mary's letter with her own and post it when they reached Lyon.

There'd be small opportunity for Mary, once they'd reached that place, to post a letter—she was not even certain she would have the chance to seize this one small moment on her own this morning—but the younger sister had a most romantic nature, and if she believed that she was helping Mary keep a secret correspondence with the mythical Chevalier de Vilbray, she might agree to take the letter.

Mary had her story all arranged: how the chevalier had declared his love, and begged that she should write to him, and told her to address her letters to another name so their affair could be kept private, and had warned her to on no account expose them to her "brother," lest he disapprove. She'd made the story pretty in her mind with several flourishes, but in the end she did not get to tell it after all, because the younger daughter was already occupied.

"Good morning," was the greeting that she brightly gave to Mary. She was sitting at a table in the little public salon of the coaching inn, a pewter cup of chocolate set before her with a plate of toasted bread, both pushed aside to make room for a dainty silver watch that lay in several pieces on the weathered wooden tabletop. The largest piece, to Mary's great surprise, was firmly held within the strong efficient fingers of the Scotsman. Sitting in the chair beside the youngest of the daughters, with her mother and her sister looking on from their position on the sofa by the hearth, he was calmly and methodically assembling the pieces of the watch with the assistance of a small-edged knife, and aided by the light of a tall candle.

He did not rise, as would a gentleman, when Mary took a step into the room, although the women from their seats paid her the customary honors with their gracious nods and greetings.

"You were quite right," the younger daughter said. "Señor Montero is not fierce at all. He's very kind. The pin of Maman's equipage broke on the stairs this morning and her watch was dropped, and truly she was desolate, but as you see he's offered to restore it."

Mary did not wear an equipage—that partly useful, partly ornamental bit of jewelry for the waist, with chains that held a whole array of trinkets: little jars of smelling salts, and sewing scissors, and, as often was the case, a watch. This one seemed far too tiny for MacPherson's fingers, but he deftly set the pieces back in place and with a final turning of his knife, clicked shut the glass and gave the watch a final wind and fastened both the key and watch again onto their chains and passed them to the younger daughter, who replied in Spanish with what sounded like effusive thanks and in her turn presented the repaired equipage to her mother, saying, "There, you see? It is as Mademoiselle Robillard assured us: señor Montero is a man of many talents."

"Indeed he is," her mother granted, in a tone that was not ready to forgive him all, "though he does keep those talents hidden well behind that most unpleasant face of his."

"Maman!" The younger daughter shot a glance towards MacPherson but he'd missed their whole exchange and was now sitting back and stretching out his shoulders slightly as though sitting working on the watch had left them stiff. The knife, Mary noticed, had already disappeared. To where, she knew not; although she was starting to think if he turned out his pockets they'd be full of nothing but blades, some more deadly than others.

He looked at her then, and before he could guess at her thoughts Mary masked her expression, not letting him see how she felt. But the truth was, she knew that her chance had been ruined. The diligence *d'eau* would depart in an hour, and the others were up now and coming for breakfast. She heard Thomson's voice on the stairs.

Inspiration struck suddenly. She held Frisque close against her midriff, close against the letter that was lying flat and snug between her stomacher and stays, and smiling at the younger sister used the same excuse that Mistress Jamieson had used to draw her out from crowded company. "My dog," she said, "needs to be taken outdoors. Come and walk with me."

CHAPTER 25

A PAGE HAD BEEN TORN from the diary. It had been done cleanly and carefully, close to the binding, without having any effect I could see on the day's entry, which ran from the page before into the following page without breaking:

...and though we are relieved of Mr. Stevens for the moment, his diversion to Dijon will put him but two days behind us, and perhaps not even that if he can find a private boatman to convey him down the river. Mr. M——, although pretending sleep, did not relax his guard all day and even now is up and walking in the next room, keeping watch, which is I gather meant to ease our worries but in my case does the opposite. He seems to never sleep as would an ordinary man, but Mr. M——, for all his faults, is far from ordinary. Were I free to tell a proper fairy tale I'd cast him as an ogre, but the tales I have been telling have no magic in them, so I could do no more than depict him as the surly captain of the guard who stood at the town gate and was defeated by my brave Chevalier.

She had written down the story, all of it, just as she'd told it to her fellow travelers on the diligence *d'eau* that day, and I'd transcribed it faithfully although I couldn't see how it would be of use to Alistair.

"She does this more and more as she goes on," I told Denise. "She makes up stories."

"They're good stories," was her judgment. I had finished reading two of them to her while she was busily assembling her *galette des rois*—the king cake for Epiphany—while I sat at the table in the kitchen being no help whatsoever, drinking coffee and complaining.

"Yes, well, sometimes they're so good I don't know if the people she's talking about are real or not. And they take as much time to decipher and transcribe as do her proper diary entries, so really I'd be happier if she'd just left them out."

"Perhaps she meant to publish them someday." She was beating the eggs for the frangipane filling now, having already rolled out the first round of her homemade puff pastry. "You said she was hoping to visit a Paris salon in her time there, yes?"

I had to think. "Yes, she mentioned it when they were first getting settled in Paris, how wonderful it would be if she could go to that salon. I'd have to look it up."

"Well, this is what the women did at that time, in salons. They told their stories. And the fairy tales for some years before that were very popular. It's obvious she read them and admired them, from the name she gave the villain in her last tale."

"Monsieur Furibon?"

"Yes, that name is from a fairy tale, a famous one by the Countess d'Aulnoy, called 'Prince Ariel.' The villain is a wicked prince named Furibon."

"I don't think I've ever heard that one."

"Well, these are not the fairy tales that we grew up with. These were written for adults, and they belonged to a distinct period of time, and a distinct group of writers, nearly all of them women of the noble class. It was a clever and subversive thing they did, to tell these fairy tales. Sometimes they would take well-known tales from folklore and adapt them, but as often they created them from their imaginations, and you see how they are commenting on how life is around them, on the world and how it limits them." She folded the ground almonds in and stirred all to a flawless paste. "The heroines of these fairy tales, their lives are often dictated by overbearing men—by their fathers and their suitors, kings and princes whom they must outwit and guard themselves against, and the fairies who helped them were usually female, and powerful. They're very feminist, these stories."

"Which is probably," I said, "why we don't hear of them."

She smiled. "Yes, very likely. There were men in these salons, too. Charles Perrault—you know, the writer of 'The Sleeping Beauty'? He was always with these women. His own niece had a salon, a very famous one. But where her princesses were strong and stood up for their rights, her uncle's heroines were meek and weak and beautiful, and needing to be rescued."

"So why," I asked, "did his stories survive all this time, while hers haven't?"

"Because he was a man. And because the society those women skewered with their stories was just as quick to skewer them for their success, for being popular. It happens still today, I think. But those women, those writers," she said, "they were really the start of the genre we now would call fantasy. Their fairy tales were not meant to be read on their own, in the way we now think of a fairy tale—they were woven into novels, into memoirs, and intended to reflect the larger themes and stories in those books. So really," she concluded, "what this girl who keeps the diary, Mary Dundas, what she's doing is a part of that tradition. She's creating, in a way, a travel memoir, and the little stories she creates are just another part of that. You can't just read them on their own, that's like trying to listen to the words of an opera without the music—you're only getting half the effect. You have to look at them in context. Like this last one, where she has her hero having to escape from his pursuers and outwit the evil merchant. I would think she's working out her own plans how to leave these people, wouldn't you? Whether she can do it or not, it's what she's wishing for, and so she puts it all into that story."

I'd never thought of it that way before. "So then she's the chevalier, when she tells these tales?"

"That's what I think." Denise filled her piping bag carefully, gave it a twist at the top, and began to pipe almond paste onto the puff pastry, filling the king cake.

I watched her with interest, wondering how she'd developed such a detailed knowledge of such a curious subject. In the end, I simply asked her.

With a shrug she said, "I wrote a paper on it once, at university. I loved studying literature, back then. I planned to one day teach it."

"Really?" That surprised me.

"Really. But I never finished university."

"Why not?" I asked. "What happened?"

"Noah happened." Glancing over, she took one look at my face and added, "No, it's fine. I didn't mind. I could have gone back afterwards and finished, but by then I'd stumbled into doing this." She spread her hands, the gesture taking in the whole room. "When I was younger I always worked summers for my aunt and uncle at their hotel, I enjoyed it. And soon after Noah was born one of Luc's friends was starting a restaurant and needed some help with the cooking, so I said I'd help. I enjoyed that, as well. And then one of the waiters, his mother came out of the hospital and needed someone to help cook and clean for her, so…" She shrugged again, turning to roll out more pastry. "I like this. I'm happy."

"But you might have been happy," I pointed out, "being a teacher."

"It's possible. But we all change, you know? When other people come into our lives, our priorities change. This is perfect for Noah," she said, "this arrangement. He comes home at lunch if he likes, and I'm here when he gets home from school, and I'm here on the days that he's ill."

I'd never had to arrange my own life around somebody else's routine, or their needs, so I thought about this for a moment. When I had been Noah's age, I'd gone next door to my neighbors most days after school and had stayed there till either my mother or father had come home from work. It had never occurred to me that, for those few years, my parents had probably had to arrange that, to make sure that I was looked after, since I'd been too young to be left on my own in the house for so long. Just like Noah. "So where does he go after school on the weeks that he lives with his father?" He didn't come here, I knew.

"This is a Wednesday," Denise said, "so Luc will be working from home. On the other days, Noah goes to play at a friend's house. His best friend, Michelle. They're like this." She held up two fingers pressed tightly together. "She's quite a character, Michelle. You'll see that when you meet her."

I sometimes found it hard to keep pace with the easy way she shifted subjects. "I'm meeting Noah's best friend? When?"

"It will be soon, I would imagine. Noah likes when all the people in his life know one another." She looked at her hands for a moment and frowned and crossed over to where I sat, holding her hand out to show me the jumble of tiny and colorful ceramic figurines. By tradition, the *galette des rois* had a single *fève* hidden inside it—the French word for "bean." In the old days, I gathered, it had been an actual bean, but as time had gone on it had slowly evolved to a small figurine. In the king cakes that I had been served at my neighbors' house during my childhood, the *fève* they'd used year after year had been Mickey Mouse, which I'd adored. And I'd twice found the *fève* in my own piece of cake, meaning I'd been the "queen" for the dinner that year, and been able to wear the gold foil card crown Ricky's mother kept tucked in a drawer, and had chosen my "king"—always Ricky, of course, out of loyalty—and for those few hours had felt very special.

Denise asked, "Which of these should I put in the king cake for Noah?" There must have been more than a dozen *fèves* cupped in her hand. "I have two little robots, a blue and a red one, or else there's this soldier. Which one do you think—?"

"The cat," I said. "It looks just like Diablo."

"So it does. I didn't even notice him. All right, then, it's the cat."

I watched her take the little figurine and press it gently down into the filling of the king cake before fitting on the final round of pastry. "But how," I asked, "can you be certain that Noah will get that piece?"

"I just do this." She was marking out shapes on the top of the cake with the tines of a fork, and she made a small extra mark over the spot where she'd hidden the *fève*.

"Oh." It made me think back to my childhood again, to the things that I'd thought had been random that actually weren't.

"I've been thinking," Denise said. "This girl with the

diary, this Mary Dundas. You said that before her brother brought her here to Chatou, she was living with her aunt and uncle, yes? And not her parents?"

"Yes. I think, from how she writes about her mother, that her mother's dead."

"Which means her father also must be dead, or else he's left her for some reason with her aunt and uncle. And her brother, now he's also left her." With the cake set to the side, she started tidying the worktop, clearing all the small unwanted scraps away. "There's a thing, you know, when children are abandoned by the people that they love. It's psychological. They start to feel they can't be very lovable, that nobody will want them as they are, and so they try to act like someone who they're not. Maybe her stories are a part of this."

I hadn't considered that, either. "You studied psychology, too?"

Smiling, she said, "No. But Luc, when his mother left, he had some trouble adjusting." She'd lost me again, only this time she noticed it, backtracking to explain: "She's an American, Luc's mother. From California. When Luc's older brother was fourteen he went to a school in America, so she went with him, and Luc stayed in France with his father. They didn't divorce, they were still all one family, but for a few years they were separate. And Luc, he was only twelve when she first left, and it wasn't so easy for him."

I was trying to follow along and make sense of this, feeling the sadness that Luc must have felt when his mother and brother had left, and attempting to draw the connection to Mary Dundas and her stories. "Did Luc act like someone he wasn't, then?"

"Oh, yes." Bending, Denise slid the king cake into the

oven of the old enameled cooker and shut the door with a decided clang before she straightened. "He turned into a tough guy. Always making trouble."

"Luc?"

"I know. He's such an easygoing person, right? Such a good man. But when we were teenagers, to those who didn't know him well, he was this very dark, bad boy."

"*Luc?*"

With a nod she poured a cup of coffee for herself and held the pot up. "More?"

"Yes, please."

She came to join me at the table. "In the end, I think it was just too exhausting for him, to pretend to be this other kind of person. People can't pretend forever."

She was talking about Luc, and maybe Mary, and I gathered from the way her voice pitched downwards on those final words that they were meant to be a statement, not to ask a question, so I only gave a nod and didn't comment. But if it *had* been a question, I could easily and from my own experience have given her the answer:

Yes, they can.

❧

I looked for some hint of the dangerous bad boy remaining behind Luc's blue eyes, but I just couldn't see it. I'd met his gaze several times over the course of the dinner, and from where I sat I could see the whole corner behind him where both walls were covered with framed family photographs, some very old and some recent and some showing Luc as a teenager, and even in the one where he was staring out unsmiling with his arms crossed he still looked like himself. He must have been either much angrier then or a very good actor to make anybody believe he was capable of doing anything stronger than mischief.

The photographs, all on their own, shone a light on the things that Luc valued. They crossed generations but focused on parents and large groups of children at picnics and sports days and holidays, everyone gathered in much the same way we were now in Luc's dining room. It was a cozier room than the one at Claudine's house. The table was neither as grand nor as long, and the food rather simpler than dishes Denise might have made, but the chicken was nice and the wine tasted good and the warm conversation was easy to follow and I felt included and very content.

"Don't you dare," Luc was telling Denise, though his grin undermined his own warning. "The boy is too young to be hearing these stories."

"He already knows you're not perfect."

"Yes, but you don't need to tell him all the crazy things I did. He might try doing them himself."

Claudine said, "Luc, that drawing in the gold frame, just behind you. Is that new? I don't remember ever seeing it before."

He nodded, taking up the wine bottle to refill all our glasses. "Yes, it was my Christmas present from my father's aunt. She's moving house and getting rid of many of her things, and she remembered how I always loved this drawing, and the story that went with it. But *that*," he said to Noah, "is another story you're too young to hear."

"Why?" Noah asked.

"It's very tragic, very sad."

Claudine asked, "Who's the man?"

Luc told her, "Jean-Philippe de Sabran, the uncle of my

great-grandfather's great-grandfather. He fought in the Seven Years' War, in America."

Noah had leaned forward in his chair, expectant, waiting for the story, but Luc stopped it there.

"Papa!"

"There's no 'Papa' about it. That's all I can tell you till you're older," Luc explained. "Except to say there's a museum in New York that keeps his sword in a display, and this"—he nodded to the portrait—"this was drawn by a young woman, an American, who loved him."

Claudine was looking at the drawing. "It's really well done, for an amateur artist."

I followed her gaze and I had to agree. It was beautifully rendered in ink that had faded to sepia tones on the plain ivory paper, and had a partly unfinished look as though the artist had been more intent on capturing the moment than the details.

Claudine said, "It's very lifelike. I would know this man, I think, were I to pass him on the street. And I would like him. She is showing us his character, his heart, the girl who drew this, and by doing that she lets us see her heart, as well. I can believe she loved him."

When she said that, I lost interest in the portrait and instead began a study of Claudine. She looked, as always, effort-lessly elegant in simple black, her dark hair with its strands of tinsel gray caught back and coiled at her nape to hold its more strong-minded waves contained. I found her difficult to read. She never seemed to show the obvious expressions on her face that let me know how she was feeling. When she smiled it was a smaller movement that might have been sad or insincere or truly happy, I was never sure. I wondered now, from what she'd said about the artist showing us her

heart, whether Claudine let her own emotions show more
clearly through the photographs she took. And that in turn
made me reflect upon the portrait I had seen of Alistair in
Claudine's upstairs studio, and what that picture had to say
about her private feelings.

I found it an interesting thought, so absorbing I wasn't
aware I'd withdrawn myself from the whole conversation
until it slowly filtered through my consciousness that plates
were clinking as Luc cleared them. I blinked hard to free my
senses from the fog that always followed hyperfocus. If Jacqui
had been with me she would have brought me right out of it
when she first saw me beginning to slide, as she always did,
saying my name before anyone noticed. I had to admit this
was nicer, though, and much less jarring to simply come out
of it all on my own.

"You were daydreaming," Noah informed me. He turned
to his father and asked, "Can we pull out the kings now?"

I'd never been part of this ritual as an adult. At my neighbors' house, because I'd been the same age as my friend
Ricky, we'd both shared the distinction of being the youngest ones present, and so every year we'd dived under the table
the same way that Noah did now, settling in to decide in a
random way who got which piece of the cake.

Claudine, as the eldest, was put into service as cake cut-
ter, setting each piece on its plate and then waiting till Noah
called out from below to say who should receive it. Even
without Denise's mark on top, the piece meant for Noah
was simple to spot from the gleam of the porcelain *fève*,
clearly visible, stuck at the filling's cut edge. Claudine deftly
maneuvered the plates to make certain that piece went to
Noah, but when he scrambled up into his seat again and
saw the cake upon his plate, he didn't look as happy as

I'd thought he would. In fact, his eyebrows drew together slightly in a frown.

It didn't last. He quickly pointed at the wall behind his father's head and said to me, "See, there's a picture of me as a baby."

I turned my head to look, and when I did, he switched our plates.

I was aware of him doing it—he had to lean across the table and there was a fair amount of clinking—but I could also see everyone smiling, and Denise winked and made a great production of directing my attention to another of the photographs, by which I understood I was supposed to make believe I *hadn't* seen the switch. I did my best to play along, and when I "found" the *fève* and feigned surprise, the look of joy on Noah's face made all of my pretending seem worthwhile.

The paper crown they brought for me to wear brought memories with it: me at six years old, or seven maybe, sitting at the table at my neighbors' at Epiphany, the Mickey Mouse *fève* on my plate, the foil card crown upon my head…

"You have to choose your king," Claudine said.

There were only two males at the table, and it really was no contest. Luc might be the one I fancied, but his son was sitting looking at me, leaning slightly forward in his chair the way my cousin did whenever she was waiting with impatience, or with hope.

So I chose Noah.

Luc seemed fine with that. He told his son—and he was smiling when he said it, so I knew he wasn't actually resentful—"I thought *I* was Sara's favorite."

"I'm sure she likes you, Papa," Noah reassured his father, using both hands to adjust his own gold paper crown, the handmade match to mine. "But like I told you, *I'm* the one who helps her best."

CHAPTER 26

Soon shall my voice be heard no more,
and my footsteps cease to be seen.
—Macpherson, "Fingal," Book Five

Lyon
February 21, 1732

THERE WAS NO WANT of helping hands to meet them on the quayside at Lyon. The diligence *d'eau* had barely settled in its berth along the river wall when it was all but overrun by men who came aboard with the audacity of pirates and proceeded to behave as though they had already been engaged as porters for the baggage. One, a burly man with a red waistcoat, took the merchant's luggage in his meaty hands and started off at such a pace the merchant had to scurry to keep up with him, and two younger and more wiry men began to jostle one another for the trunk and bags belonging to the mother with her daughters. But Thomson kept hold of his deal-box and Mr. MacPherson took charge of their two portmanteaus and the case with his long gun inside, and his unsmiling face and unyielding appearance proved more than enough to discourage the would-be assistants from seeking to deal with him.

With so many cases slung over his shoulders he should have looked heavily laden, but he stood as straight as he always did, moving with ease. In three strides he crossed the broad plank that the boatman had laid from the deck of the diligence onto the quay. Mary, walking behind him, was not so sure-footed and wobbled somewhat at the end, but she quickly recovered and clutching Frisque close to her chest stepped off onto the quay without needing MacPherson's help.

It was a foolish thing, really, to shrink from his touch. And decidedly rude to ignore the hand he held outstretched, but she felt less than civil towards him today, and with cause: he had spoiled her chances this morning of passing her letter as planned to the younger of the frilly sisters. Although the young woman had accepted Mary's invitation after breakfast to come out and walk with her and Frisque, their freedom had been limited by Thomson's warning to stay within sight of the inn, and by his assigning MacPherson to go with them for their protection.

The Scotsman, to Mary's eyes, hadn't seemed keen to leave Thomson alone when the Englishman might yet be coming behind them, but there had been no room to argue that morning, not with the younger sister understanding Spanish and MacPherson being kept by his disguise from speaking English, so he'd had to merely frown and rise reluctantly and go along while Thomson had advised them, "There are rogues aplenty in a town like this, and never can young women be too guarded."

Mary might have disagreed with that. She'd felt distinctly over-guarded strolling in the younger sister's company outside the inn along the river, with MacPherson walking just behind them. He had kept two paces back and been discreet, but she'd been ever conscious of his watchful presence, and she'd known there'd be no hope of handing off her letter to the younger woman without him observing it. Still, she knew MacPherson, even if he understood a word or two of French, had not the depth of understanding to be privy to their conversation, so she had made use of that. And as she'd hoped, the younger sister had found Mary's claim of thwarted love for the Chevalier de Vilbray to be romantic.

"Oh, you poor thing," she'd told Mary. "Can your brother not be reasoned with?"

"My brother," Mary had replied, "is quite a different man from what he seems, I am afraid."

"What will you do?"

"I have a letter." She had felt it in her pocket as she'd spoken, though she'd dared not draw it forth. "I have poured my very heart into it, and if I can but find some means to send it from Lyon, at least my gallant chevalier will be assured I've not forgotten him."

"Why, *I* can send the letter for you."

"Would you? That would be most kind." She'd tried to sound surprised, as though this had not been her own design from the beginning. "I would give it to you now, but I do fear señor Montero would inform my brother."

Glancing back, the younger sister had remarked to Mary, "*He* is not a man, I'll warrant, who would know or understand the agonies of love."

The devil had pricked mischief into Mary's heart then, and she'd said, "Oh, you are wrong. He loved a woman once with all his being, but..." She'd paused then, and pretended great reluctance to divulge the tale, but actually she'd used the pause to call to mind the details of Madame d'Aulnoy's fairy tale about the Russian prince who'd sought the fabled Isle of Happiness, where lived a magic princess and her court. Of course they fell in love and lived in perfect happiness three hundred years, until the prince had ruined things, which seemed the perfect story to reshape to fit a man such as MacPherson.

"But?" The younger woman's eagerness to hear the story had shone in her eyes, and Mary had obliged, then added:

"It ended most unhappily. This woman had a beautiful estate, where they might both have lived in comfort and contentment all their lives, but he was restless there and went to seek his fame upon the battlefield, and so chose honor over love." She'd paused again, for in the fairy tale the Russian prince was killed, but her invented story obviously could not have that ending. "When he finally did return, he found the gates of her estate forever barred to him."

"Is that why he has come away from Spain and into France?"

Mary had nodded and had neatly turned the tale back to her purpose. "And I fear the same might happen if I cannot reassure my dear chevalier that he has not lost *my* love. If I can pass the letter to you while I'm traveling, I will. If not, perhaps we could contrive to meet tomorrow, at the great cathedral in Lyon. The one that was described to us."

"The one with the celestial clock? Of course. Maman is keen to see it anyway, it will be no great trouble to persuade her we should go there. But your brother…"

"My brother will surely permit me to hear the Mass."

Frisque had concluded his business and lifting his nose from the ground sniffed the wind with a wag of his tail before turning to lead them all back by the way they had come, trotting cheerfully past the tall Scotsman who'd stopped for the moment to let them pass by him, and then had turned with them and fallen in step at their backs as before.

The younger sister had frowned faintly. "I suppose it is as Maman says: we cannot know what people truly are by their appearance. I would not have guessed your brother was a tyrant. Nor would I have guessed señor Montero had endured a tragic love affair." She'd chanced another backward glance towards MacPherson, walking with his long coat swinging and his hat pulled low. "Perhaps," she'd said to Mary, "that is why he writes such sentimental poetry."

The younger woman had in truth appeared to gaze with different eyes upon MacPherson during the remainder of their journey.

Now, as she stepped off the diligence *d'eau* and followed Mary's path across the plank, she slipped her hand most willingly into the Scotsman's, sending him a smile before she turned to shield her eyes against the lowered angle of the sun. Across the river Saône, a line of buildings stretched along the low stone wall that met the water's edge, and in the midst of them the two square towers of a large cathedral rose with prominence. "Why, look, Maman, that must be the cathedral with the famous clock, do you not think?"

Her mother paused in mid-negotiation with one of the would-be porters to look also, and inquiring of the boatman she received the answer that indeed it was the same cathedral.

"Then we ought to go tomorrow," said her daughter, adding charmingly to Mary, "Mademoiselle, will you come with us? We could meet you there at morning Mass. It would be most diverting."

Mary thought the invitation well delivered with a passably convincing spontaneity. She played her part and said, "It's very kind of you to offer, but my brother may have other plans…"

"Oh, do please let her come." The younger woman turned a most appealing face to Thomson. "We'll take very good care of her."

Thomson would make her no promise, but said, "If our schedule allows it."

He glanced once at Mary but she looked away. The bright River Saône, in its winding approach to the city, had given them such a romantic series of views that when they'd reached the rocky promontories standing as twin sentries to Lyon she had been sure there would be nothing else to rival that magnificence. But this came close. A bridge of several arches linked the two banks of the river like a graceful bow of stone, its reflection cast perfectly down by the glittering light of the sun that had just started slipping behind the high hill that created a picturesque backdrop for the great cathedral.

As her means of escape, the cathedral looked promising and reassuringly near. Something she could attain.

Mary held that thought close while they said their good-byes to the others and turned in the other direction, away from the river. The Scotsman appeared to know where he was going. The streets became a labyrinth but he took every turning in a certain and decided manner, never breaking stride but one time, when a passing horse and chaise went trotting by at speed and pressed them all into what small space they could find against the nearest wall. Frisque barked at the indignity and Mary soothed him with a soft word and a rumple of his ears, then raised her chin and squarely met MacPherson's eyes as he glanced back. He gave them no encouragement. She merely felt his gaze rest narrowly upon her as though somehow he suspected her of insubordina-tion. Then he turned again and led them on, around a sharp corner and into a street where the houses seemed ancient, all crowded together like gossips, with crooked bare timbers and old mullioned windows.

The roofs hid the sun and the street lay in shadow, and Mary prepared for the worst.

But the middle-aged woman who opened the door to MacPherson, when he finally stopped at a threshold and knocked, had a pleasant and cheerful appearance. She wel-comed them in as if they had been family. She had the complexion and hands of a woman who'd never done labor, although from her house she was clearly not noble. More likely, thought Mary, her family belonged to the merchant class.

Inside, the house seemed much larger. The drawing room into which she promptly ushered them had been designed for the comfort of guests. There were several chairs set round the room, two with footstools, a square plush-topped table for playing at cards and a table for writing, set close by the window that faced to the street. A mirror set over the fireplace mantel was flanked by a pair of gilt sconces, each set with three candles, and to either side of the fireplace itself, recessed shelves held small porcelain trinkets. And books.

Mary tried not to stare at the books while the woman moved past them to shutter the window.

MacPherson had not yet stepped into the room, but had planted himself in the doorway, immovable.

Taking no notice, the woman twitched the curtains shut as well, and said in the beautiful English of one who'd been born in that country, "I feared you might have met some misadventure, for we did expect you yesterday."

Thomson replied, "There was no misadventure. The diligence coming by land was delayed on the road by a problem with one of the horses, and so—"

Cutting over his speech, the tall Scotsman asked, "Where is Mr. Foster?"

If the woman thought him rude, she did not say so. She was poised, even gracious. "My husband has gone to Bordeaux. He departed the day before we had the news of your coming, so sadly you've only myself and my son to attend you. Ah, here he is now. Johnny, do show the gentleman where he may put all that baggage."

Her son was a young man of sixteen or so, slightly built and not tall, barely visible behind MacPherson. His nervous but polite "This way, sir" had no visible effect.

MacPherson did not shift an inch.

The woman, who presumably was Mrs. Foster, stared in some surprise till Mr. Thomson broke the tension with a charming smile, apologizing, "As you see, my friend is very diligent in guarding me. Come, sir," he told MacPherson. "I'll accompany you. Then you will be certain of my safety."

As the footsteps of the men receded up an unseen flight of stairs, Mrs. Foster said to Mary and Madame Roy, "Please, sit down. You must be weary from your travels. Will you have some wine, or water?"

Madame Roy took wine, and Mary, having no great wish for either, asked if Frisque might have some water.

"Yes, of course. A darling little dog," their hostess called him. When she brought the porcelain bowl, she added, "Put him down and let him run a little, if he likes. This carpet will not mind a bit of hair, nor even soiling. I've had two dogs of my own and lost the last just over Christmas, so I'm glad to have yours here awhile."

Mary obliged and let Frisque have his freedom. "He's very well trained."

"Unlike some," Mrs. Foster said drily, and pointedly glanced where the men had gone. "I was not given your actual names, only those you'd be using for travel, yet I presume señor Montero hails from colder climes than Spain." She let her eyes dance briefly as she looked at Madame Roy. "As do you, if I am not mistaken. You'll forgive me, but you do remind me of a woman I knew years ago at Saint-Germain-en-Laye, and she was of the Highlands. She was..." Mrs. Foster stopped, and looked more closely. "Faith, it *is* you! Euphemia Shaw!" In delight she crossed the carpet. "You'll not recognize me, after all these years, but I was Barbara Ellis then. You were my sister Ann's friend, more than mine, but even so…"

Madame Roy smiled too, as Mary had not seen her smile before. It made her look years younger. "Barbara Ellis! Aye, I see it now. You're not so changed." She stood to meet their hostess's embrace.

"Dear Effie. Are you still called Effie, or is that too girlish now? We all grow older, do we not? I'd heard that you were married to a Frenchman."

"Aye, so I was."

"And is he not then with you?"

"No." Madame Roy's features had begun to settle back into their former lines. "No, he is with our poor wee daughter, in a better place than we can know."

"I'm sad to hear it. Bless them both." She paused in a way that acknowledged and honored their passing, and then in an echo of her former cheerfulness said, "But I *am* glad to see you. You must tell me all the news from Saint-Germain. I've not been there in years."

"Nor have I," admitted Madame Roy. "I fear I have no stories I can tell ye. This lass here, she is the storyteller."

"Truly?" Mrs. Foster looked round, but whatever she may have intended to say was forgotten when she saw the focus of Mary's attention. Instead she asked, in tones that needed no answer because it was plain, "You like books, my dear? If you see one that interests you, do please feel welcome to read it. They're gathering dust these days, and there are some there you might find amusing. I have all of *Gulliver's Travels*, and nearly all of Mr. Pope's *Odyssey*—the fourth volume seems to have traveled off somewhere itself, though the fifth one is there. And there are some writ by various ladies, although my husband does think them all frivolous and less important."

Mary rose from her chair in a fine graceful motion, and in imitating the bearing of Mistress Jamieson chose to make use of her words as well, finding them fitting: "In truth, so few women write anything, that when they do it can never be deemed unimportant." And feeling great pride in the way that came out, she moved over to look at the spines of the books, spotting one title that drew her eye above all others: *Hypolitus*. Taking it in hand, she found it was indeed the novel by Madame d'Aulnoy—the same one containing the story she'd used just that morning when she had adapted the fairy tale of the doomed Russian Prince into her own new-invented account of MacPherson's sad love affair.

She said, "I did not know this had been translated to English."

"Which is that? Oh yes, her books are very popular. I also have her *Travels into Spain*, there on the shelf below." She might have said still more but Mary did not hear her, having found the comfort of remembered words that, even in another language, lightly played within her mind as though it were an instrument and every word a touch upon familiar strings that summoned forth a tune from her imagination:

Under the Reign of Henry VII, King of England, George de Neville, Earl of Burgen, had the Misfortune to be suspected of having had a Hand in the Conspiracy of Edmund Prose...

While the other women turned back to their talk of Saint-Germain, she took the opportunity to curl into her chair again and read, and so remove herself from all her greater cares and all the people causing them. At suppertime her thoughts remained within the novel, and she held herself aloof from conversation, eating all in silence and excusing herself afterwards to seek the solitary peace of sitting in the drawing room and reading, which if only temporarily allowed her to escape.

Frisque had deserted her to beg scraps of the kitchen maid with evident success, so Mary did not have the dog's attentive ears to give her warning.

She didn't know Thomson had come in the room till he settled himself in the chair next to hers, stretched his hands to the fire on the hearth, and said, "That was a very large meal. I'll be all night digesting it."

Mary said nothing. Truth was, she had decided herself to be done with all of them, and was now only counting the hours until she could effect her escape more completely and not have to live anymore among criminals, no matter how kind they might seem to be.

Thomson glanced at her. "You're very quiet. Are you feeling well?" When she nodded, he said, "Then it must, as I feared, be my company. You do not seem to be finding the same pleasure in it you once did. I'm sorry. Perhaps…" Here he stopped, looking into the fire as though seeking his words there, while Mary determinedly went on with what she was reading.

The novel's much put-upon heroine was just embracing her sister and wistfully saying: *If I knew you could keep a Secret, how pleased should I be to repay your Goodness, with making you my Confident…*

"Perhaps," said Thomson, starting over, "I could tell a story that might rival that within your hand for danger and betrayal, and might even make you feel some pity for its hero. May I do that? Would you listen?"

Mary had no wish to hear any defense of his defrauding all those people of their money. "Mr. Thomson…"

"Please."

She raised her eyes then from her book and looked at him, and that was her undoing. If a man could look more miserable, in truth she'd never seen it. Though she knew she would regret the impulse, Mary marked the page she had been reading and she set her book aside. "Very well," she told him. "I am listening."

And so his tale began.

CHAPTER 27

Dark in thought, a-while, he bends:
his words, at length, come forth.
—Macpherson, "Temora," Book Eight

Lyon
February 21, 1732

I 'VE ALWAYS BEEN," HE told her, "of an easy temper, which I am come to believe has been given me not as a gift but a scourge for my sins, for all my misfortunes proceeded from that."

The greatest of these, so he said, began when he was not yet one and twenty and against his father's good advice decided to become involved with what then seemed to be as good a company as any young man might desire to work for: the Charitable Corporation. To move from his father's offices in Edinburgh to the financial heart of the City of London had been itself exciting, and when he'd been made the Corporation's warehouse keeper he'd seen nothing in his future but advancement.

"I had already, with my father's guidance, been a man of business. Now I was a man of reputation, with not one but two assistants and the trust of the directors."

But those same directors, as he came to learn, were so infatuated with the great advantage they were making of their money that they paid no great attention to their duties, running all things in a fashion most irregular, and while they often grumbled and found fault with everything they could find fault with, not a one of them was minded to apply the rules and articles by which the corporation should be governed.

"This fatality of their affairs left things unguarded for my two assistants to indulge in schemes and speculations and to wreak so much havoc that by the time I discovered what they had been up to the damage was done, and the company was like that log there," he said with a nod to the fire, "seeming sound on the outside yet eaten away from within by the flames, and prepared at any moment to collapse."

She was not moved to pity him, for he must also have neglected his own duties to allow the damage to become so far advanced, and in her mind there would have been but one way for an honest man to deal with such a fraud. She asked, "Why did you not denounce them?"

"Because there were others involved in their schemes, men more senior than I in the company, and they persuaded me that if the losses were ever exposed and made public, the whole corporation would fall into ruin and all its investors made bankrupt. The remedy, they said, was to restore the balance of the books, and to this end they brought into our company another man: George Robinson." He spoke that name in darker tones and brought his gaze to Mary's. "Mark that name, my dear, and shun the man if ever you encounter him, for truly he's a rogue to be avoided. But the others did persuade me he was the most proper man to suit our purpose, being well-known as a broker in Exchange Alley, and a man—so they assured me—of an easy fortune."

Looking to the fire again, he watched the flames in silence for a moment, as though thinking on a memory he would rather have forgotten. In the interlude, the log he'd pointed out before as being half-consumed and on the point of falling splintered at its center and collapsed in fragments, sending up a swirl of sparks that briefly burned and just as quickly vanished.

Thomson settled deeper in his chair. "We had a plan that would have raised a profit large enough to pay back all that had been taken. To achieve this, we had but to borrow money from the Corporation's coffers for a brief time and replace it shortly afterwards, but when the time arrived for us to put our plan in action we discovered Mr. Robinson had taken all the money into his own hands and lost it by mismanagement. And so we were then worse off than before, and forced to grasp at any scheme we could to try to set things right again."

By now there were suspicions among others in the company, and some few men stepped forward to insinuate they knew the secret, and had to be paid off or dealt with otherwise.

"One man, our late cashier," he said, "had often in a merry way inquired of my assistants what they did with all that money, and as time went on he gained a sharper instinct that the funds were misapplied and had expressed himself to me more fully on that subject; even threatened to expose it. Mr. Robinson arranged to have him taken off and paid a handsome salary, which might have been the end of it, but…"

Something caught his conscience then and made him look away, and Mary pressed him. "But?"

"Our late cashier," he told her, "is now very late indeed. If you would seek him now you'd have to seek him in the churchyard, where you'll find him in his grave."

Her eyes grew wide as she made sense of what he'd just revealed to her. "They murdered him?"

"I have no proof," he said. "No proof. But you perhaps will see why I was hesitant to go against the others. With the secret having killed one man already, I feared it would kill me, too, though I was not its instrument nor cause."

So he'd held his silence, and together with the other men had latched upon another scheme, yet more ambitious than the first and every bit as certain to restore their funds, but once again their need forced them to turn to Mr. Robinson. And as before, "While we were satisfying ourselves with the prospect of repaying what we owed, he up and cut our throats a second time and sold the stock from under us, and so we all together were in debt for half a million pounds."

The number dropped into a somber silence. In the fireplace one more log fell in amongst its fellows in a slide of sparks and ashes. Mary tried to form an image of that great a sum of money. There could be no quick way to climb from such a pit, she knew. Small wonder Mr. Thomson had despaired.

"I will admit," he said, "when Mr. Robinson imposed that new deceit upon us, I was on the point then of submitting to my fate and telling all to the authorities, but he and all the others made apologies and promises, and God forgive me, I believed them."

Then upon the back of this, they'd learned the City had petitioned Parliament to make a close examination of their books and warehouses, which meant that all their losses and their schemes would be discovered. So the others had decided Mr. Thomson should abscond, and thus divert suspicion from the truth by making it appear that he alone had stolen all the Corporation's missing money and run off with it.

"And since my choices were to come abroad as they proposed or stay in London and be made to bear the blame for their misdoings anyway, I came to France and threw myself upon the mercy of my countrymen," he said. "My fellow exiles."

There was sadness in his smile, and Mary felt a twinge of sympathy.

He said, "And so you see, from being of an easy temper, and trusting a rogue who presented himself as a man of an easy fortune, I am myself become a man of a desperate one—the most unhappy creature that ever lived. And whatever the Company may in their malice and revenge say, I never was one shilling the better for them, and have lost all, and the blame of their loss laid at my door in attempting to save them." His shoulders raised and lowered in a sigh. "As for the poor investors who have lost all too, I had no intention to hurt them, and perhaps when their first fury is over and they are disposed to hear reason, I can set everything in a clear light. In the meantime, I've nothing to offer them but my regret."

He sat a moment longer with his head bent and his gaze upon the fire, no doubt reflecting on the miserable state in which he found himself. And then, as though he felt he had imposed on Mary's patience for too long, he stood. The line of buttons down his waistcoat front had gone askew and tugging at its hem he set it straight again, as though by fixing that one slight disordered thing he could fix all.

He turned once at the door before he left the room, his eyes cast down, his voice turned quiet. "And I do especially regret, my dear, that I have lost your good regard, as I've so clearly done," he said. "And caused you disappointment."

❧

Mary, when she sat before a fire, had always fancied she saw pictures in the flames. On any other night, had she been left to sit alone like this, she might have looked to find them, seeing faces and fantastic beasts and palaces that briefly danced and glimmered in amongst the burning logs. Tonight her focus was distracted by her notice of the ashes that had fallen through the grate and would be swept away tomorrow and discarded as a necessary product of destruction.

They'd once been living things, those ashes—trees within a forest, cut and shaped to suit another's purpose, and reduced now to a sad, ignoble state with no good use remaining but to cloud the water in the washing tub to keep another's linens white and clean.

So it was with Mr. Thomson, fallen from his status as "a man of reputation" to a fugitive, reviled by all and forced to shoulder all the blame that ought to have been shared with Mr. Robinson and others with the power and position to conceal their guilt.

Although he may have acted less than wisely and put faith in people who did not deserve it, and although the outcome of his actions certainly had caused harm to the innocent, there seemed to her injustice in the fact that those he'd trusted in his business had abandoned him, and Mary having heard his tale could not now find it in her heart to follow their example and abandon him as well.

She slipped her hand into her pocket and withdrew the letter she had written last night to her uncle and her aunt. And as it had upon the night when Nicolas had left her at Sir Redmond's house, her aunt's voice stirred with clarity within her memory, telling her: "You always have a choice."

She did. She had a choice. And casting her misgivings to the wind she made one now and leaning forward tossed the letter on the fire.

She heard the patter of Frisque's paws upon the floorboards

in the passage before he came bounding in to greet her with a wagging tail, his muzzle stained with gravy. Mary gathered him onto her lap, receiving his affection and returning it by laying her own cheek against his silken head, and would have made more fuss of him had not a shadow passed them both to stop before the fireplace.

Mary stiffened as MacPherson took a twisted paper spill from the container on the mantel and bent forward to apply it to the fire. She quickly looked to where her letter, nearly all consumed by flames, sat barely recognizable as such amid the logs, its few surviving edges curled and blackening. MacPherson, to her great relief, seemed not to have observed it, for he straightened unconcerned and lit his pipe, then with his unprotected fingers pinched the burning end from the long spill and set it with its fellows on the mantel.

Frisque, as though he craved the Scotsman's notice, gave a short attention-seeking bark and was rewarded by the flicker of a glance from those emotionless blue eyes, but Mary used that bark to her advantage, rising from her chair with the excuse, "My dog does need to do his necessary business."

Whether MacPherson believed her or not he gave no indication, but answered her with a brief nod that, although not completely polite, was not rude. As with most of his gestures, as Mary had found, it fell stubbornly somewhere between.

Being mindful of her own good manners at least, she returned him a smile. "Good night, Mr. MacPherson."

"Mistress Dundas."

Again, Mary thought, that fell somewhere between a "good night" and an abject dismissal, but making good use of it she turned and left the room, glancing one final time into the fire where with some satisfaction she saw that her letter had now been entirely lost to the flames and was no more in evidence.

Mr. MacPherson appeared as content as a man of his nature could be with his solitude, because when Mary had taken Frisque briefly outdoors and come in again, passing the door to the drawing room on her way up to her chamber, she noticed the Scotsman had settled himself in the chair she'd abandoned, his pipe laid aside and a book in his hand.

He remained in that chair throughout most of the next day.

She found it distinctly unnerving, him sitting there reading. At first she had found it amusing to see he'd been reading the book she had set down herself when she'd started to listen to Thomson: Madame d'Aulnoy's *Hypolitus*, with its sensational string of adventures, professions of love, and a hero who wore his emotion so openly when with the heroine that in the space of a few pages he'd gone from "bathing her cheeks with his tears" to embracing her, to—when their parting was imminent—throwing himself at her feet. Mary tried to imagine Mr. MacPherson throwing himself at any woman's feet, and failed.

And yet, he seemed to find the novel passable enough, for when he'd finished it just after breakfast he had set it down where he had found it, risen briefly from his chair to search the bookshelf by the fireplace, and resumed his seat with Madame d'Aulnoy's *Travels into Spain*, ignoring everything and everyone within the drawing room.

Thomson seemed much cheered today and in a better temper, which to Mary's mind was partly due to her deliberate effort to be kind to him. He sat now with their hostess and Madame Roy, who were playing at a lively game of backgammon and talking of their youth. It had occurred to Mary that both women, having lived at Saint-Germain-en-Laye, might well have known her parents, or her aunt and uncle, but she dared not ask them questions, for to share a common cause—as Thomson's tale had clearly illustrated—did not mean that people could be trusted. And no matter how her brother might have let her down, she would not bring him trouble for the world.

Instead she'd taken up her journal, having had neither the time nor inclination to attend to it the night before, and sitting at the table by the window she was now intent on setting down her summary of what had happened yesterday, beginning with her walk and conversation with the younger of the frilly sisters at Mâcon, continuing through their arrival at Lyon and Thomson's sad confession, and concluding with:

> *And after he had told me that and opened all his heart to me, I could not in good conscience keep my plan, and so this morning having chosen to continue with him I decided not to go to hear the Mass, despite his having offered to have somebody escort me, which I hold as further proof of his true good and generous nature. I have stayed instead withindoors with the others. I perceive that we are waiting, though I do not know for what. We are informed by Mrs. Foster that a coach stands ready to convey us to wherever we are going, but the hours pass and Mr. M— seems fixed in place with little wish to move, so—*

Mary felt a sudden pricking at the bent back of her neck, and resisting the strong urge to raise her hand to shield the spot, she turned her head instead with careful nonchalance and found MacPherson's gaze directed calmly at the pages of his book. It was the third time she had felt that he was watching her, yet either the sensation was the product of her overwrought imaginings or else he was too quick in his reactions to be caught.

It was imagined, she decided. There was nothing she was doing that would warrant the attention of the Scotsman, and he impressed her as a man who did not waste the slightest effort without need but only spent it with efficiency. Which meant that even now, when it appeared that he was idle, he most likely had a purpose known to none except himself.

If so, his face revealed no hint of it. He looked less fearsome, reading. With his gaze turned downward it had not the piercing steadiness that hardened all his features; and his mouth, although still crooked and uneven at its corners, was not set into its stricter lines. He looked almost…approachable, she thought. And while he never would be handsome and had not the will to charm, she did allow some women might yet find his hair attractive.

Having rarely seen it but by evening candlelight, and mostly in the day beneath his hat, she had observed today that in the sunlight angling through the window of the drawing room MacPherson's fair hair had a range of hidden lights within it, from a color much like honey to a reddish tone that only showed when struck directly by the sun. It might have even curled, had not he kept it gathered neatly back into the black band at his collar.

He prepared to turn another page and Mary saw the movement of his eyelids and immediately looked away before he caught *her* looking. With her head bent as before above her journal she continued:

—we can do no more than wait until he leads us onwards. I confess I would not mind to spend more time here in this house, for Mrs. Foster is a very amiable hostess and her son is—

"Sir," said Johnny Foster, entering the room in some disorder. He appeared to have just come from the outside, though Mary had not heard the front door open, so he must have entered by the back. His face was flushed as if from running. "You were right," he told MacPherson. "He did come."

MacPherson closed his book and set it to the side. "When?"

"Not a quarter of an hour ago. I recognized him easily from your description, so before he'd even had a chance to disembark I had got in before the other men and offered him my help, and as you'd said he would he asked if I had seen two men arriving with two ladies, and he gave me an account that matched you perfectly, and I replied as you instructed."

Here he stopped to draw a breath while all the others, save MacPherson, stared at him.

MacPherson waited. "And?"

His breath by now somewhat restored, the lad went on, "And when I told him you were gone away again this morning towards Avignon, he did not wait to hear another word, but told his boatman to untie the moorings and continue on. He was not but five minutes at the quayside, and once I'd watched him out of sight I ran back here to tell you, sir."

MacPherson gave a nod, which Mary could have told young Johnny was the closest he could hope to come to getting praise.

"I'm all at sea," complained his mother. "*Who* has come?"

Beside her, Thomson slowly smiled in open admiration. "Mr. Stevens," was his guess, and having read the confirmation in MacPherson's unexpressive face he added to their hostess, to explain, "We had an Englishman who traveled with us and who caused us trouble. We escaped him at Chalon, and I had hoped that was the end of him, but now I do perceive Mr. MacPherson neither shared my hope nor counted on it, for which lack of faith I am inordinately grateful."

As should they all be, Mary reasoned. With the current of the river, Stevens would be traveling much faster by the water than they'd travel by the road. They'd be behind him now and not before him, which for any hunted prey produced a great advantage.

Rising to his feet, MacPherson stretched as though to sit so long had left his shoulders stiff, and turning, said to Mrs. Foster, "Call your coachman."

CHAPTER 28

LUC SAW ME LOOKING at my watch and smiled. "He'll call us when he needs us. And it's only been ten minutes since we dropped him off. Relax."

"It isn't that." I wasn't worried about Noah. Even though he clearly didn't like to take piano lessons, he'd seemed happy when we'd left him at his teacher's house. She had three cats.

"What, then?"

"It's nothing." I could hardly tell him I was keeping track of time while I was answering his questions to make sure I wasn't monologuing. "Anyway, I'm boring you."

"I'm not bored. Why would I be bored?"

"Because it's really boring, what I'm telling you," I reasoned. He had asked me about ciphers and their history and I knew I'd rambled on a bit, but thankfully, as he'd said, it had only been ten minutes. I'd been worried it had been much longer, given that I'd only now just realized we were walking down a different street.

I really liked this little town, called Carrières-sur-Seine, a short drive north along the river from Chatou. The oldest section had retained its ancient character, with houses that had clearly stood for centuries, their walls of rustic limestone and rough plaster mellowed warmly by the weather and the years. The town was built into a hillside and its narrow streets were set on different levels, winding down towards the languid River Seine.

We passed a tight gap where a flight of stone steps steeply dropped between two houses, giving me a brief view of the roofs below, a bit of green that might have been a park, the shining silver strip of river, and a smudge of leafless trees.

Luc said, "I'll tell you if I'm ever bored."

He wouldn't, though, I knew. He was too nice. I dipped my chin a fraction so my mouth just touched the soft edge of the scarf I wore—the blue scarf Luc had bought for me a week ago in Paris. It had fast become my favorite.

"Are you cold?" he asked.

"Not really. Just my hands."

"My hands are warm." He held one out to make it clear that was an invitation, so I took it, liking how his fingers closed with care around my own.

I liked the whole sensation, actually, of walking hand in hand with Luc. Our steps matched well. We weren't so far apart in height—with taller men I had to walk more briskly to keep up, but there was no need to adjust my stride at all when keeping pace with Luc. We fit together naturally.

I would have called it "comfortable" except it wasn't. I felt too aware of him, too flutteringly nervous on the inside to be comfortable. This felt much closer to the first relationships I'd had in adolescence than the ones I'd had more recently: the thrill and the anticipation and the all-consuming thoughts that I'd begun to have of him. And then again, in some ways it felt nothing like those earlier encounters either, leaving me confused as to exactly what it *did* feel like.

Like Luc, I told myself. *It feels like holding hands with Luc.*

He asked, "What would you like to talk about?"

"America."

"America?"

"I've never been. You have."

"Yes, well, my mother's an American."

"I know. Denise told me."

"You talk about me with Denise?" He didn't seem put out. In fact, he looked a little pleased.

"Sometimes. Is that all right?"

"Of course." His fingers moved and slipped between my own until our hands were more securely linked together. "What else has she told you of my family?"

"That your mother and your brother moved to California when he went to school, and left you here," I said. "Do they still live apart, your parents?"

"No, that was a temporary situation. Now they live together, half the year in Paris, half in California."

"And your brother?"

"He's in California, still. He loves it there. He works for the same company I do, for Morland Electronics, only his job is much more important than mine."

His eyes were crinkled slightly at the corners so I couldn't tell if he was being serious or not, but since he'd told me that his brother was a programmer, I guessed that Luc was teasing.

"What's your brother's name?" I asked, acquiring details for the mental file I was assembling on Luc's family.

"Fabien."

"He's two years older than you?"

"Yes. Two years and two months. Just how much have you talked to Denise?"

"A bit. She only has good things to say about you."

Luc's mouth lifted at the corners. "Yes, I pay her well to do that. What exactly would you like to know," he asked, "about America?"

I liked the way he answered questions, so straightforward, nothing seeming out of bounds. And he was very skilled, I soon discovered, at describing things. We walked along the river for a while, along the gravel pathways of what looked to be the remnants of a formal garden, but instead of truly noticing the fountain and the fishpond I was seeing California in my mind: the rise of vineyards washed by sunlight underneath a sky as blue as Luc's own eyes, and sunsets flaming on the far horizon over the Pacific Ocean where the great waves rolled and rose and broke along an endless beach of sand.

It sounded beautiful. I said as much.

"It is," he said. "But every place has something that is beautiful about it, if you only look to find it."

We climbed another flight of steps to street level, the river at our backs now, and Luc told me, "Come, I'll show you something beautiful."

He led me up a little lane, paved red with a cobblestone gutter that ran down its center, and houses to one side that had been half-carved from the pale limestone cliff of the hill. The most lovely of these had blue shutters, a blue-painted gate, and a half-rounded wall like an old castle turret with trees growing in a dark frieze at its top.

"Denise," he told me, "has a special fondness for these houses. They're called 'troglodytes,' and in the town where she grew up, in Chinon, there are many of them carved out of the cliffs. Some very ancient. But the part I want to show you is up here."

He led me up the winding lane and round a corner where the hills and walls closed in upon us and we stepped into a dark and quiet passage that must once have been a house carved from the stone—the rotted skeletons of wooden joists and wall supports still showed in some few places—but had now become essentially a cave, with one small section of its roof left open to the sky. I stood there in the dark and felt the welcome safe embrace of walls and ceiling close around me in a hug so nearly physical it made me smile in happiness.

"You see?" Luc's voice was close, and quiet. "Beautiful. I'm sure it was a good house in its time as well, but sometimes what is left behind when something has been lost is even better than the thing that came before, you know?"

I couldn't disagree with him, not standing in that ruined place.

Luc told me, "Noah's friend Michelle thinks this would be the perfect place to keep a dragon."

"Denise says she's quite a character."

"Michelle? She is, but in a good way. Noah wants to introduce you."

"I don't think that's such a good idea."

Luc asked, "Why not?" and seemed puzzled so I tried to share my reasoning.

"Denise says Noah likes it when the people in his life know one another. Right? Well, I don't think I ought to be in Noah's life."

The light where we were standing was enough to let me see his face and know that he was frowning slightly, but I couldn't really see his eyes. "You're there already."

"But I shouldn't be."

"Why not?"

"Because," I told him, "when I leave, he'll be too sad." He must have seen how deeply Noah got attached to things, I thought. I didn't want to be responsible for making Noah sad, the way he'd been when he believed he'd lost Diablo.

Luc, still frowning in the dark, said, "When you leave...?"

"Yes, when my work is done and I go home to London."

He stayed silent for a moment. Then he told me, "You

don't have to leave completely. There are trains, you know. And planes. And roads."

"Luc."

"I'm in London every other month on business as it is," he added.

"Luc." I felt a sudden weight within my chest, a pressing sadness as I realized he was wanting something more than I could give him; something more than just a simple holiday romance. "I don't… I can't…" He mattered more than any of the others had, and so it hurt me more to disappoint him, but that only made it more important he should hear the truth. "I can't sustain a real relationship. I always mess things up." I'd meant to state that calmly as a fact, but my voice wobbled on the final words and Luc's own voice grew gentle in response.

"How do you mess things up?"

In every way conceivable, I could have told him. "I just do."

"It might not happen this time."

"Yes, it will. It always does. I'm just not capable—"

"Who told you that?" His words, still quiet, cut across my own with an insistence that I simply couldn't bring myself to answer, so I briefly closed my eyes and closed my mind against the memories.

Luc fell silent too, and when my eyes came open he was watching me. Not crowding me, but standing close enough that I was very much aware of him.

He asked me, "If you could…if you were capable of having a relationship, would you want one with me?"

"Yes."

"You like me."

"Yes."

"Good. So your plan was that we should spend time with each other, and then you would leave me?"

"Yes."

Luc gave a nod, and remarkably I saw the curve of his smile.

"What?" I asked.

"It's a terrible plan." He came closer. "No, really, you need to revise it. I'll help you." He kissed me—just lightly, but there in the dark of the cavern-like passage his touch left me buried in feelings.

I still tried to argue, "I can't change."

He rested his forehead on mine. "You don't have to. Simple math. You only have to change the value of one variable to affect the outcome of the whole equation."

My efforts to focus on logic were hampered by feeling his hands at the small of my back. "And you're trying to tell me that you're that one variable?"

"Well, of all the men you've known before, were any of them me?"

His logic made me smile a little. "No."

"Then I'm the variable." Lowering his mouth to mine, he set about convincing me, and did a thorough job of it. I wanted to believe.

He said, "You never need to change for me." His breath was warm against my cheek. My hair. My neck. "You understand? You never need to change."

It seemed he somehow needed a reply, but since I didn't have the focus or the energy to form a proper sentence, I just answered with, "OK."

I felt him smile against my skin and he pressed closer to my body in the darkness and I really didn't notice much beyond that till his mobile rang to tell us it was time to pick up Noah.

We had lunch at a café somewhere—I didn't notice much about that, either—and we took our time in getting back, so when they dropped me at the front of the Maison des

Marronniers the lights in some of the château's front windows had already been switched on against the fall of twilight.

Luc got out and came around to get the door for me, and bent to kiss me one more time with warmth, and touched my arm the way that people sometimes did when they were being reassuring. Then he turned his head and gave a nod to someone on the terrace and in English said, "Good evening."

Which alone should have prepared me.

But it still surprised me when I turned and saw my cousin standing on the top step.

She returned my hug as tightly as I gave it, and explained when I asked why she hadn't told me she was coming, "Well, I wanted to surprise you. I appear to have succeeded."

She was watching Luc's car trundle off around the circle of the drive.

"Now what, exactly, Sara darling," Jacqui asked, "was *that*?"

❧

I saved myself from what I knew would probably have been a very long and disapproving lecture by distracting Jacqui with the pages I'd transcribed of Mary's diary.

After supper, Jacqui brought the pages from my workroom to the salon, poured a glass of wine, and curled into the sofa near the fireplace. "This," she said to me, "is fabulous."

I felt a swell of pride. "You think he'll like it, then?"

"Who?"

"Alistair. Who else?"

She finished with another page and laid it facedown on the growing pile beside her. "Yes, of course he'll like it. This is really so much better than the mundane sort of stuff he was expecting. I mean, honestly. This reads just like a—"

"—thriller. Yes, you've said."

My words seemed to intrigue Claudine, who came in from the dining room to join us, switching on another table lamp as she passed by to take her own seat at the sofa's other end. She'd brought a glass of wine with her as well, and set it down now as she touched the stack of pages overturned between herself and Jacqui. "May I?"

"Have you not read it yet? Then yes, please do," my cousin said. "It's fascinating."

While the two of them were reading, I let my thoughts drift backward happily to Luc and what he'd said to me this afternoon, and how he'd held me. How he'd kissed me.

"Ooo," said Jacqui. "I've got chills."

I roused myself. "From which part?"

"Mr. Stevens."

"Has he just begun to travel with them?"

"Yes."

"Then wait," I told her. "It gets better."

For another several minutes I heard nothing but the clinking noises from the kitchen as Denise washed dishes. I'd have helped her, but the times when I had offered she had firmly told me no, then made me coffee so I'd sit and keep her company, and since I hadn't seen my cousin in nearly a fortnight I decided I had better keep *her* company instead.

Claudine said, "Your diarist—Mary? She seems quite intrigued by this Mr. MacPherson."

My cousin said, "*I'm* quite intrigued by this Mr. MacPherson." She grinned. "The allure of the Scotsman, and all that."

Claudine pointed out Mr. Thomson was also a Scot. "But she doesn't describe him in such detailed language. I can't picture Thomson at all in my mind, but I know 'Mr. M—' has fine hands and blue eyes and blond hair with some red in it."

"Yes," Jacqui said, "she does like his hands, doesn't she? Listen here: 'For all I've never seen him wearing gloves, he keeps his hands as neat and clean as any gentleman's.' And later on she writes: 'He did repair the broken watch with a dexterity that might befit a goldsmith, which I would not have believed had I not stood and watched him do it.'" Smiling, she remarked to Claudine, "So his hands are clean *and* dexterous."

"These are both good things." Claudine was smiling too, which led me to believe I'd missed some joke that had been obvious to them.

But Jacqui never let me stay outside the circle very long, and for my benefit she added, "He would be a very interesting lover."

Then I understood. I told her, "If he let you live."

"Well, yes, there is that."

"Anyhow," I said, "I don't think Alistair will care much whether Mary Dundas likes MacPherson's hands, and I don't think her stories will be useful to his research either, but there's still a lot of detail coming out about the fraud, and—"

Jacqui interrupted with, "Oh yes, her *stories*. Darling, why didn't you tell me about those? They're rather wonderful. A couple more and they would make a lovely little book all on their own. In fact, I know the perfect illustrator...she did Bridget Cooper's books." She had her tablet out already, taking notes and planning things. She told Claudine, "We ought to sit down soon and get the rights all sorted."

"Rights?"

"Yes. This diary is much more than just a simple source of research, don't you realize? It's a very special thing. Not only is it going to give Alistair one amazing book—and I'd be very surprised if we don't manage to get a television deal out of it for him—but it's the whole package: intrigue, adventure, money, betrayal. It's got the dramatic potential to make a good film, or a miniseries. And then there are the fairy tales." She had the vibrant, lit-from-the-inside look that I knew meant she was honestly excited by a project, and it made me feel a little proud my work had helped her feel that way. She told Claudine, "The diary's yours, you own it, so apart from whatever Alistair ends up making from his book, we need to make sure you get proper payment, too."

Claudine sat back. "I don't want money."

To my ears it sounded as if she had placed an emphasis on that last word, as if she wanted *something*, just not money. But I often got things wrong.

"Well, want it or not," Jacqui said, "you'll be making some, once the transcription is finished." She looked at me. "How much is left?"

"Eighty-three and a half pages. I've finished ninety-two, and there's a half a page still on my desk that I worked on this morning before I went out, but I haven't had time yet to enter it into the computer, so it's not with those," I said, giving a nod to the papers both she and Claudine had been reading. "But all they've been doing is traveling south from Lyon for a couple of days in their carriage, and so far they haven't had any real problems apart from a stubborn lead horse."

Jacqui curled deeper into the cushions and leaned on the arm of the sofa. "Well, Mary still wants to be careful," she said. She was looking directly at me. "If she'd asked *my* advice, I'd have told her that going around with strange men—even ones with nice hands and good hair—only leads you to trouble."

CHAPTER 29

Within that wood he has placed his chiefs;
beware of the wood of death.
—Macpherson, "Fingal," Book Three

Valence
February 25, 1732

THE WOMAN WAS TRYING to push him away.

Mary saw what was happening almost as soon as she noticed the man and the young woman close by the stable door, hidden by shadows. At first she'd believed they'd been stealing a moment of private affection, but now she could see that the woman was trying to push him away, to get free of his hold, and the man wasn't letting her loose.

Perhaps it was only in jest. Couples played, sometimes. She'd seen Aunt Magdalene try to recover a letter from Uncle Jacques's hands, and their struggle had ended in laughter. Perhaps this would, too. But she couldn't help feeling concern.

It was dark in the courtyard. They'd chosen this inn—the Saint-Jacques—for its being outside the walls of Valence, since that city was one of the staging points for any journey on this route by land or by water. They would have gone by it completely, but being unable to go past the city without changing horses regardless, and given that they were in want of a night's rest, MacPherson had judged this to be an acceptable compromise. And being cautious he'd ordered the coachman to slow to a walk for the final leagues so they would make their approach to Valence under cover of darkness. It helped that tonight was the night of the new moon—a good night for hunted things.

Save for the glittering hard winter stars and the glow of a pierced lantern hung on a hook just within the wide door of the stable, there was little light to be seen beyond what could squeeze out through the thin jagged cracks in the inn's tightly fastened black shutters.

The coachman was busy unhitching the horses with Thomson's assistance while Madame Roy stayed in the coach with Frisque nestled beside her, but Mary, impatient for air, had already stepped out.

"Have a care," Thomson warned when she stumbled against a loose stone in the yard. He was speaking in English. They all were now, having assumed new identities with the new traveling papers provided for them in Lyon.

"An Englishman!" Thomson at first had exclaimed when he'd seen their new papers, while they'd been awaiting their coach and its driver. "I fear that I'll not be convincing." Yet Mary, observing him since, had decided he was at least as accomplished as she was at changing his skin. He'd adapted his accent to hide any trace of inflection that marked him as Scottish, and did it so perfectly Mary's own accent seemed rustic beside it, although their new names and relationship kept that from being a problem.

Mrs. Foster had said, "If they found you in Paris, they'll know you were posing as brother and sister and that you made yourselves out to be French. And that's how you stayed on your journey to me, did you not? Which is why you're now changed to be husband and wife."

Madame Roy had not liked that arrangement at all, until Thomson had promised her he would not take it so far as to share Mary's chamber, and that they could all carry on as before, only Madame Roy was Mrs. Grant now, and Thomson and Mary were Mr. and Mrs. Symonds, and keeping on in his role as a servant, MacPherson was now Mr. Jarvis.

He made, to be sure, an unusual servant. The more Mary saw him with Thomson, the greater her wonder that anyone watching the two men together would ever count Thomson the master. MacPherson stood straighter and strode with more confidence, and Thomson looked to him always and followed his lead, yet whenever they came to an inn or an alehouse, the people they met were accepting of what they were told, treating Thomson with all the regard of a gentleman, leaving MacPherson to fend for himself. Which appeared to be what he preferred.

For the whole of their journey from Lyon, not once had MacPherson sat with them inside the coach, riding beside them instead on a series of horses he'd hired and replaced when they'd stopped to change theirs. Mary reckoned the horses he'd used must have been fair exhausted at finishing each leg of travel, from carrying not only his weight but that of his swords and his gun case. The cleverness of its design had grown clear when he'd first strapped it onto the side of his saddle: with the top half of the cylinder removed and secured behind, the now-modified traveling case made a boot into which the long rifled gun could slide and remain there at rest, close to hand if he needed it. So far, to Mary's relief, he'd not needed it. But he remained ever watchful.

When he had signaled the coach to turn in at the yard of the inn here, he hadn't turned with them. Instead he had made a complete circuit of the inn, making sure all was in order, and now with a clopping of hooves his horse drew alongside them. MacPherson dismounted and ran one hand over the horse's damp withers before he began to unfasten the straps of his gun case.

Thomson remarked, "I could do with a cup of spiced wine. I am feeling the cold in my bones tonight."

The man by the stable door had begun kissing the woman so boldly their coachman called over in French and reminded the man there were two ladies present and he would be well advised to take his woman indoors, or at least to the relative privacy of an unoccupied stall, whereupon the man called back in very bad French with a thick English accent that he and the woman were only enjoying themselves and the coachman should mind his own business.

MacPherson, at the hard exchange of voices, briefly glanced from one man to the other before lowering his gaze to the last strap and fitting the top once again to his gun case, but Thomson, affronted, stepped into the fray.

"Come now, sir. Are you English?" he asked, in that language. "If so, then you ought to have manners much better than those you display."

The man by the stable door turned so the light from the lantern nearby showed the shape of his features. "Indeed I am English, and sir, you are well met. I meant no offense." Evidently the scant light allowed him to take note of Thomson's superior clothes, because he touched his hat brim respectfully. "I've been a long time on the road and I trust you won't blame me for taking a kiss where it's willingly offered."

Which answer apparently satisfied Thomson, who having received his apology nodded acknowledgment of it and started to head for the door of the inn.

But Mr. MacPherson asked curtly, "And is it?"

The man replied, "Is it what?"

"Willingly offered."

A person who'd never encountered MacPherson might well have believed from his tone that he cared not what answer was given. But Mary had heard how he'd spoken in Paris mere moments before he had killed, and without even seeing his face she could tell he was now in a mood that was dangerous.

Having not had her experience—nor, it seemed, any great instinct for caution—the stranger allowed his own voice to grow heated. "Of course it is. Haven't you eyes in your head?"

Having finished securing the long gun and slinging the case on his shoulder, MacPherson turned round. The light from the lone lantern hanging within the wide door of the stable could not reach the place where he stood.

Thomson had retraced his steps and sought now to undo what he'd started. "Come, Jarvis," he said to the Scotsman. "The woman in truth does look willing enough, and I must get my own wife indoors and to bed. Let us not interfere with another man's pleasure."

MacPherson ignored him, and in the same tone as before told the stranger, "I'd hear it from her, and not you."

The woman had, during this interchange, kept her face turned from them, either in shame or from modesty. That she was local was plain from her clothes and the style of her headdress. MacPherson now called upon Mary, and said, "Mrs. Symonds, you speak French. Ask her."

Mary, having no experience with such a situation, was not certain what to ask, but she decided upon, "Are you with this man by choice, madam?"

The woman shook her head, her answer coming faintly: "No."

MacPherson, needing no translation, said to Mary, "Tell her she can go."

This Mary did, and the woman pushed free of the man, who this time offered no resistance but stepped back, his hands withdrawn and partly raised as if to prove his harmlessness. As the woman hurried from the stable yard, the stranger complained to MacPherson, "Now look what you've done, man. You've spoiled my night's fun." Dropping one hand to his sword hilt, he said coldly, "Let me return you the favor."

The coachman cried out and fell heavily as something moved in the darkness behind them, and at the same moment the man by the stable door came at them too.

Mary did not know if there were two men or twenty attacking.

MacPherson had laid hold of Thomson's coat and all but thrown him clear into the coach, and the quick flashes of silver and steel in his hands after that told her he'd drawn his sword and the deadly long dagger, by which time she'd dropped to the ground and gone under the coach, her heart pounding in panic.

The scuffle that followed, with harsh breaths and curses and blades clanging hard against blades in a frenzied and disordered way, started Frisque barking madly. The horses, half-hitched to their harness still, sidestepped and snorted and got in the way while the horse that MacPherson had ridden shied nervously farther away from the fight.

Mary, lying as tightly pressed into the earth as she could, had a view of the lighted door to the stables, and when the men passed between it and the coach she tried hard to make sense of the shifting confusion of legs. From the shape of his boots, cast in silhouette, she knew which ones were MacPherson's, and so she could see he had one man before him and one to the side, though it seemed to her he was the one doing all the advancing. And when the first sword fell, it wasn't his own.

With a cry sounding only half human, another man called out, "My hand! Bastard near took my hand off!"

"You still have your hand, you great coward," the first stranger taunted. "'Tis only your wrist. Now come help—"

But in that same breath he was also disarmed, and a second sword dropped to the dirt. Spewing curses, the man flung himself at MacPherson and found himself knocked to his knees for the effort, and Mary could see the long blade of MacPherson's sword lower to point at the fallen man's neck. "Are ye finished?"

The man with the slashed wrist apparently was, for he'd taken off running already, his steps growing rapidly faint in the dark.

Frisque, as always when he thought a danger had safely retreated, barked louder, until he was hushed from within the coach. Below it, Mary held her breath.

The answer came: "Not yet."

Not from the man who should have spoken, but from one who had come forward from the place of his concealment in the stables and stood now beneath the lantern in the open stable door. The light, because it was behind him, showed his shape alone, including the short barrel of the pistol in his hand, but Mary recognized his voice.

"I had much rather do this quietly," said Mr. Stevens.

He left the light, coming across to them steadily—keeping his pistol, presumably, aimed at MacPherson.

"Take his sword," he instructed the other man, who rose uncertainly.

Mary, astonished and horrified, saw the sword turn as MacPherson relinquished it.

"And the dirk," Stevens added. "A most uncouth weapon, befitting a barbarous people who can barely speak but to lie and deceive."

He was careful, she noticed, to stop his advance a few paces beyond where the Scotsman could reach, and she guessed that, like Frisque, he barked loudest and bravest when there was little real danger of his being brought to account for it.

He said, "That was quite a neat game you played back in Chalon. And a bold move to have that lad hasten me on from Lyon. Very clever. But I'm clever, too. I did ask, on my way down the river, if any had seen you stop in at the towns, and on finding none had, I deduced you had not gone before me at all, but were coming behind. In your place," he confessed, "I'd have done the same. And I would never have risked passing straight through Valence, where there might be so many eyes watching, and some of them English. No, I'd have come this way. So here's where I waited. And whether you passed by or stopped, I would have you. And him."

He meant Thomson, she knew. There was nothing but silence above in the coach. Not a snuffle or whine from her dog.

Stevens said, "I will take him, now. And I'll be having that handsome gun too, while I'm at it." He ordered the other man, "Take it. That case he has over his shoulder."

The other obeyed. Mary heard the sharp slide of one blade on another as first the man gathered the forfeited sword and the evil long dagger that Stevens had called a dirk into his one fist. They must have been heavy to hold, for she saw the sword's point touch the ground near the wheel close to where she was lying. And then she saw his boots step forward as he came between the tall Scotsman and Stevens, preparing to lift off the strap of the case.

What happened next happened almost too quickly for her to untangle its order. She heard a quick gasp and a shuddering wheeze, and then the sword point lifted and was raised beyond her line of vision as the other man was lifted too, caught hard upon whatever blade he had been stabbed with to become a human shield against the pistol Stevens held, as in a swift and fatal rush, MacPherson charged the Englishman.

The noises Stevens made while dying, while not loud, were nonetheless disturbing. Mary cupped her hands against her ears to shut them out, and when she saw MacPherson's boots returning she shrank closer to the coldness of the ground.

He crossed to the coachman, who having been cudgeled and not run through had been attempting to stand with the aid of the horse harness. "Sir, I can drive," he said hoarsely. MacPherson assisted him round to the coach step and said to the others inside, "Take him."

Then he crouched low to look under the coach, finding Mary unerringly, even in such little light. Stretching his hand to assist her, he waited.

She knew there'd be blood on that hand. There was no way his hands could stay clean when he'd done so much violence. She shook her head to tell him she did not need help, and crawled out on her own, and he moved back to let her do it. He said nothing, only looked her over briefly as though seeking signs of damage. Mary warranted he'd find none save the rough disorder of her hair and scrapes of dirt along the bodice of her gown, which were, from what she could make out, no more than he himself had suffered in the fight.

He looked away from her and said to Thomson, who was only now emerging from the safety of the coach, "Come. We've little time."

"To do what?" asked Thomson.

In a low, impatient voice that clearly felt the answer was self-evident, MacPherson said, "Hide *them*"—he nodded at the corpses—"change our horses, and be gone."

"But…" Thomson glanced towards the dark wall of the inn, and Mary saw him working through the facts to realize, as she had already done, they could not stay the night. The wounded man who'd run off minutes earlier might even now be in the city finding friends to help him seek revenge, or at the least he might inform upon them, leaving them but little time to get away before they either faced a new attack or were discovered.

With a sigh that mourned the loss of his anticipated tankard of warm wine more than the loss of life around him, Thomson helped MacPherson drag the bodies of the two dead men into the stables. From the sounds that followed, Mary guessed they were pitching hay or straw over the bodies.

Frisque whined and Madame Roy leaned from the coach and told Mary, "Will you take him? He would come to you, and I can't hold him."

Mary took Frisque woodenly and cradled him against her, but she did not go inside the coach. She did not wish to be confined. A cage, however comfortably appointed, was a cage, and left the creatures in it vulnerable to those who were outside, and she already felt too vulnerable, her senses strained and heightened to the point of pain.

So when the shutters of an upstairs window in the inn banged open, she had heard the bolt slide back beforehand, and been warned in time enough to turn her face to meet the light that speared with sudden brightness down into the yard. A man, presumably the landlord, called in French, "What's happening? What's going on? Who's there?"

She did not know how much he'd heard, or whether he'd conspired in the ambush, but she knew she didn't have the luxury of time to sort things through, and being trapped upon the spot she took a chance and played her part. "Good evening, sir. Do you speak English?"

All the furtive noises from the stable had now ceased, and she was not the only one who waited for his answer.

"Yes," he said, speaking more loudly. "A little."

"Oh, I'm glad. My uncle's fallen ill. He's had a fever half the day that's making him delirious and difficult to manage. I'm afraid, were we to stay here, we might pass on his contagion to your other guests, but as you see our horses cannot stir another step, they are exhausted. If we could but have some fresh ones…?"

"Yes, of course. Of course. I'll send the *palefrenier*."

She noticed he'd drawn back as if he feared the illness might spread upward on the air, but when she thanked him, she asked one thing more. "We'd also be most grateful for a meal, however small, that we could carry with us. Bread and cheese would do, perhaps with two bottles of wine?"

He promised those as well, and withdrew from the window, making sure to bolt the shutters as before, securely.

Mary felt her spine and shoulders sag against the stalwart lacing of her stays and breathed a little deeper in relief. Then she turned and saw MacPherson in the doorway of the stable. He was standing there and watching her, with Thomson close behind, and with the lantern hanging just above his shoulder she could see his features. He was looking at her closely, as he'd studied that small broken watch in Mâcon; as if she were made of gears and wheels and he would seek to understand her workings.

Let him look, she thought. And slipping on her calmest face, she held to Frisque more tightly so the Scotsman would not see her hands were trembling in reaction to the night of fear and trauma, as she simply said, "He's sending out the groom."

And turned away.

CHAPTER 30

Ghosts are seen there at noon:
the valley is silent, and the people shun the place...
—Macpherson, "The War of Caros"

The Bas-Vivarais, near the village of Maisonneuve
March 3, 1732

A WEEK HAD GONE BY and she still was no closer to guessing the place where MacPherson was leading them.

Since killing Stevens at Valence the Monday before, he'd been more than annoyingly secretive, and if the others knew where they were going they hadn't seen fit to tell Mary. They'd driven straight through that long night from Valence, getting what sleep they could in the coach, till at sunrise they'd come to a town called Étoile where they'd struck out on foot, crossing over the Rhône while the coachman, relieved of his passengers, carried on south with instructions to turn when he could to the east and proceed towards Switzerland, hopefully drawing off any men still in pursuit.

While the bodies they'd left in the stables would not have lain long without being discovered, it stood in their favor the night had been dark and their contact with those at the inn had been brief and thus few there got a good look at them. But there was always a risk, as they'd been well reminded by something MacPherson had come across while he'd been emptying Stevens's pockets of evidence of his identity, before concealing the bodies with hay: a page torn from the *London Gazette* from October last, giving notice that anyone capturing John Thomson would be rewarded with the staggering amount of one thousand pounds. It had given a detailed description by which any person would know him, although that description had raised Thomson's ire.

"I do *not*," he'd said, "go with my knees in. Nor are my legs 'thick.' And to claim I'm 'inclined to be fat' is no less than a libel."

He had continued irritated for the better part of that first day they had been walking, until Mary, seeking peace, had pointed out he should be grateful they'd described him so imperfectly, because it might then spare him being recognized.

But truly, she had written in her journal that same night, *apart from those few things which wounded him—and reasonably so, for he is straight of leg and while not lean is not rotund—the notice Mr. Stevens carried listed Mr. Thomson's features to the hazel of his eyes and color of his eyebrows, and it would take no great skill to match the man to that description, which if it be widely circulated could be very worrisome.*

It was, she'd thought, the reason why they had not stayed at inns since they had started this new segment of their journey, but had stopped each evening at a farmhouse of MacPherson's choosing and had paid well for whatever hospitality was granted them, most often beds on straw within an outbuilding or barn, and a good share of the plain food the families had on hand to offer. In the villages and towns through which they'd passed they'd stopped for water and bought bread and then moved on, the one exception being on the second morning when Madame Roy had insisted they begin their day by hearing Mass, because it was Ash Wednesday. There had been a short debate between the older woman and the Scotsman as to whether this was really necessary, being that the day was not a holy day of obligation on

which people were required to go to Mass, but Madame Roy
had not been swayed, and so they'd gone. MacPherson had
stood with them in the church, though Mary doubted that
the ritual—of being touched by ashes while the mournful
priest intoned they had been born of dust and would someday return to it and should no longer sin but seek salvation—
could have meant much to a man so comfortable with killing.

Thomson, as they'd left the church and started on their
way again, had pointed out a different sort of irony. "We
promise to observe a holy Lent in imitation of the days our
Savior wandered in the wilderness," he'd said. "And look
where we now find ourselves."

It was, in truth, a wilderness.

They'd traveled far enough now to the south there was
no snow upon the ground, and from the place where they
had crossed the Rhône the level plain had quickly given way
to the forbidding mountain foothills of the Vivarais. The narrow paths and drover's roads were full of rocks and stones
that rolled with unpredictability, the ways forever climbing
or descending through rough stunted trees and sheer faces of
gray stone and forested hills rising steeply to either side.

In this wild and rugged place, the Scotsman's stamina and
strength were things to marvel at. He'd passed one portmanteau to Thomson, who could barely manage that together
with his deal-box, but MacPherson kept the larger of the
portmanteaus slung over his own shoulder so it rested on his
back beside the long case of his gun. The heavy basket-hilted
sword was at his side again, the ordinary sword hung at his
other hip, his evil-looking dirk sheathed in its place along
with heaven only knew how many other blades. A walking,
breathing armory—and yet he moved in silence with a steady
gait as though he carried nothing.

Mary, walking in his wake, had often found herself lulled into calmness by the rhythmic swagger of his stride that set his coat to swinging from his shoulders like a cape. He was a fine-looking man from the back, and she thought it a shame he had not been born handsome, nor reared with more care for his manners, for he would have otherwise made a good hero.

Her mind, in such moments, had frequently wandered to thoughts of new stories, new tales of adventure…and had just as frequently been yanked back down to reality by a new volley of Thomson's complaints.

He'd deplored the poor make of his shoes, and the weight of his deal-box; the muscular soreness that sleeping on hay had produced, and the pace of their walking; the quality of the plain food they'd been eating, and his unendurable hunger, and even the sun, which in his view was either too bright or too little in evidence. Mary had once thought she never would hear someone find fault with so many things as her cousin Gaspard could, but as each day passed, Mr. Thomson continued to prove she'd been wrong. For a man who claimed to be "of an easy temper," as he'd told her in Lyon, he did not rise well to adversity.

Madame Roy, on the other hand, had shown herself to be nearly as hardy as Mr. MacPherson. Mary thought this unsurprising, since they both were of the Highlands where such walking would have doubtless been a common thing, and where—from the few woodcuts she had seen—the land was similarly rugged. Mary, healthy as she was, had felt impatient with herself for tiring so easily upon the uphill paths, and pushed herself to match the others' steps *without* complaining, though at times she'd wished she could, like Frisque, stop walking and sit stubbornly upon the ground till some-one deigned to carry her.

Conveniently, each time she'd found herself approaching that level of weariness, MacPherson had stopped anyway for varied other reasons—once to readjust the crossed straps of his sword belts, and another time to work a bit of thorn out of the top edge of his boot—and so she'd gained her moment's rest. Had she been more suspicious she'd have said that he was doing it on purpose, but it seemed such an unlikely thought that Mary had dismissed it almost instantly, remembering MacPherson did not do things out of pity.

Still, the third day in the afternoon, when she'd begun to feel her knees grow more unsteady as she climbed, she'd seen MacPherson glance behind a minute before he had stopped to reorder the portmanteau's contents as though he desired to better distribute the weight.

Thomson, seizing the chance to set down his own burdens and sit for a moment, had grumbled, "My back will be bent by the time we get out of this desolate place. Can we not find an actual bed for tonight?"

But MacPherson in typical fashion was quietly focused on what he was doing and couldn't be bothered to make a reply.

Stubborn man, Mary thought, as she'd watched his bent head, and as though she had spoken aloud he'd looked up then, directly at her.

Thomson, seeming to think that he hadn't been heard, had tried again: "Can we not stop at an inn? Plainly no one has followed us, and I would happily risk being recognized if I could sleep but one night in a bed."

After holding the silence for half a beat longer, MacPherson had dropped his gaze back to the task at hand. "If someone's following us, ye'll not see them," he'd said. "And the risk is not only to you."

As he'd fastened the straps of the portmanteau, he had

glanced once more at Mary, who had just set Frisque on the ground for a moment to stretch out her arms. The dog wasn't a great weight to carry, but holding her arms bent so long left them aching and numb.

MacPherson had watched her. And then he'd advised, "Let it walk."

"He's a 'him,' not an 'it,'" she had said, "and he's too old to walk so far."

Frisque had already curled into a tight round of fur on the hard ground, his eyes drooping shut. For a moment MacPherson looked down at him, then bending forward he scooped the dog up with one hand and, before Mary could even offer a protest, he'd put the tiny spaniel in the large and deep hip pocket of his horseman's coat. Frisque had all but disappeared, only his muzzle and eyes and ears showing, and after a brief scrabble round with his paws to align himself upright, the little dog had seemed delighted.

And after MacPherson had slung the repacked portmanteau on his back as before with the gun case and set out again, Mary could not deny it had made walking easier, not having Frisque in her arms. She was wearied at times by the weight of her cloak, but whenever the changeable clouds had rolled over the sun and the winds had blown harsh through the valleys and gorges she'd been very grateful to have it for warmth, and when sleeping she'd used it to soften her "bed," rolling into its folds in the way she'd seen Mr. MacPherson roll himself within his great horseman's coat when he lay down to rest before keeping his watch through the night.

Madame Roy says it is the particular way of the Highlanders, Mary had put in her journal, *who in their own homeland of Scotland do wear a great garment of wool that will serve as a skirt or a cloak or a blanket according to need. She says her own father and brothers oft slept out of doors while they tended the herds, in all weathers, and never knew illness until they were come into France where they all slept inside the house and in their beds.*

Thomson, she'd thought, although Scottish, could not have been bred in the Highlands. She could not imagine him sleeping outdoors in the snow, as Madame Roy had described to her—he was a man who'd spent his life in towns and craved their comforts.

When they'd passed beneath the high stronghold of Aubenas, he'd gazed up at its towers with great longing in his eyes, but they had passed it in the cold and misty dawning hour before the town had wakened, for their path was crossed here by a road that carried travelers from the west into the mountains of the Cévennes, and MacPherson had determined they should cross that road themselves before another person could be found upon it.

And then the rains had started, and they'd none of them had comfort after that.

All winter rains were desolate, but these had a relentless force that wore at Mary's stamina. Even with her hood up and her head down she'd been wetted through, the lining of her cloak proving no barrier to such an onslaught. She'd been very thankful her journal and penner were safely wrapped up in the portmanteau Mr. MacPherson had charge of, and would not be ruined. He'd seen to that when the rain first had begun to grow fierce, by arranging the cases he carried so they lay beneath his loose horseman's coat, gaining that extra protection on top of the fact that their leather was already oiled to resist the wet.

He'd moved Frisque, too. The pocket providing no shelter against the rain, Frisque had been buttoned into the warm space between Mr. MacPherson's own waistcoat and undercoat, held there with a firm hand while the Scotsman walked.

Mary had begun to wish he'd carry her, as well, and she'd suspected had she asked he might have tried it, for he seemed to have a strength that knew few limits. But her own strength had been failing by the time they'd finally reached a place where shallow clefts and deeper caves began appearing in the steep rock face beside the path, and when MacPherson had stopped in the mouth of one such cave to rest a moment, she had needed no encouragement to follow.

Thomson, dark with sarcasm, had said, "Another day of this, and I may turn *myself* in. Would they render me the thousand pounds, do you think, if I so surrendered?"

It had been a foolish question asked in jest and not requiring an answer, and so none of them had offered one. He'd peered out at the dismal rain still beating down in torrents, and remarked, "I feel a new appreciation, Mistress Dundas, for your friend the chevalier. This must be how it felt for him the time he had to shelter in that cave, when he went hunting and was caught out in that tempest. You'll not have heard that tale," he'd told MacPherson, as the Scotsman's head had turned, "for she did tell us it in French aboard the diligence *d'eau*, but it is really most remarkable."

He'd urged Mary to tell it again, but she'd shaken her head and declined, not because she was tired—though she was—but because she knew Mr. MacPherson, having read Madame d'Aulnoy's book of *Hypolitus* in Lyon, might remember the fairy tale in which the Russian prince had met the West Wind with all of his brothers, and realize it had been her inspiration.

But Thomson, not put off by her reluctance, had retold the tale himself, lending his own flamboyant style to his description of the Chevalier de Vilbray's encounter with an aged woman and her sons, one of whom had led him on a great adventure overland.

MacPherson, to Mary's relief, had appeared to be only half listening. And when Thomson had ended his story by praising the chevalier's brave resourcefulness, the Scotsman had but shrugged and said, "He sounds a fool, to me."

Mary had stirred to defend her creation. "And why is that?"

"None but a fool," he'd replied, "trusts a stranger he meets in a cave."

She'd have argued the point with him, but she'd been simply too tired from the day's walk—indeed from the nearly a week's worth of walking that had come before it—and so she had leaned her head back on the cold stone and let her eyes close. When she'd opened them, he had been watching her.

She'd felt him watching her a few times after that, when they had ventured out again into the rain, but she had kept her head down and her own gaze on the ground, to keep from stumbling. It had not been till that ground had changed from rough stones into squared ones that she'd noticed they were climbing a steep winding street into a town.

And when MacPherson had conducted them into a proper guesthouse where they'd found themselves with rooms and fires and beds with pillows, Mary had been too amazed to speak at all, much less to thank him.

Madame Roy had set out Mary's gown to dry before the fire, and had a copper tub filled with hot water for a bath. "You've been a fine, strong lass so far, but walking in the wet can raise a fever in those not accustomed to it."

Mary had obediently bathed without a protest, feeling all the aches and soreness of her body swirl away within that blissful, steaming water. She had even let Madame Roy wash her hair—a rare indulgence that stirred memories of her childhood and made Mary close her eyes. It was the second time Madame Roy had done something Mary's mother used to do. The evocation of those memories had grown even stronger when Madame Roy, having combed out Mary's hair before the fire, had tucked her warm and snug beneath the sheets and blankets of her bed, with Frisque a softly breathing weight beside her feet.

And Mary's thoughts had drifted sleepily to Saint-Germain-en-Laye—to happy days and happy evenings, and the voices that surrounded her: the lilting Scottish voices that were strange and yet familiar. Madame Roy's voice, then, had seemed to fit so well with them that Mary of a sudden had decided that a French name did not suit the older woman near as well as that by which their hostess in Lyon had called her. And so, drowsily, her face half buried in the softness of her pillow, she'd asked, "May I call you Effie?"

For a moment there'd been silence, then the other woman's hand had gently stroked the hair from Mary's face. The Scottish woman had said, just as gently, "Aye."

And Effie she had been, to Mary, from that moment on.

They had set out this morning, Monday morning, fresher in their minds and in their steps, though Thomson soon fell back to grumbling.

"You do know," he said to Mary, with a nod ahead to where MacPherson walked now with his long gun in his hand, "why he's been carrying that gun today? This region, so they told me in the town, is rife with bands of thieves and brigands, who will boldly strike by day to rob and plunder the unwary."

"Then it's a good thing," she told him, "that Mr. MacPherson is never unwary."

It was, she thought, perfectly true. Though his attitude seemed to imply he was merely ignoring them, Mary felt certain he heard and marked well every word that was said, and with her spirits rising today she had found it diverting to try to provoke him to break his unwavering silence. She hadn't succeeded, though it had been just as diverting to watch that same silence push Thomson to greater impatience.

When they came to a place where MacPherson desired them to keep to the right, he merely gestured with his hand that gripped the long gun to an outcropping of rock in that direction, causing Thomson—who'd been asking why they hadn't thought to hire a mule this morning—to stop long enough to ask, "And what is *that* supposed to mean?"

Mary quipped it was obvious. "He's saying we might as well speak to that stone as to him, for in truth it would give us as lively an answer."

MacPherson, not breaking stride, half turned his head to glance back at her and looked away in one movement, but Mary thought she glimpsed the faintest twisting of his mouth in what, incredibly, appeared to be a smile. Even more incredibly, when Effie spoke up from behind her and said something briefly in their Highland language, MacPherson replied with a short sound that came close to being a laugh.

But he said nothing more until late afternoon, when they came to a river and found it had risen with yesterday's rain, and the ford where they clearly were meant to cross now lay submerged by a shallow but swift-moving current.

The river was broad, but the bank on the far side was level with a clearing edged by trees. MacPherson, handing Frisque to Mary, had a brief exchange of words with Effie before he told Thomson, "Turn your back," and did the same himself.

Effie bent and stepped out of her shoes and stripped her

stockings off, and rolling them together took the little dog from Mary's arms. "Ye do the same," she said. "I'll help ye cross."

The men respectfully stayed standing with their backs turned while the women hitched their skirts up past their knees and stepped into the rushing water. It was freezing cold, and Mary could not help but give a little shriek, and then a laugh. Her bare feet slipped a little on the wet stones but Effie, having gathered both her skirts and Frisque into one arm, now linked her other arm with Mary's and helped her to balance as they crossed together.

"There," the older woman said, and set the squirming dog down as they reached the other bank, "go have a run, if ye've a mind to." And he did just that, in circles, snuffling happily at all the new discoveries he was making in the clearing. Mary dried her legs and rolled her stockings on, her fingers feeling numb upon the buckles of her shoes. When she was done and Effie had called over to the men to tell them it was safe for them to turn around, she turned herself and saw that Frisque had ventured near the trees. She called him back.

But he had found something. His hair was raised, his ears were back, and even while she thought she'd never seen him look like that, he started barking, and it was a fierce and frenzied sound she'd never heard him make.

She clambered to her feet and looked to where the dog was looking.

Something colder than the water of the river touched her then.

She'd never seen a living wolf. She'd seen their pelts, and even once the lifeless corpse of one that had been killed by hunters, but she'd never seen one standing like a predatory shadow with its rough brown coat concealing it amid the trees, its eyes locked with a fixed and hungry purpose on its prey.

She did not scream. She yelled, and ran for Frisque with all the speed she had, and as the wolf broke from the tree line Mary reached the little dog and snatched him up and wheeled about and went on running, with her lungs on fire.

MacPherson, from the river, yelled as well, "Get down!"

She did not understand. Her gaze in panic fell upon him, standing in the water to his knees, the long gun leveled to his shoulder as he sighted down its barrel.

"Mary!" he called out more strongly. "*Down!*"

She did as ordered, dropping with her body curled round Frisque, the wolf so close behind she heard it panting.

And MacPherson fired.

CHAPTER 31

Send thou the night away in song; and give the joy of grief.
—Macpherson, "Fingal," Book One

The Bas-Vivarais
March 4, 1732

THOMSON WAS STILL SPEAKING of it come the morning. "Flung me," he repeated, as he told the tale again to the three older children of the family where they had been taken in the night before. "Did not 'let me go,' he *flung* me on my ar—well, on my backside in the middle of the river."

"Did you drown?" The littlest boy had asked this question twice already, but appeared distrustful of the answers he'd received before. He was perhaps five years of age, with wide brown eyes. There were two children in the family younger still than him—one barely walking, and an infant in its cradle, but they were not at the table.

Thomson, having twice denied it, told him now, "I did. I drowned. But as you see, I have recovered."

He'd recovered his good humor, Mary noticed, thanks in large part to the generous share of wine their hosts had given him, together with a good hot meal of fish and bread, and a good long sleep that, while it had been on a pallet made for him beside the stove, had nonetheless been in the house and nowhere near a barn or hayloft, so had left him most contented.

He was speaking French, as they had done since they'd first chanced upon this house a quarter of a league beyond the river, since with Mary all disheveled and a little bruised and leaning hard on Effie it had proved to be much easier to make their explanations all in French, though they had kept to their identities, their English names, asserting they had lived in Paris some years and so learned the language.

Seeming satisfied at last by Thomson's answer, the small boy sat back and said, "It was not nice of him to let you drown."

"No," Thomson told him in agreement, "and I thought so at the time. As I was sinking underneath the water, I thought, 'This is not so very nice of him,' but—"

"But," said Mary, smoothly picking up the story, "Mr. Jarvis needed both his hands to hold his gun, so he could shoot the wolf."

The children all looked curiously at the Scotsman sitting in his chair. He took no notice. He'd said nothing yet this morning and indeed had spoken little since the incident itself.

He'd killed the wolf with one shot, as it leaped. She'd seen it struck and twisted by the impact in midair, and then its body had dropped heavily upon her legs and she had curled more tightly round her dog as all the trembling aftermath of fear coursed through her.

Effie should have reached her first. She'd been the nearest, and she could run strongly for a woman of her age, but it was not a woman's boots that kicked the carcass of the wolf aside, nor yet a woman's legs that knelt beside her.

"Are ye hurt?" MacPherson's voice had sounded too rough. "Mary, are ye bitten?"

"No." She had not thought her voice would come at all, yet there it was, if weak. And Effie had by then arrived and knelt beside her too.

MacPherson had said, "Search her and be sure. Be sure."

He'd risen and his boots had paced in Mary's line of vision until Effie, having looked at Mary's feet and legs and arms and hands, had told him in relief, "She's not been bitten."

He had moved away then and had stood beside the river for some minutes, paying little heed to Thomson who had finished crossing on his own and seemed much taken with the marksmanship of his protector. "Truly, I have never seen a shot like that, sir, not in all my life. Is it the rifling that does make the gun so accurate?"

MacPherson had not answered, nor said anything at all since then that Mary could remember.

"Was it a mad wolf?" the elder boy asked. He was not that much older than his little brother, but had, Mary thought, the most serious eyes.

So she soothed him with, "No, it was only a hungry one. Sometimes, when winters are long, it makes animals desperately hungry."

"And would it have eaten Frisque?"

"It wanted to." She looked across at where the little dog was lying in the elder boy's arms, reveling in all the new attention being paid to him.

This family was a young one, with the parents not yet thirty and the eldest of the children—a small girl with golden hair—no more than ten. The children had been turned out of their bed last night to bundle round their parents on the mattress and the floor, while their bed had been given to Mary and Effie, but they did not seem to feel themselves hard done by, and they'd made a great fuss over Frisque, who had abandoned Mary's feet last night to sleep among the children.

Now the elder boy stroked Frisque's soft ears and said, "*I* would not let him walk so close beside the river. It's too dangerous. You should take better care of him."

His mother turned then from the hearth, where she'd been seasoning a pot of soup. She was a tall and straight-backed woman with a pretty face. "You must not speak like that," she told her son. "It's very rude. Apologize."

He did, but put his face down so it rested on the dog's smooth head, and Mary gently said, "But you are right, I should take better care of him. He is an old dog now and is not used to such long journeys."

"You could leave him here with us," the boy suggested.

And his mother turned again. "Why don't you go and help Papa?"

"He's gone to cut more wood. He does not like me helping, when he's cutting wood."

"Then take your brother and your sister and go clean the bedrooms. Go."

"Can Frisque come, too?"

The children's faces turned with hope to Mary, and she nodded, and in a confusion of scraping chairs and dancing feet they rose and went off to their chores.

"I apologize, madam," their mother said, and smiled. "They've never seen so small a dog before. They're very taken with him."

Mary said, "And he with them. It's been a long time since he has had children he could play with." And she told the woman of Frisque's history: how he had been raised and loved by her own neighbor's children, only to be left behind without a backward glance when they had moved away. "This likely brings back happy memories for him, being here. Perhaps," she said, "perhaps he thinks *his* children have come back for him."

Effie, entering the kitchen, asked, "Whose children?" She had two herself, just then—the tiny infant in her arms, the little toddling girl in tow and clinging tightly to her skirts. When Mary answered, Effie nodded. "Yes, he'll not wish to leave with us."

Thomson said, "Nor will you, from the look of it." He smiled as he watched Effie settle herself in a chair with her charges, cradling the baby in the crook of one elbow while the toddling girl climbed to her lap to be held with the other arm. "You do that very gracefully, madam."

"I've had much practice."

The mother asked her, "Have you many children of your own?"

"I only had the one, God rest her soul, but I have been a nurse to many."

"Then," the mother said to Mary, "you must start a family soon, so she'll have children she can care for."

Mary faintly smiled and looked away. Her wandering gaze fell on MacPherson, sitting looking at the mantel of the kitchen hearth, and in English she remarked, "You're very quiet, Mr. Jarvis."

His glance slid briefly sideways, as though waiting for there to be a point to that comment, and when none was provided he looked back to the mantel. "She should wind her clock."

Mary hadn't noticed the clock, to be honest. It wasn't a large one—a wooden-cased table clock with a small handle on top and a face edged with brass. When she translated MacPherson's comment for their hostess, the young woman said, "Oh, I know. It was my mother's, but it's broken, it no longer works. It used to have a lovely chime."

Distilling this to English for MacPherson, Mary only said, "It's broken."

And he nodded, losing interest.

Mary nearly asked if he could fix it, as he'd fixed the watch at Mâcon, but his face didn't invite questions. Instead, she turned her focus to her own concerns.

There was her gown to sponge and clean; her stockings to be mended where they'd torn when she fell running to the ground. And after that, she took her journal out and brought it up to date as best she could from the last time she'd written, through their day of walking in the rain and their most welcome sojourn in the hillside town—whose name, she had since learned, had been Joyeuse, a name of happiness—and all of their encounter with the wolf, that led to where they were today.

We are to spend another night here. Mr. M— claims it is to confound any who have sought to follow us, but I believe it is because I slightly hurt my ankle in my fall and he would let me rest a little longer before I must face a full day's walk on it.

She had no rational foundation for that curious belief, nor could she think of any reason why MacPherson might have gone against his nature so completely as to change his plans so she could be more comfortable, but more and more she felt it must be so.

He'd gone out late that morning with his gun in hand, returning with a brace of rabbits and an observation. "They have a mule in the barn," he'd told Thomson. "Ask if they would sell it."

And with the deal done and the money exchanged, Thomson had said with pleasure, "At last we'll have something to carry our baggage."

"It's carrying *her*." With a curt nod at Mary, the Scotsman had set Thomson straight.

Mary, thinking it imprudent to say anything, had bent her head a little closer to her journal and continued writing her new fairy tale about a huntsman and a wolf, in which the wolf was magic, and the huntsman not at all what he appeared to be.

But she'd asked Effie afterwards, while they had worked together to tuck in the blankets of their bed, "Are all men of the Highlands so unfathomable?"

"Some." Effie smiled slightly, then grew serious. "And some like him, who've seen the wars, have depths we'll never reach or know."

"How do you know he's been to war?"

"It's in the eyes," said Effie, very quietly. "It changes them. They go to war as boys and are made men too soon, too violently, and all of them return with something lost, with something missing. You can see it in their eyes."

Mary had thought about this later, when MacPherson's eyes had briefly met her own while they'd been sitting with the others after supper by the kitchen fire, the children all in bed except the baby who, resisting sleep, was cradled still in Effie's arms.

The mother said, by way of an apology, "He does not like to sleep, this one. He is afraid he'll miss something."

"I nursed a child like that, once," Effie said. "Always watching, always thinking, with a mind that would not rest."

"It must be difficult," the mother said, "to leave the children you have cared for."

Effie, looking down upon the baby, started rocking gently in her chair. "They have their own lives, in the end. They grow, and they forget."

Mr. MacPherson, Mary thought, had not forgotten. She was watching him when Effie began singing softly to the baby in their Highland language, and she saw his eyelids close for just a second as though he'd had something pain him from within, and Mary wondered whether his own mother had perhaps once sung him that same lullaby.

But when the song had finished and she said—in English, so he'd be included in the conversation—"That was very pretty," he surprised her more than he had ever done.

He smiled.

As smiles went, it was but slight and did not show his teeth, but it did carve a line much like a dimple down his cheek and made his face look younger. "That," he told her, "was the 'Griogal Cridhe,' a widow's lament about seeing her husband beheaded."

Mary was still too surprised by that smile to respond, but it didn't keep Thomson from commenting, also in English, "And this is the sort of thing mothers will sing to their children, then, up in the Highlands? To teach them that life's full of treachery?"

Shrugging, MacPherson said, "Or where to seek their revenge."

Effie, still rocking the baby, directed her words to the Scotsman. "Shall I sing a song better matched to your mood, then?"

The shadow of the smile still lingered on his lips as he returned the older woman's gaze, his own more of a dare, thought Mary, than an invitation.

But when Effie started singing this time, nothing of the smile survived. MacPherson sat in silence with his gaze cast downward, fixed upon the hard edge of the table, and when Effie's voice had sung the final note he looked at her, and Mary thought she saw within his eyes the lost and missing things that Effie had been speaking of. Or rather, she could see the hollow places they had left behind.

He stood, and without speaking, went outside.

Soon after that they heard the steady striking of an ax blade chopping wood, and Thomson, attempting to lighten the mood, said to Effie, "Another beheading song, was it?"

The baby had fallen asleep now, and Effie replied in soft tones, "The lament of a warrior for his dead comrades and those whom he loved who lie cold in the ground and unable to comfort his wounds while he wanders alone and unloved. *Fada atà mise an déidh chàich*, it begins, and in English the verse would be: 'I have lived too long after the others, and the world yet troubles me, and there are none left to talk to,'" she said, "'of the lives we once had, in the time before.'"

The past, Mary thought, was itself a great predator, chasing you always behind in a tireless pursuit so you ran from it, or lying ever in wait for you, ready to sink its sharp teeth in the spots where it knew you were weakest.

She tried to stay sociable out of regard for their host and his wife, who were both lovely people with kind and good hearts and seemed honestly glad to have been thus imposed upon, having four new mouths to feed and their household disrupted, because it had brought them new company.

Indeed they were so generous and so keen to please that Thomson had to do no more than mention his enjoyment of warmed wine for them to hang a pot upon the hearth and start to heat some. But when all the cups were handed round and their host ladled out one more and said, "I will just take this to your man, for it is cold outside and he is doing all my work," then Mary without thinking set her own cup down and rose and said, "I'll take it to him."

It *was* cold outside, and clear, the waxing moon just past its quarter in the starry bowl of black night sky. She'd heard the ax fall when she stepped outside, but now she only heard the murmur of the dark wind through the trees that rose around the edges of this little patch of field and farmland. She could see the stump, and all the chips of wood around it, but she could not see MacPherson.

When the furtive sound came close behind her, Mary reacted as anyone might who had just been attacked by a wolf, and wheeled suddenly round.

"Do not strike me." MacPherson gave the warning in a calm tone not unlike the one he'd used to tell her those same words the morning he'd first said them to her, when he had surprised her in the kitchen of the house in Paris. Now, as then, she let her raised hand fall, dismayed to find that in her sudden movement she had spilled a good part of the wine upon the ground.

Carrying on past her, he set the short section of log he was carrying on its cut end on the stump, and adjusting his grip on the ax handle swung the ax round in a sure, measured blow. He had taken off his coat and was in shirt and waistcoat, and his white sleeves had a ghostly appearance. He glanced at the cup in her hand and asked, "Was that for me?"

"It was." Mary looked down. "I can fill it again."

But he held out his hand for it as it was, acknowledging her action with the curt nod that was also, so she'd learned, how he expressed his thanks. Which nudged her to remember her own manners.

"I've not thanked you yet for what you did. For saving me and Frisque," she told him. "Thank you."

He drained the cup. Handed it back to her. "Do it again and I'm shooting the dog," he advised her. "I telt ye that he would be trouble."

"You did." Crossing her arms to keep off the chill wind she confided, "I'm thinking of leaving him here."

She knew that MacPherson, who did not speak French, would have not heard Frisque's story on either occasion she told it, and so she repeated it now for him, adding, "He loves being here with the children. He thinks he's come home."

He said nothing. Another log splintered and split on the stump underneath the strong force of his ax.

"Anyway," Mary said, "he's an old dog, I've no right to drag him around for my own sake. He will be much safer and happier here. And these people are good. They will care for him."

"And if he pines for ye?"

"No fear of that. I am easy to leave." Mary looked skyward, at all the innumerable stars in the blackness. "And easier still to forget." She wasn't sure why she had said that. It sounded so small and so sad, and she hastened to hide what it might have revealed by diverting his focus. "Which way is your home from here?"

"What?"

She said, "Scotland. Where is it?"

He stopped work a moment and holding the ax at his side turned his own head up, searching the stars with the eyes of a man long accustomed to finding his way by them. "There." With his free arm he pointed and Mary looked too, to the land that her father had left long ago, long before he'd left her for the same cause—to follow his king.

"Do you miss it?" she asked.

It was so long before he replied that she thought he was simply ignoring the question, as he often did, but at last in a level voice he said, "There's nothing to miss." Then he turned. "You are cold. Go inside."

Mary knew he was cold as well, cold to the core, and whatever he'd seen in his youth was the cause of it, and in that moment she wanted to tell him how sorry she was for whatever he'd lost. That she knew what it was to be lonely. But nothing in his face or stance was inviting compassion, and Mary well knew there were some things so broken they could not be mended with words.

So she nodded and turned and went in.

She did not know when he came in, for she was in her bed already and asleep, but in the night she woke and turned and felt the blankets cold beside her feet where Frisque was wont to sleep, and realized that the dog was with the children once again, and as she lay there feeling empty at the knowledge she had lost the one companion she had thought would never leave her, and yet trying to be happy for his happiness, she heard the fall of footsteps in the kitchen and the now familiar sound MacPherson's swords made when he took them from their belts and laid them to the side.

Next morning when she woke she found MacPherson sleeping upright in a chair, his head leaned back against the kitchen wall, his legs outstretched in front of him. A stump of candle sat within a small dish on the table, and on the kitchen mantel sat the clock, now ticking rhythmically. And on the hour, to the delight of all the children and their mother, it began to chime.

"We could have had the mule for nothing, after that," said Thomson, as they gathered their things after breakfast, preparing to leave. But they'd paid fairly for the mule, enough to let the family buy another to replace it in the spring, when they would need it for their plowing. And standing saddled at the door and waiting for them patiently, it was a welcome sight to Mary, for her ankle had begun to ache.

Her heart ached more. She watched the children gathering round Frisque to say good-bye to him, and saw his joyful, wagging tail, and she was well aware of what she ought to do and say, and of the choice she ought to make, but it was very difficult.

She felt MacPherson watching her, his hard gaze steady on her face. He slung the gun case on his back and looked from Frisque to Mary, and he told her simply, "Call him."

Mary looked at him, not understanding, knowing that her anguish must be showing in her eyes.

He said again, more slowly, "Call him."

Mary could have told him that it was no use, that she had called her father back and it had made no difference, that if something once desired to leave you it was lost already and forever. But she yielded to the pressure of those unrelenting eyes, and cleared her throat, and called out, "Frisque."

The dog's ears perked, and his head turned towards her, and he left the children and came bounding over happily to paw the hemline of her skirt and ask to be picked up. She could not do it, for her eyes had filled quite suddenly and foolishly, and she feared if she moved at all those tears would fall and shame her. Without words, MacPherson scooped the spaniel up and placed him safe in Mary's arms and lifted both of them to sit upon the mule.

Then taking the bridle into his strong hand he remarked, "Not so easy to leave after all, it appears."

And they started to walk.

CHAPTER 32

Luc bent forward from where he was standing behind my chair, leaning his hands on the armrests and bringing his cheek close to mine as he read the transcribed pages over my shoulder. It usually bothered me when people hovered, invading my personal space, but with Luc it felt...nice.

It was comforting, actually, having the warmth of him there at my back like a shield, and the press of his arms against mine was surprisingly pleasant. I might balk at the more random contact and touching that most people took in their stride as a matter of course every day, but I liked being held by the people I liked to be held by, and how Luc was touching me now felt a lot like a hug. I relaxed deeper into it, resting my head in the strong hollow curve of his shoulder and liking the freshly ironed scent of his smooth cotton shirt.

Luc said, "He's taking care of her."

"He *is* their bodyguard."

"Well, technically he's Mr. Thomson's bodyguard, but here you see he's starting to care more about protecting her than Thomson."

He pointed a few entries back to the lines that read:

We are to spend another night here. Mr. M— claims it is to confound any who have sought to follow us, but I believe it is because I slightly hurt my ankle in my fall and he would let

*me rest a little longer before I must face a full day's walk on it.
In truth he seems to disapprove my smallest movement, and
when I stepped outside on waking to dip water from the barrel there so I could wash, he came behind and took the bucket
from my hands and would not let me carry it. And yet for all
he shows concern, he has today been more withdrawn than I
have seen him, and more sullen. Truly, never have I met a
man more difficult to fathom.*

Luc maintained it wasn't difficult at all. "She's his Achilles'
heel. He's fallen for her."

"I'm sorry?"

He smiled at my skeptical face. "It's OK, you won't see
it because you're a woman. A woman can start with a man
she might find unattractive and slowly begin to see good in
him, grow into love with him, but this is not how it happens
with men. We're much simpler," he told me. "We see and
we want."

I was still unconvinced, so my tone sounded dry. "Really?"

"Really. This bodyguard would have found Mary attractive the first time he saw her in Paris, I promise you, and
he'd have wanted her right from that moment, those feelings
won't change. But how *much* he wants her, the strength of
his feelings—he may not have realized this till he was watching her run from that wolf."

I sorted this out. "So he's been in love with her all along,
but he didn't know he was in love with her until the moment
he thought he might lose her?"

"Yes."

"And you're saying men aren't complicated?"

"We see and we want," he repeated and shrugged.
"Very basic."

"And what do you do when you get what you want?"

"We look after it." He turned his head and I felt the warm brush of his kiss at my temple. "What's this over here?" he asked, reaching to pick up a page to the side of my stack of transcribed ones. "It looks like Noah's writing."

"It is Noah's writing." He'd been in my room earlier, at first just sitting quietly and playing with the cat. So very quietly, in fact, it hadn't bothered me or hindered me from working. I hadn't even been aware how closely he'd been watching me until I'd stopped to stretch and he had asked an intelligent series of questions. "I gave him some samples of ciphers to work through."

"You're teaching my son cryptanalysis?"

"Yes, and he's teaching me how to play Robo Patrol, so it's a fair exchange."

"Hardly." He studied the page for a moment. "You made up these samples yourself?"

"Yes, why?"

"So you don't just break ciphers, you write them as well?"

"Only simple ones, like what I'm working with here. Why?"

"Have you ever done any proper encryption," he asked, "with computers?"

"A very long time ago, just as a hobby. Why?"

Luc shrugged. "No reason." And then he said, "Well, that's not true. There's a reason. You remember I mentioned my brother?"

"Fabien, who lives in California and works for the same company you do only his job is more senior."

"So you remember." He sounded amused. "Well, his job is more senior than mine because he's actually in charge of the development of all of Morland's tactical and sonar systems—a lot of high-level defense contracts—and he just called me this morning to say he was coming to Paris next week to hold interviews for his department here. I don't know all the positions he's filling, but some have to do with creating encryption solutions and cyber security for different clients, and I thought…"

"That's very specialized work. I don't have the experience."

"Fabien trains people all the time. Well, not in person, but he makes arrangements to have them trained. I think he cares more about someone's aptitude, how their mind works, than their years of experience. And your mind works well at *this*." He set the paper down again. "You said you wanted to find a job that let you work on your own, and I know for a fact some of his people do that. From home, even. I can't guarantee that he'd hire you, but I'm pretty sure I could get you an interview."

I angled my head in the warm cradle of his strong shoulder to gain a clear view of his face. He looked innocent. I wasn't fooled. I said, "You're taking care of me."

"Actually, I'm being selfish. Finding a job for you here means you'll stay close to me. But it's your choice. If you'd rather I not interfere, that's fine too."

As I studied his face I remembered the words that MacPherson had spoken to Mary, affecting her strongly enough she had written them down: *Not so easy to leave after all*. And they struck a strong chord with me, too. Luc Sabran wasn't easy to leave.

So a job in France, close to him, working alone on encryption and cyber security, sounded fantastic.

Except, "I'm not all that impressive in interviews."

"Fabien never does anything formal, it isn't his style. We could go into Paris and meet him for lunch if you like, if you'd find it more comfortable."

"At Les Éditeurs?"

"Sure."

"Could we take the Ducati?"

He smiled. "Of course."

"Then I'd like that," I said. "But I'm paying. I still owe you lunch."

I expected an "OK." Instead, he leaned lower and kissed me. I didn't complain.

It seemed almost too quiet a few minutes later when he left me sitting alone at my desk with the diary. It was new for me, but I'd discovered I didn't mind having Diablo and Noah and Luc hanging round while I worked.

And I no longer minded transcribing the fairy tales Mary kept writing. In fact, I'd begun to enjoy them.

I worked all the rest of that day on the one she'd told Thomson and Mr. MacPherson and Madame Roy several days after the wolf had been shot, and this time I could see, as Denise had explained, how the fairy tale fit with the rest of her narrative:

There once was a good and wise king who ruled over a pros-perous land, with a son—the crown prince—and two daugh-ters. The crown prince and his younger sister had good hearts and wise heads as well, but the elder daughter was envious and cruel, and thought it most unfair her brother's birth had robbed her of her chance to rule the kingdom. Calling on a fairy who was practiced in the darker ways of magic, she went about clearing her path to the throne. First she had her brother kidnapped in the night and taken far away into a distant land, from which there would be no returning. Then she had her sister, who was gifted with a rare and lovely voice, changed to a little bird and locked within a golden cage that hung beside the window. And with none to bar her way, the elder sister had her father turned into a small defenseless hare and set him to be chased at that day's hunt. But her father was clever and swift. He outwitted the hounds and the hunters and ran at great speed to a far distant forest of thorns, where he knew he'd be safe. Incensed by this, the elder sister—who had now been crowned the queen—instructed her dark fairy to pursue the hare, her father, to the forest and ensure that he was killed.

This vengeful order was by good luck overheard by the young princess, trapped now as a bird within a hanging cage, and using all her own brave ingenuity she freed herself and flew off through the open window in the same direction the dark fairy had just taken, hoping she might find her father first and somehow warn him. She found the forest made of thorns, and found her father also, in great peril—unaware that to his one side he was being stalked and threatened by a wolf, and to the other stood a huntsman with his long gun to his shoulder.

The princess sang a warning to him, but he could do no more than lie still, for time in this strange forest passed more quickly and the hare-king had already grown too old to run with all the speed he'd once possessed. The princess, to protect him, swooped down hastily and perched atop his back, and from this vantage point she saw now that the huntsman was none other than her brother the crown prince, changed as well from all his wanderings so far from friends and home, his heart grown hard and cold and merciless.

The wolf—who was of course the evil fairy in disguise— had failed to recognize the crown prince, but was quick to spot a way to deal with both the king and younger princess. Stopping her advance, the fairy cast a spell upon the "huntsman" that would make him in a single shot kill bird and hare together.

But before the spell had fully taken hold, the princess sang.

She sang a tune the prince and she had sung when they were children, and the warbling notes began to thaw his frozen heart until they became words within his mind that told him: "Save your shot, dear brother. Do not let your heart grow cold enough to kill without a cause."

And so he'd changed his aim and killed the wolf instead, and with the evil fairy dead the whole enchantment ended and the king and princess were restored to their true selves, and with the prince they left the forest and set off along the path they knew would lead them home.

❧

"That's not a proper ending," was Jacqui's opinion, when I read the tale to her over the phone.

"Why not?"

"She never does say if they made it home safely. Most readers," she said, "like a little more closure."

"Why?"

"They just do. It's human nature, I suppose. We want things to end tidily—especially with fairy tales. We want our happily ever afters."

"Not every story has one."

"Yes, I know." My cousin's voice reminded me that she, with her two less-than-wonderful marriages, knew from experience frogs sometimes stayed frogs no matter how often you kissed them. "But that's the beauty of my business, darling. We can manufacture them."

In honesty I didn't mind an open ending, one that left some room for my imagination to continue with the story line and end it where I chose, or let the characters keep living on within my mind like distant friends I could look in upon from time to time. But I deferred to Jacqui when it came to knowing readers' preferences. I did, though, feel the need to point out, "Mary's fairy tales aren't really meant to stand alone, though. Denise says back in those days women's fairy tales were woven into novels, so you're not supposed to read them on their own—you have to read them in the context of the narrative around them. That's why this one makes more sense when you know what's going on in Mary's diary, with MacPherson and the wolf attack, and when you can see how she's pulling in the other themes dealing with King James and the Jacobites."

My cousin tried rewinding me a notch. "Denise says this?"

"She studied it at uni."

"Ah. And how are you two getting on?"

"Denise and I? We're getting on just fine. I really like her. Why?"

"She doesn't mind that you and her ex-husband are…" Jacqui paused, as though in search of the right phrase.

I waited, curious to see what she'd select.

"…together?" was her final choice.

"She doesn't mind at all. She's said so." Several times, I could have added. Clearly. Unequivocally. *You're good for him*, she'd said to me this morning, when we'd stood together at the kitchen window watching Luc come up the path from the back garden. *He's so happy. Look at him.* He made me happy too, and she had commented on that as well.

My cousin said, "I see," though I suspected that she didn't. "And just how 'together' are you?"

"Sorry?"

Bluntly, because she had learned the blunt approach

was best with me, she asked me, "Are you sleeping with him?"

"No."

"Oh." There was no way on the phone that I could try to sort the blend of vocal tones in that one word. I couldn't tell if she was pleased or disapproving or surprised. "Why not?"

She wasn't being rude. She knew my pattern; knew that normally I'd meet a man and have him in my bed and out the door again within a week. I shrugged and said, "I don't feel any rush, with Luc. I feel like we have time."

She didn't answer straightaway. And then she only said, "That's good. I hope it lasts."

I knew *that* tone. "But you don't think it will."

"I didn't say that. Does he know that you have Asperger's?"

"No. Not unless you told him."

Jacqui reassured me with, "You know I'd never do that."

"Good. So, getting back to Mary and the diary…"

"Yes. Where are they now?"

"Just outside Nîmes." I named the city in Provence, just south of Avignon, where Mary and the others had been forced to break their journey. "They've been stuck there for a while now. Mr. Thomson's ill in bed. He has a fever."

"All that walking in the rain, no doubt. Or else his dunking in the river."

"Mary walked in rain too, and she isn't ill." I knew it wasn't logical for me to feel such pride in the resilience of a woman I would never meet, but I was growing close to Mary through her words and so I felt it anyway. I liked her sense of humor and her strength and her tenacity, and her determination to let nothing keep her down. She'd had no liking for the rooms they'd lodged in outside Nîmes, and Mr. Thomson with his fever had apparently not been an easy patient, yet she'd made the best of things and done her part to entertain him and Madame Roy and MacPherson in the evenings with her stories, having noted in her diary her amusement that MacPherson, when she'd told them all the story of the huntsman and the wolf, had replied with his opinion the crown prince would have done well to shoot the lot of them and gain himself a kingdom he could rule alone in peace.

For as it stands, so Mr. M— remarked, the prince is left to guide the king and princess through the forest when he might have spared himself the effort, which he said in such a tone I knew he was not serious, for though we all must be indeed a weight upon him, he appears to carry it with ease, as he does everything.

I wasn't the best at detecting emotional interplay, and I'd admittedly missed all the signs that Luc said showed MacPherson had fallen for Mary, but even I was aware of the quietly growing rapport between Mary and the Highlander. In the fortnight they'd spent stuck there waiting for Thomson to make his recovery, she'd written five times in her diary, and one of those entries was given entirely over to the day MacPherson had taken her into the city itself—to assist with translation while he bought supplies, or that at least had been Mary's belief, though I knew as well as she did Madame Roy could have done that for him as well, and with less trouble on his part, for Mary still needed to ride the mule. But she'd had a splendid time from the sound of it, looking through the shops and stalls and admiring the ancient sights.

There is a most impressive tower and a temple and, against the southern city walls, an ancient amphitheater where the Romans set their warriors to fight with beasts and with each other, now so picturesquely run to ruins that I might have wandered all the day within it had not Mr. M— refused to let me wander. He is watchful of my ankle even though Madame Roy worked a Scottish charm upon it yestereve, tying three knots in a white linen thread that she held in her mouth while repeating a verse in her language, then winding the thread round my ankle where I am to leave it until it unravels itself. She says such a charm in the Highland tongue is called an oleless, or so it does sound to my ears, and will work without fail, and in truth I confess that already I feel an improvement, and will I feel sure be quite ready to walk on my own when we leave here a few days hence.

Summarizing all of this for Jacqui now, I said, "I haven't gone beyond that, but I'm guessing that they'll still be heading south."

My cousin told me, "Yes, they're going to Marseilles. I've done a bit of sleuthing myself this week." It turned out she'd actually sent her assistant, the handsome and capable Humphrey, to Kew, to the National Archives, to search through their records for anything useful on Thomson. "Humphrey found a lot of letters flying back and forth between the government in London and the English ambassador in Paris, who had spies all over. Not the nicest people," she pronounced them. "Keep your eyes open for any mention Mary might make in her diary of two Jacobites named Mr. Cole and Mr. Warren, in Marseilles."

I jotted the names down. "Why?"

"Humphrey's been reading their letters all week, and he thinks they're both bastards. They shook Thomson's hand and pretended to be his friend," Jacqui said, "while they betrayed him."

CHAPTER 33

Now, like a dreadful wave afar, appeared the ship…
—Macpherson, "Fingal," Book Three

Marseilles
March 31, 1732

M R. WARREN." THOMSON SHOOK the Irish banker's hand with pleasure. "Kind of you to see us."

"Mr.…Symonds, is it?"

Mary had expected him to be an older man, but he was somewhere between her own age and MacPherson's, well dressed in the tidy immaculate way of most men who had dealings with money. She was glad she had taken the trouble to comb out her hair and repin it beneath the lace headdress she'd traded her spare pair of gloves for at Nîmes.

His office was in the Cours, the broad main street of Marseilles, which ran perfectly straight and was lined with twin rows of tall trees that lent shade to the benches and fountains beneath them. Mary had a clear view of the street and those trees from the chair that the banker held graciously out for her, close to the window.

He turned to his clerk. "Would you be so kind as to go call on Mr. Thomas Cole and ask him if he's able to attend us? Thank you."

When the clerk had gone, the banker closed the door and turned to them and smiled. "Now then, Mr. Thomson, let us have a proper introduction, sir. I'm glad to meet you."

As they shook hands for a second time he added, "I'm sorry I wasn't here when you arrived in town. I had expected, you see, that you'd come down through Avignon, and having business myself there just lately I tarried awhile there in anticipation of your coming. But you did not come through Avignon?"

MacPherson, standing quietly behind them, gave the answer. "No."

"I see." The young man looked up at the Scotsman with a quick assessing eye and wisely chose not to pursue the matter. "Are there only three of you?"

"Four, actually," said Thomson. "We've a maid, who's stayed to watch our things this morning. And our dog."

"You have a dog as well?" The Irishman raised both his eyebrows slightly as though not sure how to manage such a curious assemblage. "Never mind, I'm sure we'll find you something suitable. You wish to go by sea, I take it?"

"If we can. It will be quicker," Thomson said.

"Indeed. And very much safer," the banker replied. "You'll avoid going through any other Dominions on your way to Rome, for 'tis sure the English ministers in Genoa and Leghorn have been told to keep a watch for you."

MacPherson said, "We did not mention Rome."

"Well no, you didn't, fair enough. But that is where the king lives, is it not?" asked Warren. "Also, I've a letter from your banker, Mr. Wogan, writ from Paris with advice that if a package comes for you after you've left here, I'm to send it on to Rome. So I assumed." His smile, self-deprecating, sought to charm, and seeing it had no effect upon the Scotsman he said in a mock aside to Thomson, "Has he always been this trusting?"

Thomson laughed. "Come now," he told MacPherson,

"surely we can let our guards down among friends. We're all of the same party, and truly I'm weary of watching my back."

Mary privately thought he could hardly have cause to complain or be weary, when Mr. MacPherson had been the one doing the watching for all of them. But she said nothing. Her mind had been all but consumed by that single word: *Rome.*

They were going to Rome.

Where the king was. And where her brothers and father had gone. Where her father was, still.

Mary kept her face turned to the window and gazed at the street without seeing it, hearing but little of what others said. She recovered herself for a moment to nod a polite greeting to Mr. Cole—Mr. Warren's good friend and associate—when he came in, and she noticed the clerk had been sent off again on an errand to leave them in privacy, but beyond that she retained little interest for what else went on in the room.

She was vaguely aware they were speaking about the affair of the Charitable Corporation, and Thomson's sad part in it, although there seemed to be differences in how he told the tale this time around, and those differences gradually drew Mary's focus away from the window and back to the men.

"…and having the management of the whole, we contrived to bring up all the stock into our own hands with the Company's money, and in that time got the stock augmented fivefold, to £600,000."

"And how did you manage that?" Warren had leaned forward in his chair as though he found the story fascinating.

"Why, sir, as such things are always done. By bribing several members of Parliament to pass acts allowing it," Thomson said drily. "Yet clearly we did not bribe widely enough, for we could not keep the directors of the great companies in London, who found our traffic a prejudice to their own, from persuading Parliament to enter into an examination of our Corporation's affairs, by which means all our schemes were defeated and I obliged to come abroad."

"A disappointment to you," Mr. Cole commiserated.

"Yes, indeed. For had Parliament not interfered, I should soon have had in my hands four or five hundred thousand pounds with which to assist the king."

"And how much have you now?"

Mary waited for Thomson to answer Cole's question, trying to reconcile what he'd just said with the tale he had told her in Lyon, confused by the details that would not be matched. Glancing over her shoulder she saw that MacPherson was still standing stone-faced beside the room's door, and she could not tell from his expression how much he himself knew about the affair.

Thomson smiled at Warren and Cole in his charming way. "Enough," he told them both, "to get to Rome, if you can find a ship to carry us."

Which brought them back to business.

In this, Mr. Warren deferred to his friend, who seemed better acquainted with all of the various ships in the harbor.

"I know a man, Vilere—a very good man, comes from Avignon, who is an officer of the galleys, and could possibly arrange—"

MacPherson cut him off. "No galleys."

"Ah. Well then. I would not send you by felucca at this time of year, their crews are not so seaworthy and often unreliable, and you have women with you…" He thought for a moment. "There's one ship might suit you quite well, though the captain's a bit of a rogue." To MacPherson, he said, "Have you any objection to sailing with Spaniards?"

"None."

"Right. Let me see, then, what I can arrange for you."

Thomson and Warren and Cole shook hands all round and Warren in parting asked once more, as though to be sure, "So you do not need money?"

Thomson assured him he did not. "But when I return, if I have any business, sir, rest assured you'll be the first man to know it."

The young banker found this of interest. "And when do you plan to return?"

But his clerk, having finished his errand, chose that exact moment to enter the room. Thomson said in a jovial tone, "Very soon, I should think, for we plan but to travel a few leagues from town and return hence as soon as we can before Easter week."

Men and their secrets, thought Mary, as she rose to follow MacPherson and Thomson out into the sunlit street. Men and their lies. And yet…

She lifted her chin and the Scotsman looked down at her as she asked bluntly, "Was this the plan from the beginning, to take us to Rome?"

He replied, "Would it matter?"

To no one, she reasoned, except very possibly her. Nicolas had said, straight out, if anybody wanted something from their father, they would have to go to Rome to ask him. And perhaps her brother had been speaking more to her than to her cousin, when he'd said that. Just perhaps, this had been Nicolas's and her father's own design from the beginning. Mary dared to let a tiny seed of hope begin to try its roots within her at the thought that maybe, as she'd called to Frisque that morning, so her father was now calling her. And asking her to come to him.

That seed had grown yet larger by the afternoon, when Mr. Cole sent word for them to meet him at the quayside and be ready to depart.

"A ship," said Effie, with a note of resignation in her voice. "It would be."

Mary, neatly wrapping up her journal, felt deep sympathy. "It was too cruel of them," she said, "to send you on this journey when you suffer so from motion."

"No one sent me on this journey, dear. I asked to come. Do you have your other stockings? Those ones, aye."

"But why?" asked Mary, as she passed the stockings over to be packed.

"Because you'll need a dry pair close to hand, once we're aboard the ship."

"No, why would you have asked to come?"

"I had my reasons," said the Scotswoman, and kept them to herself, as seemed increasingly to Mary to be something of a habit of the Highlands, for MacPherson too said next to nothing as they made their way down to the quayside.

Marseilles was a pretty town, built at the edge of the land with the sun shining hard to the south on the Mediterranean Sea, and the hills ringing all round behind with their dotting of villas and country estates. The long harbor, while not large, was made safe by sheltering rocks and at this hour of day was a bustling place with the breeze bearing scents of wet wood and warm canvas and salt from the sparkling sea. Tall ships idled and creaked at their moorings, some seeming impatient to leave while still others seemed peacefully slumbering, glad of the rest, while around and amidst them bobbed smaller boats carrying produce and merchandise, sailors and passengers, men of all races and languages mingled together.

For Mary, who had only read of such sights in the pages of books and imagined them in her own mind, this bewildered and thrilled her and filled her with wonder.

It was only when they had met Cole at a table with benches set near to a hut by the water, where they were served small cups of coffee by a man who wore, Mary saw to her horror, a fetter and chain on his leg, that she started to notice the other men like him who shuffled in chains, often linked two together, the chain borne between them, and all of them wearing some form of the same sorry uniform: red coats that looked more like peasants' frock shirts, partway open in front and designed to be pulled on without any buttons; and coarse linen shirts and brown breeches and red caps to cover their heads, which appeared to be generally shaved.

"Galley slaves," Cole explained, when he saw her reaction. "A common sight here, I'm afraid, and one that's most distressing to we men—and ladies—born to British freedom, though I'm told there are but half as many galleys now as there were in the old king's day."

Mary took no comfort from that, for as she looked round the harbor she saw far too many ships with rows of dreadful oars set on their waterlines. So many ships that she knew for each pair of men she now saw laboring beneath their chains, there must be hundreds more imprisoned in the dark and crowded decks who had not even that small scrap of liberty.

Thomson answered smoothly, "British freedom is a drink that has a different taste depending where you're served it. I suspect that what my countrymen have tasted would to you taste much like servitude."

Which drew a glance from Effie that might well have been approval. It was difficult to know, with Effie. She sat to the table's end, declining coffee for her stomach's sake, in preparation for the trial by sea that was to come.

"Just so," said Mr. Cole. "I'm sure I did not mean offense. 'Tis only that my friend Vilere, who long has been an officer aboard the galleys, tells me that our sentiment affords these men more sympathy and pity than they do deserve, for most of them are criminals so vile that in another Christian country they'd be put to death for what they'd done."

"This is a death," said Mary, with her gaze still on the galleys. "Slavery is a kind of death."

"But see now, that is sentiment," said Cole, to prove his argument. "And not all slaves are chained below and beaten. Some have leave to work at trades, you see their huts along the quay here. And this man, this Turk"—he nodded to the man who'd brought them coffee—"he was taken in a war, and so is treated better than the others, for the French would have his people see this when they come to port, in hopes the Turks will treat their own French prisoners in like fashion. He can work, and if he works hard he perhaps can save enough to pay his ransom, and return to his own homeland. So you see, you are quite wrong to let your sentiment paint everything a single shade of black."

MacPherson, who till now had sat in stoic silence on the bench across from Mary, said, "She has a right to think as she decides."

Her upward glance was only meant to show him she was grateful he'd defended her, but what she saw in his eyes when she met them put her in a great confusion, for in place of their accustomed frost-like calm she glimpsed a pain so deep and dark it was as if he'd briefly torn a bandage back to show a violent wound. It vanished even as she looked, but left her troubled.

Thomson said, "Come, let us speak of less afflicting things. Which is our ship?" He turned a little in his seat to view the tall, three-masted ship that Mr. Cole was pointing to.

Cole said, "That's it. The *Princesa Maria*."

"A good name," was Thomson's opinion. He asked Mary, "Would you not agree, my dear?" His kind voice and warm eyes sought to restore the peace, an effort he extended now to Cole. He looked around and said, "I should imagine this is yet a very pleasant place to live."

"It is. When you return, sir, you should think to settle here or someplace nearby where you might employ yourself in trade, for I do recommend it. That is, if you can remain here, unmolested in this kingdom."

A man was approaching them.

Middle-aged, heavily built, with a brown coat and shiny brass buttons, he held out his hand to shake Cole's and surprised them with English. "Well met, sir. Well met. And would these be my passengers?"

Mary's first thought was that this man looked neither a rogue nor a Spaniard, but part of the mystery was solved when, as Mr. Cole started to make introductions, the man said, "No names on the quayside, sir. Captain forbids it. I daresay he'll get them all sorted out once they're on board. This is all of your baggage, then? Right. Come along."

And with no more ceremony, they were gathered up and led along the quayside to the waiting ship, though Mary noticed that MacPherson, as the others took their leave of Mr. Cole, pressed something in the Turkish war slave's hand that left that man staring dumbfounded at his open palm for half a minute afterwards.

She glanced up at the Scotsman as his long and easy

strides brought him beside her, and she asked, "Did you just pay his ransom?"

He didn't answer, only gave a nod at Frisque within her arms and said, "Take care he doesn't get a ducking."

She held Frisque as firmly as she could while they were boarding, and more firmly still when they were standing on the deck and all the ropes were being cast away, for she had never been aboard a proper ship and was not used to how it rolled and subtly played against her balance as the sails were set to catch the early afternoon's fair wind and take advantage of the tide to draw it surely out to sea.

Frisque wagged his tail and pushed his forelegs on her arm to thrust his nose into the wind that blew more strongly once they'd come clear of the harbor. Mary had to fight the urge to do the same, for it in truth was an exhilarating feeling, but she had a sense that it would look undignified to all the crewmen standing within sight of them, some staring as if they'd not carried passengers before.

When they had rounded the great rock that stood guard at the harbor's entrance, the brown-coated man who'd helped them all on board before instructing them to wait there while the ship got under sail, returned and showed them all a cheery smile.

"Now," he said, and looked from Thomson to MacPherson brightly, "which of you is Mr. Symonds?"

Something—some small inner instinct—stabbed at Mary then. It must have stabbed MacPherson too, for his reply cut over Thomson's. "I am."

"Right then, Mr. Symonds." Without altering his tone or smile the man drew out a pistol. "I'll be taking both those swords, sir, if you please."

CHAPTER 34

But, now, the night is round thee:
and the winds have deceived thy sails.
—Macpherson, "Fingal," Book Three

Marseilles
March 31, 1732

H E STOOD HIS GROUND, as she had known he would, and did not yield.

"Perhaps, sir, you misunderstand the situation," said the man in the brown coat. His heavy face gave him a jolly and benevolent appearance that was strikingly at odds with what was happening. Behind him, other men had now begun to shift position so they formed an almost ordered rank, and Mary saw that other weapons had been drawn. "'Tis Captain's orders that none other than his crewmen carry weapons on this ship, so I will have them even if I have to shoot you for them, sir. But if I shoot you, what will happen to these ladies?"

From behind him, someone made a crude remark in rustic French that would have told him to the letter what would happen to the ladies, had he understood that language. Mary knew her face had whitened, but she would not show her fear to men like these. She pressed her back against the railing of the ship and held Frisque tightly.

She could see MacPherson thinking. That was good, she told herself, because he'd always found a way to get them out of trouble in the past. He'd always taken care of them. He'd always—

Once again the rude French sailor made a lewd insulting comment, this time aimed with specificity at Mary, and she held her head up higher, though her knees began to tremble slightly underneath her skirts.

MacPherson moved his head a fraction till his gaze was leveled on the man who'd spoken. "If you wish to lose your tongue, together with that useless part you think to violate my wife with, I suggest you speak again." He said it quietly and calmly. And in perfect French.

She nearly did fall, then, from sheer surprise, but he'd already switched back into English and was saying to the man in brown, "I'll let ye have my swords if ye will let me have your word my wife and servants won't be harmed."

The man replied, "And I will let *you* live, sir, if you let me have your swords."

They were at an impasse.

Mary watched MacPherson weigh the varied outcomes, then he took both sword hilts in his hands and drew them out and held them, harmless, for the men to take from him. Her heart sank very slightly but she knew from having seen him kill the man who'd been with Stevens at Valence that he had blades where none would find them, and that even when he seemed unarmed to most, he was yet deadly.

"And those pistols," came the next instruction.

Mary hadn't known he carried pistols, and she hadn't ever seen them. How the man in brown had spotted them she didn't know, but there they were, a pair of them, with silver inlaid handles, being turned and handed over.

"And the long gun on your back."

He slipped the gun case off as well, without resistance.

"And the dagger."

There was movement in the ranks of men behind

the man in brown who held the pistol, and a pleasantly inflected male voice with a Spanish accent said, "That is no ordinary dagger."

Mary watched the men part like a river when it meets a rock, and saw their captain—since from how they had reacted, he could be no other—casually approach. He cut a daring, gallant figure, in a coat of forest green with gold braid trim, and more gold on his waistcoat and the brim of his black hat, with falls of lace at cuffs and collar. He was very handsome, and the sharply trimmed dark beard that matched the long curls of his hair lent him an air that was not totally respectable.

He told them all, "*That*, to the men of the mountains of Scotland, is one of their weapons most sacred. A weapon of honor." He stopped at the side of the man with the pistol, not blocking the other man's aim but not hiding behind it. He challenged MacPherson, "Do you have this honor?" His tone was a gauntlet thrown down by a man who, beneath all his charm, was yet dangerous. "Or are you a…how do you call them in your country? Broken men, isn't it? One of those broken men, who live beyond the law."

Coldly, MacPherson said, "I am no broken man."

"Then you may keep all your weapons, if you swear an oath on your dagger that they'll not be used against me or my men."

"I'd first have your word ye'll harm neither my wife nor our servants."

This seemed to amuse him. "And what shall I swear by?"

"Your word as a Spaniard will do."

Thomson made an incredulous sound like a snort. "Come now."

"Given," the Spaniard replied, as with interest and

something approaching respect he looked on while MacPherson drew the sharp dirk from his belt and raised it level to his lips to kiss the blade and seal the oath. And then the captain gave a nod and turning told his men, "Stand down. And give him back his weapons."

Coming forward with a swagger in his step that nearly matched MacPherson's, he said, "May I see your papers?" With the papers in his hand he sorted through them. Glanced at Thomson. "So then you are Mr. Jarvis, yes? And this is Mrs. Grant." He showed some sympathy for Effie, who between the motion of the ship and this upsetting incident was looking ill. "Oh, Mrs. Grant, you are not well. I'll send Emiliana to look after you. She is good at looking after people." He studied MacPherson's hard features, and in a dry tone said, "Your name is not Symonds, I think, Mr. Symonds."

"It is while I'm on board your ship."

"Fair enough. And your wife, this is truly your wife? She is lovely. And look, she has brought me some dinner." He grinned both at Frisque and at Mary's expression. "I'm not being serious. See how she looks at me now? You and your dog are both safe, Mrs. Symonds, I promise." Returning the papers to Mr. MacPherson, he swept off his hat. "I am Marcos María del Rio Cuerda," he said, "at your service."

He bowed, Mary thought, with the grace of a gentleman. But in his eyes shone the devil's own mischief.

"Now," he said, clapping a hand on MacPherson's back as though they'd long been friends, "let's get your wife and your servants below, and we'll go have a drink."

❧

Mary wasn't convinced that the captain, del Rio, was someone to trust.

He had kept his word, taking them safely below where he'd shown Mr. Thomson and Effie to two little cabins tucked into the prow of the ship, which while cramped were at least clean and private; and as he had promised, he'd called a young woman to come sit with Effie and make her more comfortable. Then he had given MacPherson and Mary a much larger cabin beneath his own, set in the stern down a half flight of steps.

She'd barely had time to adjust to the fact that she would now be sharing this room with MacPherson, alone, without Effie, when Captain del Rio had ordered MacPherson again to come drink with him. Mary had not been sure which prospect she'd dreaded most—being left with MacPherson, or left on her own. But before he had left her, the Scotsman had taken one silver-edged pistol and folded her hand round it, telling her low, "Keep that aimed at the door and if anyone enters but me, shoot them."

Not the most comforting manner, thought Mary, in which to be left.

But she'd known from his tone and his words he was doing the best that he could to protect her, and so she had nodded and made no complaint when he'd gone with the captain.

That had seemed like a lifetime ago.

She'd been left with three candles, all cheerily burning; a narrow berth set in the wall, with a curtain to close out the rest of the room, and a table with two chairs nailed fast to the floor. For a while she had sat in one chair holding Frisque, till he'd fallen asleep and she'd shifted him onto the berth where he would be more comfortable. Then she'd been free to move restlessly round the confining space, hearing the tramping of feet and the voices of men while she listened as hard as she could for MacPherson's. It struck her she might not be able to pick his voice out from the others so easily if he were speaking in Spanish. Or French.

He spoke French.

That discovery rushed back on her with its full weight of embarrassments and implications, and Mary could feel her cheeks flushing although there was nobody else in the cabin. She cast her mind miserably back to the times she had spoken when she had been sure he would not understand her. She thought of the things she had said. And she tried to feel angry with him for deceiving her, only he hadn't—he'd never once actually told her he didn't speak French. She'd assumed it, and if he had then played along with it she could not fault him for that, since had *she* been a man sent to guard a collection of strangers, she might have, like him, sought to keep that advantage. It was in many ways like her own choice to not reveal it when she'd had carte blanche while playing cards at Fontainebleau—because it would have laid her own hand bare to her opponent. Mary, too, had kept her secrets. But she wished she had not told the frilly sisters, in her teasing way, that he was sentimental and wrote poetry. And that, like Madame d'Aulnoy's Russian prince, he'd suffered through a tragic romance.

It was at least a credit to her storytelling that she had made anyone believe such things about him, for to take a man as hard and stern-faced as MacPherson and convincingly portray him as the hero of a love story was something that took more than an inspired imagination.

Or at least, she thought as much until she heard the steps of two men coming down the stairs, and then the cabin door swung open and MacPherson ducked beneath the lintel while Captain del Rio leaned a shoulder on the door frame for support and said, "I still do not believe you."

And MacPherson *laughed*. A sound she'd never heard before. A deep and rich and rolling sound that woke the sleeping dog and made Frisque answer with a happy woof.

For Mary's part, she could do little more than stand and gape, because the Scotsman looked so different in this mood that she could scarce believe it was the same man she had so long traveled with. Had she looked closely at his eyes she might have seen the quiet warning in them, but she only noticed that his smile had carved creases at their outer corners in a way that really was attractive, so she wasn't in the least prepared when he advanced without a hint of hesitation and embraced her with the sureness of a man who need not fear rejection. Low, and for her ears alone, he murmured, "Do not strike me."

And he kissed her.

At the first touch of his mouth on hers she inhaled quickly in surprise and then stopped breathing altogether, having for some idiotic reason lost all knowledge of the way that it was done.

She had read books. In Madame d'Aulnoy's stories, lovers met in secret, shared languishing looks and sighs, and then the hero kissed his lady's hands, always with tenderness and passion.

There was tenderness and passion in MacPherson's kiss as well, but it was nothing like the books. No room for languishing. His hold was firm and solid, and she felt as though she'd suddenly been wrapped within a blanket of sensations. She felt his hand warm on the curve of her jaw, felt the hard calloused strength of his fingers at rest on the side of her neck where her pulse beat. She felt when those fingers slid into her hair, and continued to slide till his whole hand was cupping the back of her head and supporting her, while her own hand, having lifted in reflex, encountered the sleeve of his coat and could do nothing more than to cling to it or be caught tightly between them as his other arm settled possessively into the curve of her back, a secure weight she felt through the bones of her stays. And she felt…oh, she *felt*—only that, and the other words all fell away from her.

Mary heard Captain del Rio say something she didn't quite catch and the cabin door creaked and MacPherson released her, a movement she felt but did not see because she discovered her eyes had closed. It took a great deal of focus to open them. And a great effort and one more deep breath to look up.

He stood close, and the gaze angled down to her own was as difficult to fathom as the reason he had kissed her. Yet she knew there must have been a reason. He would never have done such a thing at random.

Mary guessed the answer lay in what del Rio had remarked when he came in, and as the Spaniard's steps retreated to the upper deck she asked, "Was that designed to help convince the captain we are married?" It heartened her to find she had a voice, although it seemed to lack the force or will to rise above a whisper.

"Aye."

As someone accustomed to playing a part, Mary had to admit he'd been very convincing. The taste of the wine he had drunk lingered still on her lips, and she had to resist the irrational impulse to touch them, as if to revisit the feel of his kiss. Since that would only embarrass them both, Mary tried instead to show him she had taken it in stride, and lightly asked, "And does he plan to sell me in the marketplace at Tunis, or to keep me for himself?"

MacPherson promised, "He'll do neither."

"But he only gave his word he would protect your servants

and your wife," she added, with a nod of understanding. "So if I am not your wife, he'll not be bound to give me his protection, nor to keep me safe."

He stood a moment longer, silently assessing her with eyes that shielded all his thoughts. And then he said, "I'll keep ye safe." He sounded very sure.

And she believed him.

Mary was not sure when she'd stopped fearing him. She thought it might have started when he'd shot the wolf to save her, though she owned it might have started even earlier. In Valence, when he'd cared to intercede to save the honor of a woman other men would not have valued. Or in Lyon, when she'd watched him reading Madame d'Aulnoy's books. Or perhaps earlier than that, in Mâcon, when he'd fixed the broken watch.

She pondered this in silence later, while they shared the supper that was brought to them, and after, while MacPherson stood outside the cabin door to give her privacy to undress to her white chemise and shake the dust and wrinkles from her gown and slip into the berth and draw the curtains closed. She went on thinking, after he'd stepped back into the cabin and she'd heard him getting ready for his own "bed" on the floor against the far wall, and the candles had been snuffed to leave the cabin in a darkness so complete she could see nothing but the images that rose within her mind.

Frisque sighed, and stirred, and snuggled deeper in the blankets next to Mary as the ship rolled to the rhythm of the midnight tides.

She kept her voice low as she said, "I do not know your name."

The Scotsman stirred as well against the far wall, and she knew he was listening.

"If I am meant to be your wife, I ought to know your Christian name. What is it?"

"Hugh."

It fit him well, she thought. A simple name, and solid: Hugh MacPherson.

"And how many languages *do* you speak?"

There was a pause, and his tone held a thread of indulgence that seemed to acknowledge the reason she'd asked. "Counting English? Four."

"So, French, English, Spanish, and…what do you call your own language?"

"The Gaelic."

"The Gaelic," she echoed. "And nothing else?"

"Not really. No."

Mary let that one pass. "And how did you learn to fix timepieces?"

Once more the pause, and then, "It was my trade."

Surprised by that, she turned her head towards him even though she could not see him in the dark. "You were a clock maker?"

"A watchmaker's apprentice."

"Truly?"

"Aye."

Her first thought was to ask him what had happened, why he hadn't carried on to become master of that trade, but she was checked by her remembrance that the late rebellion more than sixteen years ago had happened when MacPherson would have been about the age of an apprentice. She'd been sheltered, first at Saint-Germain-en-Laye and then at Chanteloup-les-Vignes, as were many of the second generation exiles who lived insulated from the brutal fighting in their homeland, but MacPherson, with the war in

Scotland, clearly had been made too soon a man, as Effie had observed, and Mary wondered what things had been lost to him because of it.

Instead she asked, after a pause of her own, "Why did you not take the letter away from me?"

"What letter?"

"You know what letter. The one I intended to post from Lyon."

If a silence could shrug, Mary thought, this one did. He told her simply, "Who was I to come between yourself and the Chevalier de Vilbray?"

She wasn't fooled. With his sharpness of mind, he would easily have figured out, from what she'd said while he was present, what she had been planning. And from his dry voice, she knew *he* had not been fooled by all her stories about the chevalier. So what she said next was a matter of fact to them both: "You knew I meant to leave."

When no reply came, Mary asked, "Would you have stopped me, for fear I'd expose Mr. Thomson? Or would you have let me go?"

"Which is the answer that makes ye stop talking?"

"I believe you would have kept me from leaving. I think you'd have killed me," she said, "if you'd needed to. Wouldn't you?"

The silence lasted so long this time Mary thought for certain he had gone to sleep. But then she heard him move, his voice less clear as though he'd rolled to face away from her. "The letter's burnt, and I've not killed ye. Let the past be past."

An easy thing to say, thought Mary. Far less easy to accomplish.

But she tried, and she was drifting with the peaceful, lulling rocking of the ship when one last question struck her.

"Hugh?" she asked him, softly. "What's a broken man?"

No answer came except his steady breathing; but she had the sense that he, like her, was not yet sleeping, only lying silently and staring at the dark.

CHAPTER 35

"Come thou," I said, "from the roar of ocean, thou rider of the storm.
Partake the feast within my hall. It is the house of strangers."
—Macpherson, "Fingal," Book Three

The Mediterranean
April 1, 1732

S HE COUNTED TWELVE KNIVES at the table. Eight pistols. A
sword at the hip of each seated man; two on MacPherson,
which made five in all. And the wickedly pointed gilt handle
of the heavy walking stick held by the ship's first mate could
have quite easily cracked a man's skull, so the whole party
gathered for dinner looked dangerous.

Mary smiled faintly as she raised her cup of wine, thinking of her brother Nicolas telling her back in Chatou there
was no danger in her assignment, and that he would never
consent to a scheme that would place her in harm's way. And
yet, here she was, having traveled these past weeks from Paris
with danger her constant companion, and sitting down now
to a meal with a pirate.

"Pirate *hunter*," was Captain del Rio's correction of
Thomson's remark as they started their first course, a rich
fish stew served with brown bread. "It is true, in my younger
days I was more reckless, maybe less discriminating in the
ships I took for prizes, but my government like yours has
learned there's nothing better than a thief to trap another
thief, and so now I protect the *flota*—all our ships that cross
together every year from the Americas—and in the other

seasons I hunt the corsairs of the Barbary Coast. *They* are pirates," he added, and pointed with his knife at Thomson to emphasize. "It's a good thing you are with me, they do not dare to attack the *Princesa Maria*."

He'd been very gracious, inviting a man who he thought was a servant to join them at table, but Mary had already noticed that Captain del Rio did not keep to social conventions. When she'd asked him earlier if Emiliana—the pretty young woman who'd been so attentive to Effie—was his wife, he'd grinned and said, "Yes, all right. Why not? My wife." And the young woman sat near the top of the table now, at his left hand, although she wore no ring on her own.

Mary, realizing she herself had no ring either, tried keeping her hand out of sight, finding frequent occasion to feed scraps to Frisque, who lay under her chair, but the captain had sharp eyes. "Your husband does not like to part with his money, I see, Mrs. Symonds. He gave you no wedding ring."

"Actually," Mary said, "I had a lovely ring, but it was lost in our journey through France."

"Ah. I see. A shame." He seemed amused. "My wife's was also lost." Looking to Hugh he advised, "You must buy her a new one in Rome, Mr. Symonds. They have many goldsmiths. This is your first visit to Rome? Then I envy you. It is a beautiful city—the river, the bits of antiquity, and the pope's palace—to see it all for the first time is a thing to remember."

His first mate, the man in the brown coat who yesterday had come to fetch them and then drawn his pistol upon them, said, "All things considered, I find Rome too crowded. I much prefer Genoa."

Del Rio agreed it was also a beautiful place. "But at this time we Spanish are not so well liked in Genoa, since our great Admiral Don Blas de Lezo threatened to bombard that republic with our fleet if they did not return the money they had taken from us. Two million pesos, they held in their bank, that was rightfully ours, so he was justified in making threats, but it is not my way, the bombardment. So messy." He dipped his fingers in the bowl of water set beside his plate, and wiped them.

Thomson took an interest in the talk of things financial. "How would you have got the money back, then?"

"There are always ways to take back what belongs to you." The Spaniard shrugged. "Take this affair now of the London corporation that is causing all the panic, all the bankruptcies—this, what do you call it? The Charity...the Charitall..."

"The Charitable Corporation." Thomson supplied the name casually, but he shifted slightly in his chair and Mary saw the movement draw del Rio's eyes although the captain did not pause before continuing,

"Yes, that's the one. The men who are behind that, it is said they are Jacobites." He looked at Hugh. "That they stole all this money to give to the king who's in exile at Rome. But the money they stole, if you look at it one way, it's not really stolen, I think."

Thomson asked him, "And why do you think that?"

"I'm not good with stocks," said del Rio, "and things like that. Those are for bankers. But my understanding, this money they stole, they first raised it on shares in the York Buildings Company, yes?"

Mary could see the bold gleam of intelligence lying behind the apparently guileless dark gaze of del Rio, and guessed he knew more than he cared to reveal, but he waited for Thomson to verify what he'd just said before carrying on,

"And the York Buildings Company holds all the lands

that were seized from the Jacobites, after the last war. This is how it makes its profits, selling off estates that have been stolen from their owners. So I think it is not such an evil thing these men have done in London." Leaning back, he took his wine cup in his hand and held it lightly. "All they did was steal back what the English stole from them. It isn't theft, when you steal something that belongs to you already."

"That's certainly one way of looking at it," Thomson said. He lifted his own cup and took a drink.

"No," del Rio countered with a smile, "it is the right way. I am always right about such things."

His first mate drily said, "And always very modest."

"Naturally." The captain looked across at Mary. "But what were we speaking of before? Ah yes, Rome. You will enjoy it, Mrs. Symonds. It is an enchanting place for lovers—it perhaps will be an inspiration to your husband to show you more affection, yes?"

Mary had briefly considered what role she should play with this man. She had wondered if she should be lively and just a bit foolish, like the younger sister who'd been in the diligence with them, or maybe more confident like Mistress Jamieson, but having just watched him closely now dealing with Thomson, she judged that her best defense would be to play no role, for he would surely be able to spot that she wore a disguise, and it would do no more than increase his suspicions. So when she replied to him now she was none but herself. Only Mary.

"Affection," she said, "need not be on display to be deeply and honestly felt, and sometimes it is all the more honest for being held privately."

He raised one shoulder slightly in a gallantly amused shrug that permitted her to score the point. "This may be true. It's

certain Emiliana and myself hold many things in private."
Reaching out, he stroked the Spanish woman's forearm
where it rested on the table, let his fingers linger on her skin
beneath the lacy ruffle at her elbow, and his touch seemed
genuinely loving. "She knows all my secrets, yes?" He shared
the smile Emiliana turned to him, and then looked back at
Mary. "As I am sure you know your husband's."

Sitting back, he waited while one of his servants took
their plates away and served the main course of what looked
like chicken pieces drowning in a dark-red sauce with vegetables and rice. And as the servant made the rounds to fill
their cups with wine, del Rio said, "For instance, you would
know this scar your husband has just here." He touched his
own neck briefly at the back, above his collar. "You would
know where he acquired it."

Mary felt the warning pressure of Hugh's leg against her
own beneath the table, and she knew del Rio was now testing her and this would be the first of who knew how many
attempts to trap her into saying something that would show
they could not possibly be married. She'd seen the scar,
of course she had, but she had never asked about it, and
although she could have very probably devised a story on the
spot explaining it, she could not know for certain whether
Hugh himself had told del Rio yesterday, while they were
drinking, how he had received the wound. She felt Hugh's
deep frustration at not being able to advise her, guide her,
keep her safe, and Mary knew a sudden rise of anger, not on
her behalf, but his.

She set her cup down on the table. Met del Rio's eyes.
"My husband carries many scars," she said, "as all men
who have lived a life like his must do. There are some
scars that show, and there are many, many more that he

keeps hidden, and when you've discovered all of *those*, then you may try to test me on how well I know my husband. But until that day comes, Captain, I have little time for games." Her tone was calm, but even she could hear the tremor of her righteous anger running underneath the words. "My husband is a private man, as is his right, and I'll not take his secrets and expose them for the sake of proving something that his word alone should be the proof of. I'll not do it. He's a better man than any I have met in all my life, and if you choose to doubt the truth of our attachment you will have to doubt it, Captain, and be done with it, as I am done with answering your questions. He has told you what we are."

The captain's dark eyes slowly warmed with admiration. Gently he said, "And now you have told me also. Thank you, Mrs. Symonds."

⋇

There were no more questions. No more tests.

They did not meet the dreaded Barbary corsairs, but on the second night the winds had changed and so the ship was held there wind-bound for above a week, with little they could do but find new ways to pass the hours and days, though Mary did not mind.

She found she liked this woman she had chosen now to be—this Mary Dundas, who had traveled and seen trouble and been changed by it; who had no longer any need to feign or borrow confidence but only sprinkle water on her own and pull the weeds that had been choking it and watch it grow each day a little more towards the sun. One evening at the captain's table Mr. Thomson prompted Mary to retell one of her tales of the Chevalier de Vilbray, which she obliged him with, and then she offered, "Shall I tell a new tale? One entirely imaginary?"

And del Rio had thought this a splendid entertainment. "But the hero," he had said, "must be a pirate hunter."

"Quite the best of pirate hunters," Mary had agreed.

"And you must name him..." He'd paused a moment in pretended thought, his dark eyes smiling in his very handsome face.

Mary had played along. "Marcos María del Rio Cuerda?"

"An excellent name," he had told her, and settled back into his chair with his wine cup in hand while she'd started her story.

So that had been woven then into the pattern of all of their days on the ship, and each evening she'd told a new part of the tale of brave Captain del Rio outwitting corsairs and a Genoese bank and the whole British navy. The captain had greatly enjoyed this, except on the one night she'd tried to end one of his many romantic adventures in tragedy.

"No," said the captain, "he never would leave the *condesa* like that. You must make a new ending."

Mary had found that amusing. "What, just like that?"

"Why not? You are the one who is telling the story, the ending is yours to choose."

"I choose the sad ending."

"No one," the captain had told her, with certainty, "would choose to leave the *condesa*. She's very appealing. Now, tell that part over again, but this time let the captain find someone to cure her incurable fever. It will be much better this way."

She had done as he'd asked.

"But," she'd said to Hugh later that evening, while she'd

played with Frisque in the cabin, "it really was better the first time I told it."

He hadn't replied. He'd been sitting at one of the chairs of their small table, with all three candles together before him, head bent above some little nautical instrument he'd found the day before that was not working. She'd looked at the gleam of the brass pieces held in his hands, and the small parts scattered over the top of the table, and she'd asked for interest's sake, "Would you have chosen to stay with the countess?"

"No."

"Why not?"

"She fainted too much."

"So you like a strong woman, then?"

He had glanced up very briefly, then down again. "Aye."

And that glance had made Mary feel warm inside.

They had not touched since the night he had kissed her. He'd kept to his side of the cabin, and stepped out when needed to give her the privacy that she required, and behaved in all ways like an honorable man. But there were times she wished…well, she wished…

He'd distracted her thoughts by beginning to fit the brass pieces together again, turning screws with the point of his small knife and assembling the instrument till it was all as it ought to be, tidy and whole in his capable fingers. He'd set it down neatly upon the scarred wood of the table.

She'd said, "I would ask you a question."

"Now, there's a surprise."

"How do you go from *that*," she had said, nodding towards the small instrument, "fixing things, making things work, to—"

He'd finished the thought for her. "Killing them?"

"Yes."

In the light of the candles she'd watched his mouth twist in the ghost of a smile, deep with bitterness. She had expected his words to be bitter as well, but instead she had heard resignation in his level voice as he'd answered her, low, "Step by step."

She had thought about that. "But surely, if you marked the steps as you made them, you could then turn round and retrace them and find your way back to the place you began," she had reasoned. "Like taking the road that you left by, and letting it lead you back home."

He had looked at her quietly. "Home is not always," he'd said, "where ye left it."

And that had been all he had said on the subject.

❧

"A broken man," Effie had said, "is a man who has left his clan, or been cast out of it. An outlaw."

She had looked comfortable early the next morning, bundled in her hammock in the tiny cabin fitted in the ship's prow. There was color in her cheeks again, and she'd had energy enough to make a thorough explanation of the system of the clans within the Scottish Highlands, each belonging to its lands and bound by ties of loyalty and blood, with a chief who looked after the whole of the clan and could claim all its members' allegiance, the chieftains of various branches below him, and all of the other clan members arranged below that. "But a broken man," she had concluded, "is shunned by his kin and no longer belongs to the land he was bred upon, and has no shelter or comfort but that he can scrape for himself."

Mary had tried to absorb this. "But Hugh…that is, Mr. MacPherson says he's not a broken man."

"Then he is not. And it's Hugh is it, now?" Effie's eyes

had been knowing. "What else has your Mr. MacPherson been telling ye, there in your cabin at night?"

"That I talk too much." Mary had smiled and refused to be shamed. "He has made no improper advances, if that's what you're asking."

"It is, and I'm glad of it. But I'll be gladder still," Effie had told her, "to finally be back on dry land."

She had found her wish granted three days after that, when at last having caught a fair wind, the *Princesa Maria* came safely to Civitavecchia.

Captain del Rio insisted on coming ashore with them. "I know the coachmen here who can be trusted to bring you to Rome. Also those who are not worth your trust, and in harbors like this there are many of those. You will have to be careful," he said, "for I hear that the man at the root of this scandal in London, a man named John Thomson, is even now heading to Rome with a borrowed name."

Mary could see, as before, the intelligence lighting the depths of his playful dark eyes.

"There will be many people, both here and at Rome, who are watching for this man," del Rio remarked. "The reward is a large one, a great deal of money, for one who can capture him. Here, I have this from Marseilles." Reaching into his pocket, he took out a cutting of newspaper, tidily folded. "It is his description, in case you might see him yourself." The quick flash of his grin let them know beyond doubt he had known Thomson's name all along. Maybe theirs too, thought Mary.

But when he bent gallantly over her hand, having found them a suitable coach that would carry them down from the harbor to Rome, he still said, "Mrs. Symonds. It has been a very great pleasure to know you. If ever you're captured by corsairs, it would be my honor to rescue you."

"Thank you." Mary had carried her fur-lined cloak over her arm, while Hugh carried the dog and the bulk of their other things, but now she folded the softness and passed it to Captain del Rio. "For Emiliana," she told him. She no longer needed it. No longer needed to borrow the plumage of some other bird when she'd learned how to fly on her own. "It's a present, for taking such kind care of Effie. Please tell her I'm grateful."

Kissing her hand with a warmth that would have done great credit to one of Madame d'Aulnoy's heroes, del Rio straightened to face Hugh. "I'm thinking, Mr. Symonds, you must buy your wife the finest wedding ring in all of Rome, for how you won the love of such a woman I will never know. How did he do it?" he asked Mary.

Mary thought a moment, then she raised her chin and told the truth. "He watched me from afar when he believed I could not see him. He followed me when he believed that I was not aware of it. One day my gloves were stolen in the street, and he returned them to me. And," she told the captain, simply, "that was our beginning."

Feeling she could do no better for an ending to this chapter of their voyage, Mary turned towards the coach. Hugh stood beside its open door, his hand outstretched to help her. And he waited. For the first time, Mary laid her hand on top of his, and felt his hand turn so her fingers were enclosed within his own, a masculine protective touch that left her feeling cared for. Safe.

And Mary needed all of that to give her strength this morning. For by day's end she would be in Rome, preparing for a meeting with her father. And the king.

CHAPTER 36

I DIDN'T LIKE INTERVIEWS. DIDN'T do well at them.

Luc had assured me, "It's only my brother."

Which hadn't been helpful. The fact that the man I'd be meeting at lunch *was* Luc's brother made it imperative I do my best to impress him, since he wouldn't only be judging me as a prospective employee but as someone worthy of Luc. When I'd tried to explain this last night, Luc had hugged me. "He'll like you, don't worry. Just be yourself."

"I don't have the right clothes for an interview."

"Fabien's very informal, he'll be wearing jeans. So should you, if we're taking the bike. He'll care more about what's in your head than what outfit you're wearing."

That still hadn't stopped me getting up early this morning and trying on all of the clothes in my wardrobe before I had settled on one combination I liked, and then taking a full sixteen minutes to tie and retie the blue scarf Luc had bought me in Paris, until its folds lay in a perfect arrangement. The clock on the chest of drawers had been my lifeline, and when I had later gone downstairs to wait, I'd relied on the stately and competent pendulum swings of the old longcase clock in the dining room, and at 10:50 precisely I'd stepped out to wait on the terrace, deferring in turn to the time display that I refreshed on my mobile with rhythmic, predictable clicks.

I could see the top part of Luc's house from here, over

the wall at the back of the garden. I'd hear the Ducati start; hear when he rode up the lane and around to come fetch me.

He'd said he would fetch me. He'd said, "If we leave at eleven, we'll get there in plenty of time."

I had managed to stay fairly calm till the moment the time on my mobile read: 10:58.

Because if he were going to start the Ducati and ride it around to collect me, two minutes was really the minimum time he would need.

I refreshed the display again: 10:59.

I had started to pace. He was coming, I told myself. Ordinary people weren't hung up on time in the same way I was. I should try to stay calm.

I should go *there*. It was now exactly 11:00, and Luc's house was so close I could cross the garden and go through the door in the wall and be there at his door in the time it would take me to text him or call him. Yes, that's what I'd do. I had already paced to the end of the terrace, so walking the final short distance across the back garden and through the door into the lane seemed a logical step.

The Ducati was parked in its place at the side of Luc's house so I knew he'd be home when I knocked at the door, and before I could start with my pacing again he had answered it.

He had his hand to his ear and it took me a second to realize that he was midway through a phone call. "Hang on a minute, Geoff," he told the caller, and muted the mobile to kiss me hello.

"It's 11:02," I said. "We need to go."

"Yes, I know. Sorry. My boss," he explained, as he held up the mobile. "Come have a seat. We're just finishing up now, it won't take a minute." He turned as he said that and crossed to the dining room table to study the screen of the laptop computer on top of it while he unmuted his phone and continued, "Thanks. Now, read me the numbers he gave you?"

He didn't understand, I thought. Unless we left *now*, we'd be late. It wouldn't matter what his brother thought of me, of how my mind worked—no one hired a person who turned up late to an interview.

I tried to breathe more normally, feeling in my pocket for my pen and my Sudoku puzzles, only to discover I'd forgotten them.

The last time I'd worried this much about being late, when I'd first come to Claudine's and my cousin had taken her time getting ready for breakfast, at least I'd been able to take matters into my own hands and go down alone, but that wasn't an option here. I wasn't in control of how I got into Paris. I had to rely on Luc.

"We need to go."

I wasn't sure if I'd said those words audibly, my mouth had gone so dry, and Luc seemed not to have heard me.

The hall was too narrow. I took a step into the sitting room but that was worse. There was music here playing from some source I couldn't see, not loud but vaguely discordant, like jazz. And the trees outside made moving shadows across the wall next to the window, so that to my eyes the light seemed to be flickering. Squeezing my eyes shut, I fought back the impulse to cover my ears.

No, I told myself silently. *No, no, no, no...*

I couldn't have a meltdown. Not in front of Luc. Not here.

I rarely had them anymore. I'd learned to recognize the warning signs and knew the ways to calm myself before things overwhelmed me, but already I was losing my ability to concentrate. I knew Luc was still talking on his mobile but I couldn't hear the words. The sounds around me blended into one confusing jumble, and I started trembling as the feeling of compression settled over me, as though the air around me had grown thick and heavy, closing in. In panic I clenched and unclenched my hands, making tight fists and releasing them, trying to keep control.

Forcing my eyes open, I braved the stabbing bright pain of the light as I focused on Luc and said urgently, "We need to *go*."

He turned then and looked at me. Quickly he spoke again into his mobile and ended the call but he didn't approach me. He stood there, his figure distorting and wavering like a mirage. He was saying my name: "Sara? Sara, I'm sorry. It's OK. I'm here. It's OK."

But it wasn't OK, and I knew it. I said so. "It's not OK." And like a wheel spinning round in a rut I repeated it over and over: "It's not OK. Not OK. Not OK. Not OK…"

And then sensation and pain flooded up and took over and I was in meltdown.

I felt the hot tears overflowing and knew I was yelling at Luc but I wasn't aware anymore of the things I was saying, although I could hear the accusing tone of my own voice. I heard him asking me quietly whether I wanted him to leave the room, and I told him I didn't, I screamed it, and then I was curled on the sofa, my arms locked around my bent knees while I rocked myself, sobbing and sobbing, unable to stop…

Until slowly, like floodwaters draining by steady degrees, it began to subside.

I felt shaky. My head ached. My eyelids felt swollen and my throat felt raw.

I had folded myself into the furthest corner of Luc's leather sofa. The light in the room now was blissfully dim, and he'd taken the armchair across from me, where he sat quietly waiting. His voice when he spoke was incredibly calm. "Sara? What do you need? Can I get you a blanket?"

I nodded and he rose and left the room, returning with a blanket of the perfect heaviness so when he draped it round my shoulders it was like a reassuring hug. And then I wanted one of those, as well. I asked him, "Can you hold me?"

"Sure." He sat and I curled myself into his arms and the feel of them round me was perfect as well—just the right weight and pressure.

We stayed there like that without moving. Without saying anything. Slowly the floodwaters lowered still more and were followed behind by a dark seeping current of shame.

It went deeper than simple embarrassment. I couldn't even imagine what Luc must be thinking; how much his opinion of me must have lowered.

I said, "I'm so sorry." My voice hurt.

"You don't need to be sorry."

"Your brother..." I had no idea how much time had passed, but I knew I had ruined our plans for the lunch with his brother in Paris. My chance of a job.

"There's no problem. I texted him. He understands."

He was trying to make me feel better. I shook my head. Ordinary people, I knew, wouldn't understand something like this. "No, he doesn't. How could he? How—?" I was about to say, "How could you?" when I stopped talking because for the first time I'd noticed what lay on the table in front of the sofa: a booklet of Sudoku puzzles, with a pencil laid on top of it. It wasn't *my* puzzle book, but one that looked a lot like it, and it was set out so tidily within my reach that it couldn't have been a coincidence. Taking a moment and trying to think, I looked once more around the room, noticing all of the things Luc had done.

He had turned off the music. He'd closed the curtains to dim the light. He had stayed close but not too close. Kept calm. Moved quietly. Brought me a blanket.

I shifted my head on his shoulder to look at him. Study him.

Luc went on holding me. "Fabien understands melt-downs because he still gets them himself, sometimes. Not very often. He usually shuts down instead. But his meltdowns were very…spectacular, when we were young."

What seemed strangest to me wasn't what he was saying but how he was saying it, in the same tone people used when they talked about commonplace things like the weather.

I asked, to be perfectly certain, "Your brother has Asperger's?"

"Yes."

His brother who was, like me, a computer programmer. A skilled one, apparently, to have been put at the helm of developing Morland Electronics's tactical and sonar systems. "And when did you…how did you…?"

"When we had breakfast," he said. "That first morning, when you told me all you had learned about Jacobites."

I felt my face flushing as I recalled how I'd monologued, talking and talking till Jacqui had signaled me. "You must have thought I was crazy."

He turned his head then and looked down at me with those incredible eyes that could hold my world steady. "I thought you were beautiful."

Just for that moment, while I looked at him and he looked back at me and those words hung suspended between us, I felt in my heart it might truly be possible, what we were try-ing to do. But the tear that I felt slowly trailing its way down my heated cheek hadn't been caused by my meltdown. I brushed it away.

"I can't do this," I said. "Not to you. Not to Noah. I ruin things, Luc. I'm not capable—"

"Who told you that?" he asked quietly, as he had asked me that day in the old ruined troglodyte house, when I'd tried to convince him the first time that I couldn't do real relationships. "Was it your cousin?"

"No." Jacqui had always looked after me, guarded me, watched out for "friends" who were taking advantage of my lack of social awareness, my need to be liked, for their own ends—to help with their homework or do little chores for them. "Real friends," she'd told me once when she had rescued me from a posh restaurant where four girls had taken me out for a birthday lunch and left me stuck with the bill, "don't just take from you all the time. Real friends look after you." She'd been especially watchful of boys, though there hadn't been many. My few teenage boyfriends had not hung on more than a couple of months before backing away in what quickly became a predictable pattern: they'd promise to call me and then never would, and I'd wait while my hopefulness slid into heartbreak.

"Why do they always leave me?" I'd asked Jacqui through my tears one night. "What's wrong with me?" And she of course had reassured me there was nothing wrong with me at all, but even though I hadn't yet been diagnosed with Asperger's I'd felt my difference painfully.

When I'd started university, my cousin had been going through the first of her divorces. It had been a messy battle that had claimed much of her energy. I'd felt alone, and lonely. And in one of my computer science classes, I'd met Gary.

He'd been captain of the rugby team, a golden boy in

every way, blond haired and so incredibly good-looking that the first time he had spoken to me I'd assumed he'd done it by mistake. But he had asked me out and taken me to dinner and he'd danced with me and kissed me and by half term I'd been totally in love. So when he had assured me that a programming assignment we'd been given was supposed to be collaborative, I'd believed him. I had reasoned I must simply have misunderstood the lecturer's instructions, wrongly thinking we were meant to work on that assignment independently. Instead I'd worked with Gary and another classmate, Erica.

She'd been a friend as well. We'd worked together as a team before, and Erica had commented on how well Gary treated me, and I'd said I was honestly amazed that he had chosen me at all, and even more amazed he hadn't left me yet, as all the others had. We'd talked of past relationships, and Erica had told me that I ought to have more confidence. "He really likes you," she had said of Gary. I'd believed her, too. And being—as I often was—the first to solve the problem of the program we were working on, I'd freely shared my code, only to find myself called up before the head of the department, charged with cheating.

As I told this now to Luc, he settled back into the cushions of the sofa, with his arms still round me firmly and protectively. "They stole your code and passed it off as theirs."

My nod was slight. "We weren't supposed to work in teams. They lied."

They'd changed the code in tiny ways to distance it from mine, but code could be as individual as handwriting to some discerning eyes. And then of course I'd told the truth, because I could do nothing else.

I had been very fortunate. I'd been believed. My marks

had been reduced as a small penalty for not taking enough care to be sure of the assignment's true requirements, but I had been cleared of cheating. Unlike Erica and Gary, who had been kicked off the course.

"Stupid bitch," was what Gary had called me before he'd left. I hadn't seen him again after that. Erica had been more vocal, coming round to tell me in great detail what she thought of me. She'd weaponized the private things I'd told her, flinging all my insecurities back at me with a force that made them sting. "You know why all your boyfriends leave? Why no one ever stays with you? Because you're weird," she'd told me. "You're not normal. You're not capable of having real relationships because you'll always end up letting people down, the way you've let down me and Gary."

Saying those words over now to Luc still stung a little, even now. "But she was right," I said.

"No, she wasn't. They're the ones who took advantage of your trust. They let *you* down."

"But—"

"There's no 'but.' She lied to you about the course assignment, right?"

"Yes."

"And have I ever lied to you?"

"You said it was tradition for a man to take a woman out to lunch at New Year's."

I could feel the movement of his mouth against my hair. Perhaps a smile. "Apart from that."

I thought back through the time that I had known him and admitted, "No."

"Then which of us does it make sense to believe?" he asked. "Me, or someone who was angry and out for revenge and had already lied to you?"

It wasn't the most perfect logical argument. I couldn't know if a person had lied to me until that lie was exposed, but I knew in my heart Luc had always been truthful. And so I said, "You."

"Then believe what I'm telling you. This, what we're having, is a real relationship. You're more than capable. You're doing fine. Every couple," he told me, "has moments that challenge them, but when you're with the right person, a person who loves you, a person you love, you work through them together. Those others who left you, who hurt you, they weren't the right men for you, that's all. And just because *they* left, that doesn't mean I will." He gathered me closer, as though I were something of value. "I'm not going anywhere."

I leaned against his chest and shut my eyes and sorted through what he'd just told me, trying to decide if he'd been speaking hypothetically or if he had just said he loved me.

I thought of what Denise had told me when she had explained about their marriage and divorce: "He deserves to be properly loved," she had said. And I wanted to give him that, wanted to be the right person for *him*. Still with my eyes closed, I told Luc, "I love you."

"I love you, too." Easily, simply, with no hesitation.

He gently smoothed the tangled hair back from my forehead and I lifted my own hand to hold his there, to press it firmly to my eyes because it felt so comforting, the steady rhythm of his heartbeat strong and soothing at my temple where my face was resting on his shirt.

Recalling something else Denise had said about Luc's family, I asked, "Was that why your mother took your brother to America to go to school? Because he has Asperger's?"

"Yes, it wasn't so well understood in France. The

opportunities were better in America for Fabien to get the education that was suited to his way of learning. And he met his wife there, so it's good he went."

"He's married?"

"Very happily."

"With children?"

"Yes. Three daughters. Why?"

I hadn't expected that. Hadn't allowed for it in my own life, having long since resigned myself to the idea of being alone like the single computer that Jacqui's psychologist author had used to explain how my mind was wired—one little Mac in an office of PCs, unable to fully connect. Incompatible. But when I tried to explain using this same analogy now to Luc, he pointed out, "But Macs can do things a PC can't do. And in my office, Macs and PCs share the same network."

"You're not ever going to let me win an argument, are you?"

"Do you want to win this one?"

"I don't know." I suddenly felt very drowsy. "I don't know what I want." Then I thought for a moment and added, regretful, "I wanted to meet your brother."

I felt Luc's shrug. "He's in Paris for two more days. We can try again tomorrow."

"But tomorrow's Thursday," I reminded him. "You'll be at work."

"I have a very understanding boss. I'll work from home. We'll try again, same time. I won't be late," he promised.

"I don't know."

"I'll leave it up to you." His hand felt warm against my forehead. Safe. "It's your choice."

I was half asleep already, sinking fast beneath the weight of the exhaustion that so often struck me after meltdowns. "My choice..."

He bent his head to mine again, and when he spoke it stirred my hair and sang within my ears above the restful rhythm of his heartbeat. "Always."

CHAPTER 37

The king of the world sits in his hall,
and hears of his people's flight.
—Macpherson, "Carthon"

Rome
April 22, 1732

I T PROVED TO BE a difficult decision, choosing what to wear to meet the king. She knew it was ridiculous, with all she had encountered and endured, that such a silly detail now should hold her all but paralyzed, yet in the days they'd been in Rome it had become a problem. Both her winter gowns from Paris were too warm for such a climate, where by afternoon the hotness of the sun even so early in the season kept most people shuttered in their rooms and houses, and the scents of sun-warmed stone and brick and plaster fought the drifting perfumes of the hanging flowers, and the carriage horses by midafternoon stood drowsy-eyed in harness in the shade cast by the ancient buildings of the many squares— called by the people here *piazzas*—that were set like little beads within a lacy web of narrow, twisting streets.

Their piazza had a fountain, and a very ancient structure called the Pantheon, or sometimes the Rotunda, built to honor all the gods that had been prayed to in the old Rome of the Caesars, with a dome that Mary marveled at, so perfectly constructed that it stood without the benefit of buttresses. It had become a church now and there was but one God honored there, but Mary felt the weight of all the old forgotten gods still pressing round her in the shadows when she entered in that building, where the daylight and the moonlight shone by turns from a great open circle at the very center of the dome. She had a good view of the massive pillars of its portico and front from the tall window of their room in the hotel, where she was wont to lean each morning and again at evening, simply listening to all the splendid sounds of Rome and drinking in the sights.

And she was at that window now when Effie called to her.

Frisque barked, and Mary shushed him, lest the other guests of their hotel complain about the noise. Frisque had been out of sorts since their arrival here, and Mary had at first blamed it upon the warmer weather, but she'd seen him pacing round the room at night as if in search of something, and she now believed it was because he had grown used to having Hugh close by, and missed him. As did she.

Since the name *Symonds* had so clearly been discovered at Marseilles, their names had changed again, with papers Hugh had drawn from a compartment in his gun case before burning all the others. She was back to being Mr. Thomson's sister, with their surname being… Well, it hardly mattered, Mary thought, for it would surely change again.

"Come try your gown," said Effie from the cool and airily high-ceilinged room they shared. The room that Hugh and Thomson had was over theirs, up one more pair of stairs, and while she often heard them walking round she rarely saw them but at meals. She found it hard, having grown used to sharing nearly all her hours with Hugh, to have him now so separate from her, and to see him only in the company of others where she could not draw him into conversation nor enjoy his calm companionship without another person intervening.

With a sigh she turned and went to Effie.

"Now," the older woman said, "I've done my best with it, but I'm no seamstress."

They had found the gown by sheer good fortune, having gone in search of a mantua maker and stumbled upon one not many streets distant who had been about to reuse parts of this one in making another. It was somewhat plainer than her Paris gowns—not a new *robe volant* but a simply cut bodice set over a closed skirt, and it had been torn at the seams in three places and missing its laces, but made of light silk in a pale frosted blue Mary found very calming.

A fine trade, she thought, for the plum-colored gown. And with Effie's repairs and a length of new ivory silk ribbon to thread through the sides of the bodice across the plain stomacher, matching the trimmings of ivory lace showing around the low neckline and under the gathered sleeves from her fine linen chemise, Mary thought the effect very pretty.

"You're sure you won't come?" she asked Effie.

"I've seen the king often enough in my time. And who else would look after this bundle of mischief?" She nodded to Frisque. "He would ruin the room if ye left him alone in it. There now, that's done. Not too tight at the elbows? Good. Then all ye need is your cap. Here, I've finished that too."

She had crafted a new cap from one of her own, adding small bows she'd fashioned from scraps of silk ribbon that matched the frost blue of the gown.

Mary, keeping her head still while Effie adjusted the pins through the lace of the cap, felt a twinge of uncertainty. "What is he like, the king?"

Effie appeared to be sorting through words to describe him and settled on: "Kind."

It wasn't what Mary expected, but it eased her worries a little since she hoped to ask his assistance in finding her father. She'd thought, when they'd first arrived, she might just find him—that he would be easy to locate, but Rome was a crowded place, and while they'd waited for King James to make his reply to the letter that Thomson had sent to acquaint him with their arrival, she had not been at liberty to ask around in her own name, to learn where her father might lodge.

But in front of the king, she'd be able to be her own self.

Effie told her, "Now mind what I telt ye, about how to pay him your honors, and how ye should speak. Let me see how ye curtsy."

For Mary, the long years rolled suddenly backwards and just for a moment she felt a small girl again. *Show me your curtsy*, a woman's voice spoke in her mind from a great distance, followed by praise. *There's a clever wee lassie.*

She curtsied.

It satisfied Effie, who turned to rummage in the bottom of their portmanteau, and drew out something wrapped within a handkerchief. "I've had this," she remarked, "since I was your age, when I lived at Saint-Germain-en-Laye, which makes it near as ancient as that fountain ye keep staring at outside. So have a care when ye first use it or the dust might make ye sneeze."

She took the lace fan Effie handed to her, and the voice stirred for a second time, in gentle warning: *Have a care, ye'll raise the dust and make your mother cough.*

She had to look away from Effie; fight the siren pull of shared experience. *I used to live at Saint-Germain-en-Laye*, she longed to say. *My father served the king there as a wig maker. Perhaps you knew him...?* But she'd grown too good at keeping secrets. She said nothing.

Till she spread the fan to open it, releasing a familiar scent that made her briefly close her eyes.

"What ails ye?"

"Nothing." Mary shook her head. "It's…lavender. My mother smelled of lavender."

The curtains lifted on a breeze that carried to her ears the lovely dancing sound of water in the fountain at the heart of the piazza, its continual cascades forever falling to be gathered and borne upwards once again in sparkling mimicry of life.

The older woman reached a gentle hand to rearrange a curl of hair so it trailed artfully along the line of Mary's neck. "Your memory's playing tricks with ye. Your mother, rest her soul, used naught but rosewater. The lavender was mine."

Mary stood silently a moment, not quite certain she had heard those few words properly, and then her eyes came open and she turned to meet the Highland woman's gaze. "You were my nurse?"

A pause, as though a final threshold waited to be crossed, and one that seemingly could not be crossed with words, because instead of saying anything in answer, Effie nodded.

Mary's eyes began to fill. "Oh, Effie. *That* is why you came? Because you…oh—" She broke off, bringing one hand quickly to her mouth in sudden pain. "And I forgot you! Effie, how could I forget you?" And uncaring of propriety, she flung herself at Effie in the same impulsive way she knew she must have done in childhood, when she had been hurt and wanted comfort.

Effie's own arms folded round her, sturdy and yet tender, and she stood there rocking Mary as she might have soothed a baby.

Mary, clinging to the older woman, whispered, "I'm so sorry."

"Hush, now. Hush, there's nae harm done. Of course

ye'd not remember me, ye were a wee small thing. I never thought that ye'd remember me."

"Then why?" asked Mary. "Effie, this was such an awful journey for you. Why would you agree to it, if I could not—?"

"Because," said Effie, "when your brother found me— and that was no easy thing for him to do—and when he telt me he was sending ye to Paris and had need of one to watch ye, I knew well enough whose hand it was that sent him there." She laid her hand on Mary's hair. "God always gives us people for a reason, lass. He takes them from us too, but when He puts them in our path and gives them back to us again, we would be great fools not to realize that He means us to belong to them."

❧

She met Hugh's eyes again across the confines of the coach and tried to smile, but could not. Partly because she had just now realized why the frost blue color of her gown had drawn her so compellingly—because it was the same shade as his eyes.

He wore new clothes as well, and they were like no clothes she had seen a man wear. His shirt and stock and cuffs were as they'd always been, but over them in place of his usual long coat he wore a short gray one with sleeves slashed to show strips of darkly green velvet, and one sword belt slung over that, from which his fine Scottish broadsword was hanging. And in place of a gentleman's breeches he wore the Highland garment made of checkered wool in green shot through with white and red and gold, that had been wrapped and belted so it covered him from waist to knees and wound up over his left shoulder like a folded cloak, to freely fall and swing behind. His Highland dagger in its sheath hung at the front edge of his belt, as did a hanging pocket, and his legs to just below his knees were cased in stockings of a different checkered pattern, with his feet in buckled shoes.

If she had read those clothes described on paper she'd have thought that any man who wore them must look feminine, but Hugh MacPherson sitting with his strong legs bare looked more a man than Mr. Thomson did in proper breeches.

There was nowhere else to safely turn her gaze but to the lace fan she held folded in her hands. She would have hoped to see the streets through which they rattled and she had so wished to have a view of the king's palace, having overheard it being highly praised by an Irish priest at their hotel who'd been talking at breakfast last week to another guest, one of his countrymen.

"I do confess," so the priest had admitted, "'tis nowhere so impressive as his French palace at Saint-Germain-en-Laye, being not set apart in its own grounds or park, and the building itself is not nearly as large, but it yet has a fine situation, and shares the same Square of the Holy Apostles with the palace of that noble family of Colonna who are cousins to our king." Moreover, so the priest had said, whatever the king's palace here in Rome lacked in its outward beauty, it was very fine within. "There's a grand courtyard and an even grander staircase, and the Chapel Royal where His Holiness our last pope did baptize the younger of the little princes. You should see it if you're able," he'd advised the other Irishman. "I'm told there are yet many people daily, even Englishmen, who come to pay their honors to the king."

But those, thought Mary, like herself, who had to come in secret, must come also unobserved, which meant the coach was closed, its curtains drawn so none could peer inside and see them, and this meant they neither could see out.

She guessed when they had entered through the palace doors by how the sound of rolling wheels and clopping hooves began to echo closely, telling her they now had come into a passage. And she heard the swing and creak as heavy wooden doors were closed and barred behind them, as the coachman brought the horses to a halt.

Suddenly nervous, she raised her head and looked again at Hugh, and in his steady gaze found reassurance.

The coach door, when it opened, swung towards the unseen coachman who was holding it, and came to rest against the wall of the dim passage, serving as a screen of sorts to shield them from the eyes of any who might seek a view of these new visitors. And in the wall, another door now opened inward, to admit them to a secret stair. The man who held that door was evidently known to Hugh, for they shook hands in silence as they met each other. Once they were inside, the secret door was closed again, and Mary heard the coach wheels rumble onward down the passage and proceed through what was probably the courtyard.

The man who had met them appeared to be in his midthirties and carried himself like an officer. He said nothing to begin with, only led them up the narrow stairs and into a long gallery with tall grand windows and a vaulted ceiling that was decorated beautifully in intricate designs that fooled the eye. At the end of the gallery four narrow steps took them up into a private receiving room, where the high and rounded ceiling had been painted very cleverly to seem to be the sky, viewed through a realistic garden trellis with bright vines of tiny blue flowers trailing all round it, and Cupid-like *putti* at play in the leaves.

Here the man turned to face them and greeted Hugh in a more good-natured manner. "I see the clothes reached you. Lord Marischal hoped they would."

"Aye. It was kind of His Lordship."

"And you must be Thomson." Not waiting to be introduced, the man held out his hand. "I am Captain Hay."

The name appeared to register with Thomson, for he smiled in pleasure. "Not the famous Captain William Hay who once sailed in the navy of the late tsar in St. Petersburg? My brother is a merchant there. George Thomson. He speaks highly of you, Captain."

"Very kind of him, I'm sure." His gaze moved on politely. "And this would be…?"

Hugh said, "Mistress Mary Dundas. She's the sister of Nicolas Dundas."

"Ah, Dundas, yes. So that's why you asked me about the wig maker. I was able to—" But he was brought up short by footsteps in the gallery. He turned, and Mary turned as well.

The king had come.

Seeing him actually there in the room with them struck her at first as a thing overwhelming. It took her a moment to drop into her finest curtsy the way she had practiced, and keep her head bowed in respect until he gave them all leave to rise.

He was tall, with a wig of pale gray and a suit of gray silk a shade darker, trimmed richly with gold braid and lace, his chest crossed with the ribbands and medallions of his varied royal orders, though she knew not what they were. She looked to match the features to the portrait she had studied at Sir Redmond Everard's—the portrait of the king when he had been a boy, his hand upon his hip with confidence, his gaze fixed with keen interest on some distant sight. This older King James had the same stubborn chin but his dark eyes had grown more resigned. And when he smiled, it was the faintly weary smile of a man who had seen much and could not be easily drawn to react to what others might view as intriguing.

Still, when he saw Hugh standing proudly in Highland dress, King James appeared to be moved.

He said, "I know your face, do I not?"

Captain Hay introduced Hugh more formally, and the king nodded. "Of course, I remember now. Mr. MacPherson. You came here to Rome years ago with the Earl Marischal and his brother on their way to Spain."

"I am honored, Your Majesty, that ye'd remember."

"I trust I shall always remember my brave and faithful Highlanders, and particularly those of a name so sincerely attached to me. Believe me, Mr. MacPherson, I know how loyally you and your clansmen are inclined, and I'm glad of the help of so many brave men, at a time when honest hearts and hands were never so much wanted."

Thomson, when the king's gaze moved to him, remarked, "Your Majesty, I can assure you there are honest hearts and hands in all three of your kingdoms."

"Mr. Thomson. Our worthy friends in Paris have mentioned you more than once to me."

"Then you'll know there is nothing I would not willingly undergo for your service. I have never failed to assist my fellow Jacobites in England financially whenever I could, and in Paris Mr. Robinson and I were pleased to be able to give some of your principal men great sums out of our joint stock. I also gave, out of my own pocket, upwards of eight hundred pounds, and there is more that can be got to help prepare for your return to England to take back your rightful throne from the usurper."

"A rebellion?" The king's wise, indulgent expression put Mary in mind of her uncle's face whenever one of her cousins said something that showed want of thought or experience. "I have myself been expecting such things all my life," he said, "and they have never happened with success."

Thomson assured him this time would be different. "I promise you, Your Majesty, you have many friends right now in London. Why, some of the aldermen serve as cashiers for the money collected to support your cause, and the city is ripe for revolution."

"I cannot raise a revolution on the money taken from the hands of those my birth and duty binds me to protect." The king, though only in his middle forties, looked a good deal older as he paused for thought, and finally said, "I once believed as you do, that rebellion was the only way; that violent diseases must have violent remedies. But those remedies, Mr. Thomson, cause very real suffering, most usually to others than ourselves."

Mary stole a glance at Hugh, whose face betrayed no measure of his thoughts, and she remembered how his eyes had looked the night Effie had sung the haunting sad lament about the warrior who wandered all alone with all his loved ones in the ground, and something told her Hugh knew well the truth of the king's statement.

"I am glad indeed," the king went on, "to find you were endeavoring to aid my cause, and I suppose you took the best measures you could for that effect, but the truth is I did write some months ago to General Dillon and the rest, that I could not condescend to such proposals, that such a means of raising money was not all in keeping with my conscience, and that I had rather leave matters as they are without compromising myself, and wait till it shall please Providence to restore what does belong to me. And to my sons."

The small painted *putti*, like children themselves, gazed down from the gold scrolls of the flower-wrapped trellis adorning the lovely curved ceiling, the "sky" rendered with such a skilled imitation of light that it seemed there must truly be sunshine behind the pale clouds.

The king said, "Prince Charles will, I hope, be one day both a great and a good man, and I would advise him and his brother as my father once advised me—nay, required me—to treat all our subjects with fairness, and never to molest them in the enjoyment of their religion, rights, liberty, and property, for a king can never be happy, lest his subjects be easy." He leveled a decided gaze on Thomson. "And it seems I must now be unhappy, for you will not be so easy for this next while in the place where I must send you."

Thomson asked, "And where is that, Your Majesty?"

"You understand that I cannot appear to be condoning this affair. And I suspect my subjects who have lost all through this misadventure would much blame me if I showed myself indifferent to their suffering. As a simple formality, it will of course be the pope who arrests you, but it will be known to be done by my orders."

Thomson raised his eyebrows. "You are having me arrested?"

"Not for long. And should you want for anything while you're confined, you may apply to Captain Hay or to my secretary, Lord Dunbar." Turning to Hugh he said, "I shall direct you where he should be taken, and then I am sure the Lord Marischal will have new work for you."

Then his gaze settled on Mary. "I thank you," he told her, "for coming to Rome. I have little these days I can offer my subjects, when even my ailments increase with my age, but I still thank God my heart is good, and that will never fail you."

He was turning away, but she summoned her courage and managed to speak up. "If it please Your Majesty," she began.

The king paused to look back at her.

"My father, William Dundas, served Your Majesty at Saint-Germain-en-Laye, and came with you to Rome, and still resides here. I've not seen him for some years, and I am hoping very much to see him now, if he desires it."

King James looked to Captain Hay, repeating, "Dundas... William Dundas... Ah, the wig maker. Of course. But he did leave us, surely?"

Captain Hay confirmed this for Mary. "He parted from hence with your brother Charles, only last Michaelmas. I have been making inquiries but have not yet learned where they might have been bound."

Mary schooled her face carefully, not wanting anyone to see the great chasm that had just opened within her, exposing the sharp jagged edges of her disappointment. So then their whole journey had been done for nothing, and she had again been cast off, left behind. Mary felt all off balance and strangely deflated, as though she had opened a gift to discover it empty inside.

The king watched her, and in his eyes Mary saw the deep kindness Effie had spoken of. "It grieves me that my friends in Paris did impose upon you, madam, so unnecessarily, and brought you here by ways exposed to accident and danger, and that the circumstances of my court force so many brave subjects and old servants, like your father and your brother, to seek elsewhere for their bread. I hope in God that better days will come when friends and honest people will not be forced at so great a distance from one another." His small smile was also kind. "Till then, I will neglect nothing that lies in my power," he told her, "to see you are sent safely home."

Mary curtsied again as he left them, but when he had gone she looked up at the high rounded ceiling with new eyes from which the romance had been stripped, so she saw the gold trellis not as a beautiful frame but a cage, that some cruel hand had opened to trick the small painted birds into imagining they could find freedom against the wide blue of that sky. But it wasn't a sky, after all. It was nothing but plaster, and those little birds would be beating their wings on it endlessly all of their lives without anything changing, the more fools for trying to fly in the first place.

CHAPTER 38

M Y FATHER SAID, WE *do not always get the things we want.*
I had transcribed that line an hour ago, and now
it resonated in my memory as I stood in Claudine's studio upstairs and looked with interest at the photographs of
Alistair. Claudine, at the table behind me, was sorting the
black-and-white prints of a wedding she'd photographed
into an album for one of her clients. She asked me, "And
why would he be disappointed?"

"I don't think he'll like the way it ends." Assuming, I
thought, he had even learned how it had started. I wasn't
convinced that my cousin had actually told him Mary hadn't
gone to Saint-Germain-en-Laye. Jacqui never lied to me but
neither did she always tell me everything, especially when
she thought it was better for me not to know, and having
thought back over our discussion on the phone when she
had promised she would tell him and I'd said I'd wait for
her to ring me back and she'd replied by text to tell me to
keep going, I had realized there'd been wiggle room in that
exchange for her to *not* tell Alistair and still not tell a lie. And
when she'd been here last, her talk had been all about her
own excitement and plans for the book, with no mention of
his. "There are things unexplained and unfinished."

"As with real life," Claudine pointed out.

Thinking of Alistair's unfinished trilogy, that for the

moment would have to remain so, I looked from the mutely accusing eyes of his framed portraits to those hung beside it, my gaze unexpectedly finding another familiar face.

"Wait," I said. "Is this…?"

"Madeleine Hedrick," she named the famous actress. "Yes, she was one of my first assignments when I went to London. Such a wonderful woman."

"You worked in London?" Which explained, I thought, how she had learned to speak such perfect English.

Claudine said, "When I was starting out, yes. By the end I worked all over—New York, London, Rome— although I think I spent more time in airports in those days than anywhere."

Surprised by all of this, I turned and asked, "What did you photograph?"

Claudine, fitting another of the wedding prints into the album, shrugged. "My specialty was high-end advertising and fashion, but for a few magazines I also did some celebrity portraits. That one of Alistair, second one down on the right, I took that for a magazine."

I looked. It wasn't the portrait of him I liked best—the quiet one where he was sitting by the window, reading. Here he was more energetic, standing midway up a hill in what appeared to be a Scottish glen, the sky behind him streaked with clouds that cast long shadows on the curving land below. "And was that how you met?"

"No. Alistair wasn't a celebrity, when we first met. We had mutual friends," Claudine told me, "in London, and sometimes when I'd go to parties he'd be there, and one day he said he was writing a book about the Scottish exiles in the Netherlands, and asked me would I like to take the pictures for him? All our friends were teasing him because they knew my fees were too expensive for him, and he looked so embarrassed that I told him yes. I had the time. I took the photographs. I didn't charge him much. And when he came to write the second book, the one at Saint-Germain-en-Laye, I took the photographs for that as well. *That*," Claudine told me, "was an even better job, because my aunt was living here, you see. This was her house. I played here as a child, I always loved it. So we stayed here, Alistair and I, and did the research for his book. It was…"

She paused, and I turned round again and saw she'd stopped her work and wore a faint frown like the one my cousin sometimes wore when trying to decide what words to use, describing something.

Claudine said, "For years I'd been so busy. Always traveling. But here… It was like coming from a crowded place to somewhere I could breathe. Does that make sense?"

I nodded. I felt that way here, myself.

She said, "I found I liked to breathe. I liked the person I became when I was here. I think we all wear masks we show the world, and here I didn't have to wear it. It was very…"

"Liberating," I supplied, when once again she seemed in search of the right word. I wasn't thinking of Claudine, though, when I said it. I was thinking back to yesterday, and how I'd woken in Luc's sitting room in early evening to find Noah sitting at the far end of the sofa, being careful not to lean against my feet which were still covered in the blanket.

He'd been playing Robo Patrol, without the sound on. When I'd stirred, he'd turned and told me, "Papa says I need to let you sleep."

I'd blinked, and focused. "That's all right. I've slept enough."

"He says you had a meltdown."

Children were direct. I liked that. I had given Noah a plain answer. "Yes."

He'd set his game down, seeming to find me of greater interest. "Did he give you ice cream? Uncle Fabien feels better if you give him ice cream."

"No," I'd said. "He didn't."

"Uncle Fabien punched a hole right in the wall once, when he had a meltdown. Do you punch through walls?"

I'd thought he'd looked a little hopeful I would say I did, as though I had a kind of superpower.

"No. I just cry, mostly. And I'm very loud."

"Oh. Well, next time you have one, be sure that you have it when I'm here," had been his advice, "because *I'll* give you ice cream." And having said all he had wanted to say about that, he had held out the Robo Patrol game. "Want to try the next level?"

I'd felt something new in my chest, like a fullness around my heart. "Yes," I had said, "I would like that."

I felt that same fullness now, holding it close as Claudine gave a nod at the word I'd suggested.

"Yes," she told me, "liberating. Alistair had moments of that here as well, I know, but his career was on the rise. His second book did very well. It made him famous, and he had to travel. For a while I tried to do it with him, but I couldn't be that person anymore. Sometimes you try a coat on that you used to wear, and it just doesn't feel the same. The style, the cut—it's not that you've outgrown it, but it doesn't really fit. So you stop wearing it." She bent her head again above her work. "He didn't understand that. I'm not sure he ever will."

She fell silent again for a moment. I didn't say anything either. I'd been curious about Claudine's relationship with Alistair, and apparently today she felt inclined to talk about it, but I'd learned through observation it was sometimes best to not leap in with questions. Questions sometimes went unanswered. But faced with a stretching silence, people often sought to fill it.

Claudine finally said, "Success, for him, is something that you win, that other people have to give you. But if other people give you something they can take it back. For me, the work itself, just being able to create—that's what I want. I don't need all the high acclaim and recognition. Capturing a wedding, this is not less than a fashion shoot. In many ways, it's more important. More worthwhile." She slid the final print in place and closed the album, keeping one hand on its leather cover. "You've met him, have you? Then you'll have seen how he's restless; how quickly he walks."

I thought of my cousin's complaints as we'd kept pace with Alistair all through the woods of Ham Common.

Claudine went on, "Always he's looking for something, he's chasing it. Always the neighbor's grass is greener, somewhere else, over the next hill." Her smile was slight. "My grass is green enough."

I looked around the room, at all the many pictures in their frames, with new appreciation for the scope of what she had accomplished, what she had abandoned.

When my gaze returned to rest upon the single photograph of Alistair, relaxing with a wineglass in his hand, head bent above his book, my first thought was: *He isn't walking.* And my second was: *He looks content, and happy.* And then I noticed something that I hadn't before.

I had already guessed Claudine had been the person sitting in the empty chair, who'd left her wineglass on the table while she'd snapped the photograph, but now I looked beyond the curtain at the casement window by his shoulder, lifting in the

faint suggestion of a summer breeze, and saw the outline of a
peaked roof framed by trees. Luc's roof. The chestnut trees in
the back garden. The same view I saw myself each day when
I looked out the window of my bedroom.

"This was taken here," I said. I wasn't sure why that surprised me.

Claudine said, "It was." And then she said, "I had hoped…"

But she didn't finish, didn't tell me what she'd hoped. She
only stood and smiled and said, "Come, let's go down and
have some coffee with Denise. We ought to celebrate your
finishing the diary."

❧

"Darling," said Jacqui, "you're not making sense. What do
you mean, he'll have to come to France?"

"Not only France. He'll have to come *here*, to Chatou.
It's what she wanted him to do from the beginning."

"Now you've lost me. Who wanted, and why? And
what does any of this have to do with some drawing from
America?" The force of her sigh made me hold the telephone
briefly away from my ear.

I tried again, purposely slowing my speech as I took things
a step at a time.

"The drawing," I said, "is of one of Luc's ancestors.
It was drawn, so the story goes, by a young woman who
loved him."

"The ancestor."

"Yes. And when Claudine first saw it, she said that the girl
who had drawn it had shown us her heart in the drawing,
had shown us she loved him."

"The ancestor."

"Yes."

"I'm just trying to follow along," she explained, in response to my tight reply.

"There is a photograph in Claudine's studio," I said, "of Alistair."

"Ah."

"Have you seen it? The one where he's reading?"

"I think so."

"Well, *I* think Claudine, in that photograph, showed us her heart," I said. "She was in love with him then. She still is." I tried backing my opinion with a summary of everything Claudine had said, and finished with: "That's why she bought the diary in the first place, don't you see? Not because she values it for what it is—she doesn't—but because she hoped that it would bring him back here. Back to her."

"I see."

I wasn't sure she did. I found it frustrating to talk like this, unable to see Jacqui's face. I might not be able to read everyone's expressions but I'd studied Jacqui's long enough to guess, most times, at what she might be thinking. But her tone of voice was lost on me.

She said, "It seems a complicated way for her to do that, don't you think?"

I thought most people did things in a way that was ridiculously complicated, coming at them sideways all the time instead of saying what they wanted. "Look, just get him here, all right? And if you haven't told him yet what's in the diary, then for heaven's sake don't tell him now. Don't give him any reason to decide he needn't come."

"What makes you think I haven't told him?"

"Have you?"

Jacqui hesitated. "No."

"There you are, then. Just as well. He can decide if it's

of any use to him when he's had time to read it. If it isn't, he won't have to pay me anything." I took note of the time on my computer screen and said, "I have to finish up here. Promise me you'll bring him over. Those exact words."

Jacqui sighed. "I promise I'll bring Alistair to Chatou just as soon as it can be arranged. All right?"

"This weekend would be nice."

"I'll do my best." When I'd accepted that, she asked, "So, how does Mary's diary end?"

"It doesn't," I replied. "It doesn't end."

"I'm sorry?"

"You can see it for yourself," I said, "this weekend."

Ringing off, I gave my concentration back to the computer, typing in the final lines of what I had transcribed this morning:

On the 15th after breakfast Captain Hay did call upon us with the message Mr. Thomson wanted me to visit him.

Which, it appeared, was the first thing of any real note that had happened since Mary had seen the king. She'd given a full and colorful account of *that*, down to a detailed description of what they'd all worn to the palace, but afterwards her entries had grown sparser, and more dull.

Her days seemed duller still, and while she tried to keep herself amused by telling stories to her fellow guests at the hotel at mealtimes, from what I could tell they were the old tales she had told of the Chevalier de Vilbray, and not her newer, more original creations. She referred to them, but did not write them down.

A week before this final entry, on May 9, she'd written:

So at dinner told the story of the storm, which was well liked by all, and Effie later said to me in private she believes if the chevalier ever comes to Rome he will be most amazed to find himself so celebrated here for his adventures. Her remark did make me smile, which pleased her, for she holds I am become too melancholy. When I answered that it was a melancholy thing to wait so long at someone else's whim, she gently did remind me that had been her whole life's lot, and that she meant to wait upon me longer yet, and stay with me as long as she was wanted, which I told her would be always. I am glad to have her with me, but I count it still a hard thing that we are not free in life to choose our road, for Hugh must go wherever the Earl Marischal would have him go, and I must go where I am sent.

And there, I thought, was Mary's problem written in a sentence: she no longer had MacPherson.

If she'd seen him since she'd seen the king, she'd written nothing of it, but the fact that he had gone from being "Mr. M—" to being "Hugh" since they had shared the cabin on the pirate hunter's ship gave me good reason to believe his absence was the root cause of her melancholy.

Captain Hay had been the only visitor she'd mentioned, and this visit—after breakfast on the morning of May 15, in Mary's final entry of the diary—was the first time he'd brought any news that she had deemed worth noting.

He will return this afternoon and take me to the place where Mr. Thomson is confined. I cannot think why Mr. Thomson would desire to see me, nor am I assured what he might say to me should be believed. Each time he has spoken of coming abroad he has altered the facts in small ways yet without seeming less than sincere. In truth he is more a chimera than I am, and I know not whether to count him a friend or a villain.

*In truth there is but one man in the whole of Rome whose
honor I am certain of, whose friendship I have come now to
rely upon, and if it were my choice to make I would lay all my
heart before him and refuse to leave his side. My father said,
we do not always get the things we want, and he was right;
for though my aunt once reassured me I would always have a
choice, if there is one before me now I do confess I cannot see
it, so instead I must—*

And that was where the diary ended.

I would never know what Mary had felt she must do, or
what I would have done in her predicament, but where she
had not had a choice, I knew I had a simple one.

I made it now.

I read the time again on my computer, switched it off, and
stood, decidedly.

"I won't need lunch," I told Denise as I passed through
the kitchen on my way to the back door. "I'm going out."

"All right, then. See you later. Mind the cat," she warned.

Diablo had been lying like an obstacle outside the door. He
walked across the garden with me, weaving round my legs, but
when we reached the door within the wall, I aimed him back
towards the kitchen. "Go on, then. Go home," I told him,
and because I thought that good advice, I carried on into the
lane myself and ducked beneath the low-arched tree branch,
climbed the few steps of Luc's porch, and rang the bell.

The door swung open right away. He had been in the
entry hall, and waiting.

"Hi," he said.

I looked at him and understood what Mary had been feeling when she wrote: *I would lay all my heart before him and
refuse to leave his side.*

"I'd like to go to Paris now," I said. "I'd like to meet your brother."

Luc stood looking down at me a moment, then he kissed me very gently, almost carefully, and straightened with a smile that made the whole world disappear except the two of us. "OK."

CHAPTER 39

M Y COUSIN DIDN'T TRY to catch the bride's bouquet. She knew me well enough to know I wouldn't try to throw it to her, either.

Luc and I were married the first Saturday in June, having decided that was time enough to let my family settle from the shock, although my father had still seemed a little dazed when he had walked me up the aisle, between the chairs in Claudine's garden, and my mother, when she'd watched Denise set out the cake and cutlery, had asked no fewer than three times, "And *who* is she again?" as though the tangle of relationships was mystifying.

We had kept the guest list small—no aunts and uncles—so the day thus far had been an easy one to manage, though in honesty I knew that I'd remember little else beyond the look in Luc's blue eyes as we'd exchanged our vows.

The bouquet went to Noah's friend Michelle, who made a most impressive dive to catch it, ending with a grass stain on her frock to the resigned amusement of her mother, and preventing open warfare among Fabien's three daughters.

They were clever lively girls and close in age, the eldest being thirteen and the youngest just turned nine. The middle girl was very clearly on the spectrum like her father and like me, for having failed to catch my bouquet she at first turned gloomy, blaming her own clumsiness and uselessness, until her sisters rallied round to cheer her with a hunt for spiders in the garden.

"Spiders," said her mother to my cousin, "are her current special interest."

"Oh, I *know*," said Jacqui, picking up on something in the other woman's tone that I had evidently missed. "With Sara, it was snakes. We had to visit them at zoos. I had to pet one."

I sat patiently through all of this till Fabien's wife went across to supervise her daughters. With indulgence I remarked to Jacqui, "You might try *not* talking as though I weren't here."

Smiling, she said, "Sorry. I suppose I've just got used to it, having you so far away."

"Not so far." She had kept popping over at weekends as though to be certain I hadn't made some huge mistake, though her visits were less frequent now, which I took as a sign of approval.

She asked, "You're still liking the job?"

"I am loving the job."

"You're not finding it lonely?"

I thought of the room I now worked in at Luc's house—*our* house—with my desk and the chair and the second chair next to it where Noah sat after school and did homework. I said, "No. I'm not lonely."

My cousin's head turned and she looked at me, then she reached over and clasped her hand over mine, briefly. "I'm glad. I *am* glad for you, really." She blinked very quickly and slid on her sunglasses even though we were in shade underneath the big chestnut trees. Looking away, she said, "Luc's brother seems like a good man to work for."

He was. He was brilliant. I said so to Jacqui and followed her gaze to where Fabien stood near his daughters, head stoically bent to my mother as she rattled on about something. I did love my mother, but she talked a lot.

Jacqui asked, "Should I rescue him, do you think?"

"He's fine." I turned my head to smile at her. "You don't need to be managing things all the time. Relax."

"It isn't in my nature." But she leaned back in her chair, to please me. "He doesn't look much like his brother."

"No." Fabien looked more like Luc's mother, I thought—the tall build and fairer hair. Luc had his mother's blue eyes but in all other ways he was like a young clone of his father. I'd found myself several times watching his father and thinking how Luc's hair would lighten like that and turn gray one day, and how I'd be there to watch it. I twisted the broad band of gold on my ring finger, liking the feel of it, finding it soothing.

My cousin asked, "What have you done with your husband?"

"He's taken my father to see the Ducati. They're bonding."

In French from across the lawn, Noah called: "Sara? Michelle wants to know if the bouquet means she'll be the next to get married."

When I confirmed that was indeed the tradition, Michelle gave a shriek and the bouquet was promptly tossed upward again and kicked off a great game in the garden, all the children catching it and passing it as though it were a hot potato no one wanted to be left with, but when it came round to Fabien's middle girl she caught it tightly and proudly and held it, not letting it go.

"There, you see?" I told Jacqui. "Things always work out as they're meant to."

"I suppose they do." She was looking, I noticed, not at Fabien's daughter, but at Alistair, who sat not far away from us, discussing something with Luc's parents. "I never thought I'd see him so relaxed."

"He's like that all the time, here."

In the five months he'd been living with Claudine he'd made a good start on his new book, having given us a moment of suspense at first when he'd first read the transcribed pages of the diary, all in private, on his own. Emerging from the study he had crossed to the salon and fixed his gaze on me, and then on Jacqui, and had said, "It isn't what I'd thought it would be."

Jacqui had said, "No, I—"

"It's so far beyond my expectations," he had cut her off. "I really...I can't tell you how incredible this is."

The names that had meant little to the rest of us when reading through the diary had been well-known names to Alistair, who'd sought to educate us all that evening in the throes of his excitement. "You see here, this Martin O'Connor who's mentioned when Mary's at Chatou? Well, he was with the Mine Adventurer's Company, and he went down just after this to mine for silver in Provence. And Robinson, George Robinson, he set up with some other men to run some mines in Burgundy, and what they all were *really* doing was..."

And so the diary we had feared would disappoint him had instead surpassed his hopes by shining new light on the efforts of the Jacobites to find a steady source of income for King James's court in exile.

"He had no way," so Alistair had said, "of raising money like most kings. He had a crown but not the country or the taxes to go with it, only subjects who were landless like himself, and looked to him for their support. And having to rely upon the pope to give him money was humiliating. So..."

And he'd been off again, explaining all the details of the silver mines and lead mines and attempts at trade, and efforts that went well beyond what Thomson and his cohorts did, or didn't do, depending on one's view of things. But I'd been watching Jacqui's face, while Alistair had talked, and I had asked her later on why she'd been smiling.

"Because when a writer gets like that," she'd said, "so fired up, I know the book they write for me will be amazing."

He was still fired up.

I reassured my cousin of this now, while she was watching him in conversation with Luc's mother. "He's decided to use Mary's diary, Mary's story, to tie all the parts together and give readers someone personal to root for, to connect with."

"Well, he always likes the little people best himself, does Alistair. The kings don't hold his interest like the commoners."

I had to side with Alistair. In all that I had read about— the great financial scandal and the treachery and intrigue and betrayal—what had captured me the most was the small story of two people who'd been caught in the machinery of politics and history without knowing it, and brought together for a little while before the wheels had turned to separate them once again.

My cousin said, "It's too bad Mary's diary doesn't have a proper ending."

"Well," I said, "I think she just stopped writing. She was sad. And Thomson did go back to Paris when they let him out of prison, so I think they very probably sent Mary with him. Maybe that was why he sent to ask her to come visit him. To tell her they were going back."

My cousin agreed that made sense.

"Yes, I know," I said. "Alistair thinks there's a whole other diary. He thinks that they went into Spain."

"Why Spain?"

"He says the Earl Marischal went to Spain later on that year, and he thinks Mr. MacPherson went with him, and both Luc and Alistair think that MacPherson had fallen for Mary, so they think he married her and took her with him."

"I see. So your husband's a romantic, then."

"A hopeless one." I watched as Claudine came to sit with Alistair, her hand linking so naturally with his. I added, "One of us is right, or maybe neither of us is and she went somewhere else entirely, or stayed in Rome. We'll never know for certain."

We both pondered this in silence for a while. And then I said, in case my cousin hadn't heard, "Claudine and Alistair are going to take a road trip in the autumn, traveling the same path Mary took, so Claudine can take photographs of all the places Mary wrote about, from Paris all the way to Rome. We're going to watch the dog," I told her, "while they're gone."

"Diablo won't be happy."

"He'll adapt."

They had declared a brief truce for my wedding day, apparently, the cat keeping watch from the terrace while Alistair's dog Hector ran with the children.

My cousin said, "Hang on. If Alistair thinks that they all went to Spain…"

"Yes?"

"He hasn't roped you in to doing research on your honeymoon, I hope?"

"No. We're not going to the part of Spain that interests him. We're going to the north," I said. "Luc's boss has a house there he's letting us have for the fortnight."

Jacqui looked at the dark-haired man who sat on the far side of Alistair. "Luc's boss," she told me, "is rather incredibly hot."

"Yes, I know." He was not, to my eyes, as good-looking as Luc, but I saw the appeal. "He is also incredibly married."

"But happily?"

"Yes. Very happily."

Jacqui pronounced that a shame. "I could use the male companionship," she said. "I've been abandoned." She nodded to where her assistant, the gorgeous and affable Humphrey, was standing beside Denise, chatting and helping her set out the glassware.

"He'll have to get in line," I said. "Denise's current boyfriend is quite fierce."

"She didn't bring him?"

"He's in Canada," I told her. "Climbing something, I believe." Still, watching Humphrey now in action I decided I should give him even odds. Denise did like a man who wore a suit with style.

"Oh well," Jacqui said, "it will do Humphrey good, getting out a bit. He's worked long hours these past few weeks. We've got the fairy tales scheduled to come out next spring, did I tell you? You want to see some of the paintings that Julia's done for them. Simply amazing. She's done this incredible cage with a songbird to put on the cover—you know, from the tale with the wolf and the huntsman who's really the prince, where the princess is turned to a bird."

I said quietly, "That one's my favorite."

It spoke to me on a deep personal level, that tale of the princess who'd rescued her brother and father when they had been lost in the forest of thorns.

I remembered how lost I had felt sometimes, out of my element, and how my cousin had always been there for me, leading me out of the labyrinth, keeping my feet on the path.

Now I looked round the garden at everyone—Fabien once again trapped by my mother beside the geraniums, and his adorable family—*my* family—still hunting for spiders, and

Noah at play with Michelle, and Denise flirting madly with Humphrey, and Geoff and his wife talking politics now with Luc's parents while Claudine and Alistair sat holding hands, and my father and Luc coming through from the lane, and it all seemed so wonderful I felt my eyes stinging hotly. I closed them. And opened them.

Jacqui asked, "Are you all right? Do you want a Sudoku?"

Shaking my head I said, "Jacqui?"

"Yes, darling?"

"I love you."

I wanted to thank her for not giving up on me. Thank her for making me take the job Alistair offered; for keeping me on the straight path that had brought me here. Thank her for leading me out of my personal forest of thorns. But there were too many words that needed saying all lodged in a jumble somewhere in my throat, so I didn't say anything.

And yet she heard me.

"I love you, too," Jacqui said simply, and turned her attention to Luc, who was crossing the garden towards us, the sun on his hair. "Now, let's see if this beautiful, romantic man of yours knows how to mix me a decent martini."

CHAPTER 40

He stood like a cloud on the hill, that varies its form to the wind.
—Macpherson, "Fingal," Book Five

Rome
May 15, 1732

I T HAD BEEN BUILT as a tomb and it felt like one. Back in
the time of the Caesars, this massive and stern tower had
been the tomb of the emperor Hadrian, and his bones lay still
beneath them as they climbed the broad shallow staircase of
herringbone bricks that ascended the cavernous space.

Mary was glad of the company of Captain Hay, who had
come to collect her this morning at her hotel, walking beside
her the whole way and over the broad stone bridge guarded
by pale sculpted angels who'd seemed to look down with as
much melancholy as could be felt within the heavy walls of
the Castel Sant'Angelo, this fortified and impenetrable place
that was at once a mausoleum and a prison. She felt small and
cowed in its echoing passages. They had passed small dismal
rooms and dark cells behind barred doors and wooden ones,
and heard the coughing and shuffling below in the dimness
their sight could not penetrate.

Captain Hay said, "It is better than this further up, do
not fear."

She did not tell him she was not afraid. These past
weeks while she'd waited at the hotel, she had found herself retreating to that place behind the shields she'd used

so long and which had always served her well when she felt vulnerable.

At first, when Thomson had been sent to prison here and she had been taken back to Effie at their hotel in the piazza close beside the Pantheon, she had not realized how much things would change. She'd thought that Hugh would still be staying there to guard them, but he had not even come back with them in the coach, and on the next day men had come to clear his few things from the room upstairs, and all she could assume was that he now was lodging closer to the palace or within it, where his patron the Earl Marischal could call upon his services more readily. She'd hoped he might come pay a visit to them when he'd settled in his duties and could find the time to spare, but he had not. At least, not in a formal way. One night as she'd looked down upon the fountain in the square beneath her window, she had thought she'd glimpsed the faint red glow of a lit pipe from deep within the shadowed darkness of the great tall pillars standing at the porticoed front entrance of the Pantheon, but even as she'd tried to look more closely it had vanished.

She had seen him in the street a few days later—he'd been walking at the shoulder of an elegantly dressed man slightly older than himself, and although the other man was talking to him, Hugh had glanced her way instead. Their eyes had met. But when she would have nodded to acknowledge him he'd shaken his head slightly, and she'd yielded to the warning and passed on, though she had not been able to resist the urge to look behind, to find the other man had turned his head as well to look at her with interest.

"Was that the Earl Marischal?" she'd asked Effie that night.

"Aye. A man of great influence, of an old family that long has supported the king and has lost their estate back in

Scotland because of it. My clan and Mr. MacPherson's are bound to the earl's noble family by ancestry, and there's not one of my kin would not rise if he called us."

Mary had only a small understanding of the complex obligations binding one man to another in the Highlands, but she understood enough to know that Hugh, by virtue of his duty to the earl and to the king, was now departed from her life as fully as her father and her brothers were. In weaker moments, lying in her bed at night, she'd wondered what might happen if she called to him as he'd advised her once to call to Frisque—and then she pushed the thought aside because it was a foolish one, and even had he wanted to, she knew he could not stay.

No more than she could stay that happy woman she had been aboard del Rio's ship. If it were true, as Mistress Jamieson had said, that any man deserving of her love would see her as she truly was and need no more from her than that she should be nothing but herself, then Hugh was more deserving of her love than any other man could hope to be, for through some subtle alchemy his presence had allowed her to *be* who she truly was, and now, without him there, she could not manage it at all. She did not try to reason why, nor did she let herself admit she loved him—only told herself that having never been in love, she could not know for certain it was love that had consumed her thoughts and heart. Besides, since Hugh had moved beyond her sphere it made no sense to feel towards him anything but gratitude and ladylike affection, for to love him could but lead to greater heartache when she left.

She'd cloaked her sadness in the old familiar fashion and become again that lively, undemanding, and flirtatious person who at Chanteloup-les-Vignes had been so entertaining;

though she found that skin now fit her much less comfortably and left small holes and gaps that sometimes showed along the seams.

She tried to hide them now, and answered Captain Hay's kind reassurance that the dark Castel Sant'Angelo was less oppressive on its upper levels with, "I'm glad to hear it. I feared Mr. Thomson might be inside one of these cells."

Captain Hay said, "He was for a time, which we had not expected, but luckily he wrote Lord Dunbar to tell us and we were then able to have him moved into more comfortable rooms. As you'll see."

It was indeed completely different on the upper levels. From a long, protected courtyard that stood open to the sunlight, they climbed up another flight of steps and into a curved loggia with lovely vaulted ceilings painted with frescoes in beautiful colors, where airy breezes blew through open archways framing views across the hills and roofs of Rome.

Thomson's new "cell" was a spacious room, soaring and square with fine leaded glass windows and elegant curtains and, set at its center, a table at which he'd been writing. He rose as they entered.

She'd been of two minds when the captain had called at her hotel this afternoon, bringing her word Mr. Thomson was asking to see her. She did not know what to believe about Thomson.

Each time he has spoken of coming abroad he has altered the facts in small ways yet without seeming less than sincere, she had written this morning in her private journal. *In truth he is more a chimera than I am, and I know not whether to count him a friend or a villain.*

This afternoon, he seemed the same man he'd been when she'd met him in Paris, his pleasure at seeing her genuine. "I am so glad you could come. Thank you, Captain, for bringing her. And for the paper you sent."

Captain Hay, with a nod at the table, remarked, "I can see you have put it to good use."

"Indeed." Thomson's tone was well satisfied as he looked over the neat stacks of letters and papers himself. "I have written a private memorial for His Majesty's use, as well as the one for his banker…Signor Belloni, is it? Yes, I thought so. For Signor Belloni to send into England, to Parliament. And I am just now writing to my father, to tell him I'm well and expect to be soon set at liberty." Turning to Mary, he added, "But I did not wish to depart, my dear, without this meeting." His eyes, though they held not the depth of loneliness they'd held in Lyon, still craved her esteem.

Captain Hay asked, "Have you reached a decision on where you will go when you leave Rome?"

"I expect I'll return by the same way I came, though I trust that the journey will be somewhat easier. I'm told there is an order from the cardinal to prevent my being seized in any part of France, so I need have no fear of going back. At any rate, I am obliged to go to Paris, for till I have seen my friend Robinson I cannot know the true situation of my affairs."

The captain nodded understanding, and seemed on the cusp of saying more when they were interrupted by a short respectful knock upon the outer door. Excusing himself, he went to answer it, and after speaking briefly with the guardsman who had knocked, the captain turned back to them, told them, "Forgive me, I won't be a moment." And stepped out.

"An interesting man," Thomson said. "And a brave one. My brother in St. Petersburg has told me stories…but I wander too far from my purpose." With a slight and charming smile, he turned as well and crossed the room to where his deal-box sat atop a lacquered table in the corner. "I've given up most of my papers and things, for the sake of appearances, you understand—so our king may be seen and believed to have done all he could to restore what the people in England believe I have taken. But some things are left to me still."

Mary, while he was saying this, took a step closer herself to the table at which he'd been writing, her gaze falling to the still unfinished letter he'd told them was meant for his father. He had a clear hand. It was easy to read.

"Where the devil…ah, here they are."

Mary looked up and stood waiting while Thomson approached with a tiny bag of softest velvet nestled in his hand.

He said, "These are a gift for you, my dear. To thank you for your help."

Inside the bag were earrings made of gold and set with opals fashioned as small teardrops. Mary looked at them, and not at him. And then because she could not hold her silence any longer she asked, quietly accusing, "Who in London is now bankrupt for the want of these?"

"No one, I can promise you. They are my own to give," he told her earnestly. "I bought them years ago as an investment, and I wish for you to have them as a token of my gratitude and friendship."

Friendship. Mary turned her hand a fraction, watching how the opals changed their colors in the light. "This friend of yours," she said, "this Mr. Robinson you told the captain you must see in Paris—would that be the Mr. Robinson who came away with you from London?"

She did not raise her head to seek the truth in his expression, for she knew she would not find it there, and anyway, his silence was itself an answer.

Still she carried on, "The man who swindled you? The man you warned me in Lyon was someone I should shun were we to meet for he was nothing but a rogue," she said from memory, "and a liar?" On that final word she did look up, and met his wary gaze with one that did not try to hide her disappointment. Nor her growing anger. "I am sorry, Mr. Thomson, I cannot accept your gift." She slid the earrings in the velvet bag and gave it back to him. "Nor would I claim the friendship of a man who could write *that*," she added, pointing at the letter on the table.

He looked down as well, and at his frown of faint confusion Mary took the letter in her hand and read the passage that offended her, as evidence might be read out in court to the accused: "*A report (which I never heard of) it seems was spread when I went abroad that I had carried all off in money to the Pretender, and that reached this place, and sometime after my arrival I was taken up and everything I had seized. If my intention had been to assassinate the Pope they could not have used me any worse.* This is what you write, sir, to your father. From this room, *this* room, where you are kept and fed and sheltered by the kindness of that king you would deny as a pretender." Mary was so angry at this new betrayal she could feel the paper trembling in her fingers, and she dropped it as though it were poisoned.

"But my dear. You must consider what I'm writing may be opened, may be read." He was trying to calm her, she knew. To cajole her. "And you of all people should know that one tailors the tale to the listener."

She paused and collected her thoughts before answering, knowing in one sense that what he'd just told her was true, and yet knowing it was for that reason she could not believe him.

"The thing is," she said, in a voice that surprised her with how small it sounded, how sad, "it is one thing to tailor the tale, and another to tailor yourself—for by doing the first you may only lose sight of the truth, but by doing the latter you stand then to lose your original form so completely you are become naught but a cipher, a nothing, that changes as smoke changes shape on the wind, and is lost and forgotten as quickly."

"My dear."

Mary steeled herself against the part of her that even now sought to pity him, seeing the good in him, wanting to think what he said was sincere. She said only, "Good-bye, Mr. Thomson."

And turning, she left him alone with his writings that may or may not have been speaking the truth.

❧

Captain Hay was in the courtyard, talking to another man whose back was to her, so she could but guess from his expensive suit of clothing that he was a man of some importance, with a fine and educated voice that, like the captain's, had retained its Scottish intonations.

"—likes it very well indeed," the man was saying. "He is missing the company of the Duke of Liria, naturally, for they were always very close, but General Lacy keeps him well amused and our friend Admiral Gordon is as kind to him as ever. I have just in fact sent several pounds of snuff by ship from Leghorn to St. Petersburg for Admiral Gordon to pass to my brother."

"If he does not use it first." The captain smiled. "I miss the admiral. Though I dare say he has not the opportunity for mischief he once had. When last he wrote me, he was waiting for his granddaughter's arrival on a ship from Leith, and I believe Sir Harry Stirling and the admiral's daughter Nan now have two children of their own to keep him busy in St. Petersburg."

"All men must settle, in their time. And I am glad to see the admiral so well set in Petersburg, and General Lacy too, for they are worthy of it. Better they rise by their merit in Russia than molder away here." His voice had grown cynical. "To see some of our old gentlemen, once clever men, turned to old women here in Rome is a melancholy sight. 'Tis why I am so often in the country."

"Where was it this time?" asked the captain.

The other man named the place, which meant nothing to Mary, adding, "You ought to have come with us. It is only twenty miles from Rome, and the shooting was excellent."

"Next time." The captain had noticed her now.

Through all their talk she'd stayed discreetly to the side, not wishing to intrude, but when the captain greeted her it made the other man turn too, and Mary recognized him then, for she had seen him walking in the street with Hugh— the Earl Marischal.

Mary's curtsy was low, from respect for his noble rank, but also because it allowed her to divert her gaze from his, which for some reason seemed to be trying to measure her. "My lord," she greeted him when they were introduced.

"Mistress Dundas." The earl was a well-formed man of about forty years old, with a long nose and strongly arched eyebrows and keen and intelligent eyes. "Do forgive me for detaining Captain Hay with gossip."

Captain Hay said, "I have been detained by more than that, my lord. I've been told I must wait for a messenger sent by His Holiness, who would have me carry something in private to give to the king, so I very much fear," he told Mary, "we cannot go yet. If you're anxious to leave, I could try to have one of the guards—"

"I can take her." The Earl Marischal had a genuine smile. "If she'll have me as escort."

She looked at him and took his measure in her turn, and took his arm.

She was glad to be free of the Castel Sant'Angelo. Glad to be free of its sighs and its sufferings, and of the darkness that seemed such a part of its stones. Outside its walls the air felt softer and a little warmer even though the afternoon was coming to its end, the angels casting longer shadows on the bridge while golden light spilled down the ripples of the River Tiber. The prospect of the great church of St. Peter's in the distance was so lovely Mary could not help but keep her eyes upon it while she walked, in hopes that she might fix within her memory how it looked with the sun striking it at just that angle, turning it to something from a dream.

The earl looked down at her. "This is the first time you have been in Rome?"

"It is, my lord."

"And what is your impression of it?"

"I've not been able to see much of it, but what I have seen has been very beautiful."

"'Not able to see much of it'?"

"Why yes, my lord. I've been with my companion at the hotel for the whole time of my stay here, and we could not venture far afield without a man to guide us."

"So you've been here all this time and not seen any of the greatest sights?"

She told him, "I have seen the king."

He looked at her again as they stepped off the bridge, and stopping for a moment asked, "Are you in a great hurry to return to your hotel? Because if not, we might walk back the longer way along the river. You should at least see something of the place before you leave it."

Mary said, "I'm in no hurry to return."

He was an easy man to walk with. Mary wondered what her cousin Colette would have thought, to know that she had traveled all the way to Rome and was now strolling by the ancient River Tiber, with an earl.

He asked her, "Have they arranged your passage back to Paris?"

She would not have thought a man of his estate would take even a passing interest in her own affairs, but she supposed Hugh might have spoken of them, and being a gentleman the earl was merely asking now to be polite. "Not yet, my lord." It must be soon, she knew. The king, for all his goodness, could not pay their keep indefinitely, and she and Effie surely were a burden to his finances.

"No word yet of your father?"

"No, my lord."

She did not wish to talk about herself. An hour before this, Mary might have played her practiced part and tried amusing the Earl Marischal with lively conversation, but she no longer had the heart for it—not only because she half feared she might become like Thomson and change shape so often she no longer recognized her true self, but because she only really wanted to discuss one thing.

She asked, "Did Mr. MacPherson go with you, my lord, to the country?"

She felt him glance down at her, but if he thought it a bold or a curious question he did not remark on it, only replied, "Yes, he did."

"And were you very long away?"

"A fortnight, more or less."

Which made her feel a little less forlorn, explaining why she had not lately seen Hugh here in Rome.

The earl continued, "I do not believe he much enjoyed the country, to be honest, though as usual he did so well at shooting that the rest of us were forced to stand in awe of him. Except," he said, "when it was wagered that he could not hit so small a target as a sparrow. You have seen him shoot?"

She had a vivid memory of it. "Yes."

"So then you know how safe that wager was, particularly since the sparrow was at rest upon a hedge. I laid my money down as well," he said, "and lost it all."

"He missed the shot?" She was amazed.

"He did not take it. With the sparrow in his sights he changed his mind and set his gun down, and would not be moved to fire. A thing I've never seen him do."

"Did he say why?"

"I asked him that, believe me, after I had paid his losses and my own. He said that when the sparrow chirped he reckoned it was telling him to save his shot, and so he did."

"He said that? Those exact words?"

"Yes."

She thought about the story she had told while they had waited near to Nîmes for Thomson's fever to subside—the story of the crown prince who'd been exiled far from home and had become a huntsman in the forest full of thorns, and who had nearly killed his father and his sister in disguise until the princess had made use of her enchanted songbird form to sing and stir the memory in the prince's heart of what he had once been. She'd told him: *Save your shot, dear brother. Do not let your heart grow cold enough to kill without a cause.*

The earl was walking closest to the river, and the sun

was angled low behind him so she could not easily observe his features, but she knew that he could see her own. She bent her head. "Did it surprise you," she asked, "seeing him compassionate?"

"What actually surprised me was the fact he spared the effort to explain. He does not bother, as a rule."

Mary matched his dry amusement with a small smile of her own. "You've known him long."

"I've been acquainted with him long. I'm not sure anyone can know MacPherson." He looked at her. "He has not had a very pleasant or an easy life, you understand. Would you like me to tell you what I know of it?"

She nodded, and he told her, in the simple way that men were wont to tell things, without sentiment.

And broke her heart.

CHAPTER 41

He afterwards walked the hill. But many and silent
were his steps round the dark dwelling...
—Macpherson, "Fingal," Book Two

Rome
May 15, 1732

HUGH CAME FROM THE Highlands near Inverness, born the third son of a weaver. He was but a lad of fifteen in the year fifteen, when the rebellion began and he rose with the rest of his clansmen in favor of King James and marched with his father and brothers and cousins on Preston, just over the border with England.

They came into Preston in early November, proclaiming the king in the marketplace, and for a handful of days all was easy—until they had word that the government of the usurper was sending up troops from the south to attack them. The Jacobites dug themselves in and prepared for a battle. They got one. Hugh's father fell in the first hours of the fight with the government troops, on a Sunday, while shooting down over the barricades from the upper window of an occupied house. Hugh, lying next to him, picked up his father's dropped musket and carried on firing.

"He lay on his belly the whole of that day," said the earl, "and through all of the night, with his father there dead at his shoulder."

By nightfall the town was in flames, and next morning the government forces received reinforcements that let them surround the town, trapping the Jacobite army within. Still, the men were for staying and fighting, but some of the gentlemen officers voted instead to surrender, and Hugh, just like all of the other brave Highlanders, was told by his own commanders to lay down his weapons. His father was thrown in a ditch to be buried, and Hugh and his brothers and cousins and all of the others were taken up prisoners.

Numbers were hanged. For the rest, several hundred men crowded all into the jails where they lay upon straw with no covering, there was but fever and sickness and suffering through the raw winter months until their trials.

"I know not what horrors he saw there," the earl said, "but one of his cousins died and the surviving ones were, with his brothers, condemned to be transported to the Americas and sold for slaves for seven years."

Mary remembered the depth of the darkness and pain she had glimpsed in Hugh's eyes in Marseilles, when he'd looked at the galley slaves. Now she knew why.

"How was he spared?"

The earl said, "He was not." Then more quietly, "He was not spared."

Hugh, the youngest of his family captured and condemned to transportation, was so dangerously ill when they were sent on board their ships his brothers feared that he would not survive the voyage, so they gathered what they could among them—all they had remaining—and they bribed the captain to set Hugh down on the coast of Ireland. He was too ill and unaware to raise a protest, or to even see them before they were gone across the sea without him, and he never after heard if they were taken to America or to the harsh plantations of Jamaica and Antigua. They were simply gone and lost to him, with neither trace nor word.

The rebellion meantime had been lost, and the earl with his own younger brother had made his escape through the Highlands to wait in the western isles until the king sent a ship out of France to collect them. Hugh's own passage was less direct—from Ireland he found a boat to carry him to Cornwall, where he fell into the company of free traders who, unable to set him down in Scotland, took him safe instead to Spain.

"We met him there, my brother Jemmy and I," said the earl, "when the Governor of Palamos assigned him to us as a guard against the robbers on our road, when we arrived ourselves upon the coast of Catalonia in the first months of the year nineteen. Hugh and his clan are of the same origin as my family, if old tradition does not fail, so I did take a real concern in what regarded him, and finding him a loyal lad I hired him myself to guard my brother."

Then in the summer of that year the Jacobites made another descent upon Scotland, landing a body of soldiers, some Spanish among them, near Inverness. Hugh was one of the first men ashore, keen to finally return to his home and his family—what little remained of it—after his three years in exile.

And then came the Battle of Glen Shiel.

"The whole affair was poorly done," the earl admitted. "We advised the Spanish to surrender, and ourselves made a retreat. I managed to get off the coast in safety on my ship, but Jemmy and MacPherson with some others were cut off and forced to escape as they could to the mountains."

Hugh led the way through the wild passes and mist-shrouded heights and made straight for his home. The earl's brother, fighting off illness through all this time, spoke of it afterward—how Hugh encouraged him, telling him what they would find at the end of their climbing: a cottage slung close to the earth, with a roof of fine thatch that would keep out the rain that now plagued them; a fire to warm them, and beds soft with blankets Hugh's father had woven himself on the loom that at one time had seemed to be always in motion; Hugh's mother and sister within the door, waiting to welcome them.

Then they'd come over the last of the hills and found... nothing.

A ruin.

A hollow of stones where the cottage had been, partly tumbled and blackened by fire, and the wind blowing lonely and weeping across the scarred earth.

The earl said in a somber tone, "I'm told MacPherson said nothing. Did nothing. He stood and he looked, that was all."

For what else could he do, Mary wondered, when all of his memories and hopes had been struck from the place where they ought to have been? When the light in the window that beckoned him home had been naught but a false fire that died in the darkness? She saw him again standing out in the night at the farmhouse near Maisonneuve, chopping at wood as though killing the demons that Effie's sad Highland lament had released, the song of the warrior who had outlived all his loved ones and had none left now who could comfort him. *Which way*, she'd asked him that night, *is your home from here?* And he had looked to the stars and had pointed the way. *Do you miss it?* she'd asked. And she understood now why he'd answered, *There's nothing to miss.*

The earl told her, "The *saighdearan dearg*—that's what they call them in the Highland language. The red-coated soldiers, the government soldiers, not all of them English unfortunately. In the wake of the Fifteen, they punished those men who'd come out for the king."

Little knowing or caring that Hugh's father lay dead already at Preston, the red-coated soldiers had burnt both his home and his livelihood, setting the loom ablaze, and finding no men to punish they'd turned to the women and…and…

Mary could not imagine the terror and pain that Hugh's mother and sister had suffered. Nor what he'd suffered in learning their fate, knowing he had not been there to shield and protect them.

Again a small piece of the puzzle that was Hugh MacPherson fell into its place, and she knew why he'd stepped in where others might not have, to safeguard the honor of one who had none to defend it, that night in the yard of the inn at Valence.

"He carried but two things away from his old home," the earl said. "A piece of the wood, not yet burnt, from the loom of his father, and part of the blade of the sword that was left for his mother to use to defend herself if need be, that he found broken and left in the dirt. You'll have seen both these things if you've spent any time with him."

Mary knew where. He had fashioned them into the dagger—the dirk—that he wore at his belt. The wood-handled dirk that he used when he killed to protect those he guarded. The blade that he touched to his lips when he swore an unbreakable oath.

Mary nodded and looked away, seeing the golden light scattered like small shattered dreams on the river they strolled beside. She'd asked Hugh on del Rio's ship how he had made the journey from a man who liked to fix things to a man who killed. And he had fallen silent and his mouth had twisted in the smile that was not like a smile, and he had told her: *Step by step.*

And walking now beside the Tiber while the earl

continued telling her the story of that summer, Mary pictured in her mind the steady striding steps Hugh would have taken while he was half helping and half carrying the earl's ill brother through the rugged Highlands, every one of those steps taking him a little farther from the man he might have been, and leading him along the path to what he would become.

He got the earl's brother to safety and a ship across the Channel, and the three men meeting up in the Low Countries had then found their way again to Spain. For nearly nine years after that, Hugh guarded the earl's brother through his various adventures in the Spanish service, into France and out of it, and all through the five-month-long siege of Gibraltar, until the earl's brother, on finding that being a Protestant stood in his way of advancing his rank, finally went into Russia to join the service of the empress there.

"It is not an easy thing, gaining admittance to Russia," the earl said. "The invitation sent to Jemmy was for him alone, and so MacPherson could not follow."

Since then, these past few years, Hugh had been serving the Earl Marischal, loaned out upon occasion to his friend the Duke of Ormonde, who at length had heard from Paris that a trusted man was needed there to guard the warehouse keeper of the Charitable Corporation.

"And from there," the earl said, "I believe your knowledge of MacPherson's actions will be fuller than my own."

They walked a little ways in silence. Then the earl remarked, in tones more casual, "He'd kill me if he knew that I had told you this."

She glanced at him. "Why did you tell me?"

"I could say, because you asked me to," he speculated. "Or because I thought that you should know what manner of a man had brought you here from Paris, though I rather think you know already, do you not?"

She told him, simply, "Yes."

"Then I could say I told you of MacPherson's life because he would not tell you it himself. He did not tell *me* most of it, I learned it secondhand and sometimes even that was difficult. He is a very pri—"

"Private man," she finished for him. "Yes, I know."

She felt his gaze upon her face but kept her own steadfastly on the river and the dancing play of light.

"Then let us say," the earl said finally, "that I told you what I did because he would not kill a sparrow."

Mary did not know if the Earl Marischal had heard tell of her story of the huntsman, or if he had somehow guessed at her connection to Hugh's unexpected show of mercy, and the earl did not choose to enlighten her on that count for already he had moved on to a newer subject.

"But I'm meant to be showing you some of the sights of Rome," he reminded her.

They had by this time come round a long bend of the river and were now approaching a small island set in the Tiber, attached by an ancient arched bridge to the shore.

"There's a bridge on the far side to match it," the earl said. "The island itself was shaped into the form of a ship, with this end of it here as the stern, and the bridges at each side are set as its oars, which itself is a pretty arrangement."

There were several buildings clustered on the island—a church, he pointed out to her, and a hospital, warm plastered walls and uneven tiled roofs in a picturesque huddle, but Mary admired the bridge most of all. It was not very wide, and curved up and across in a gentle arc. Built in the time of the Caesars, its softly red bricks showed the signs of their age, but the parapet where she was leaning felt very strong. Doing his part as her guide, the earl showed her the twin pillars set on the parapets, one very near to the place where she leaned—a squared stump of pale marble with faces set round it, their features now worn by the years and the weather.

"These were not set here when the bridge was first built, but some few hundred years ago. I have been told they are meant to show Janus."

The god of the Romans who stood at the gates with one face always turned to the future, and one to the past.

"'Tis an emblem well fitted for Rome," said the earl, "for although it is beautiful here, it seems always some part of this city must stand as a monument to what has already passed." The earl moved to lean on the parapet next to her, looking as Mary did down at the river that flowed swiftly under the arches beneath them and folded itself on the rocks into two white-laced currents that sent up a sound like the roar of the sea.

Mary knew what he meant. She felt it herself here, the strange juxtaposition of ruins and life, of things all at once moving and stuck in their place, like this oar of a bridge and the ship of an island beside them that held but the shape of those things and would never go anywhere, held fast forever in bedrock and mud.

"'Tis an emblem as well for the court of our king, at the moment." The earl spoke more gravely, and when she glanced over he showed her a half smile. "I always have and always will do what I can to serve King James, but you will find it is an open secret here that I do not approve of his reliance on Lord Dunbar, and I will not stay where such counsels prevail as cannot frankly be told to an honest man; where none but mean servile souls are welcome, and those who have spirit are forced to be silent."

She focused on one part of that speech alone. "You are leaving?"

"We are. I have written by this last post to my friend the Duke of Ormonde, to help us get away with the least noise, so as not to do hurt to the cause nor the king. As soon as it is possible, I hope before this month is out, MacPherson and I will return to Spain."

Her heart became a heavy weight that dropped a fraction lower in her chest and pressed against her ribs until it caused her pain to breathe. She raised a hand to shade her eyes, although the sun by this time was behind them, sinking ever lower, and deliberately she looked ahead and asked, "What is that bridge?"

It was not properly a bridge, for it did not go all the way across the river, having fallen at its middle and collapsed so that it only touched the farther bank.

"That," he said, "they tell me is the oldest stone bridge left in Rome. It has a proper name but you will hear it called most often here the *Ponte Rotto*, meaning 'Broken Bridge.'"

A view that, at the moment, seemed appropriate, so Mary thought. A bridge that none could cross, that nevermore would lead a traveler home. She moved her hand to shield her gaze more closely, blinking back the stinging of her eyes. "Why is it broken?"

"Because it stands just where the current is strongest. No matter how often they try to rebuild it the river keeps beating away at it, taking it piece by piece."

"And yet it stands." She said that in a small voice that was nothing like her own, and she was not sure why she said it.

It was only that just then, she felt a kinship with that ancient bridge that was forever being carried off in tiny pieces by the unrelenting current, and yet did not have the sense to yield, to let go of the shore and simply fall. It stood, as she had done her whole life, trying to stay hopeful in the face of what she'd lost; and as their king had done through all the changes in his fortunes that had brought him to this distant place. As Hugh had done, so stubbornly repairing things and setting them to rights when all he loved had been reduced to ash and memories.

The Earl Marischal had turned towards her, unable to hear her for the rushing of the river underneath them. "What was that, my dear?"

She told him in a stronger voice, "I said the bridge still stands." She let her hand fall to her side and looked at him. "And surely every broken thing can be rebuilt."

The earl stood regarding her much as her uncle regarded a wine that surprised him with quality.

"Yes, Mistress Dundas, I'd like to believe so."

She noticed his gaze had gone past her, and turning she saw the tall man now approaching the bridge from behind her.

"I'd very much like to believe so," the earl said again, as he lifted his hand and called out to MacPherson, who'd noticed them both by this time and was coming towards them with slow, even strides.

CHAPTER 42

No more shall I find their steps in the heath, or hear their voice…
—Macpherson, "Fingal," Book Three

Rome
May 15, 1732

M ARY TRIED TO COMPOSE herself, grateful the light was now softening so if she turned from the lowering sun Hugh might not have a definite view of her features, for although her traitorous moment at hearing the news he would soon be departing had passed, and she was in control of her face and emotions, she could not be certain he'd not see some lingering trace of it and she had no wish to show him such weakness.

He wore not his fine Highland clothes but a more common suit of a deep earthen red that looked well with the old Roman bricks of the bridge as he set foot upon it. His own face gave nothing away of his thoughts.

The Earl Marischal greeted him first with, "Did you find the man you were after?"

"Aye." Hugh looked at Mary, and he gave the short nod of greeting she'd come to miss while he'd been gone. Then he turned his impassive gaze back to the earl as a pupil might look to his tutor to lay bare the meaning of something inscrutable.

The earl offered nothing but, "And did he finish the work that you paid him to do?"

Hugh nodded curtly.

"Good. All is well, then." The earl, with an elegant ease that told Mary he was long accustomed to facing Hugh's silences, added, "I feared I might have missed the time I'd told you I would be here, for at the Castel Sant'Angelo I chanced to meet Captain Hay and as usual we fell to talking. A fortunate delay, as it turned out, for it gained me the company of this enchanting young lady." Smiling briefly at Mary, he told Hugh confidingly, "I see now why you were so disapproving of the men put forward to escort Mistress Dundas back to Saint-Germain, and why you did advise Lord Inverness he should choose none of them, for had I been her guide so long, as you were, I would also wish to choose with care the man who was to take my place."

He might as well have spoken to a statue but he did not seem bothered. He cast an unhurried glance skyward and lifted his eyebrows. "But it appears my delay, although fortunate, makes it impossible for us to do as I'd planned, for I have not the time for it now, else I'll risk disappointing the little duke." He turned to Mary. "Have you had the pleasure yet to be presented to our two young princes? No? The younger, Henry, Duke of York, is serious for one so small. I never saw any child comparable to him." His tone held indulgence. "The Prince of Wales, his brother Charles, is already unruly, but the little duke is so determined to be on his good behavior that he's ordered a journal be kept of his actions, that I may see and tell the world how well he does behave. He made me promise to buy him a special book just for this purpose and bring it to him before bedtime tonight, so I must buy one now else he'll count me a man of no honor at all." Looking at Hugh again he asked, "There was not a stationer's shop, by chance, near to your silversmith?"

In watching Hugh, Mary had noticed a faint line that showed in his hard cheek when he was amused or, much more commonly, exasperated, and she saw it now. He told the earl, "No."

"Ah."

Mary said, "There is a stationer quite near the Corso, where I bought a journal for myself just yesterday." Bound with bright colorful boards and tooled leather it was much more decorative than the one Colette had given her, and yet she doubted she ever would hold it so dear.

She thought of Hugh standing at Fontainebleau holding her journal within his hands, and wondered what he would think, with his practical Highland ways, of the impractical manner in which she had ended that book today, writing:

In truth there is but one man in the whole of Rome whose honor I am certain of, whose friendship I have come now to rely upon, and if it were my choice to make I would lay all my heart before him and refuse to leave his side.

A most foolish sentiment, surely, she told herself, and one he'd hardly have welcomed, but as she had gone on herself to acknowledge, her father's dour philosophy of life had been a true one: *for though my aunt once reassured me I would always have a choice, if there is one before me now I do confess I cannot see it, so instead I must—*

And here, having run out of space in the first journal, Mary had opened her new one and inked her pen carefully and marked the date again and carried on:

—content myself with having briefly touched that wider sky that Mistress Jamieson did speak of, for being brought to earth

again I'd rather have the memory of flight and bear the pain
of losing it, than to have never flown at all.

Brave words, she thought, and tried to match her
actions to them now as she gave the Earl Marischal directions to the stationer's.

He thanked her and bowed gallantly and kissed her hand
and said, "I have enjoyed our walk. I trust MacPherson will
at least approve himself to be your escort back to your hotel,
since he seems loath to recommend another."

With a final nod to Hugh he wished them both a pleasant
evening and walked off in the direction of the Corso and the
palace, leaving Hugh and Mary standing on the bridge.

She watched the earl's departing back and thought she
understood why Hugh would serve a man like that—a man
of decency and honor and intelligence. And given that the
earl belonged, as he himself had owned, to a more noble
branch of Hugh's own clan, by serving him Hugh could
quite rightly claim to be no broken man, but one who was
yet bound by faith and duty to his family.

She had gained a deeper understanding of MacPherson
this past hour, as these past weeks had given her a deeper
knowledge of her feelings for him, yet she could share none
of it but held it all within her as she faced him in the fading
light. Behind him the whole western sky had now softened
to pink streaked with turquoise, and Mary knew they would
not have long to talk, so she wasted no time.

"If you truly are given a say in whom Lord Inverness will
select as my guide, I would ask you a favor."

He neither denied nor confirmed his involvement, but
waited with evident patience for her to continue.

Mary said, "I would not give you trouble…" Then she

caught herself, remembering the times she'd been a bother to him on their journey down, and added, "Though I do suppose that it is rather late for that."

Again the line showed for a moment in his cheek. He told her, "Name the favor."

"Mr. Thomson claims he will be set at liberty quite soon, and I would rather not be sent to travel in his company."

Hugh did not ask her to explain, so she was spared the complicated task of giving voice to her unsettled view of Thomson and his character; her indecision whether he was a good but misguided man or a dissembling traitor.

Hugh said only, "Then ye'll not be. I will see to it."

She thanked him, and although she'd learned in childhood that no good would come of prodding at a wound, she could not keep herself from saying, "It is too bad the Earl Marischal is not inclined to travel north to Saint-Germain-en-Laye, instead of south to Spain."

Mary thought she saw a small change to the angle of his head as though he counted it of interest that the earl would so divulge their plans. He took a step towards her, thoughtfully. "The earl," he said, "prefers a warmer climate, and he has few friends at Saint-Germain."

She sympathized. "In that respect, the earl and I are equal."

He'd come to a spot an arm's length from her, and now he stood there and studied her face. "You were born there."

"But I have not lived there since I was a child." She had not intended the words to sound wistful, but Hugh seemed more focused on what she had said than the way she had said it.

He frowned. "When I took ye from Paris, ye told me in plain terms ye were to go back to your family. The whole way to Lyon ye seemed fair determined," he said, "to go home."

Mary gave a little shrug and looked deliberately away. "Home, as you once told me, is not always where you left it."

She did not wish to speak to Hugh about her family. He already knew—had known from the beginning—who her elder brother was, and doubtless he would then know something of her family's past. And having made inquiries here in Rome about her father and her other brothers, he would also know how little she had figured in their lives. He did not need her to remind him of how easily they'd left her, for he was about to do the same himself.

Hugh had said nothing in reply, and Mary—knowing he had no great love of conversation—took that as a sign he wished to bring an end to this one and deliver her to her hotel in safety, for the sun had crept yet lower and the turquoise color in the sky was bleeding through the softer pink and washing it away, and soon the twilight would descend.

"Shall we start back?" she asked him with a brightness that she did not feel. "I'm sure that Frisque will be beside himself with joy to see you, he has been so bored these past weeks." *As have I*, she nearly added, but she held her tongue.

"I have a gift for ye."

It was, as speeches from the Scotsman went, so strange and unexpected that she was not sure she'd heard him right. "A what?"

He did not bother to repeat the comment, for he had already pushed his sword hilt to the side to gain him access to the pocket of his dark red coat, from which he drew his hand out in a half-closed fist. He held that fist towards her, and his fingers opened to reveal a thing so purely beautiful that Mary could do naught but stare.

It was an equipage—a silver clip of four open-work hearts so set together that they seemed to form a butterfly, and hanging from them by three dainty silver chains she saw a tiny watch key, and the little watch that went with it, and something small and round suspended in a cage of silver wire.

She looked at it and could not speak.

She thought of what the earl had asked him earlier, about whether the man Hugh had met had completed the work he'd been paid for, and vaguely her mind resurrected the earl's idle mention of shops and a silversmith, but it seemed incredible that Hugh would go to so much trouble and expense on her account. And then she looked at the watch and another thought, still more incredible, struck her. She asked him, "You made this?"

He nodded. "I had a man here do the chains and the clip for me, for I had not the right tools."

Any words she might have said at that moment all seemed to be caught in a lump at the base of her throat, so she did not say anything, letting Hugh show her the watch—how the glass front would open, as would the bright silver-cased back, and the way it was meant to be wound with the key.

With his head bent, intent on instructing her, he said, "It must be wound once a day, though it will run for six hours beyond that if ye do forget it."

She managed to say in a small voice, "I will not forget."

She did not mean the watch, but she stared at it anyway, noting the miniature scrollwork that weighted the delicate hands on its white porcelain face with the numerals marked simply in black.

"The face is a plain one," said Hugh, "but the workings inside will not fail ye."

Her gaze lifted slightly and focused on Hugh—on the serious line of his brow and the slash of a shadow his eyelashes made on his strong angled cheekbones, and Mary could not then imagine how she could have ever thought Hugh unattractive. "It is a handsome face," she told him, and again she was not speaking of the watch.

He took no notice, gathering the bits of silver and the chains that ran like liquid over his hard palm, and passing all into her smaller hand.

The turquoise sky was flaming now to duller gray, and Mary had to lift her hand to see the details of the silver chains and what they held. She gently rolled the little silver cage to better see the flattened ball within. "Is this a bullet?"

"It is."

She glanced up, mutely questioning, and Hugh explained, "I killed the wolf with that shot. It protected ye once, and it may yet have power to keep ye from harm."

Her eyes started to fill and she quickly looked down. She'd been cared for and loved by her uncle and aunt, but she'd never had anyone show such concern for her welfare as this hardened man of the Highlands, who'd taken the trouble to fashion a charm with the sole aim of keeping her safe in the time when he would not be able to do it himself. When he would not be there at her side.

Blinking hard at the butterfly hearts, she began to believe she had seen a design like that somewhere before…and then suddenly she knew exactly where she'd seen those hearts, and her gaze slipped in mixed disbelief and dismay to the basket-like hilt of Hugh's sword, and the open space where now one piece of the wrought silver basket was missing, then back again to the increasingly valuable gift in her hand.

Her fingers closed around it and she had to fight and concentrate to keep the tears from spilling over from her blurring eyes, and it was all for naught because a single tear squeezed through her lashes anyway and slowly tracked a path down her averted cheek. She blinked again to force the others back and breathed a steady breath and willed herself to show him nothing but the strength he'd told her he admired.

Hugh was watching her. He asked, "Is something wrong?"

Everything's wrong, Mary wanted to say. *You are going away.* But she shook her head. Found her voice. "No." Not *exactly* her voice, so she cleared her throat lightly and tried again. "No, it is only that this is a beautiful gift, and I've nothing to give you at all in return."

There was silence a moment, as though he were thinking. "A story will do."

Mary brought her head up at that, grateful he'd given her something to smile at. "My stories," she said, "are in no measure equal to this, and you know it."

He looked at the silver that gleamed in the hand she'd held up as her evidence, and with a stubborn shrug told her, "I'd count them above it."

The gift of his approval was as precious to her as the silver equipage she fastened with great care upon her gown before she turned to lean again upon the parapet, uncaring that the twilight was now properly upon them and there was no view to see beyond the ghostly outline of the broken bridge against the darkness of the shore and hills beyond. And looking at that battered bridge and at the dark gray water surging at it from beneath the place she stood, she felt a sudden desperate need to bravely stand against the current that was so uncaringly attempting to tear one more piece away from her. "What tale," she asked him, "would you have me tell you?"

He considered this. "The one ye told at Mâcon."

She had only told one tale she could remember at Mâcon, and it embarrassed her to think of it: the tale she'd told the younger of the frilly sisters while they'd walked and talked in French, when she had thought MacPherson could not understand that language, and she had made sport of him by fashioning a fine dramatic tale of tragic love, with him its hero. The stone beneath her hands was cool and weathered, pitted like old bone, and Mary pressed her fingers to it. "I have long since owed you an apology for what I said at Mâcon."

Hugh stood watching her a moment longer, then came slowly forward on the bridge and bent to lean beside her on the ancient parapet. "And why is that?"

"You know why. I should not have told that story."

With another shrug he said, "I liked it well enough. All but the ending."

Mary turned her head so she could see his profile in the dimness. "It was not my ending. Nor even my story, for all that. You read the original version in Lyon, in Madame d'Aulnoy's book, you must have noticed. The tale of the Russian prince."

"Aye. Yours was better," he said. "Tell it over."

She sighed. "Hugh."

"It starts with him lost."

She could not refuse him, not when he had given her such an incredible gift of his own, so relenting she started the story and tried to repeat it the way she had crafted it when he'd been walking behind her at Mâcon, a shadow she'd longed to be free of. And yet, as she told the tale over again to him, Mary could not keep from noticing all the small points of connection to how things had happened with them in real life—from the earliest part where the hero had gazed upon his lady and had followed her without her ever noticing him in return, to their first meeting when the hero's lady had dropped her scarf and he'd returned it, to the time when he had kissed her and her world had been forever changed, until Fate cast a pall upon their happiness and forced him to decide between remaining with his lady or returning to the battlefield.

She stopped the story there, because she found it struck too close to home. The twilight now had settled all around them and the lamplight gleamed within the windows of the tile-roofed buildings clustered on the little ship-like island that would never leave its moorings, never know another shore.

Hugh said, "Go on."

"You do not like the ending," she reminded him. "You told me so yourself."

He turned his head towards her then, his face so far in shadow now she scarce could see his eyes. "Then write a different one."

Mary was not sure at first that she understood what he was asking.

Until quietly he told her, "Write a better one."

She realized he was speaking in the same tone he had used at Maisonneuve to tell her she should call to Frisque. And hope—a tiny twisted knot of it—began to loosen and expand within her. She remembered what she'd written in her journal so despondently this morning: *If it were my choice to make I would lay all my heart before him and refuse to leave his side.* And he was making it her choice.

Beyond his shoulder she could see the paler marble outline of the Janus pillar with its faces turned in all directions and so worn by time and weather they were featureless, that no one now could know or guess at who they might have been. So it would also be with them, she knew—when time had turned and people of an age to come would stand upon this ancient bridge and she and Hugh would be but faceless shadows then themselves, and none would know they'd ever been there.

None would know that on a mid-May evening, with the stars beginning to appear and glimmer in the darkening deep blueness of the arching sky, a young and lonely woman had put all her heart within her hands and laid it full before the silent man who leaned beside her.

"Then he told her," Mary said, "that he must leave, for he could not neglect his duty nor his honor. And his lady sighed with sadness, but she understood, and said to him, 'Your honor and your duty are so very much a part of you I could not ever ask you to abandon them, but neither do I think I can endure it, sir, if you abandon me. So what to do?'" She could not hold Hugh's gaze although she could not truly see it, so she looked away again, repeating, "What to do?"

A night bird in the trees along the river's edge began to trill, and Mary drew her strength from it.

"And so it happened," she went on, "a fairy of the nearby forest heard the lady's mournful speech, and being deeply moved by it, the fairy turned the lady to a falcon that could ride into the battle on her true love's hand, and so they rode away together and had many fine adventures, and he carried her forever with him and she spent her life content, for she had wings to spread and fly with and the man she loved to hold and keep her safe."

There was no sound or movement for long moments but the rushing of the river and the night bird calling.

And then Hugh asked, "What adventures did they have?"

She found it difficult, with all of the emotions of her speech, to make a calm reply. "I do not know."

He thought this over. "Then ye'd better come to Spain," he said, "and live them for yourself."

She turned to look at him, and saw that he was straightening to stand at his full height before her in the semidarkness, and the faint light from the windows of the little island at her back showed her his steady gaze was serious.

Her heart became a trembling thing within her as she straightened too and faced him, and the night air grew alive between them, though she could no more have guessed his thoughts than she had done when they'd first faced each other in the Paris street. Except his eyes now were not cold, she thought. Not cold at all, and no longer impenetrable.

"Marry me," he said.

She had to smile at his tone, for it could not be helped. "That's not a question."

"No," he said, and bent his head towards her. "It is not."

And then her smile was covered by his kiss and Mary, wrapped within the warmth of it, could care for nothing else.

Let currents flow and kingdoms fall and time move onward, Mary thought—this moment was for them. Those people of an age to come who stood upon this bridge would never know how long she'd stood tonight in Hugh's strong arms, or what he'd said to her, the quiet simple words that had been spoken from his heart and were for her alone; nor would they know what she had answered back, and how he'd smiled and gently tipped her chin up with his hand to kiss her longer and more deeply; nor how he had finally held his hand to her outstretched and she had taken it with happiness and followed him.

It mattered not that no one else would bear that moment witness nor remember it, for if the future could not know them, neither could the past confine them, and the choice was always theirs to make, the tale their own to finish, as her aunt had once assured her. And her aunt had been right also when she'd laid her hand on Mary's heart and said, "I think that always here you've had a little voice that calls to you." For Mary knew the voice that she'd heard calling to her for so long had been Hugh's own, and now had come the time, at last, to let it lead her home.

THE END

ABOUT THE CHARACTERS

Once upon a time, a baby girl was born at Saint-Germain-en-Laye.

Her father, William Dundas, was a wig maker who'd been born at Pencaitland in the Scottish Lowlands, and who'd come across as a young man to serve King James VII at his exiled court in France. It was there William married his French-born wife, Marguerite Paindeble. Their son Nicolas was born within the year, and in due course was followed by other sons—Charles and Jean [John]—and at last, at the end of July in the summer of 1710, came their daughter.

They named her Marie Anne Thérèse.

Her baptism, on the twenty-fifth of July of that year, was recorded in the register of the parish church, where I came across it while doing my research, and being in need of a heroine for my new book, I decided she'd fill that role wonderfully well.

I tried to leave her family as it stood—her mother's sister, Magdalene, was also in the parish records with her husband, Jacques Laurent—but as I could find little record of the family after Mary's birth, I took some liberties.

I don't know when her mother died. I don't know for a fact that her father and brothers followed King James VIII into Italy, but many of the male courtiers from Saint-Germain-en-Laye did so, both after the failed 1715 rebellion and in the years following the death of James's mother, Queen Mary, when the already diminished former court at Saint-Germain was reduced even further by financial hardship and lack of support from the French.

Following an exiled monarch into an uncertain future wasn't without risks, and it was common for the men to go alone. It would have been a kindness, in a caring father's eyes, to leave his tiny daughter safe behind with family; so in setting William Dundas on the path so many other men were forced to take in those times, I allowed him to leave little Mary with her aunt and uncle, where he could be certain she'd be cared for.

I don't know where the Laurents lived, but there were only two locations close by Saint-Germain-en-Laye where I could find both surnames—Paindeble and Laurent—intermingled in the records of that period, so I chose the village whose name I liked best: Chanteloup-les-Vignes, giving Mary the view across the forest towards Paris that would leave her primed to step into my story.

That story, to be honest, started taking shape much earlier, while I was doing research for another book, *The Firebird*, and stumbled on a stray mention in Paris correspondence of a Mr. O'Connor—"a reputed Sharper" suspected of being a Jacobite spy. Thinking it might be the Edmund O'Connor I was writing about in *The Firebird*, I dug deeper, only to find it was not him, but Martin O'Connor, a man with connections that led me to one of those somehow forgotten true stories from history I love to discover.

Martin O'Connor was an Irishman, and by his own admission when he first came over to the Continent he went into Flanders and mixed with the Jacobite soldiers there, many of whom were his relations. Whether one of these relations was in fact Edmund O'Connor I don't know yet, but Martin himself certainly became a great champion of the Jacobite cause.

An ardent Freemason—as were many of the leading Jacobites—he was also the Secretary of the Mine Adventurers Company, and whether on his own initiative or at the company's behest he appears to have been working to establish mines as part of a larger and organized Jacobite effort to find a steady source of income for King James VIII.

James, as a king in exile, was in the difficult position of having all the expenses of maintaining a court and government without any of the usual resources for raising the money to do so. He couldn't collect taxes, and most of the people who followed him were in no position to contribute to his cause. In fact, many of them—particularly in the wake of the disastrous 1715 rebellion—had lost their own estates and crossed over the Channel as refugees, looking to King James for pensions and financial aid. James repeatedly wrote in his letters of his desire to help them and his frustration at not being able to fulfill what he felt to be an obligation to assist those who had suffered because of their loyalty to him, but "the truth is," he wrote to the Duke of Ormonde in 1719, "we are in a terrible way as to money matters."

Well aware of this, his supporters continued to search for new avenues of income, and while permanent and sustainable ones—such as mines—were highly desirable, no stone was left unturned, and various schemes were proposed.

The idea of using the stock market was a recurring one. As early as October 20, 1717, Father Graeme (whom any readers of my book *The Firebird* may recognize as being the son of Colonel Patrick Graeme, who featured in both that book and in *The Winter Sea*) was writing from Calais to King

James's chief adviser, "Will you only allow a well-wisher to the good cause to put a trick on the stockjobbers by sending over a counterfeit *Paris Gazette* with news in it to make their stocks either rise or fall, as shall be found most convenient, and you may have a million sterling in a week or two without running any risk?"

I came across several other examples of similar offers in the correspondence I was reading, but the king invariably turned them down. Nonetheless, his followers continued to intrigue, at times without his knowledge, let alone his blessing.

By the summer of 1731, it had become apparent to one of the British informers placed in the household of a prominent Jacobite in France that some new plot was in the wind. Several people, including Martin O'Connor, had been traveling with regularity between London and Saint-Germain-en-Laye, where they were meeting with General Dillon, who, although he was no longer part of King James's inner circle, was still a loyal Jacobite and viewed by both the king and those around him as an honest man.

Whatever General Dillon and O'Connor and his friends were up to, it pushed the bounds of honesty enough that the informer's Jacobite employer was concerned, and King James—when he learned of it that summer—reportedly wrote to the general himself and instructed him not to proceed with the plan.

That this plan involved the stock swindle that would give rise to the Charitable Corporation scandal is certainly suggested by the fact that the informer repeated this detail in almost the same words the following April, while writing to his British spymasters about the affair of the Charitable Corporation. "O'Connor and others," he told them, "have assured me that the Pretender had writ some months ago to the principal people concerned, in a very great Secret, that he could not condescend to such proposals…"

At any rate, the king's instructions came too late. The wheels of the scheme were already in motion.

There were so many people involved in the scandal, and their interconnections and dealings were so intricate and well-concealed, that I could probably spend decades trying to work my way through that labyrinth without ever finding my way to its center. Even now, when I have reached a basic working understanding of the things they did and how they did them, I can't claim to fully understand their motivation.

Of the two men who shouldered the bulk of the blame for it—the banker, George Robinson, and the warehouse keeper, John Thomson—I chose to write about Thomson, not only because he left behind a greater wealth of correspondence, but also because the more I read of it, the greater an enigma he became.

Each time he recounted his role in the Charitable Corporation affair—in his personal correspondence, or in conversation with people he trusted, or in his official testimony to the Parliament committee investigating the scandal—he told a different version of the tale, and I found it increasingly impossible to tell which one, if any, was the truth. With three centuries between us, and without a better knowledge of his character, I could not say with certainty if Thomson was a victim, zealous Jacobite, or fraudster. I chose instead to have him, in this novel, give the varied explanations that he gave in life, pulling his dialogue in those scenes directly from his letters and conversations and leaving it up to the readers to judge, from his own words, which story they ought to believe.

While I may not know Thomson's true reasons for

getting involved in the stock fraud, I do know for a fact that in October of 1731, reportedly accompanied by Martin O'Connor, he fled London, crossing to France.

There was, in France, a long established Jacobite network extending from the old court of Saint-Germain-en-Laye to most of the primary cities and towns—Boulogne, Bordeaux, Marseilles, Lyon—and of course Paris, where the body of King James VII lay in state at the Church of the English Benedictines in the rue Saint-Jacques, still unburied years after his death, awaiting the restoration of his son to the British throne so the dead king's body could be given a proper state funeral at Westminster Abbey, within his own kingdom.

I have no direct evidence Sir Redmond Everard played any part in the move to assist and conceal Thomson that winter, but he was closely connected to some of the people who did, and I found the coincidence of his house being at Chatou—the same town where I'd placed my modern-day characters—too great to let it pass by without using it, just as my discovery of the real-life arrest, imprisonment, and examination of Mrs. Elizabeth Farrand, the Jacobite courier carrying messages between Paris and London, seemed to me the perfect opportunity to give a walk-on part to Anna Jamieson, a favorite fictional character of mine from my novel *The Firebird*, whose nature made it likely she'd have stepped in to take up the dropped baton of Mrs. Farrand. It was also in keeping with Anna's nature that, once on the page, she decided to turn that walk-on part into a proper cameo appearance and leave a more meaningful stamp on the story line.

By the time of Mrs. Farrand's arrest by the British, John Thomson had been hiding in France for three months, and the British ambassador in Paris, James Waldegrave, had been doing what he could to have him found and brought to justice.

Waldegrave was, interestingly enough, a grandson of King James VII by one of his mistresses, which made Waldegrave's mother King James VIII's half sister—but while he was not above using his family connections to gain information, paying visits to his uncle the Duke of Berwick at Saint-Germain-en-Laye from time to time, there is no indication he felt sympathetic at all to the Jacobite cause. On the contrary, he had a far-reaching web of informers and spies used to counter their efforts. He put them to use in hunting for Thomson.

There were, in that winter, no certain reports of where Thomson was actually staying. Waldegrave's spies reported having seen him in a hired coach in November and speculated that he was staying with the Jacobite Abbé Dunn at Boynes, south of Paris—which he probably was, since some of his papers were later discovered there and in January one of his associates claimed to have visited him in a little village outside Paris.

But by the thirtieth of January, Thomson was writing to a colleague in London: "Write but seldom for three months, and expect to hear but seldom from me in that time…" And a letter he wrote to his cousin in Edinburgh, dated that same day, was written from Paris.

So I put him in Paris.

One of the difficulties of doing research in this period, incidentally, is that at the time, England was still using the Old Style calendar while France and Italy used the New Style, so when the newspapers in England announce on the ninth of the month that someone is setting out for France, that person is actually setting out on the twentieth in the New Style, which adds eleven days. For the sake of simplicity

I kept all the dates in this novel in New Style, as my characters would have used them on the Continent.

In Paris, I chose to put Thomson on the rue du Coeur Volant for three reasons. First, that particular street had changed little since 1732, allowing me to visit it, stand where my characters would have been standing, and gain what impressions I could, which is always an integral part of my research. Second, because the real-life timing of that part of the story meant events would be happening at the same time as the annual Fair—the old *Foire Saint-Germain*—I deliberately chose a street close to the Fair site, so it could be used in the story. And finally, the rue du Coeur Volant was very close to where George Robinson—John Thomson's fellow fugitive—had stayed while he was hiding out in Paris (at the Petit Hôtel de Normandy in the rue Taranne).

For descriptions of the city at the time, I turned primarily to memoirs of the travelers who stayed in Paris in the early eighteenth century and who thoughtfully recorded all the fascinating details they observed, from public executions to the lamps that hung above the streets. As is my custom, I tried when I could to move my characters within existing dates and real events—the pantomime they go to watch (the evening Mary's gloves are stolen, when she first encounters Hugh) was actually performed on that one evening: Wednesday, February 13, and its plot is detailed in a French newspaper of that month. While such minor things might be of little importance to most of my readers, they help me to anchor my characters, real and imagined, within their historical landscape.

Because Thomson, whenever he'd been spotted somewhere in France by the British ambassador's spies, had been always in company with noted Jacobites, never alone, I considered it very unlikely he would have been left on his own while in Paris.

I gave him Mary, with her imagined former nurse, Effie, to help with his camouflage and, for added protection, created a bodyguard for him in the person of the fictional Hugh MacPherson.

Just as Mary Dundas stands, in part, as an example of the displaced second generation of Jacobites, born in exile and without a land to truly call their own, so Hugh MacPherson represents the many Highlanders who left their homes to fight for James, and paid a higher price than most.

Hugh's story, as told by the Earl Marischal, is entirely true, in its various parts. It was drawn, down to the burning of the cottage and the loom, from the memoirs and letters and firsthand accounts I read in my research, and while I cannot say with certainty that all those things happened to one man, I can say in honesty all of them happened.

Hugh's surname was intentionally chosen to place him with a family of MacPhersons from near Inverness whose names are recorded as being among those men captured at Preston and transported to the Americas and the West Indies for seven years' slavery.

As for Hugh's Highland dress, worn to the meeting with King James in Rome, although standard clan tartans weren't used in those days, I made Hugh's plaid, in pattern and colors, identical to the one worn by a previous MacPherson chief, in a portrait painted a few years earlier.

Finally, since Highlanders were known to go everywhere heavily armed—it was common for a visitor to the Highlands in those years to see a man "walking with a dirk and pistol at his side and a gun in his hand"—I allowed Hugh to do likewise, giving him the best gun he would have been able to find on the Continent in 1732.

I was surprised to find in my research that the first rifle was reportedly invented by Gaspard Zollner of Vienna as early as the fifteenth century. In 1498, at a Leipzig competition, most of the marksmen reportedly used rifles—guns with grooves cut into the inside of the barrels to improve accuracy—although those grooves appear to have remained straight until the use of spiral rifling began to take hold around 1620. By the mid-1600s, companies of chasseurs, or riflemen, had been incorporated into most of the armies of what is now Germany, and by the end of that century their use had begun to spread, but in 1742, they were still enough of a novelty outside mainland Europe that Benjamin Robins, writing in his book *The New Principles of Gunnery*, felt it necessary to write of rifles: "…these pieces, though well-known on the Continent, being but little used in England; it is necessary to give a short description of their make…"

Robins's book makes fascinating reading, as he tries to figure out the scientific reasons why such rifling might make guns shoot with more accuracy. At the end of his book, Robins makes the prescient statement that:

"Whatever State shall thoroughly comprehend the nature and advantages of rifled barrel pieces, and…shall introduce into their armies their general use with a dexterity in the management of them; they will by this means acquire a superiority, which will…perhaps fall but little short of the wonderful effects which histories relate to have been formerly produced by the first inventors of firearms."

The English army didn't formally adopt the use of the rifle until 1794.

The rifle Hugh carries is a duplicate of an actual circa 1730 sporting rifle sold at auction at Christie's in 2009.

It might have proven useful while he was guarding Thomson in Paris, as the danger I describe was real. Even though the French police were apparently in the pay of the Jacobites, a fact bemoaned by Waldegrave in his letters to his superiors, the bounty on Thomson was a large one, and attempts were being made to find and capture him.

I made use of this reality to set them on the road south.

The journey from Paris to Rome was a commonplace one in those days, part of the established path of the "Grand Tour" many British tourists traveled at the time. Most of them either brought their own coaches across the Channel or hired one when they reached the Continent, but a very few used the public transportation of the diligences, both of land and water, and the *coches d'eau*.

Conveniently for me, the routes and schedules of the diligences and their stopping places are preserved within the "Almanach [*sic*] Royal" for 1732 (a new one was printed each year), which lists also the feast days and saints' days, the hours the sun and moon rose and set each day, and myriad other small details that helped me re-create the trip as accurately as I could.

Diligences were built to carry ten people inside, and even in winter it would have been unlikely for my characters to be the only passengers, so I created traveling companions for them.

I also created a villain.

It's one of my personal quirks that I can't make a person a villain unless I'm convinced, from the records available, that's what he was. However long dead these people might be, they were—and remain—people first, and as such they deserve to be written about with respect.

The friend "by the name of Erskine" mentioned by Stevens as planning an attempt to seize Thomson in Paris was in fact William Erskine, accused of planning such an attempt in early March, forcing the British ambassador Waldegrave to reassure the French authorities his government "did not encourage the practice of carrying people off by stealth."

But it's impossible to tell from the surviving documents whether Erskine was indeed working for the British or for the Jacobites or, as he claimed, on behalf of a kinsman owed money by Thomson. I can't even be sure which William Erskine he was, as there were several men of that name mentioned in the correspondence of the time.

So instead of making him my villain, I created Stevens.

But the wolves were real.

I read about them in *Some Observations Made While Travelling through France, Italy, &c., In the Years 1720, 1721, and 1722, In Two Volumes*, by Edward Wright, Esq., printed at London in 1730—one of the travel accounts that I read in the course of my research. A bibliography of those accounts would stretch to several pages, but Wright's was one of my favorites, along with *The Household Book of Lady Grisell Baillie* (edited by Robert Scott-Moncrieff, WS, and printed at Edinburgh by the University Press for the Scottish Historical Society in 1911), which chronicles a tour that lady made of Europe from 1731 to 1733, meticulously noting the exchange rates between the French *louis d'or* and the British pound as she went, and giving helpful tips such as how to smuggle your Protestant prayer book past the customs men at Rome.

These books and many others allowed me to re-create a landscape that, in some cases, no longer exists.

At Valence, for example, I was able to lodge my characters at the same inn, which was fondly remembered by

Jean-Jacques Rousseau in his *Confessions* and, although long lost, is well described in the *Annales de la Société Jean-Jacques Rousseau*, published in 1905 at Geneva.

Beyond that point, I remained conscious of the need to keep my travelers away from the common path of the tourists, especially avoiding Avignon—a city under the protection of the pope—where there was a sizable Jacobite community and, consequently, a number of Waldegrave's spies.

Beginning in Marseilles, however, I had a written account of what Thomson said and did to go by, provided by the British informer Thomas Cole.

The aliases I gave to Thomson and the others for their time in Paris and the first part of their journey south were fictional, but from Thomas Cole's letters I know for a fact that Thomson came to Marseilles that spring traveling under the name "Mr. Symonds." I also know he met the banker, Mr. Warren, who had been expecting him.

I altered facts in one regard, by having Thomson meet Mr. Cole at the same time, when in actual fact it appears the two men didn't meet until later on that summer, when Thomson returned to Marseilles on his way back from Rome. Introduced by Warren, Cole became friendly with Thomson and promptly sold all the information he'd learned (and continued to learn) from their conversations to Waldegrave. Mr. Cole became such a success as a British spy that he went from simply reporting what he'd learned to actively trying to "trap" individuals, a policy that backfired upon him rather spectacularly in 1735, when a man he informed against to the police turned the tables and claimed Cole had been his accomplice. Cole was tried, found guilty, and sentenced to the galleys. I cannot say I did not find that justice.

I'm not sure how John Thomson traveled from Marseilles

to Rome, but I do know King James sent him back again by sea, and since many of the travelers whose accounts I was reading used ships or feluccas for this final leg of their voyage, I sent Thomson that way as well, taking the opportunity to introduce my own fictional addition to the pirate hunters who at that time kept a watchful eye out for the Barbary corsairs.

In Rome, I put my travelers in the Albergo del Sole al Pantheon, which has been a hotel since the fifteenth century, with its windows that look on the fountain and Pantheon now, as they would have done then.

The modest Palazzo Balestra that once housed King James and his court lies a short walk away.

I have been to the palace. I've gone up the once-secret staircase, but the king's rooms are now a private apartment, so I was shown through the rooms just above it. Fortunately, Professor Edward Corp of the University of Toulouse had been able to visit the king's rooms previously and shared his impressions with me, as well as some beautiful photographs he had taken of the painted ceiling as it yet remains, with Mary's birds still beating hopefully towards the false sky.

At the time of Thomson's visit, those rooms and the ones around them would have echoed with the footsteps of the two young princes, Charles and Henry, and the trusted courtiers who included Captain William Hay—again no stranger to the readers of my book *The Firebird*—and the Earl Marischal.

Writing to their mutual friend, Admiral Thomas Gordon, from Rome in February 1732, Captain Hay claims the Earl Marischal "may be justly stiled [*sic*] the hero of our cause."

Having read the earl's own letters to Admiral Gordon, together with those to his brother, his niece and her family in

Britain, and those preserved within the Stuart Papers, I agree with William Hay.

The earl's fondness for Prince Henry and the journal Henry kept for him were things I found endearing, and I've relied on his own account of where he'd been and what he had been doing at that time in Rome to guide Hugh's movements also.

I don't know if the earl met Thomson, but I do know Thomson met the king. Their conversation was repeated by John Thomson to his "friend" at Marseilles, Mr. Cole, who promptly relayed it to Waldegrave, as I've relayed it to you, in the same words. In fact, nearly all of King James's words used in that scene are his own, taken mostly from letters he wrote to his family and friends.

Thomson was imprisoned. I haven't been able to find where he was actually held in the Castel Sant'Angelo, only that he claimed to have been moved from a poor cell into a comfortable apartment there, so I gave him the same apartment used half a century later for another man embroiled in a scandal: the self-styled "Count of Cagliostro."

The letter to his father from there on the fifteenth of May was a real one, and I've quoted it verbatim. He also used his time in prison to write a full confession of his part in the scandal, addressed to the British Parliament, and in typical fashion the two letters tell different stories.

Released from prison that summer, he made his way back through Marseilles to Paris and eventually home to London, where in April of 1733 he testified to the Committee in charge of the Charitable Corporation affair in return for a percentage of whatever money they were able to recover by his evidence. It must not have been much. According to the *London Gazette*, a statute of bankruptcy was awarded against Thomson on September 2 of that year, and afterward he largely disappears from history.

Interestingly, though, he turns up in St. Petersburg a few years later, happily engaged in business with his brother there and continuing to annoy the British by setting up a manufacturing house for wallpaper in Russia, thus undercutting the British exports to that country. He appears to have still been there in the 1770s, and I continue to keep my eyes open for new references to him, though he remains as enigmatic to me now as he was when I first began to read his letters.

As for the money? At the time, it was estimated that the swindle involving the Charitable Corporation resulted in profits to the conspirators amounting to half a million pounds, yet only a tiny portion of that was ever recovered.

I have an idea—completely unproven—where some of the rest might have gone.

In the summer of 1732, shortly after Thomson's release from his prison in Rome, Martin O'Connor—who had led me into this tale to begin with, and appears to have been involved in the stock scandal from its beginning—began to develop new mines in Provence with his partners—mines that were presumably intended as a source of income for King James—with O'Connor personally investing 20,000 *livres* of capital.

And in 1733, Thomson's fellow fugitive, George Robinson, joined a number of fellow Jacobites, at least two of whom had also been involved in the scandal, to form a company aimed at developing mines in the province of Burgundy. *Their* starting capital was 360,000 pounds.

I could go on to say that neither venture ended in the way the Jacobites had wished, but it lies within the power of each storyteller to decide where best to end the story—a truism that would have been well-known and understood by Madame d'Aulnoy.

Her own story is a fascinating one, too long to recount here, but well worth searching out and remembering. For my part, I'm happy to see the woman who was not only arguably the writer of the first modern fairy tale, but also one of the most popular and successful novelists of her age, slowly being discovered again and restored in some part to the place she deserves in the canon.

I found it rather poignant that, in her novel *Hypolitus, earl of Douglas*, with its fairy tale about the Russian prince, Madame d'Aulnoy has the prince exclaim, when he first learns three hundred years have passed since he last saw his homeland: "When I come there again, who will know me? Or how shall I know any Body; My Dominions are, doubt-less, fallen into the Hands of some strange Family? I can't suppose there will be any left for me; so that I am likely to be a Prince without a Principality; every Body will shun me as if I were a Spectre…"

She might have been writing of King James VIII.

I could tell you the end to *his* story, but I have a sense I'm not done with him, or with his followers, yet.

So let me finish where I started:

Once upon a time, a baby girl was born at Saint-Germain-en-Laye.

Her name was Marie Anne Thérèse Dundas.

Her baptism, on July 25, 1710, was written down into the parish register…as was, in the very next entry, the note of her death, on the fourth of September that year. She had lived only six short weeks.

She wasn't given a chance at a life. So I gave her one.

Writers can't truly change history, but we can decide, as I said, where a story should end.

Not being fond of the ending of Mary's tale, I wrote a different one.

I wrote a better one.

READING GROUP GUIDE

1. "Mistress Jamieson" tells Mary when they meet: "My mother likes to say some people choose the path of danger on their own, for it is how the Lord did make them, and they never will be changed." Do you agree? Was it more true in the past than today? Did Mary purposely choose a path of danger? Who else?

2. The author has people in her own life with Asperger's syndrome who helped her with Sara's character. What was it like to be in the point of view of a person with Asperger's syndrome? Did you have any preconceived ideas about Asperger's? Did they change?

3. Journeys (physical and otherwise) are a prevalent theme in many of Susanna Kearsley's books. What journeys can you identify in this book, past and present? How do they differ for female and male characters?

4. Mary takes "Mistress Jamieson" as a role model. "She closed her eyes a moment…and allowed the poise and grace of Mistress Jamieson to settle round her shoulders like a robe before she turned." Is there anyone you use as a role model in this way? Why do you think it's helpful?

5. Why does Mistress Jamieson teach Mary the cipher?

6. Susanna Kearsley has said, "Never underestimate the power of an animal to reveal character within the story." How does the dog Frisque further the plot? What does Frisque tell us about Mary? About Hugh? In the present, how does the cat Diablo serve these purposes?

7. *I fear the man across the street...* What did you think of MacPherson when he is first introduced? Did you have him pegged as a hero? If not, when did you begin to change your mind? When did Mary stop fearing Hugh? When did you? Can you identify what makes you feel safe or not safe around someone?

8. Hugh was a man of his time. If he lived in the present, what sort of job would he have? What role in society would he fill?

9. Compare the meeting of Mary and Hugh with the meeting of Sara and Luc.

10. It is Luc who points out to Sara that Hugh has fallen for Mary, long before she realizes it: "A woman can start with a man she might find unattractive and slowly begin to see good in him, grow into love with him, but this is not how it happens with men. We're much simpler." Do you agree?

11. In fiction, as in life, what people appear to be may differ from what they are. While Hugh first appears as a

sinister character, "Jacques" appears to be a charming gentleman, but is he? Do you think Thompson is a good man or a bad man?

12. By "seeing" the story as it unfolds in the past, the reader is not only a step ahead, but also often has more knowledge than Sara as she deciphers the journal. How did this affect your reading of the story in the present?

13. If you're familiar with Susanna Kearsley's writing, you may recognize a number of references to characters, both in the past and the present, whom the author has introduced in other novels. Did you recognize anyone? (Hint: Characters also seen in *The Winter Sea*, *Mariana*, *The Splendour Falls*, *Season of Storms*, and *The Firebird*.)

A NOTE OF THANKS

No book of mine is ever written without the help of a number of people. It might take a book of its own to thank all of them, but here are some who deserve special mention:

I'm grateful to Catherine Heymann and Jacques Chiaffrino, my hosts for my time in Chatou, who graciously allowed me to use their Maison de Chatou as the model for my Maison des Marroniers; and to their neighbors, Colette and Marcel Saby, for allowing *their* house to be Luc's for this novel.

I owe a great debt to the film director and writer Franco Amurri and his wife, Heidi, who generously helped arrange for my personal tour of the Palazzo Balestra—the former palace of King James VIII in Rome—and to Veronica Schiavulli and Oscar Garibaldi of Volpes Case, for being my guides through that building and showing me all of the corridors, stairways, and rooms they were able to.

I'm also indebted beyond measure to Edward Corp, professor of British history at the University of Toulouse. Not only for his books *A Court in Exile: The Stuarts in France, 1689–1718* (Cambridge: Cambridge University Press, 2004), *The Jacobites at Urbino: An Exiled Court in Transition* (London: Palgrave Macmillan, 2009), and *The Stuarts in Italy, 1719–1766: A Royal Court in Permanent Exile* (Cambridge: Cambridge University Press, 2011), all of which have proven invaluable to me in my research, but also for his great kindness in sending me his personal photographs of King James's rooms, which Professor Corp took on his own private tour of the Palazzo Balestra in 2011, and which included brilliant color images of the painted ceilings in the king's gallery and cabinet.

And finally, as ever, my thanks to my mother, who, born with a natural editor's eye, always makes my books better.

ABOUT THE AUTHOR

New York Times and *USA Today* bestselling author Susanna Kearsley is known for her meticulous research and exotic settings from Russia to France to Cornwall, which not only entertain her readers, but also give her a great reason to travel. Her lush writing has been compared to Mary Stewart, Daphne du Maurier, and Diana Gabaldon. She hit the bestseller lists in the United States with *The Winter Sea* and *The Rose Garden*, both RITA finalists and winners of RT Reviewers' Choice Awards, and won the RITA in 2014 for her novel *The Firebird*. Other honors include National Readers' Choice Awards, the prestigious Catherine Cookson Fiction Prize, and finaling for the UK's Romantic Novel of the Year Award. Her popular and critically acclaimed books are available in translation in more than twenty countries and as audiobooks. She lives in Canada, near the shores of Lake Ontario.